A Kendall O'Dell Mystery

BENEVOLENT EVIL

A Kendall O'Dell Mystery

BENEVOLENT EVIL

SYLVIA NOBEL

Phoenix,
Arizona

Phoenix, Arizona

1st Printing October, 2020

For information, contact Nite Owl Books
11801 N. Tatum Blvd #143
Phoenix, AZ 85028
602-618-0724
E-mail: beverlyniteowlbooks@gmail.com
www.niteowlbooks.com

ISBN 978-0999835166

Cover Design by
Christy A. Moeller, *ATG Productions, LLC.*
www.atgproductions.com

Library of Congress Control Number: 2019953888

ACKNOWLEDGMENTS

****

The author wishes to thank and acknowledge the following people for their invaluable assistance:

Dr. Carl Gassmann – Scottsdale Surgical Arts
Kelly Powell, Mgr. Bumble Bee Ranch
Pete Gorisch – Long Haul Trucker
Jill – Trail's End Large Animal Removal & Disposal
Rebecca Williams, Globe, AZ
Mary & John Stemm, Globe, AZ
Bryan Thomas- Crime Prevention Officer,
Yavapai County Sheriff's Office
Leo Scott, Prescott AZ
Tamra Brice, Bagdad, AZ
Donna Jandro, Editorial Services
Tina Williams, Editorial Services
Kelly Scott-Olson and Christy A. Moeller,
ATG Productions, Surprise, AZ

and

My husband, Jerry, for his encouragement and for driving endless miles on Arizona's lonesome back roads to assist in my research.

TO MY LOVING FAMILY,
CHERISHED FRIENDS
AND
DEVOTED FANS

THANK YOU FOR YOUR
CONTINUING
ENCOURAGEMENT
AND SUPPORT

ADDITIONAL TITLES IN
SYLVIA NOBEL'S AWARD-WINNNG
KENDALL O'DELL MYSTERY SERIES

Deadly Sanctuary
The Devil's Cradle
Dark Moon Crossing
Seeds of Vengeance
Forbidden Entry

Also
Chasing Rayna
A Scent of Jasmine

Published by
Nite Owl Books
Phoenix, Arizona

CHAPTER 1

Ca-chink! *Ca-chink*! The sharp ring of hammering combined with the percussive whoosh of nail guns interrupted the pristine silence of the desert, echoing off the nearby coral-blushed cliffs, masking the soft thud of hoofbeats on the sandy terrain. Breathing in the invigorating air, I reached down and gave my mare a comforting pat on the neck. "Easy, girl," I murmured in a soothing tone, noting the startled movement of her ears. I reined her to a sedate walk, marveling at the sea of yellow and orange Mexican gold poppies. Hard to believe it was February—technically still winter, but the mild weather felt more reminiscent of late spring mornings back home in Pennsylvania. Had it actually been only ten months since I'd arrived here? For a host of reasons it seemed as if I'd been here much longer, perhaps because so many remarkable events had transpired in that short time period.

My escape from living a debilitated life with asthma, plus a heart-crushing broken engagement in Philadelphia had unexpectedly landed me smack-dab in the middle of the sweltering Arizona desert where I'd accepted the reporting job at the *Castle Valley Sun*. On day one, I had jumped feetfirst into my first precarious assignment, which was immediately followed by four more mind-blowing stories that had shocked the residents of not only Castle Valley, but also the entire country. Now, here I was, engaged to Bradley James Talverson, the sexiest, wealthiest rancher in the state. Not too shabby.

Adjusting my wide-brimmed hat, I shaded my eyes against the blinding rays of early-morning sunlight and squinted at the framed-in skeleton of our new house rising majestically on the western slope of Sidewinder Hill. *Our new house*. A thrill of anticipation rocketed through me as I envisioned the completed dwelling Tally and I would soon share. Not only would it be a grand, four-thousand square feet, far more spacious than any place I'd ever lived in my entire twenty-nine years before, but the view—the commanding view of the rugged mountains and cactus-dotted landscape of the Sonoran desert we would relish each day left me in total awe. Perhaps most importantly, after the wedding we would be living a full mile and a half away from Tally's not-quite-right-in-the-head mother. For me, that was not nearly far enough. As my dad had jokingly suggested, another ten miles further would have been preferable. Good, but fifty would be even better! I could not suppress the surge of mischievous delight. "You are so evil," I chided myself.

Fifteen minutes later, as we began our ascent up the rock-strewn slope, the din grew progressively louder. Starlight Sky continued to toss her head nervously as we angled higher along the newly-graded road that just weeks before had been a narrow horsetrail and would soon be a paved driveway. Ahead at the job site, an assortment of pickup trucks—all makes, models and colors—along with two white panel trucks stood parked at odd angles in any available spot. The place bustled with contagious energy to the contrasting strains of Mexican and country-western music. At least a dozen men, some wearing hard hats and others ball caps, scurried about carrying out their appointed tasks.

I looked around. No sign of Tally yet. I fished my cell phone from my jacket pocket while reining in Starlight Sky. Eight-fifteen. Crap. Was he going to be a no-show to discuss the house plan changes with our architect? He had been saddled up and ready to join me before Jake, his long-time ranch manager, had shouted from the barn that one of the horses appeared to be sick. Tally had quickly signaled for me to go ahead and promised to join me as soon as possible. Afterwards, we planned a leisurely ride back to the ranch before I headed into the newspaper office, officially ending my well-earned three weeks away from work. During that time, I had completed physical therapy after having the cast removed from my left arm, broken during my last harrowing assignment. Tally and I had taken a rare vacation to the coast together where I'd made a concerted effort to stay away from my phone, ignore the news and allow my mind and body to relax. Now, back at the Starfire Ranch astride my gorgeous black-and-white dappled appaloosa, I felt ready to tackle the world again. I fired off a brief text to Tally. EVERYTHING OK THERE? STILL COMING?

"Howdy, Miz. O'Dell!"

I glanced up to see Bob Stockman, the stout job foreman, ambling towards me waving, an amiable grin lighting his round face. "Morning, Bob." I dismounted and kept a firm grasp on the reins as my skittish mare paced, the bedlam obviously distressing her. "I guess Tally is going to be a little later than expected. Is Neil here yet?"

"He's over there waitin' for ya," he said, nodding towards the construction trailer.

Sudden crashes sent Starlight Sky lunging sideways and tossing her head in agitation. "Whoa, baby!" I tightened my grip, mentally scolding myself. Perhaps bringing my high-strung mare up here was not such a good idea. "Would you tell Neil I'll be with him in a few minutes? I'm going to tie her up over there in the clearing away from this noise," I stated, pointing towards a pile of giant boulders.

"Sure thing." He touched the bill of his cap and I led my prancing horse to a secluded clearing behind the rocks where lush green grass had sprouted up from the recent rains. The construction noise now considerably muffled, Starlight Sky seemed visibly more relaxed as I tied the reins firmly to the trunk of a scrub oak tree and let her graze in the soft morning breeze.

My text tone chimed and I glanced at Tally's message. VET'S ON THE WAY. NOT SURE I'M GONNA MAKE IT. CALL U IN A BIT. My heart fell. That did not sound promising. I texted him back. SORRY! ☹ Seconds later I got his thumbs up emoji.

"Damn it," I murmured. Oh well. Might as well make use of the time.

I tapped out the office number and after two rings heard Ginger's cheerful, "Mornin', sunshine! Must be nice havin' banker's hours while the rest of us are here slavin' our buns off."

I smiled at her lighthearted teasing. "It is. Are you slavin' your buns off?"

A faint giggle. "Not hardly. It's been deader 'n a doornail, especially with you and Tally both bein' gone." Her protracted sigh sounded wistful. "It sure ain't gonna be the same here without him paradin' his fine-lookin' backside around the office."

I couldn't help but laugh before admonishing her tongue-in-cheek, "Ginger! I'm going to have to check, but that may be a sexist thing to say in the workplace."

"Aw, flapdoodle. It's true an' you know it," she fired back, snorting her infectious laughter.

It was true. I'd miss him being at the office as well, although he had only been working two days a week the past few months. Tally's decision to retire from his position as senior sportswriter to return full-time to ranching had saddened the entire eight-person staff. "Okay, I admit it. He has a great butt. But I think Jim's a pretty happy camper to be stepping into his shoe…ah…boots."

"Happier 'n a pig in a pile o' you know what! You think Tally's gonna miss us?"

"Of course! But, he's been super busy at the ranch and he's got his hands full getting the horses ready. He's going to be slammed this week with buyers coming in from all over the country—all over the world actually."

No response. "Ginger?" I glanced at the phone. Had I lost cell service? "Did you hear me?"

"What? Oh, yeah, yeah." She sounded preoccupied. "Sorry, dumplin', I been checkin' out this website. Did you know that we all have a twin someplace in the world?" Before I could respond, she gasped, "Oh m' Gawd! Will ya look at her? I uploaded my picture about an hour ago and my twin's picture just popped up!"

"And is she your doppelganger?"

"My what?"

"Your mirror image?"

"Mmmm, sort of. This gal's got freckles, dang near the same strawberry-blonde hair color, but she looks to be about 30 pounds thinner, a whole lot younger and appears like she might be about 6 inches taller 'n me. Otherwise, we pretty much look identical."

My burst of laughter startled Starlight Sky who eyed me warily. "Ginger, you are priceless and definitely one of a kind."

"Am I takin' that as a compliment?"

"Absolutely!"

"You want me to upload your picture and see what we git?"

"Not really," I answered solemnly. "We've already seen my twin. Remember?"

"We have? When? Where?"

"Have you forgotten how much I resemble Tally's… late wife?"

Silence. Then, "Oh, mercy me. How could I ever forgit that?"

I certainly had not forgotten the shocking outcome of my first assignment and all the ramifications for me, for Tally, and for the benevolent new publisher of our newspaper, Thena Rodenborn. Who could have known that my investigation into the disappearance of my predecessor and two missing teenage girls would uncover a diabolical scheme that would result in the death of her only son? Because of his culpability in the horrifying crimes committed, it had been not only a personal tragedy but, because of her vast wealth and social standing in the town, a mortifying experience as well. Since that fateful day, her behavior towards me had been cordial and yet reserved. I wondered if she would ever truly be able to forgive me. "Anyway," I continued, "I'm gathering if you've got time to surf the Web, it must be another slow news day. Boy, as much as I've enjoyed having some time to myself, I feel as if I've been on the moon these past three weeks. Anything noteworthy happened?"

"Not much. Phone ain't rung but a couple a times today."

"Well, that's just dandy." It wasn't really. The *Castle Valley Sun* was suffering from the same death spiral most print publications faced—plunging subscribership and advertising revenue. Even after our big staff meeting in January, where we'd all put our heads together and brainstormed imaginative ways to increase online subscriptions and advertising revenue, my co-editor, Morton Tuggs had somberly reminded us that print newspapers nationally continued to fold at an alarming rate and that drastic changes might have to be employed. Our failing financial situation had constantly gnawed at the back of my mind during my hiatus, siphoning away what should have been a blissfully relaxing time. What we desperately needed was another infusion of cash from Thena in order to stave off personnel reductions and stay afloat until we could implement some of our ideas and turn things around. Or, I thought morosely, *if* we could turn things around.

"I hear ya, girl," she replied, audibly yawning. "I'd much rather have the phone ringin' off the hook like the old days." Pausing, she tacked on, "I guess our fate is in your hands again."

"Why mine?"

"You know why. We all know you ain't happy unless you're chasin' down one of them creepy stories you love so much. You git yourself in a world o' hurt an' subscriptions go way up for a spell!"

She was right. Each new undertaking had infused me with an adrenaline high that I was beginning to crave again. "You handed me my last scoop. Maybe you can dig up a new one up for me. The news has been duller than an old butterknife these past two months."

"So, ya ready to git back in the saddle again?" she inquired playfully.

I glanced over at Starlight Sky chomping on a mouthful of grass. "Not yet. I just got off this gorgeous horse about five minutes ago."

Ginger's tinkling laughter resounded in my ear. "I don't mean for real. I got a little tidbit ya might want to check out. Don't know if it will go anywhere, but then again, it might."

That tickled my curiosity bone. "What's that?"

"I heard tell Nelson Trotter's back in town."

"Who?"

"You ever hear of the notorious Trotter twins?"

"No. And they're notorious why?"

"Well, they ain't really twin twins," she prattled on, not actually answering my question, "they're more like Irish twins. I think him and his sister are the same age for five days, but anyway, I'm more 'n happy to share all the juicy details. It's kind of a long sad story, two actually—no wait, if you go back far enough, there's three."

"I have no idea what you're talking about, but is there something in particular among everything you've just told me that I might find interesting?"

"Oh, yeah. How much time ya got, sugar?"

"Right now, not much."

"How 'bout I tell ya about 'em later, oh and before I forgit, Tugg told me to tell you that Thena's gonna be here around noon today."

Surprise jolted me. "What? I thought she wasn't coming until tomorrow." It had been my plan to meet with Tugg before her visit to finalize our ideas and settle on the best strategy with which to approach her.

"Nope. Today. Better shake it, sugar!"

"I guess I'd better. Bye."

"Hang on a second! I plum near forgot. I do have some news," she added breathlessly. "You know that new beauty clinic, Youth Oasis, the one that opened up about a month ago where the old American Legion Hall used to be over yonder on Buckskin Trail?"

I swatted a bee away from my face. It seemed as if bees and hummingbirds were always dive-bombing my hair, thinking they'd happened upon a big, fuzzy red flower. "Yeah, what about it?"

"Al just told me this mornin' that they bought a whole page ad for Wednesday's edition."

"A full page!" I repeated, feeling a surge of reassurance. "That is awesome."

"Well, snap my garters!" The sound of crinkling paper reached my ears, a short silence, then, "Listen to this," she announced gleefully, her voice brimming with excitement. "I'm proofreadin' the ad copy now, an' you can git yourself a face-lift, a neck-lift and all kinds of skin treatments. They got coupons for a whole passel of creams, lotions, potions and best of all there's a brand new procedure called *Skin Deep Beauty Elixir*. I guess it's kind of like them HGH injections only it says here it's waaaaay better. Some magical ingredients added." She stopped to take a breath, finishing with, "Good Lord, girl, if what they're saying is true, we can all look half our age!"

I dearly loved her effervescent personality combined with her colorful Texas idioms, which she always used to maximum effect. "Ginger, what are you talking about? You're only thirty-three and don't have a wrinkle on your face."

Sounding dubious, she firmly declared, "Maybe you don't see 'em, but I sure do. Any hoot, it says here they're open until six tonight. Colleen, Margery and me are fixin' to head over there after work to check it out. You wanna come?"

"I don't know. It sounds too good to be true."

"Suit yourself. But if you ask me, there ain't a one of us couldn't use a little sprucin' up every now and then, don't ya think?"

"I can't commit right now, but we can talk about it when I get there. I gotta go. See ya!" I tapped the screen, smiling. Bless Ginger King. Known affectionately as the town gossip, not only was she often a valuable resource, she was also endlessly entertaining and had become my dearest friend. In December, she had taken the bull by the horns and thrown us the most amazing engagement party. Now, she was ensconced in the role of my wedding maven, enthusiastically assuming most of the extensive list of details that needed attention while lamenting the fact that she wished she was planning her own wedding, but couldn't seem to get her boyfriend, Doug, off the dime.

I shoved the phone in my pocket, heartened to see that Starlight Sky had settled down. Gently swishing her full, black tail, she munched contentedly on the lush winter grass. Confident she would be okay I double-checked the knot and then retraced my steps to the construction site. No sooner had I rounded the boulders than I heard the shouts of angry male voices. A small cluster of workers stood gathered around two men, one young, tall and lanky, the other muscular, older and shorter, but nonetheless, practically nose-to-nose. Gesturing wildly towards a maroon-and white-colored pickup and a newly-arrived flatbed truck piled with lumber, the young guy shouted a lengthy string of ear-blistering expletives and threatened, "You're gonna pay! You're gonna pay me for every cent of damage you done!"

"You backed into me, dumbass," the older man snarled. Thick brows furrowed in anger, his sparsely-bearded chin protruding like a bulldog, he strong-armed the younger man backwards onto the ground. When he came up swinging, a full-on fistfight ensued.

Seconds later, Bob burst from the trailer and charged over to the wrestling duo. "Hey! Hey! Break it up, you two!" he commanded harshly, inserting himself between them. "Justin, what the hell's going on here?"

"This shit-for-brains just wrecked my new truck!"

Curious, I walked closer and listened as the accusations flew back and forth. "All right, all right, that's enough!" Bob demanded. "Take it up with the insurance companies. Now everybody get back to work!"

Justin wiped blood from his nose onto the sleeve of his shirt. "Freakin' dirt bag pervert! Your lazy ass belongs back in jail!"

My interest level inched higher. Pervert? I was usually on top of people and most events in Castle Valley, especially crime statistics, but I'd never seen this guy before. The older man reacted to Justin's comment with red-faced rage, lunging at him again. At that point, I whipped out my phone and tapped out a few photos and a short video. Bob intervened again, grabbing his arm. "Cool it!" He pushed Justin in the opposite direction before addressing the older man. "I don't want to have to get the sheriff involved and I don't think you do either." Bob turned to the gathered crowd. "Show's over! Get this lumber unloaded."

Glowering, the truck driver yanked his arm from Bob's grasp. In a harsh, gravelly tone he barked, "I never did nothing wrong! Those charges were bogus." before stomping to his rig and vaulting into the cab. Bob yelled after him, "Try not to be two hours late next time!"

Intrigued, I wished I had time to follow up on Justin's accusation, but at that instant, my cell phone rang. It was Tally. I retreated to a quieter spot. "Hey cowboy, you on the way, I hope?"

"Nope. Still waiting on the vet."

Mild exasperation flared in my chest. "Really? What's the problem this time?"

"Not sure. Could be the flu, but I'm more worried about EHV."

"Can't Jake take care of this?"

"Nope."

Tally was indeed a man of few words. "Why not?"

"Because," he stated matter-of-factly, "It's Rain Dancer and there are a couple of other situations going on."

Exasperation turned to agitation. I loved Tally with fierce intensity, but sometimes his preoccupation with the horses left me feeling deflated. I hated playing second, third and fourth fiddle. Of course, he always countered that *my* fixation with pursuing a stimulating story, sometimes at the risk of my life, surpassed by a mile any devotion he had for his Appaloosa horses. Ruefully, I had to admit that he was often right when he complained that he felt reduced to an afterthought. I'd been working really hard to correct that perception. However, I was also keenly aware that besides his gelding, Geronimo, Rain Dancer was his favorite mare. I sometimes kiddingly reminded him that he paid more attention to her than he did to me. His good-humored rejoinder was that her high-spirited, headstrong personality constantly reminded him of me, so shouldn't I be flattered?

I fought to maintain a dispassionate tone. Cool. Stay cool. "I'm sorry. I know how important she is to you, but this is important to *me*. You know today is the deadline to make all the major changes we want on the house if we want it finished before the wedding and because of your schedule it's the only time we both have open for the next two weeks." No response during my short pause. "So, what do you want me to tell Neil?" He obviously heard the undercurrent of frustration seeping into my voice and answered soothingly, "You decide. This is your dream house."

"It's going to be your house too!" I shot back.

"I trust your judgement."

I inhaled a deep, cleansing breath, hoping to tamp down my escalating temper. "All right then, you won't mind me adding a wrap-around porch, a wine cellar and perhaps a turret?" The moment the words left my mouth, I realized how petulant I sounded. This generous, ultra-patient, intelligent and caring man had captured my heart from the first moment I'd laid eyes on him, yet he possessed the uncanny ability to light the fuse on my short temper better than anyone else. I sincerely believed that he enjoyed our electrically-charged verbal exchanges, which ranged from mild to volcanic.

"A turret?" he parroted with a tinge of humor. "Are you trying to replicate your grandmother's house?"

Stung, I muttered, "Very funny." However, his mocking words revived indelible memories of her stately one-hundred-fifty-year old Victorian back home in Pennsylvania that spawned my continuing fascination with old houses and buildings. To me, it was magical and truly looked like a castle. What fun it had been staying overnight nestled cozily in that high four-poster bed in what I had always called 'the round room,' and, oh, how I missed my tenacious, barb-witted grandmother along with that remarkable house.

Wasn't it only yesterday that I'd delighted in exploring every nook and cranny of that spacious house with my two brothers? With a thrill of elation, my imagination would run wild as we climbed the steep staircase to explore the musty contents of the attic. We spent countless hours poring over boxes and trunks filled with old stale-smelling books, papers, photos, clothes and other captivating relics of the past. All antique treasures to us. Looking back, I felt sure those long-ago experiences fueled my desire to become either a detective or an investigative reporter.

His mellifluous voice now brimming with mischief, he responded, "Well, if you think a turret will go with our contemporary western design, go for it, m'lady."

M'lady? I bit back a scornful response as my grandmother's wise Irish proverb, *"A kind word never broke anyone's mouth"* echoed in my mind. I also thought about Ginger's theory that our diametrically-opposite personalities combined with our intractable natures, each fighting for dominance in the relationship, kept the fireworks sizzling. I'd definitely met my match this time. "So, you're not coming to the meeting."

He cleared his throat. "Um…it's not looking good."

"Does this have anything to do with Ruth?" Was his crazy mother badgering him again about me stealing her precious son away from her?

"No, no…it…um…doesn't." Was I imagining it or did he sound distracted?

"Listen, I've got other problems brewing here. What's that?" His words trailed off as if he had moved the phone away from his ear, then grew louder again. "Hang on a second, Kendall."

I could hear unintelligible female voices in the background, then his firm, "I told you I'm not getting in the middle of this. Ask her yourself."

I frowned. Ask who? "Tally, what's going on?"

A long sigh of frustration. "You'll find out when you get here."

CHAPTER 2

Following his cryptic words, only dead air met my ears. Mystified, my thoughts tumbled over each other as I slid the phone in my pocket and reached over to stroke Starlight Sky's silky hindquarters. What in the world had that been about? I was 90% certain that one of the background voices belonged to his reclusive sister Ronda. The second person could have been his mother or perhaps Ronda's lifelong friend, the ubiquitous Lucinda Johns, who detested the ground I walked on—and the feeling was certainly mutual. Even though Lucinda was now in a relationship with one of Tally's ranch hands, I still suspected she had never wavered in her amorous quest of thirty years to snag Tally's affections. Her cunning decision to buy and board her horse at the Starfire provided her with endless opportunities to flaunt herself in front of Tally. The woman was like a leech—a giant, triple-D-breasted leech strutting around in her super-tight jeans, managing to attach herself to him at every opportunity.

My throat tightened with irritation and the familiar burn of jealousy turned my stomach sour. Stop it! Maybe I was getting myself all worked up into a lather over nothing. I swung around, marched over to the trailer and spent the next hour and a half explaining the changes we had in mind to our architect—adding extra counter space in the kitchen, a fireplace to the master bedroom and making several modifications to Tally's man cave, before I trekked back to remount Starlight Sky.

Beneath the infinite dome of sapphire blue, the warm sun at my back, I loped my spirited mare most of the way back to the ranch still slightly vexed at being stood up by Tally and unable to stop wondering what awaited me. But, I thought as the stables popped into view, my suspicions could be wrong and Ronda just needed a personal favor. If that were the case though, what prompted Tally to emphatically state that he did not want to get involved?

A glow of pride warmed me at the sight of at least two dozen stunningly beautiful appaloosas grazing peacefully behind the long white-pipe fence as I trotted into the clearing and reined in my horse at the hitching post. Sometimes I still had trouble believing that I would soon be Mrs. Bradley James Talverson and, at that time, I would be vacating my cozy rental house to begin a new life on this magnificent ranch.

At the opposite end of the barn amid the cluster of horse trailers, I spotted Tally's pickup, Ronda's crappy, old brown Jeep, and the vet's dirt-covered red pickup along with a white U.S. Fish and Wildlife truck. Next to the corral gate sat another white pickup with a large covered trailer attached. What was going on? I wondered just as Jake stepped out of the tack room. He tapped the brim of his dog-eared Stetson with one finger, a friendly smile lighting his crinkled, sun-bronzed face. "Mornin', Miz. O'Dell, I'll take care of her for ya ifn ya like."

I dismounted and handed him the reins. "Thanks, Jake, I'd appreciate that." Normally, I loved currying Starlight Sky after an invigorating ride, but if I were going to make it to the office before Thena arrived, I'd best get home soon. "How's Rain Dancer?"

"Doc thinks she's gonna be ok," he informed me with a lopsided grin.

"Oh, that's good news!" I said, breathing a sigh of relief, which turned out to be short-lived when I noticed his blue eyes darken and his grin compress into a frown. "Something wrong?"

"Well, Tally's feelin' real good about Rain Dancer but I'm bettin' he ain't none too happy about them other two hitches."

I tensed. "What's happening?"

"Doc had to put Dolly down about an hour ago."

"Oh no!" I exclaimed, acute sadness invading my heart, "Not Dolly."

"Yep," he answered, lifting his hat to scratch his balding scalp. "Her arthritis had got so bad she couldn't get up this mornin'. Tally and Ronda decided, since the vet was here anyway, they'd best git it over with," he concluded with a despondent sigh before securing his hat once again.

Tears burned my eyes and heavy guilt coiled in my gut, remembering how I'd given Tally the business about missing the meeting with Neil. This tragic situation definitely took priority. It slowly sank in that I'd never see the ranch's beloved donkey again, never hear her clownish bray, delight in her quirky personality or admire her ability to instantly bond with people and horses alike. As much as I'd miss the Starfire's resident mascot, it wouldn't be nearly as hard on me as on Tally and Ronda since she'd been around since they were children. "What's the second problem?"

"Ray Sutter's settin' in Tally's office right now chewin' his backside 'cause Vernon shot one o' them so-called, endangered Mexican gray wolves last night. That pack's been stalkin' the cattle for a couple of weeks now and finally killed a mama cow and her calf yesterday. Right over there on the far side of the south corral," he commented, pointing a gnarled forefinger. "Messed 'em up pretty bad."

I grimaced and glanced beyond the bucolic scene of grazing horses, but couldn't see anything from my vantage point. "That's awful." Tally was not a man to suffer fools gladly, especially fools from the government. He was particularly incensed about the Agency pushing the bizarre idea that somehow the wolves and cattle were now going to learn to peacefully coexist. I had to agree. How do you alter nature when wolves are natural predators to livestock? The Agency's suggestion to shoot rubber bullets at them was apparently not working. "I'm sure he's royally pissed about that."

"Yeah," Jake nodded, sagely. "Pretty pissed."

Both Jake and I turned at the sound of a car door slamming and saw Ronda with her back to us, gesturing and talking to someone sitting in the white pickup. The rising wind made it impossible for me to hear what she was saying. "Who's that with Ronda?" I asked Jake.

He squinted into the distance. "Somebody from The Last Roundup."

"What's that?"

He shot me a questioning look. "You know. Them's the people who come pick up and dispose of dead animal carcasses."

"Oh. Of course. For Dolly."

"Yeah, her and the cows."

"Really? All this time I thought you just left the cattle out in the desert to decompose."

"We normally do that, but seein' how we needed 'em to pick up Dolly, Ronda decided since we got a passel of people coming this week, she didn't want folks to see the cows' remains. On top of that, they're gonna start to stink here pretty soon and the vultures will be swarmin' all around. Might scare the tenderfoots." A wink accompanied his wry smile.

"No doubt," I muttered. Not very far removed from tenderfoot status myself, I had no doubt that would be a stomach-turning sight for most people. Tally and I had come across more than one bloated, fly-covered animal carcass on our rides across the Starfire property and adjoining BLM grazing lands. Certainly not a pleasant image, but something ranchers accept.

A twinge of melancholy flowed through me as I watched the pickup make a wide turn and head out of the driveway pulling the covered trailer that I now knew held Dolly and whatever remained of the mother cow and her calf. Disposing of dead animals did not sound like the kind of job I would ever care to have. "Thanks again, Jake," I said, touching his arm briefly. "Catch you later." I walked a few steps, but turned back adding, "Tell Tally I'm going into work and I'll contact him later."

"Sure thing." He touched the brim of his Stetson again and led Starlight Sky into the stable. I pulled off my hat, fluffed out my unruly curls and had almost made it to the Jeep when I heard a shout.

"Kendall, wait up a minute!"

I swung around to see Ronda running towards me dressed in her usual worn jeans and scuffed boots. "I need to ask you something." Breathing hard, she fixed me with those unreadable brown eyes and swiped a thatch of auburn hair from her forehead. Even after knowing Tally's sister for ten months now, I felt I'd never really *know* her. She was less than forthcoming most of the time, preferred the company of animals to people, and I feared she had inherited some of her mother's bipolar tendencies, although Tally assured me she was not yet to the point where she needed medications. While part of me was marginally curious about whatever it was that she wanted to ask, a glance at my phone confirmed that I had no time for chitchat.

"Hi Ronda, what's on your mind?"

Appearing ill at ease, she chewed her lower lip a few seconds. "I need a favor."

"Name it."

She shifted her weight, avoiding my gaze. "Um… it's not really a favor for me exactly."

It was an effort not to roll my eyes. "Your mother?"

The slight hesitation confirmed my fears. "No."

Oh, crap. "Lucinda?"

She nodded somberly.

"Is she here?"

"Yep."

"Why doesn't she ask me herself?"

Ronda looked down and drew a circle in the dirt with the tip of her boot. "Lucy said she's afraid."

I looked at her askance. "Afraid of what?"

"You. Lucy knows she's not your favorite person, but maybe just this once you could call a truce or something and listen to what she has to say."

"She's not exactly crazy about me either," I remarked coolly. For the life of me, I could not understand why Ronda liked her, but then because of her reclusive nature, Ronda did not appear to have many friends. I knew the two women had been inseparable since preschool. Maybe she was aware of some positive personality trait I missed. Brash, duplicitous, insensitive, disrespectful, mouthy—to me, Lucinda had not one redeeming quality. Well, perhaps one. The Iron Skillet restaurant, operated by Lucinda and her Aunt Polly, whom I did like, served the absolute yummiest food in town.

"I'm kind of behind the eight ball for time today. Can't this wait?"

"So, you can't spare her even ten minutes!" Usually so low-key that I hardly noticed her presence most of the time, her indignant declaration startled me. "Look, I wouldn't normally ask you to get involved, but...this is different. Maybe life or death."

Seriously? Life or death? I hesitated, thinking her request seemed a bit overblown but at the same instant, her statement had definitely captured my attention. "Ten minutes."

Her eyes softening with gratitude, she stepped forward and enveloped me in an awkward embrace. Disconcerted, I patted her shoulders, her unexpected response invoking a sense of cautious uncertainty. What was I getting myself into this time? Hadn't it been just a few months ago that I had been trapped into this very position with Ruth? Her fervent insistence that I follow up on the murder of an old family friend had produced a bombshell story but also disgorged a clattering multitude of unwelcome skeletons from the Talverson closet that they were still coping with to this day. How was I ever going to blend into this dysfunctional family? "Thank you, Kendall." She drew back and thumbed over her shoulder. "She's waiting inside."

I hesitated. "I'm really sorry about Dolly."

Instant tears glistened in her eyes and she blinked rapidly. "Thanks. She's been a part of our family for forty years. I'm going to miss her."

"Me too." I started towards the barn, dragging my feet. If I could pick anyone on earth, Lucinda would be the last person I would choose to grant a favor. Wary, but also curious, I strode inside wondering what she could possibly want from me while mentally calculating how long it would take me to shower, dress, check on my cats and get to the office before Thena arrived.

The pleasantly pungent aroma of horse manure and hay greeted me as I paused to allow my eyes to adjust to the low light. Within seconds, I spotted my nemesis loitering near the tack room, her back to me. "Ronda said you wanted to talk to me."

She swung around abruptly, her coffee-colored eyes wide with surprise. "Yeah." She continued to stare at me as if I were a ghost. Clearly, she had not expected me to come. "Did…a…Ronda tell you anything?"

I eyed her with suspicion. "Only that you needed to talk to me about something and she indicated it might be of a serious nature."

"It is." She fidgeted nervously with a hoof pick before setting it on the nearby shelf. Closing her eyes momentarily she inhaled deeply as if steeling herself. "Listen, um…I…I know that we…uh…that I've not exactly been—"

"Lucinda, get to the point. I only have a few minutes."

She swallowed hard. "Okay. My sister Holly is missing."

I leaned my head to one side, narrowing my gaze. "I didn't know you had a sister."

"She's my half sister actually. I guess because she's twelve years younger than me, we were never all that close and—she's had a lot of pretty bad problems in her life."

"How long has she been missing?"

"Two and a half months."

I looked at her askance. "That's a long time. Why are you telling me about this now?"

She cast me a melancholy glance. "She's run off a lot of times before. Sometimes she'd be gone for weeks… but this time feels different."

"In what way?"

"I don't know. Usually, somebody in the family would hear from her every so often, a call, a text, something. She always needed money, she'd swear she was coming home in a few days." A tiny shoulder hitch. "Sometimes she did, sometimes she didn't."

"When did you hear from her last?"

"The day before Thanksgiving."

I pondered that briefly. "What about her social media pages? Any posts since then?" I knew that a missing person's digital footprint was critical for law enforcement.

Her forlorn sigh filled the space between us.

"Nothing."

I watched her absently twist a ring on one finger. "I'm assuming you've posted her photo and profile online already?"

"Oh, yeah, on a bunch of those missing persons websites, including the Missing Arizonans Facebook page. My mom and me even went to the Missing in Arizona Day event. We had posters made up and handed out a bunch of them, but so far there's been nothing, not one word even though we're offering a $1000 reward." Appearing more downcast than I'd ever seen her, her voice quaked as if she were holding back tears. "It's like she…I don't know, dropped off the face of the earth. My mom and Aunt Polly, we're all scared shitless something god-awful has happened to her and…and....well look, I admit I've been a total bitch sometimes and you don't owe me the time of day, but I was wondering, *we* were wondering if…." Her expression stricken, she burst out, "If you could try to find her for us?"

It took supreme willpower not to gawk at her. Was this for real? After all the months of putting up with her insolent, insufferable behavior towards me, my initial reaction was *hell*, no! Why should I lift a finger for this manipulative woman?

I groaned inwardly. I really, really did not want to be in the position of having to interact with her on a regular basis for any reason, but was I allowing the rivalry between us to cloud my judgment? "We can run a piece on her, but you should have contacted someone at the paper sooner. This information could have been disseminated a long time ago."

Her scarlet lips turned down as her shoulders drooped. "She's been in a lot of trouble since high school. I don't know, maybe it was my mom's divorce. Whatever, she started hanging out with some real low-lifes and it just got worse and worse. It's been a…huge embarrassment to the family and…I guess we didn't want everybody in the world to know about it."

I fixed her with a perceptive look. "Drugs?"

"And other… things."

"Such as?"

"You name it. She's been busted for DUIs, theft, dealing and…doing, well, whatever she needed to do to get her drugs, if you get my drift," she stated, grimacing.

"Yeah, I got it."

A tiny ember of sympathy stirred inside me. Hadn't my whole family and I just been through hell trying to deal with my brother's drug problem a few short months ago? There were thousands of tragic stories like Holly's all over the country every single day, but was there anything newsworthy about yet another young person who had stupidly thrown her life away and was living on the street or in a crack house right now? Who wanted to read about more of that?

As Ginger would often say, there were "slim pickin's" for select assignments in a town as small as Castle Valley and the possibility there could be an even darker side to this story loomed large—human trafficking. Unfortunately, I'd had personal experience with that appalling subject. Last November, I'd broken a horrific human-trafficking story at the border, and it seemed that the nationwide epidemic of kidnappings had become ever more pervasive, especially in Arizona. But, I needed a hook, something to differentiate this incident from just another missing girl case. I'd promised Ronda I'd hear her out; still, I hesitated, reluctant to involve myself with Lucinda under any circumstances.

Responding to my silence, her dark eyes grew misty as her throaty voice took on a plaintive tone. "We're all getting pretty frantic. She's never been gone this long before."

"Can you remember the longest stretch of time that you've had no contact from her in the past?"

Her gaze pensive, she hesitated before answering. "Probably two months?"

"So, we're only talking about two additional weeks of radio silence at this point, correct?"

I think she sensed my skepticism, because she quickly tacked on, "Did I mention she's got a husband and two darling little girls living in Bagdad that need their mommy?"

I studied her anxious expression. No doubt, she was feeling as uncomfortable as I was. At that instant, I realized that my disdain for her boiled down to raw jealousy based on her hard-to-hide lust for Tally. Other than that, what reason did I have to dislike her? Moreover, it occurred to me in those fleeting seconds that I didn't really know much about her personal life because I had not wanted to waste the time and energy trying to find out. "Where's Bagdad?" I'd heard of the small copper-mining town, but couldn't remember its exact proximity to Castle Valley.

"Um... about an hour north of here."

"I'm assuming you've been in contact with Marshall." I surmised, referring to our local sheriff, Marshall Turnbull.

"Yeah. He says Duane and him have followed up on every lead and all of them have gone cold. If you ask me, I'd say they've given up looking, so…that's why I'm…I mean we, my whole family, is asking for your help," she persisted with a beseeching gaze. "I figured you'd understand considering you just went through those problems with your own brother."

Her highly-personal reference to my brother Sean's drug issues irked me, but then he had stupidly made himself a focal point of my last mind-boggling assignment so it was hardly a secret. I stood in stony silence, weighing my options. While I felt a measure of compassion about her missing sister, I could not get past my stubborn dislike of her. I gave her a dismissive shrug. "I'm sorry," I stated crisply, "it's going to be all asses and elbows at work with Tugg gone the rest of this week, but I can certainly assign this to Walter…"

Thunderclouds formed in her eyes. "No! I don't want Walter. I mean, don't get me wrong. He's real nice and all, but Tally said finding missing people is *your* specialty." She paused, shrewdly assessing my reaction. When I remained stoic, she quickly added, "He promised me you'd do it."

What? He *promised* her. So much for him not getting involved. Cheeks on fire, I struggled to suppress the sarcasm creeping into my voice. "Oh, he did, did he?"

"Yeah. He did. He thinks you're the best reporter on the planet." A hopeful gleam shimmered in her dark eyes as she squeezed out what I suspected was a totally fake smile in her lame attempt at flattery.

I could have walked at that moment, but something made me stay. It was true that the bulk of the five stories I'd uncovered this past year revolved around people gone missing. While four of them appeared to have no connection to the human-trafficking problem, nevertheless countless poor souls, including men and children, seemed to just vanish into thin air in Arizona—an abundance of them. Was it because the vast stretches of open desert provided an inviting place to hide or bury bodies, along with the plethora of abandoned vertical mines that scarred the sometimes-barren landscape? I peeked at my phone. "I'll look into it." I said tersely, the reporter-half of me intrigued, the resentful-female-half angry at Tally for putting me into this untenable situation.

Gratitude flashing in her moist eyes, she pressed her palms together in a prayer-like gesture. "I…we all can't thank you enough."

"I'll check with Marshall and we can talk again when I have more time." I swiveled around, then stopped and turned back, adding as I handed her my business card, "Any other information that might help locate her would be useful and I'll need a recent photo."

"I can show you one now!" She pulled her phone from her back pocket, scrolled and pointed the screen towards me. I tried not to gasp. While Lucinda was not unattractive, this girl had one of the most strikingly beautiful faces I'd ever seen—long dark hair, turned-up nose, flawless skin, full sensuous lips and large almond-shaped brown eyes fringed with thick lashes. She could have easily passed for a top model or movie star. What a tragic waste of a life. Acute dread chilled me imagining the worst of what might have happened to her.

"Send me that photo and I'll get back with you." I turned to leave when she reached out and touched my arm. "Thank you." Gone was the hard glint of malice usually emanating from her eyes. Instead, the angst reflected in her gaze appeared genuine. I was having trouble processing her sudden transformation from queen of snark to this unrecognizable woman in need of my help.

"I can't guarantee anything," I answered, keeping

my tone noncommittal.

"I know. I know. I promised my family I'd at least try."

"And you're positive about her not posting anywhere on social media?"

She shook her head sadly. "Nothing. Not even once since November." She swiped a tear from her cheek. "It's just plain shitty not knowing what happened to her, especially since we were all super excited about her coming home."

"What do you mean?"

She hastily scrolled through her phone again. "Wait!" she announced breathlessly. "I almost forgot to tell you the most important thing." More frantic scrolling, then, "She called Lynnis the night before Thanksgiving from a truck stop just this side of Kingman."

"Who's Lynnis?"

She looked up at me. "Her husband."

"Which truck stop?"

She glanced again at her phone. "Roadrunner."

"Did he give any details of the conversation?"

"He told us that she swore she was done with drugs forever and promised to get sober and…and…she begged him to come and get her."

I raised a quizzical brow. "And did he?"

Lips crushed in a straight line, she shook her head. "He told her to go pound sand, so she told him to go screw himself and that she'd hitch a ride to Bagdad." Her expression morose, she said faintly, "Holly was less than two hours away but we haven't heard from her since."

While the scenario sounded worrisome, I remained dubious. Was Lucinda plotting to send me on the proverbial wild goose chase so she could resume her pursuit of Tally with me safely out of the picture? Playing devil's advocate, I countered, "You said this has happened before quite a few times."

Chewing her lower lip, she shifted her weight, appearing uncomfortable. "Yeah, it has."

"So, is it possible she changed her mind and took off again?"

Her fixed gaze reflected bemused annoyance. "I suppose it's possible. Anything is possible, right? But... Deputy Potts left me a weird message two days ago that makes no sense to any of us."

That centered my attention. "What?"

"He said they have surveillance footage proving Holly was at the Family Dollar store in Aguila about 8:30 pm the same night she called Lynnis."

"And that's weird why?"

"Because Aguila is the opposite direction from Bagdad."

CHAPTER 3

I rolled—or rather, skidded into the gravel parking lot at the *Castle Valley Sun* at exactly 11:55 am, exhaling a short sigh of relief when I did not see Thena's vanilla-colored Mercedes. All right! I congratulated myself for arriving ahead of her. After leaving Lucinda, I'd mulled over every detail she had shared. I had taken a few minutes to check the Arizona map online and it did seem more than a little peculiar that the last sighting of her sister was two hours from Kingman in the opposite direction from her home. I hurriedly showered and dressed, wolfed down a handful of trail mix and then stopped to schmooze for a few minutes with my orange cat, Marmalade, and her best bud, my latest rescue, three-legged, coal-black cat, Fiona, before bolting out the door and practically hydroplaning my Jeep along Lost Canyon Road, kicking up an impressive rooster tail of dust.

Tugg and I were both keenly aware of the importance of presenting a united front. Somehow we had to convince Thena that we would work like dogs to make sure we could keep the paper up and running and profitable. Nevertheless, I feared she might not be as eager to agree to another injection of new capital considering the steep drop in advertising revenue the past few months. Maybe Ginger was right. Perhaps I'd better jump on this missing person story, even though it made my skin crawl to think I'd have to interact with Lucinda.

I slid from my Jeep, skirted by the overgrown clumps of fountain grass waving in the brisk wind, and headed for the front door thinking that Tally would be getting a piece of my mind when I saw him later this evening. Why in the world would he promise Lucinda that I'd be willing to consider her appeal without even discussing it with me first? Yes, my logical mind accepted the fact that Lucinda was Ronda's best friend and that Tally had known her since they were both children. If he had any romantic interest in her, wouldn't he have acted on it by now? His response to my poorly-concealed jealousy towards her was one of mischievous amusement, which irritated the shit out of me, while on the other hand he appeared to tolerate Lucinda's brazen behavior towards him with equal parts of good humor, aplomb and a hint of empathy, which also irritated the shit out of me.

I shook off the disconcerting thoughts and stepped inside the lobby of the *Sun*. The door sensor buzzed, announcing my entrance. While I had sorely needed the three-week hiatus, it felt good to be back at work—or back in the saddle, as Ginger had so aptly described it.

"Straight-up noon and here she is!" Ginger crowed, jumping up from her desk to practically squeeze the breath out of me with her enthusiastic hug. "We've missed ya, girlfriend!"

A blaze of affection radiated through me as I returned her embrace. "Yeah, I've missed all of you guys too."

"How's your arm doin'?" She pulled back, her eyes filled with sudden concern.

"I think it's pretty much all healed."

Her sunny smile lit up the room. "Sugar, that's the best news ever!"

The phone rang and she broke away to answer it on the fourth ring. "Castle Valley Sun." She held up a finger indicating I should wait. "Sure, Elmer, come on in. We're here until five, but not a minute after!" She hung up and fastened inquiring ginger-colored eyes on me. "Hey, I know Tugg's waitin', but when ya git a minute, take a gander at the links I forwarded you about them Trotter twins we was talkin' about earlier. Especially Nelson. Whooeee! Talk about your bad apples. I'd plum forgotten half the details."

"Thanks. I'll check 'em out later." I gave her a thumbs-up and breezed down the narrow hallway, stopping to stick my head in the doorway to my old office that Tally, Jim Sykes and I had once shared. A wave of nostalgia washed over me, realizing those days were now gone forever. Neither Jim nor Walter Zipp was at his desk, so assuming they were both out on assignments, I continued around the corner just as Tugg looked up from his computer screen and beamed me a welcoming smile. "Hey there, Kendall!" He rose, enveloped me in a fatherly hug, and then held me at arm's length, his expression turning serious. "How's that arm? You all back to normal?"

Smiling, I flexed my left arm in several directions. "Good as new. I'm ready to rock n' roll. What about you? You look a little tired." Because of his on-going health issues,

Mary, his excessively-protective wife, had pitched a fit when he'd announced his wish to ditch retirement and return to the high-stress job. She had reluctantly agreed only if I promised to take on co-editing responsibilities. Now I both loved and hated my job. I could definitely do without the hassle of running a small, financially-strapped newspaper, preferring the challenge, stimulation and yes, sometimes risk, of being out on assignment, but fully realized that if I had not consented to her terms, the paper would have folded and none of us would have a job. That commitment weighed heavily on my shoulders.

He waved away my concern. "I'm doin' okay for an old codger. Hey, I'm glad you got here before Thena." He sank into his squeaky chair once more. "It's gonna be tough convincing her to pony up this time around. I'm thinking that you and I might have to sweeten the deal by taking a pay cut. Maybe everybody else too and cut the print edition down to once a week."

"Well, I guess if that's what it takes, but let's try to stay positive. We've got other options to try." We reviewed all the major talking points we intended to introduce to her—live videos on the website and social media pages featuring local events such as parades, city council meetings, live weather reports and teasers for future editions. We also discussed a plan for securing advertisers for sporting events, sponsored content, creating a phone app and perhaps starting a new column featuring interesting tales from Arizona's past and focusing on Castle Valley's rich history.

"Let's hope she goes for it," Tugg mused thoughtfully, absently smoothing the remaining tufts of gray hair above his ears, "or I'm afraid we're toast."

"It's going to work," I assured him, keeping my tone optimistic as I shuffled the papers into a folder. "These are all innovative ideas and if we can implement them soon they are bound to increase revenue, don't you think?"

Tugg hitched his shoulders, his expression conveying uncertainly. His phone jangled and he squeezed out a hopeful smile before answering. I was halfway through opening the mail piled on my desk when I heard Ginger's dramatic whisper on the intercom. "Hey, sugar pie, she's rollin' into the parking lot right now."

Oh boy. Show time. I set the mail aside, stood and nodded at Tugg who was still engaged in conversation. Thumbing towards the lobby, I mouthed silently, "I'll go get her." He widened his eyes in response and I hurried along the hallway, still mentally rehearsing what I planned to say.

I squared my shoulders and entered the lobby just as Ginger declared in her most exaggerated Texas drawl, "Kendall, darlin', would you take a gander at this amazin' lady! Does Miz Rodenborn not look ten years younger than the last time we seen her?"

I cringed inwardly, thinking that a woman as perceptive as Thena would quickly see right through such a superficial show of adoration and fired a *cut it out* glare at Ginger who wore a look of genuine astonishment.

"Thank you, dear heart. I feel ten years younger, maybe fifteen." She turned towards me and a little shock sizzled through me. I'm pretty sure my mouth was hanging open as I stared in amazement at the refined seventy-eight-year-old woman I had not seen for over two months. I'd heard she had recently been to Los Angeles several times during that time period, visiting her great-niece who was an aspiring actress. I scrutinized her face carefully, and although I had never thought she looked her age, she actually did appear younger than the last time I'd seen her. Substantially younger. A face-lift perhaps? Botox or other filler injections? Perhaps it was the elegantly cut mauve designer suit or the fact that she was wearing her snow-white hair in a shorter, upswept spiky style. Or could it be that her blue eyes seemed clearer, brighter, that her skin seemed to radiate with a youthful glow?

"We all got to know your secret," Ginger remarked dreamily, brushing a strawberry-blonde curl away while she examined her freckled face in the mirror that hung on the wall next to her desk. "Lordy, look at these wrinkles! I need a gallon of whatever you're usin'!"

"Don't be silly," Thena stated with a little shrug of dismissal, "you look just fine to me, but there's certainly no reason we gals shouldn't try to always look our best. None of us is getting any younger."

"That's for dang sure," Ginger remarked mournfully, scrunching her face in different directions as she continued to critically study her reflection.

Still blown away by her rejuvenated appearance, I nudged myself back to the pressing matter at hand. "Hello, Thena," I interjected with a warm smile advancing to greet her, "you do look wonderful."

"And you too, Kendall. I'm glad to see your arm is all healed up." We clasped hands, touched cheeks and then I motioned towards the hallway. "We're ready for you in my office."

"Of course." As she passed by Ginger's desk, she leaned towards her and whispered loud enough for me to hear, "Youth Oasis."

"I knew it!" Ginger gasped, flicking me a sassy grin. "Too good to be true, huh?"

I made a face at her and then accompanied Thena along the hallway chatting about the interior improvements she'd made possible with her previous investment in the *Sun*. We also discussed the additional exterior work that still needed to be done on the façade of the timeworn building—fresh paint, repairs, a new roof—and also her proposal to pave the parking lot and plant new landscaping.

"Thena! Thank you for coming. We really appreciate you taking the time to meet with us," Tugg boomed, greeting us in the doorway with a cheerful grin. It was fun to observe the startled look on his round face as he reacted to her youthful transformation. Being male, it was unlikely he would express an effusive compliment like the one Ginger had. After a few seconds of perceptive silence, he concluded with, "The world seems to be treating you exceptionally well."

Her complexion flushed rosy with obvious delight; she thanked him as he seated her at the round table we often used for our editorial meetings. She eyed the only item on the table, a bright yellow folder that contained our proposals. "What have you got for me?" she queried crisply, getting right to the point. As an astute businessperson who had accumulated great wealth as a result of four financially-rewarding marriages, she listened attentively, inclining her head every now and then as Tugg and I enthusiastically explained our blueprint for saving the newspaper. When we concluded, I was heartened to hear her say brightly, "Your proposals sound very promising, especially your idea to bring the remarkable history of this area to the public's attention."

Tugg and I exchanged a quick glance of relief, but then my insides contracted with apprehension when she resumed with, "But as of this moment, the paper is failing to produce enough revenue to break even and it sounds like it may take some time to execute these changes, am I right?"

"It's possible we could turn things around within six months," Tugg suggested, maintaining an optimistic tone and expression. "So, we're thinking a short-term investment of this modest sum would be sufficient to sustain us." He pointed to the six-figure number on the sheet in front of her and we held a collective breath.

She viewed it for what seemed an eternity before pinning us with an enigmatic stare. "That seems reasonable, but I may actually be able help you generate a considerable amount of advertising revenue while these improvements are being implemented."

Again, Tugg and I swapped a quizzical look before he said earnestly, "We're listening."

"Have either of you ever heard of Dr. Asher Craig?" Her coy *cat ate the canary* expression both puzzled and intrigued me. Responding to our negative headshakes, she leaned forward, her face animated. "He's a renowned Beverly Hills plastic surgeon. Everybody who's anybody goes to him. My great-niece, Danielle, introduced me to him more than a year ago. She's an up-and-coming actress, you know."

"You showed us her picture," Tugg remarked with an indulgent smile. "Very pretty young lady."

"Thank you, I think so too," she said, pride shining in her blue eyes. "Anyway, Dr. Craig and his business partner, Dr. Raju Mallick, who is a prominent East Indian dermatologist in his own right, are the developers of a miraculous new anti-aging product and Youth Oasis is their newest endeavor." Preening like one of my cats after a thorough bath, she held up a hand, proclaiming jubilantly, "Now, I know you're both speculating, but I did not have a face-lift, even though Dr. Craig receives glowing testimonials from his patients regarding his expert surgical skills in that field. I must confess I did discuss the possibility with him, but he had another proposal for me," she continued, her face animated. "After carefully researching the published results of their clinical trials conducted during the previous eighteen months, I chose to participate in one. I received injections of their secret cell-regenerating serum once a month at his Beverly Hills clinic and I think you can now judge the results," she professed, framing her face with her hands. "And I also want you to both be aware that I'm currently in discussions with my attorney and accountant regarding my intention to make a substantial investment in Youth Oasis which, as you know, has already purchased a full-page ad in our newspaper and I expect there to be much more to come soon."

Tugg sat up a little straighter. "Now that's something to get excited about."

"Indeed! Right now, they are only open a couple of days a week, but think about this. As the word spreads about the success of these miracle injections, Youth Oasis will become a prime destination. People will come from everywhere to spend their money, not only at the clinic for treatments and elective surgical procedures, but they will also be introduced to all the other wonderful services available in Castle Valley." Counting on her fingers, she added,

"Restaurants, retail shops, gift shops, motels, sight-seeing tours and gasoline, just to name a few. In short, everything our fair town has to offer, not to mention the benefits of new job creation which will translate into increased population growth for the community." She paused, lowering her voice to a confidential tone. "This is off-the-record, but I've heard through the grapevine that several famous celebrities from Hollywood, who are anxious to avoid the paparazzi and maintain their privacy, have already secretly visited Youth Oasis for treatments."

"That's mighty impressive," Tugg declared vociferously, his ruddy complexion reflecting his growing interest.

It *was* impressive, but how was this going to work? Dr. Garcia and his nurse, Hilda, were the only two medical professionals in Castle Valley, which prompted me to ask, "So, who's staffing this place? Correct me if I'm wrong, but I'm not aware of any people in Castle Valley who have the kind of specialty medical training required to perform these types of procedures."

"A keen observation," she remarked, bestowing me a look of admiration. "From what I understand, Dr. Mallick brought some of his own people with him who will help out until additional medical personnel, perhaps from Prescott or even Phoenix, relocate here to work on a full-time basis."

"What about Dr. Craig?"

"For the time being he's bringing nurses and other trained staff with him when he flies in from Beverly Hills."

Tugg leaned back again, hands steepled beneath his chin as he eyed her with thoughtful appreciation. "We'll get right on this." He switched his gaze to me and said with an undertone of barely-contained excitement, "What do you think, Kendall? We do a big write-up, interviews, photo spread, video for the online edition, the whole shebang."

"I'm on it."

"The timing could not be better," Thena exclaimed, clapping her hands. "The grand opening is this Saturday and Dr. Craig informed me that he'd be flying in sometime tomorrow if weather and his schedule permits."

"Any chance you could arrange for me to interview him while he's here?" I inquired, jotting down a few notes.

"I'll make it happen."

"Great."

"And you're going to absolutely *love* Dr. Craig," she gushed, her palms cupped together. "As I said before, not only is his work highly regarded, he's a refined gentleman and…a fine-looking man as well if I do say so myself." Blushing, she tacked on reverently, "and he told me once that it's been his life's goal to help people look as beautiful outside as they feel inside. Isn't that a lovely sentiment?"

Tugg flung me a lightning-quick look of amusement and I knew what he was thinking. Thena Rodenborn might be pushing eighty but she wasn't too old to have a crush on her doctor, who, as altruistic as he sounded, was most likely commanding hefty fees for his surgical expertise. Moreover, if the results of the miracle injections proved to be as successful on everyone as they had on Thena, he'd be "settin' purty" as Ginger liked to say. I penned a few more questions I'd be asking him.

"Damn!" Tugg crowed, looking happier than I had seen him since starting at the paper last spring. "This could be a major development! It's going to put our little cow town on the map."

"Oh, I'm just getting started," she said with a look of sly satisfaction stealing over her features. "There's more."

As she explained the positive aspects of the clinic, which included everything from skin revitalization treatments and injections to outpatient surgeries, I savored the sensation of tension seeping from my body as the magical phrase *increased advertising revenue*, the lifeblood of all newspapers, danced in my head. We were going to be all right. No salary cuts and no staff layoffs and if we were lucky we might be able to afford to give pay raises and hire another reporter. *Hallelujah*!

Soft footsteps approached and we turned to see Ginger peering around the doorframe proffering three water bottles. "Talkin' a whole bunch does parch the throat. Y'all probably need somethin' to drink." Based on her ultra-innocent expression, I suspected that she had been eavesdropping. So Ginger. So transparent. I stifled the desire to laugh aloud.

"Thank you, my dear," Thena said, accepting the bottle with a delighted smile. "How thoughtful." She twisted off the cap and sipped while studying our proposal again.

My reproving look locked with Ginger's impish one before she exited the room. No doubt, she would be reporting her findings to the rest of the staff within nanoseconds. While waiting to hear what Thena had to say next, I surreptitiously typed Dr. Asher Craig's name into my phone. I scrolled through his website and Facebook page, absorbing the images of his impressive office, the list of medical services offered, scores of glowing reviews, and took a few seconds to study the photo of him—a distinguished- looking man with pleasant features, wavy silver hair, wire-rimmed glasses and who looked to be in his mid-fifties, perhaps older.

"Now you both know that one of my passions as president of the Castle Valley Historical Society is to try and save our few remaining treasured buildings from the wrecking ball, vandalism and neglect," Thena continued. "Kendall, you certainly know how hard I worked to get the old mission on Lost Canyon Road listed on the National Register of Historic Places."

"Yes."

"And the many obstacles we had to overcome to save the Hansen House, and that we're still fighting to get final approval on the old Ice House in Yarnell, which I'm sure you won't ever forget."

Tugg and I traded a solemn glance. "Not any time soon," I remarked softly, remembering the sickening discovery I'd made while working on a story that ended up taking a bizarre and fatal turn. "You've done a remarkable job of securing historical designation for so many endangered buildings and homes."

She accepted my compliment with a gracious nod. "Thank you. I try." She leaned forward, her eyes brightening. "Are either of you familiar with the old Catholic church located on the Double G Ranch property?"

I shook my head *no* but Tugg murmured, "Yeah, I know where it is, but last time I saw the place vandals had done real a number on it."

"Unfortunately true," she grimaced, her nose wrinkling in distaste. "I abhor people who destroy and deface for their own entertainment. There are actually two structures on the ranch that deserve to be protected and preserved."

"What's the other one?" I asked with mild interest.

"The Gold Queen mansion. Named after the old gold mine, of course. Marvelous house, marvelous architecture." Her voice rose with excitement. "It's well over a hundred years old and I'd give my eyeteeth to get my hands on it too, but for now, I am focusing on the church and," she admitted, heaving a deep sigh, "I have to concede that it's going to be my biggest and most challenging project to date. But, it has a captivating history, good bones and I believe it can be restored with elbow grease and, of course, money."

I gave her a polite inquiring look, not knowing where she was going with this. "And how exactly will restoring this old church affect us?"

She then launched into the history of the church, built almost two centuries ago. Founded originally by the Spanish as a monastery long before the ranch was there, she recounted harrowing tales of how first the monks—and a century later, the priests had survived tremendous hardships including drought, disease, fire and marauding Indians. "The church has gone through several iterations since the Catholic Church sold it about three years ago."

"Sold it?" I inquired, giving her a quizzical look. "Why would they do that?"

A petite shrug. "Apparently it was too small to accommodate the growing Hispanic population in that area so I understand a much larger, more modern church is in the planning stages now and will be closer to Castle Valley. Since that time, Our Lady of the Desert served briefly as an Episcopal church, after which it sat empty for a time, and most recently as the non-denominational Healing Heart Fellowship. I really liked the new pastor. He and his lovely family relocated from somewhere out east but they weren't there very long when he suddenly closed his ministry, put the property up for sale and moved someplace up north, I believe."

"Really? Why?" I queried, sensing a possible story.

An introspective look clouded her eyes before she murmured, "I'm a bit fuzzy on the details, but I believe that his wife and two of his children were bitten by spiders while they were sleeping."

Envisioning the horrifying scenario of spiders hiding in my bed gave me a royal case of the shivers. Since childhood, I had struggled with my irrational and illogical fear of the eight-legged creatures. My father often expressed amazement that I had no fear of snakes, frogs, lizards, mice or chasing down murderers, but the smallest spider would send me into a screaming panic. Much to Tally's amusement and my embarrassment, I had to admit that I had not overcome that fear as an adult.

"And shortly after that," Thena added, "there was a fire at the rectory when a propane tank blew up. Luckily, the family was not home at the time."

"So, that building is unoccupied as well."

"Correct. Last year, the Double G Ranch acquired the entire twenty-five acres of church property soon after Glendine Higgins passed away, God rest her poor, suffering soul." She crossed herself, then paused in reverent silence momentarily before resuming with, "I asked her daughter, Wanda, what they planned to do with the building and if she would be interested in pursuing historic designation."

I shrugged my confusion. "This is all fascinating information, but I'm confused as to how this would benefit the *Sun*."

"Me too," Tugg chimed in, looking as puzzled as I felt.

"Allow me to explain," Thena told us with an indulgent smile. "In addition to having Dr. Mallick at Youth Oasis, I've convinced Dr. Craig to visit at least twice a month to offer his expertise in consultations and perform scheduled surgeries. Can you imagine the distinction of having a cosmetic surgeon with his outstanding credentials practicing in Castle Valley?"

I continued to eye her with skepticism and cleared my throat. "I don't mean to throw cold water on your plans, Thena, but why would it be worthwhile for a doctor of such…ah…prominence to travel from Beverly Hills to… such a small out-of-the-way place as Castle Valley?"

"For one thing, he already comes to our fair state several times a month to enjoy our fresh, clean air and get away from the hubbub of the big city, so that's where the third leg of my vision comes in." She paused and I got the impression she was enjoying keeping us hanging on her every word. "Because Youth Oasis has limited space, my plan is to purchase the property and renovate the church to serve as an exclusive, high-end, luxury spa specializing in top-notch aftercare for people of means recovering from all manner of illness, but mainly for patients who have undergone surgical procedures at Youth Oasis and desire a secluded spot to recuperate. Furthermore," she tacked on with forceful emphasis, "the small private airpark just a few miles to the west will make it convenient to fly in from anywhere." She hesitated again, obviously judging our reactions before adding, "And I'm hoping Dr. Craig will agree to invest in my vision, as I'm planning to invest in his."

Tugg and I exchanged an apprehensive glance. I knew we were thinking the same thing. Energetic, sophisticated and persistent, Thena appeared to be in full possession of her faculties, but this idea seemed as far-fetched as opening an outdoor ice rink in the middle of the desert in July. "So, I'm assuming you've already discussed this…idea with Dr. Craig? What does he think?"

Hesitating, she dropped her gaze briefly before reconnecting with us, her periwinkle-blue eyes shadowed with uncertainty for the first time. "Let's just say that he is not as excited as I am; however, he does like the concept of patients having access to the healing powers of those amazing mineral springs that are within walking distance of the church."

Tugg frowned skepticism. "You think Glendine's family would be willing to part with that piece of property? It's a pretty spectacular, one-of-a-kind place."

Thena nodded. "My point exactly. It may be a challenge to convince them, but I feel it's essential to have it in order to fulfill my vision of creating an exclusive place where people of prominence can relax and heal in a unique setting they can't find anywhere else."

"Gotcha. You're thinking of making it a destination like one of those high-dollar resorts in Sedona."

"Exactly!"

I caught her eye. "It sounds promising, but if that's the case, why isn't Dr. Craig more enthused about it?"

Her exasperated sigh permeated the room. "I don't think he's in love with the idea of renovating the church. I am fully aware that there will be some roadblocks ahead to make this work, but I'm not one to give up easily, as you know."

Personally, I had to agree with the doctor. Why spend a gazillion bucks to renovate a two-hundred-year-old building when there had to be more suitable properties available closer to the clinic, or why not design and build a new place?

Tugg sat silent, looking thoughtful before remarking with an undertone of restrained endorsement, "It will be a monumental undertaking, but hey, if you think you can pull this off, more power to you."

Smiles all around. While I hugely admired this gutsy, intelligent, entrepreneurial woman, something about her idea sounded just a little off. Thena's project seemed feasible but it had a "pie in the sky" feel to it, and what if Youth Oasis did not draw the volume of customers buying products and seeking cosmetic surgeries necessary to support such a recovery facility? Tugg was right. It would be a monumental undertaking. "What's in it for the ranch owners? If they just bought the property, what's the incentive to sell?"

She met my questioning gaze. "As I mentioned before, I approached Wanda immediately after I discovered they had purchased the property because the family has had a strong connection with the Catholic Church for generations." She paused, appearing pensive. "At first she seemed open to the idea of historical designation, especially since her grandmother was the music director there for many years and her great-uncle was the parish priest. She told me she might consider selling, but since then she appears to have had a change of heart."

Tugg shifted in his chair. "Why do you think that is?"

"Well, now, she claims that on her deathbed, Glendine requested that they never part with the church under any circumstances."

Tugg looked even more puzzled. "What good

is it doing them just sitting there all boarded-up and deteriorating?"

She nodded affirmation. "Exactly my concern. It's nothing but an albatross around their necks. And, I've heard from other people that the ranch is struggling financially and they've had ongoing problems with vandals and trespassers."

"That doesn't make any sense," I interjected. "If they're having financial trouble how were they able to buy the property?"

A slight shrug. "I'm assuming an inheritance from Glendine, but then I'm not in a position to know for certain. If Wanda can be persuaded to agree to my offer, even considering her past difficulties, I would try my best to convince Dr. Craig to offer her a position at the clinic." I fleetingly wondered what difficulties she was referring to but didn't want to interrupt her train of thought. "But, if that isn't feasible, we could certainly offer her a position at the new recovery facility and there could be employment opportunities as well for her brother and son, if they so choose. Or, we might be able to offer them a situation where they could receive continuing income from our facility. Either way, it could be a win-win-win situation for everyone!"

Her zeal was contagious. Even though I was now feeling cautiously optimistic, I felt compelled to express my concerns. "It does sound promising, but why not find a building that doesn't require so much time and expense to renovate? What about the other place, the Gold Queen mansion that you mentioned earlier?"

She gave me a deferential nod. "We do want to preserve both structures, but historic designation alone will not necessarily be enough to save them from eventual demolition or destruction by other means. The mansion was definitely a consideration, but it's got several drawbacks."

"Such as?"

"Neglect, it's remote, lacks the ambience and most importantly, it does not offer access to the hot springs, which to me makes the church property unique and far more appealing for our purposes."

Nodding, I murmured, "I see."

"Once our application is approved," she went on, her tone growing more vibrant, "the building can be utilized for a *commercial* venture. That allows us to take full advantage of the Historic Preservation Tax Credit program; the minimum criteria being that it's reserved mostly for rural communities and that we show a positive impact on state and local revenues generated by the project."

Tugg absently drummed his fingers on his desk. "Sounds like you've got your ducks in a row."

"Almost. There will be a few...shall we say logistic challenges to deal with, but I'm sure we'll be able to conquer them." She shifted her weight slightly in my direction. I don't know if Tugg noticed the subtle change in her body language, but I did. While her expression remained composed, I perceived a veiled light behind her speculative stare. "And that is where you come in."

Dumbfounded, I blinked surprise. "Me?"

"Yes, you. What I need right now is an advocate to act on my behalf. Your idea of starting a column highlighting the history of Castle Valley could tie in perfectly with my project. If you can publish a series of persuasive articles written in the same vein that motived the Hansen heirs to relinquish their house for restoration, we can repeat that success."

Her reflective stare continued to bore in on me until, all at once my skin tingled as a profound sense of realization flowed through me. The message she conveyed was unmistakable. It was payback time.

CHAPTER 4

Apparently I must have still appeared skeptical, because Thena pressed ahead on her sales pitch with renewed passion. "This is a fabulous opportunity to research the colorful history of this extraordinary old church and play an integral part in preserving a valuable piece of Arizona's history. At the same time, you can employ your powers of persuasion to convince Wanda to sell it to us." She sat back, wearing a look of smug assuredness, and clasped her hands in her lap. "Consider this as well. The advertising revenue produced from Youth Oasis, in tandem with this new entity…" She paused, looking thoughtful, and posited, "perhaps I'll call it Skin Deep Rejuvenation Spa or some such thing…anyway, it will be a boon to the newspaper's financial health and the community."

Tugg jumped in, "It's sounding better and better to me!"

I locked eyes with him, tensing slightly as her velvet trap closed around me, draping a heavy mantle of responsibility around my shoulders. Talk about pressure. It sounded like a tall order, but then I was always game for a new assignment. "I'm not sure Wanda will be any more receptive to me than she was to you, but I'll sure give it a try. How soon do you want me to get started?"

"Immediately."

I hesitated, remembering my commitment to investigate Lucinda's missing sister, which actually sounded loads more intriguing than writing about some musty old building. Oh well. Pleasing Thena commanded top priority. Somehow, I would have to split my time between editorial duties and both assignments. I grinned at her. "Deal."

"Excellent. I suggest you begin by visiting Clara Whitlow over at the library. As you know, she is a lifelong resident of Castle Valley, vice president of the Historical Society and a veritable fountain of knowledge concerning the history of this area. She can provide you with a wealth of background information on the origins of the church and other related materials. I'll call her this evening and let her know that you'll be contacting her soon."

"That would be great."

She pulled her phone from her purse, scrolled with one finger and then scribbled something on a slip of paper before handing it to me. "Here is Wanda's phone number. The main entrance to the church is now boarded up so you'll have to call and let her know you're coming so she or one of the other family members can let you inside."

"I'll get started tomorrow."

Tugg and I performed an enthusiastic high-five after we had escorted her out the front door, assisted her into her Mercedes and watched her drive away, bouncing across the railroad tracks towards downtown. Was I imagining it or did the desert breeze smell a little sweeter, the skies appear bluer, the mid-afternoon sun brighter? The meeting had turned out far differently than I had expected—no salary cuts, no layoffs and offered a decent chance to salvage and grow the newspaper. My heart swelled with gratitude at the unexpected turn of events. I squared my jaw. Now I'd best get my ass in gear and make it all happen.

When we stepped inside, I inhaled a sharp breath, stunned to see the entire staff crowded into the lobby. Ginger clapped and sang out, "Here they come to save the day!" as everyone else broke into wild applause.

"Woo-hoo! You guys are freakin' awesome!" Jim Sykes shouted, punching a fist skyward.

Harry and Rick chimed in with "Damn straight!" and "You did it!" Walter and Al rounded out the bedlam with a chorus of loud whistles.

Red-faced, but displaying a triumphant grin, Tugg reached for my hand and held it up as if we were prizefighters, then motioned them to settle down. "Thank you, everyone! I'll tell you what, if Mary wasn't expecting me home right after work, we'd be celebrating tonight, so, let's plan for Friday after work at Buster's. Drinks and dinner on me!"

Stomping of feet and more hooting followed before everyone reluctantly returned to their desks. Heady with exhilaration at the challenge of a new assignment, I found it hard to concentrate as I dove into work, aware that I only had the remainder of the afternoon to catch up on accumulated tasks, organize my thoughts and prepare to be on the road again. I consulted with Tugg on the assignment sheets for Jim and Walter, caught up on emails and snail mail before I laid out a strategy for my own assignment, which included a list of people to interview and locations I would need to visit.

I did a quick Google Earth search, locating the Double G Ranch twenty-two miles northwest of town. It appeared to be a good-sized spread with miles of serpentine dirt roads, massive, irregular rock formations and a number of vehicles and structures including the old church, which I was now itching to inspect in person, along with the Gold Queen mansion. I zoomed in on the far eastern end of the property, taking note of a substantial structure tucked against a rocky hillside. I could only assume that I was seeing the old house. Tally knew most of the ranchers in the area so I'd ask him what he knew about the ranch and the Higgins family when we met up later this evening. A little shock reverberated through me. Holy crap! I'd forgotten to text him.

"I'm calling it a day," Tugg announced, yawning loudly, pushing away from his desk. "What about you?"

I looked up from my screen, surprised to realize it was already four-thirty. "Soon. I just want to finish a few more things. Hey, listen, I made a commitment this morning to work on another possible story before this assignment from Thena came up."

"Oh, yeah? Whatcha got?"

I told him about how I'd been cornered by Ronda and pressed into agreeing to follow up on Lucinda's missing sister and his eyebrows shot skyward. "Are you shittin' me?" He pinned me with a skeptical glance. "You two girls finally call a cease-fire?"

"I wouldn't go that far. In my mind it's more of a favor to Ronda and frankly, from what Lucinda has told me so far, it does sound somewhat intriguing. I can have a short piece ready to post online sometime tomorrow and we can run it in both print editions this week."

"Sounds good," he said, shrugging into his coat. "Too bad about Holly. God gave that girl a beautiful face and she seemed smart enough, but man, she sure managed to screw up her life."

I stared at him. "It seems like everybody in town knew about her but me."

He gave me a knowing look and chuckled. "Well, it isn't like you haven't had your hands full these past few months, being up to your eyeballs breaking those kick-ass stories."

"True."

"Sounds to me like Thena wants you to jump on this preservation thing right away."

"If I do that, I'm not going to be in the office much. I feel terrible leaving again when you're supposed to be off the rest of the week."

"Hmmm. I do have one little problem. Wednesday morning I have a dental appointment in Phoenix that's been scheduled for months. I can't miss it and Mary's already got plans to stay overnight so she can do some shopping and visit with friends on Thursday morning."

"Well, then, this can wait until next week."

"Not on your life! Thena's wishes come first." He fell into momentary silence but I could see activity dancing in his eyes. "How about this. If you can be here Wednesday and stay until at least noon on Thursday, I'll be back by then."

"You're sure about that?"

"You bet."

"And if you need more time on Friday as well, just let

me know. Right now, this assignment is far more important than me sitting around the house, or worse, having Mary badger me about all the stuff needing fixed."

"She's going to be annoyed and give you a world of grief," I said, shooting him an apologetic grin. "We'll probably both pay a price."

He started for the door and then turned back to me, his brown eyes glowing with humor. "Someday, she'll thank you for doing this and the only price I'll have to pay is finally agreeing to take her on that Alaskan cruise she's been bugging me about for ten years."

I smiled. "That doesn't sound like a bad thing. Especially if you get out of here in August when it's 150 degrees!"

"Amen to that!" he called, waving backwards over his shoulder.

I picked up my phone and tapped Tally's number. Five rings later, he answered. "Hey. Been wondering what the plan is for tonight."

"Sorry," I said, expelling a tired sigh. "I meant to text you earlier. It's been kind of a crazy day. I'll tell you all about it at dinner."

"Yeah, I had kind of a crazy day myself."

"I figured." I reminded myself that I was supposed to be pissed off at him for foisting Lucinda's predicament on me, but my irritation had subsided after Thena's unexpected request, diminishing my need to rake him over the coals. At least for now.

"Speaking of dinner, I'm not going to have time to cook so are you okay with takeout? I can pick up burgers and fries or Mexican on my way home." At the mention of food, my hollow, rumbling stomach reminded me that I'd never eaten lunch. Mexican, definitely Mexican—chips, salsa, guacamole, tacos, tamales, oh yeah!

"Whatever's easy." A brief silence, then, "I kinda liked you not working. I could get used to your home cooking every night."

I laughed to myself. My cooking was average at best but compared to his mother's wretched culinary skills, which I'd had to endure several times, it must taste awesome. Thank goodness, Tally and Ronda had been fortunate enough to have Gloria, their longtime Hispanic housekeeper, there to rescue them from suffering the stomach-wrenching torture of having to ingest Ruth's strangely-prepared meals every day. How she could take perfectly good ingredients and ruin them was a mystery to me.

Tally had told me stories of how he and Ronda would face her wrath if they dared complain and how they would hide food in their milk, underneath their dinner plates, in napkins and even slip pieces to the dogs in order to be excused from the table. Later, after their parents had retired for the evening, Gloria would sneak them warm tortillas filled with mouthwatering ingredients along with tantalizing pastries. Another in the long list of reasons I would be glad when our house was finished. I could imagine a day when I would never have to experience another meal prepared by her.

"Oh, I see," I said, playfully, "so you're only marrying me for my cooking?"

"One among many of your desirable attributes." His lightly suggestive tone sent a pleasurable chill surging through me, as if he were gently caressing my body.

"You're not so bad yourself, cowboy. Meet you at

my place in an hour?"

"I'll be waiting."

"Oh, one more thing. Could you feed my feline babies when you get there?"

"Consider it done."

Sighing contentedly, I slipped the phone in my purse and hopped online to order takeout from Angelina's. After I cleared off my desk, I grabbed my jacket and arrived in the lobby just as Ginger was pulling on her coat and wrapping a frilly pink scarf around her neck. "Wind's pickin' up. The weatherman is predicting thirty-to forty-mile-an-hour gusts tomorrow and it's supposed to be colder than a well digger's…knee tomorrow night."

"Yeah, I heard another low pressure front was moving in and we might get more rain or even a few snow flurries."

"Hey, hey, before you git away," she urged, searching on her desk for a few seconds before extending me several pieces of paper, "here's a list of places that still got space available for y'all's weddin'. The nicest ones in Sedona and Scottsdale book up years in advance, so these are the best I could find for October unless you an' Tally want to push the date out a couple o' months."

"Are you kidding? You've been after me forever to set a wedding date and now you want us to change it?"

She widened her eyes expressively. "Not really, but I could book a much fancier place if I had a little more time. Nine months ain't a lot of time if y'all want to find someplace really special."

I glanced at the list of places, then back at her. "You know, I really appreciate all your efforts, but, to be perfectly honest, I don't really care that much."

She drew back and stared at me as if I'd lost my mind. "Excuse me?"

I swiped a hand over my forehead. "Look, my mother spent a fortune putting on the wedding of the century for me the first time around and then wanted to do something even more extravagant before Grant and I broke up, so a simple venue is fine with me."

"You sure about that?" she queried me with a sharp glance.

"Positive." I handed the papers back to her. "Whatever you pick is fine."

Sighing, she stuffed them in her purse. "If y'all want simple, how 'bout this. Lots o' couples are gittin' hitched in national parks nowadays. How does that sound?"

"Huh? Interesting. I'll run that by Tally," I said, zipping up my jacket.

"So, you comin' with us gals to check out Youth Oasis?" she inquired, her expression turning hopeful. "It'll be fun! But, we gotta bust buns 'cause they're only open 'til six."

"I can't right now."

"Suit yourself," she sniffed, obviously disappointed. "You'll be sorry. In a few days I'm gonna look ten years younger and you're gonna be so jealous."

I grinned. "I'll definitely be checking it out soon." I tilted my head slightly and shot her a droll look. "So…ah… is there anything in our meeting that you *didn't* overhear?"

She met my gaze with an innocent yet mischievous glimmer in her amber eyes. "I might've missed the last few minutes. Why? Is there somethin' else I need to know?"

She was delightfully incorrigible. "Just that I'll be out on assignment tomorrow and possibly Friday as well."

"Oh yeah?" she said, slinging her purse strap over her shoulder. "Where ya off to this time?"

"Thena asked me to write up a story on the old church at the Double G Ranch."

Her expression changed from mild interest to wide-eyed disbelief. "Well, shut my mouth," she gasped. "That is one mighty strange coincidence."

"What is?"

"Sugar, you do remember me tellin' you about them this mornin', don't ya?"

I stared at her. "Who?"

"The Trotter twins."

"What about them?"

"The Double G is their ranch."

CHAPTER 5

Twenty minutes later, I arrived at Angelina's Mexican Kitchen. I hastily collected the food, started out the door, halted, and then turned around. Perhaps I should pick up a gift card now. I had a feeling I might need it soon. Driving out of town, I was tortured by the mouthwatering aroma of warm tortilla chips, tamales and refried beans wafting from the plastic bags. I could swear my empty stomach was whistling almost as loudly as the rising wind now buffeting my Jeep. I held out as long as I could. Unable to control myself a second longer, I dug into the chips and munched several handfuls as I cruised along the highway towards home, my mind busily sorting through all the tidbits of information imparted by Ginger. Even though we had both been in a hurry to leave, she bent my ear all the way out the front door to the parking lot, insistent that I know a few salient facts before going to the Double G Ranch.

During the short window of time available to us both, she had proceeded to give me the CliffsNotes version of the trials and tribulations of Nelson Trotter, his sister Wanda Trotter Keating and her twin sons. Breathlessly, Ginger explained that Wanda had once worked as a nurse at the hospital in Prescott until she'd been accused of murdering her husband's lover by deliberately administering the wrong meds in the woman's IV. She went on to say that Wanda's brother was a registered sex offender who had spent time in jail for allegedly kidnapping an underage woman and keeping her locked in a room at their ranch against her will. Each sibling had vehemently denied any wrongdoing. Wanda's case had been dismissed due to lack of clear evidence and Nelson had served time in jail only to have the charges dropped when his accuser failed to show up for the preliminary hearing and subsequently vanished. Free for the past year, he had returned to the ranch shortly before the death of their mother, Glendine. Ginger was about to launch into what she coined the "bad luck curse" that had dogged generations of the long-time ranching family, including one of Wanda's sons, when I held up a hand. "Ginger, I am sooooo late! I gotta go and so do you!"

She glanced at her phone. "Oh, flapdoodle. I got lots more stuff I can tell ya about that family."

Hair whipping across my face in the erratic wind, I reached for the door handle on my Jeep. "Cool! I have something to tell you too but we'll have to talk later, okay?"

"You betcha, but do not be fooled," she had warned in an ominous monotone, squinting into the dimming light of the evening sun. "Them two may have got themselves a get-out-of-jail-free card, but from what I hear around town, they're nasty tempered, potty-mouthed folks and some say Wanda's brother's crazier than bat shit, so better watch your heinie!"

I thought that while the information was noteworthy, none of it seemed particularly germane to my writing a series of articles on an ancient church, other than having some idea as to the types of personalities I would be dealing with soon. Although, I must admit, Ginger's remark regarding the supposed Higgins family bad luck curse, piqued my curiosity. Could that have been what Thena meant by her vague reference to Glendine's "poor, suffering soul"?

These thoughts were still percolating in my mind as I swung east onto Lost Canyon Road, but quickly evaporated as I stared at the dazzling spectacle of Castle Rock bathed in radiant, burnished copper, its jagged spires of iridescent coral and gold sandstone thrust boldly skyward into a luminous turquoise sky filled with billowy clouds of rose pink and magenta contrasted by splashes of deep purple. So awesome! It looked like Nature's paint box had exploded.

I glanced in the rearview mirror in time to catch the last fiery rays of the sun before it slid into a bank of molten salmon-and-lavender-flecked clouds. Chills raced up my arms. I'd only experienced one other example of what I dubbed a "mirror sunset" or "bounce" since my arrival in this extraordinary place. In my opinion, Arizona sunrises and sunsets were unparalleled anywhere else in the world.

Ten minutes later, as I pulled into my driveway, a mild pang of melancholy touched me when I stepped out onto the uneven gravel. Even though in a matter of months, Tally and I would be living in our spacious new home, I would miss the ambiance of this comfortable ranch house. In the fading apricot glow, I stood listening to the soft serenade of mourning doves before spotting Tally as he rose from the porch swing. He strode out to greet me, looking as lean and handsome as ever in form-fitting jeans and a sheepskin jacket, topped off with his well-worn ivory Stetson. Definitely hot. My heart overflowed with supreme gratitude that I had met this extraordinary man who was not only the sexiest man I'd ever met, but now the love of my life. "Was that a phenomenal sunset or what?" I asked, closing the distance between us.

"Pretty spectacular," he responded, pulling me into his arms. "Kind of like you."

I melted into his muscular frame and savored the sensation of his sensuous kiss that even after all these months still sent warm desire pulsating through my body. I returned his kiss with fervor, remembering what Ginger had said to me recently after we'd had another one of our sizzling disagreements. *"Don't be sqattin' on your spurs, missy! You do realize how lucky you are, right? How many of us gals ever git the chance to marry a tall, dark, handsome cowboy? And rich to boot!"* Ruefully, I had to admit she was right.

I think we would have continued our passionate embrace longer if it hadn't been for my loud, complaining belly. I could not contain the giggle that rose to my throat and he released me slowly, his dark eyes twinkling with mirth. "I guess my plans for you are going to have to wait until after you've been fed."

"Been fed?" I repeated, with mock indignation. "Like one of your horses?"

His hand slid down my back and he swatted my behind lightly. "Exactly."

Laughing, I rolled my eyes and pushed against his chest, commanding, "You, sir, can bring the bags inside," before I marched through the front door and then stopped in open-mouthed amazement. "What the..." I whispered in awe, staring at a large vase filled with yellow roses and a bottle of my favorite Pinot Noir sitting beside two wine glasses on the coffee table. At the sound of rustling plastic and the sharp click of his boots, I whirled around and met his meaningful gaze. "Are these for me?" I asked stupidly.

"No, they're for the cats," he deadpanned, breaking into his signature sideways grin. "Of course they're for you. Just a little something to make up for me not…um…being there with you this morning."

Our eyes locked and I knew. I knew it was more than that. The impetuous me, the hot-tempered me, famous for acting and speaking in haste, ached to confront him with "Thanks a pant-load for colluding with Lucinda behind my back!" but, at this point, what would such caustic words accomplish other than to ruin the moment? I bit them back and they lay dormant on my tongue like ground glass, for once in my life left unspoken. Instead, I closed the space between us and murmured, "Damn, it's hard to stay mad at you," before planting a long, seductive kiss on his lips. Unfortunately, my growling stomach spoiled the mood again. I pulled away with a reluctant sigh. "Sorry. You open the wine while I get comfortable," I said, tugging off my boots, "and then you can tell me about your crazy day."

While ice-cold margaritas would have probably been more appropriate with Mexican food, the wine was a fine substitute and I was feeling mellow by the time we'd polished off the meal and Tally had recounted the events of his day. Happily, Summer Rain was only suffering from a common cold and had been isolated to the south barn. On a sour note, he and Ray had gotten into an intense argument on how to best handle the ongoing gray wolf problem. The once almost-extinct animals were protected under the Endangered Species Act, which pitted him and most of his fellow ranchers against the Federal Government. "If you ask me, ranchers are the endangered species!" he complained hotly. "We're all fighting with U.S. Fish and Wildlife Services and a number of environmental groups threatening lawsuits all because we're trying to defend our livestock and our way of life."

He also admitted to being depressed about having to witness the vet put Dolly down, and stressed about all the work associated with preparations for the horse buyers who would begin arriving in the morning. "Guess we'd better make the most of this evening," he lamented, "I'm not going to get to see you much the rest of this week."

"Well, actually the timing is good for me," I remarked, finishing off last few salsa-laden tortilla chips while explaining Thena's strategy to acquire the old church and her subsequent vision of financial achievement for the community and the newspaper, and how my assignment would contribute to the success of her endeavors. "She suggested I talk to Clara at the library for background information on the church and other local history, but before I head out there tomorrow, I was wondering what you can tell me about the Higgins family."

A slight headshake before he answered thoughtfully. "Not much."

I looked at him askance. "Really? I figured you knew most of the ranching families in this area."

"For the most part, but the Higgins clan always kept pretty much to themselves. Still do. My dad was friendly enough with Glen Higgins, before he died."

"Glen," I repeated, almost to myself. "So, I'm

guessing Glendine was named after him."

"Probably."

"Do you know anything about this so-called bad luck curse hanging over the family that Ginger told me about?"

Tally lounged on the couch with both cats now ensconced comfortably in his lap, kneading and purring up a storm. At my question, his eyes narrowed, deepening the cleft between his dark brows. "Curse? That sounds like something Ginger would say." A nonchalant shrug. "There've been stories circulating over the years, some maybe true, some maybe not." His gaze turned inward as if in deep thought. "I know twins ran in the family. Glen had a twin brother named Gary and Glendine had a twin sister named Gwyn."

"Thus the Double G Ranch?"

"Yep. Clara will be a far better resource than I am." The faint lines around his eyes crinkled with humor. "She's got a few years on me."

I laughed. "No kidding. But, listen, Thena said something today that caught my attention."

"What's that?"

"She said, and I quote, 'God rest Glendine's *poor, suffering soul,'* not just God rest her soul, as most people would say. Why poor and suffering? Got any idea what she meant?"

He paused, again looking introspective. "Come to think of it, there were quite a few unfortunate accidents that happened over the years and then...um...did Thena mention that Glendine was a recluse?"

"No. Tell me more."

Absently stroking Marmalade's orange fur while

scratching Fiona under her chin, his brown eyes grew distant. "I'm not quite sure of the order, but I think it was her sister who got sick and died first, then her husband and not long after that she lost her father. Just, boom, boom, boom, all in a row, within a year or two. After the last funeral she had some kind of a mental breakdown…"

"Well, no wonder. That's a heavy load to bear."

"Yeah, well that wasn't the end of her troubles."

Now thoroughly intrigued, I leaned forward. "Meaning what?"

He held up a cautioning hand. "Again, this may or may not be true, but word around town was when she started waiting tables at the Rattlesnake Saloon, apparently she wasn't too picky about seeking male companionship."

"Understandable," I murmured. "She was probably very lonely."

He nodded agreement and continued. "At some point, she got romantically involved with a truck driver who gave her some sob story about his two-timing wife, so she let him and his kid move in with her. From what I remember hearing, he turned out to be a hard-drinking, jealous son-of-a-bitch. The rumor is he came back unexpectedly one night and found her…ah…in a compromising position with one of the ranch hands."

"Oh no," I groaned. "This sounds like a bad ending."

"Pretty much. Evidently, there was a hell of a fight. He beat the shit out of the cowboy first, and then he went apeshit and told Glendine he'd fix it so no man would ever want her again."

I tensed at his ultra-somber expression. "Uh-oh. What happened?"

"The story is he cut up her face with a broken beer bottle…I think I remember hearing that she was blinded in one eye…"

Imagining the horrifying scene, an icy chill coursed through me. "Oh, my God! That's…awful. Where were Wanda and Nelson when this all happened?"

A look of doubt crossed his face. "Mmmm. I'm not sure."

"I assume Glendine filed charges against him."

"Take it for what it's worth, rumor, innuendo, small town gossip. Supposedly, he skipped town afterwards and disappeared."

"So…she didn't file charges."

"I don't know if she ever got the chance."

I pondered that, muttering almost to myself, "I wonder if there's anything on file at the sheriff's office."

Shrugging, he said, "Again, not sure. You could ask Marshall if they keep records that far back." He stared into the distance for a few seconds. "I think the sheriff back then was Jack Hughes."

"Is he still around?"

"Nope. Died five or six years ago."

I sighed heavily. "Poor Glendine. I'd like to hope the bastard got caught and is still rotting in prison!"

"I never heard what happened to him. Like I said, the Higgins family was always a pretty close-mouthed bunch." Tally cracked a knowing smile and tilted his head to one side. "You are hands-down, the most curious woman I have ever met."

I returned his grin. "You know me, unanswered questions and unsolved mysteries drive me crazy. So, is that it? Is there anything else?"

"Well, after that, Glendine withdrew from the world. She closed herself away inside the old mansion and the townspeople started calling it the 'Shut-away' house," he intoned solemnly, crooking his fingers into air quotes. "Supposedly, she was never seen in public again, but, hey, that may not be true either."

I couldn't explain the heavy, anxious feeling coiling in my gut. Call it sixth sense, whatever, something told me that Glendine's tragic story, which had no bearing on my current assignment, sounded far more intriguing than writing about the church. Then, something he'd just said clicked in my brain. "The old mansion? Are you talking about the Gold Queen?"

Nodding, he said, "Yep," and then he straightened up, his eyes brightening. "You know, I'd almost forgotten this, but when I was…ten, maybe eleven, a bunch of us kids went out there on a dare one Halloween night. It was dark as pitch except for a couple of candles burning on the second floor. Spookier than hell. Anyway, one of the older kids swore he saw Glendine standing in one of the windows looking down at him and said he just about crapped his pants."

"Why?"

Tally leaned towards me, his eyes shining with devilish mischief. "He said she didn't have a nose."

I stared at him disbelieving. "What? You're sure he didn't just make that up?"

"Maybe, but, I'll tell you what, we hauled ass out of there pronto."

"That's a really tragic story…and captivating." I studied his earnest expression and leveled him a suspicious look. "You're not screwing with me, right?"

"Talk to Clara," he suggested. "She probably knows more than anyone."

I cocked my head sideways. "Why is that?"

"Her cousin was the housekeeper out there for many years. She can give you the inside scoop."

"Is that a fact," I mused, my imagination catching fire. "Now all I have to do is verify that what you're telling me is all true."

He stretched his arms over his head, yawning. "Knowing you, I have no doubt you'll be on the hunt until you find out for sure."

His offhand comment triggered the recollection of Lucinda's remarks from earlier, and before I could stop myself, I impulsively blurted out, "Because I'm the best investigative reporter on the planet, right?" I said it with an impish smile and tried to keep my voice light and flirty, but perhaps just a tiny hint of sarcasm seeped in? I could tell by his flinty expression that he knew what I was referring to and his chest swelled with a resigned sigh.

"I knew you weren't going to let that ride," he growled, his lips flattening into a thin line. "I don't want to get into a row over her tonight."

Realizing that I was dangerously close to spoiling our romantic evening, I quickly reversed course. "And I don't either. I just need to know what possessed you to promise that I'd get involved without discussing it with me first. That was so not cool."

"Honestly, I tried to stay out of it," he went on, combing his fingers through his thick, blue-black hair, "but the two of 'em caught me at a bad time and frankly leaned on me hard. I meant what I said about you being the best at what you do, but I didn't really promise them anything other than I'd at least mention it to you." He had the grace to appear just a little sheepish. "Look, I know how much you despise Lucy, but just this once you may want to set your differences aside. From what she told me, I think she and her family have every right to be worried. I would be."

I sighed. Was there any point in scrapping with him? As my shrewd grandmother used to say, *"Words in your mouth are like water in a pitcher. Once they are spilled, they cannot be recovered."* I took the opening.

"Okay. How well did you know her sister?"

"Not well. I met her when she was just a kid and saw her a few times with either Lucy or Polly in the last couple of years. Exceptionally pretty girl, but a little on the wild side."

"What about her husband? Do you know him?"

"Nope. I'm not going to be much help. You're going to have to work with Lucy if you decide to pursue it. And you're not under any obligation." He gently set the cats aside, rose from the couch, reached for my hands and pinned me with a critical stare. "Let this go, Kendall. Lucy is someone I've known my whole life. She is a friend and nothing more. Okay? She holds no attraction for me whatsoever. End of story."

"Well, maybe you aren't interested in her," I said with mock severity, "but given the chance, she'd jump your bones in two seconds."

His lips twitching with humor, he pulled me into his arms and kissed me with such ardor a fiery tingle raced through my whole body. Breathless, we drew apart and he held my gaze, saying softly, "There's only one woman's bones I have any interest in jumping and if a certain beautiful redhead would just shut up for two minutes, I'd show her just how much I care."

My heart overflowing with radiant sunshine, I slid him a provocative smile, laid my fingers across closed lips and pulled him towards the bedroom.

CHAPTER 6

The following morning, erratic wind gusts, strong and cold, accompanied me throughout the drive into Castle Valley. I pulled into the sheriff's substation parking area a few minutes before eight and when I spotted only Duane's patrol car parked outside the front door, my stomach tightened with annoyance. "Shit." I always felt far more at ease if Sheriff Marshall Turnbull or even their compliant dispatcher/receptionist, Julie, was present when Deputy Duane Potts was around. The man was a competent-enough law enforcement officer, but as a human being, he sucked. Well-known around town as a "skirt chaser", his constant attempts to furtively hit on me always left a sour taste in my mouth. The fact that he had a very sweet wife—albeit a bit overweight and perpetually exhausted from taking care of their four small children—never seemed to deter him. Duane had apparently missed the memo regarding sexual harassment, but rather than cause a stink I preferred cajoling him, and secretly enjoyed putting him squarely in his place whenever possible. Moreover, it would not serve me well to antagonize him. He had often been useful, providing me with information that I could not always get from Marshall and I wanted to keep it that way.

Following last night's earnest discussion with Tally, and after sending him on his way with a heartfelt kiss just as the crimson light of dawn was brightening the eastern horizon, I made the decision. As a favor to him and Ronda, I would pursue the disappearance of Lucinda's sister. Fulfilling Thena's wishes at the same time would load up my plate, but I was eager for something other than boring city council and school board meetings, local sporting events, and other small town news stories that did nothing to fire up my enthusiasm.

Before leaving the house, I had taken a few minutes to check out the Yavapai County Sheriff's Media Release page. Under the heading, **YCSO Seeking Whereabouts of Female/Probationer,** the incident report stated that Holly Mason, age 24, of Bagdad, Arizona had been reported missing by family members after she failed to return home for Thanksgiving. Her husband, Lynnis Mason, alleged that he received a phone call from her the prior evening, but she failed to appear at the family residence. Lynnis Mason had also reported her missing twice during the previous year. During one absence, Holly had been arrested in Tucson for driving under the influence of drugs and alcohol in a stolen vehicle, which she claimed was merely borrowed from a man she had met several days earlier. Deputies reported the man had an extensive criminal record, including arrests for drug trafficking, assault and armed robbery. Lucinda was right. She appeared to be involved with some unsavory characters.

Released under electronic monitoring, Holly had only stayed at the residence in Bagdad for three months before running away once more.

I studied her mug shot, again struck by the young woman's ethereal beauty, diminished somewhat from the photo Lucinda had shown me by her gaunt appearance—ashen skin, disheveled hair streaked with green and magenta and prominent charcoal circles beneath her expressionless eyes. The report continued with the fact that Holly, on active probation, had somehow removed her ankle bracelet. My throat tightened with irritation and I looked up from the screen, thinking that was a rather damning detail for Lucinda to have neglected to tell me. It meant, of course, that Holly was now in violation of her probation, and knowing that made me wonder if had she gotten cold feet and decided at the last minute not to return home.

All I could do was surmise her fate at this point, so I gathered what information I had together, including her photo, and wrote and then filed my story. Perhaps someone reading the online edition of the *Castle Valley Sun* could provide more information on the whereabouts of the elusive Holly Mason.

Curiosity about her surreptitious escape led me to check out several websites only to find out the GPS tracking devices were almost impossible to effectively remove without triggering the monitoring service. How in the world had she successfully accomplished that difficult feat? She must have had assistance from someone. I closed my laptop, rose and set out bowls of food for both cats. I pulled my phone off the charger and suddenly remembered that I'd never checked out the link Ginger had forwarded to my email.

Munching on toast and peanut butter at the kitchen counter, I almost choked when the mug shot of Nelson Trotter appeared. I stared agog. It looked like the same rough-looking dude I'd seen at the job site yesterday fighting with the younger man. I switched to my photo app and scrolled through the pictures I'd taken. Unfortunately, because the men had been moving, the images were blurry and I could not clearly make out the facial features. Same with the video. No matter. I felt certain it was the same person. Talk about another bizarre coincidence.

I swiped back to the website. Nelson Trotter, considered a Level 2 Sex Offender (Intermediate risk), had been imprisoned on charges of kidnapping and sexual misconduct with a minor female. Okay, that explained why the younger man had called him a pervert. His current address: Double G Ranch, 170 Dry Creek Road, and he was not wanted by the Yavapai County Sheriff's Office at this time. I dug a little deeper and discovered that he had an extensive criminal record beginning as a juvenile. Those records were not readily available, but he'd later been arrested for disorderly conduct, drug possession and aggravated assault. Not exactly a stellar citizen.

I tapped the second link and studied the face of the woman I hoped to meet with sometime today. Nelson Trotter and Wanda Trotter Keating bore close resemblance to one another. She had the same snub nose, square-jutting chin, heavy-lidded, close-set eyes and disagreeable frown. She also had quite a mustache thing going on. It looked almost as thick as her brother's did. I shook my head, thinking the woman was in serious need of a lip wax or a maybe a shave. While her eyes glittered cold sea green, his were a defiant ice blue. Each had the same grayish blond hair—his receding, hers lank, straight and shoulder length. There was scant information on the website other than she had been accused of murdering her husband's girlfriend but then exonerated for lack of evidence. Unreal! I thought of Thena's benign remark about overlooking the woman's past difficulties. Difficulties? That was putting it mildly to say the least. As much as I respected Thena, I could not help but feel a pang of disappointment-laced annoyance that she had glossed over such a serious charge. The fact that she appeared so willing to employ the Keating woman at the new retreat regardless of her questionable past signaled clearly that her desire to acquire the old church and surrounding land was much stronger than I imagined, which made it vital that I be successful in convincing Wanda to let go of the property. Not just a tall order, it suddenly seemed like a gargantuan task and all at once, I felt a little breathless, like a titanic weight had settled against my chest. There was no way on earth I could ever make up for my role in the inadvertent death of Thena's only son, so this was the golden opportunity, perhaps my only opportunity, to do something to soothe my conscience. My reporter's intuition warned me that this assignment would be far from easy, but then failure was not in my DNA.

I stepped down from the Jeep and the chill wind slapped my cheeks like a cold wave. Nearby, an American flag high on the pole flapped noisily. Arizona winters were definitely unpredictable; warm one day, freezing the next. I trudged across the dirt lot towards the Sheriff's Office, eager to learn additional details about Lucinda's sister and more background information on the Trotter siblings. Better to be forewarned before entering the lion's den. I pushed inside the door, trying to corral my majorly windblown hair and Duane, who had his nose buried in his phone, playing video games no doubt, glanced up at me like a startled deer. "Well, hey, Kendall," he gasped, unceremoniously dropping the phone on his desk as he sprang to his feet. With his usual lustful stare glued to me, he miscalculated when he rounded the desk and cracked his knee against the corner. I'm sure it hurt like a son-of-a-bitch, but he did a masterful job of concealing the pain, wincing only slightly, but never breaking stride as he rushed up to greet me like a long-lost relative. "I didn't expect to see you this morning," he panted, his eyes glazed with hopeful expectation, along with the patina of discomfort.

"Apparently." I dug my fingernails into my palms, mustering every ounce of self-discipline to keep from bursting into hysterical laughter. Suppressing the mirth swelling in my throat was physically painful. Smarmy dork. But, oh so predictable. "Duane, I need to see the files for Nelson Trotter and his sister, Wanda Keating." I held my breath. Wait for it. Wait for it.

"Sure thing," he replied, puffing his chest and treating me to his predictable tongue click accompanied by the gun-like pointed forefinger and thumb gesture along with what he presumed was a sensual wink. "You know I'm always happy to help you out anytime with…anything." Then, he just stood there wearing a foolish grin. He was like a broken record. Did he actually think that if he used that line on me repeatedly, I'd finally respond favorably? I cooled my heels for another few seconds or so before forcing an artificial smile.

"Today, Duane?"

"Oh, yeah. Yeah. For sure." He swiveled around and disappeared into the back room, returning within minutes. He handed me two files and made certain his fingers brushed mine. "Anything else I can help you with?"

The silky insinuation in his tone really frosted me, but I contained my ire, stating brusquely, "I'll let you know shortly."

I retreated to a small table near the front window and opened the file on Wanda. I could still feel his eyes on me and the back of my neck prickled with irritation. I whispered, "Jackass," under my breath as I began reading details of the first-degree murder charge levied against her. When I finished, the takeaway left me feeling vaguely unsatisfied, even though it appeared understandable how such a slip-up as administering the wrong medication could have happened. What were the odds that two female patients, both admitted on the same day, would share the same name? Wanda claimed that a subordinate had botched the paperwork, causing her to administer the wrong medication and that it had been an honest mistake. She did admit to knowing that Carolyn White, age 33, had been having an affair with her husband. After Wanda had administered the medication, the woman suffered a severe allergic reaction, went into respiratory failure and died several days later. The incident had been dismissed as an unfortunate error until several months later when a nurse's aide reported that she had overheard a violent argument between the two women prior to the patient's death, which subsequently led to Wanda's arrest. Over the objections of her public defender, her bail had been set at five-hundred thousand dollars and she had sat in jail until one of the leading defense attorneys in the state, Darryl Cook, had stepped in to represent her.

I looked up from the file and stared out the window at the distant mountains for a minute while I digested that intriguing detail. Curious. How had Wanda been able to afford a high-powered defense attorney if they were having financial issues?

The remainder of the information covered the trial and the state's inability to produce sufficient evidence that it had been anything other than an accident. The jury delivered a not guilty verdict. Her husband, Clement, had divorced her soon afterwards and moved to Virginia with one of their twin sons.

Whew! Quite a story. I closed Wanda's file and moved on to the specifics of her brother Nelson's charges, which were even more disturbing. A long-haul truck driver, he had been accused of picking up and holding a teenage girl hostage at his ranch. Krystal Lampton, age 16, told authorities Trotter had befriended her and promised to drive her to a relative's home, but instead, had taken her to the Double G Ranch where he allegedly confined her with zip ties and repeatedly assaulted her against her will. She claimed that after two weeks, she had managed to finally escape, sustaining injuries after jumping from a second story window. She reported that she had run barefoot with a broken ankle for miles through the desert before flagging down a car along the main road. After his arrest, Nelson Trotter had maintained that the girl was flat-out lying. He told authorities that she had approached him in the restaurant of Mick's Travel Stop. I drew in a sharp breath. Wait a minute! My heart rate quickened as I re-read the last sentence and silently mouthed the words "truck stop". Holy crap. Was this scenario disturbingly similar to Holly Mason's disappearance or what? I picked up my phone and did a quick search only to be disappointed. The truck stop in question was not on the road to Kingman but near Quartzsite, about twenty-two miles from the Arizona-California line. Damn. Thought I was onto something.

I returned to reading the file where Trotter claimed the girl had told him she was eighteen, had lost her job, and was hungry and broke. He informed authorities that he had bought her a meal, some clothing and personal items, and that she had told him she needed a place to stay for a while. He insisted that he'd done nothing wrong, swore that he had not known that she had been untruthful regarding her age and claimed that they'd only had consensual sex.

Gross. The mental image of this fifty-five-year old brutish-looking, depraved dude with a sixteen-year-old girl sent shivers of distaste rocketing through me. Eventually, he had been charged with kidnapping, false imprisonment, and one count of criminal sexual conduct. I skimmed through the rest of the report because I had already read most of the other particulars online regarding the fact that Krystal, the only witness against him, had vanished shortly thereafter. Her foster mother in Los Angeles told authorities that Krystal and a younger sibling had been taken into state custody after their parents were charged with child abuse and later arrested for cooking and selling methamphetamine. The foster mother described Krystal as a troubled young woman with severe emotional issues who regularly used drugs and had a history as a runaway. After her miraculous escape from the Double G Ranch, Krystal's foster mother stated that she had received a tearful phone call from the girl promising to return to Los Angeles where she planned to enter drug rehab and chart a new path for herself, but instead she had not heard from her again. Like Holly, there remained the possibility that she had changed her mind and decided to continue her risky lifestyle somewhere else.

Tapping my pen against my chin, I sat back to consider the problematic facts. The timing of the young woman's disappearance certainly seemed suspicious to me. I turned the page and viewed the photo of a very pretty, exceptionally mature-looking sixteen-year-old with long auburn hair and sultry, brown eyes. I picked up my phone and recorded her photo, thinking it was understandable why Nelson Trotter might mistake her for eighteen or even older. She wore an excessive amount of dark eyeliner and heavy blush. Her crimson lips faintly lifted on one side conveyed a sassy smirk.

In the process of closing the file, I halted when a familiar name jumped out at me. Well, now. How fascinating was this? Nelson Trotter had spent six weeks in jail before Wanda had finally bailed him out and retained Daryl Cook to represent him. With no victim to testify against him, the serious charges had been dropped and he'd been released, though he still had to register as a sex offender because Krystal was under the age of consent.

I shut the folder. How fortuitous that the supposedly hard-up Trotters had been able to afford one of the best defense attorneys in Arizona to get them both off the hook. Not once, but twice. And in addition to the bail money, they had miraculously come up with additional funds to buy the old church and surrounding property. Something very odd was going on here.

"You find everything you needed?" Duane inquired, sidling up beside me and resting his hip against the table. I looked up.

"Not quite. I'm also looking into the disappearance of Holly Mason."

He nodded sagely, his lips curled in a suggestive grin. "Lucinda's kid sister? She's a hot little number."

Not responding to his insolent observation, I said, "I understand you have surveillance footage placing her at a store in Aguila the night she vanished."

He leaned in closer. "Anybody ever tell you that you've got really pretty eyes?"

"Anybody ever tell you that you've got really bad breath?"

His eyes rounding in horror, he jumped backwards like a scalded dog, holding one hand over his mouth. "Damn that woman! I told Ada she put too much garlic in the spaghetti sauce last night. Sorry about that."

Stifling a giggle, I sweetly insisted, "I'd really like to see that footage."

He hesitated. "Well, I don't know if Marshall would approve that. It's still an open investigation and not everything is available to the public until he says so, you know."

"I do know that."

His eyes belied an expression I could only interpret as cunning. "Well, I could make an exception in your case. I'd be going out on a limb, but I might be able to do you a favor," he said, stroking his thin mustache with one forefinger. "And you know what they say about favors, right?"

I eagerly took the bait, stating with wide-eyed

sincerity, "What *do* they say about favors, Duane?"

He sniffed and tilted his head to one side. "That they have to be repaid."

I stood and faced him squarely. "You're right, Duane. Favors should be repaid." His expression of startled expectation had me holding back the cascades of laughter. He looked so supremely cocky I could have punched him, but I maintained eye contact as he swallowed repeatedly.

"What did you have in mind?" he finally asked, his narrow face flushing brick red.

Demurely, I reached inside my purse, removed the gift card to Angelina's and held it out to him with great fanfare. "This!" With effort, I displayed an enthusiastic smile. "You can take Ada and all four kids out to dinner for a great family evening on me." I rejoiced inwardly, watching his face fall and his ultra-confident, macho attitude dissolve before my eyes. Such fun and so well-deserved.

He cleared his throat, tapping the card on the palm of his hand. "Well… thank you. That's…real nice of you."

I forced a smile. "Don't mention it. Now, how about that surveillance footage?"

"You got it! You got it!" He rushed over to his computer and soon beckoned me to his desk. He motioned for me to sit in his chair, but then retreated several feet away, apparently nursing his wounded ego. Again, I had to stifle a laugh. Mission accomplished.

CHAPTER 7

After watching the surveillance footage twice, I returned to the small table with Holly Mason's file and mulled over what I'd just seen. On the November night in question, there appeared to be only four other customers visible inside the Family Dollar store besides Holly Mason. A young man with shoulder-length hair and wearing a long, black coat roamed the aisles, while an older white-haired man who looked to be in his 60s or 70s stood at the checkout counter talking to a young Hispanic man who appeared to be the only cashier on duty. Another man with a ball cap stood in one of the aisles perusing greeting cards, while an elderly woman, with Hispanic or Native American features, her steel-gray hair gathered in a tight bun, pushed a cart along the aisles choosing groceries, paper plates and other small items. The man at the counter gathered his merchandise and left. Holly entered the store at 8:29 pm. Wearing blue jeans, sneakers and a short dark jacket, she stopped at the counter and talked to the cashier who motioned towards the back of the store.

She then made a beeline for the door marked RESTROOMS. Moments later she emerged and strolled along the aisles, finally stopping at the children's toys section. Even though her face was slightly blurred, her frenetic movements seemed to convey excitement or perhaps tension as she rushed up and down the aisles grabbing more items, including children's clothing. Then, smiling with delight, her arms stuffed with merchandise, she piled her purchases on the checkout counter before digging in her pockets. She pulled out wads of folded bills, which the cashier unfolded and counted twice. He then said something that caused her expression to change from joy to confused agitation. His expressive gestures seemed to indicate that she did not have sufficient funds. She protested, appearing to argue with him and then stormed out the glass door. The fuzzy, flickering light reflecting off wet pavement clearly showed that it was raining.

The cashier looked after her and began stacking the items on the end of the counter. He waited on the long-haired young man, who then exited the door.

Within a minute, Holly reappeared and slapped additional bills in front of him. Dutifully, he added it to her total, but again shook his head and held up four fingers, signaling that she was still short. There looked to be another exchange of angry words. Holly swiped tendrils of wet hair from her face and ran outside a second time. The cashier checked out the elderly woman next. They talked and laughed, indicating that they knew each other and then, clutching two plastic bags in one hand and her umbrella in the other, the woman pushed outside into the downpour. She paused in one spot for long seconds, staring into the distance at something before a car pulled up next to her. The driver reached across and opened the passenger door for the woman who ducked inside before the car pulled away out of sight.

Again, the cashier began gathering the remainder of the toys and clothing when Holly, now drenched, darted inside and plunked down more money. This time it was apparently enough to pay for everything and then some. She pointed towards a glass case behind him. He strode over, unlocked it and extracted two packs of cigarettes, which he added to her order. While the man bagged everything, she rocked back and forth, hugging herself as if she were jittery, cold or perhaps both. Was she on something? Appearing overly anxious, she glanced to her left out the glass door and then hastily snatched the bags, ran out and blended into the mist, vanishing into the night without a trace.

Frowning, I studied the footage once more, thinking that, to me, there did not seem to be anything significant that would provide clues as to what had happened to her. I got the impression that Holly was a hyperactive yet persistent young woman. Why else would she endure two trips in the cold, driving rain to apparently borrow money from the person she had hitched a ride with if she wasn't dead serious about delivering the toys to her kids?

I sat back in the chair, watching the palo verde trees outside whipsaw in the blustery wind, feeling vaguely unsatisfied. So, what did happen to Holly Mason? Why had the person she met at the truck stop that night promised her a ride to Bagdad, but instead driven her to Aguila, two hours in the opposite direction? To me, Holly had appeared restive, but not frightened in any way. Lucinda was right about one thing. The whole scenario was definitely weird. It also seemed curious to me that a total stranger would agree to pony up money to pay for toys and clothes for someone else's kids. Was it just the benevolent conduct of a Good Samaritan the night before Thanksgiving?

Another thought struck me. Maybe nothing had happened to her. Had she simply changed her mind? I thought again that perhaps she had gotten cold feet and decided not to face the consequences for violating the terms of her probation. Hadn't Lucinda said her history of truth-telling was dubious at best? It would be easy to dismiss this latest disappearance as her usual pattern, but for whatever reason I could not shake the feeling that maybe, just maybe, this time was different.

I flipped through Holly's file. Marshall and Duane had questioned Holly's husband, mother, and the staff at the Roadrunner Truck Stop restaurant. A server by the name of Kelly Simms had loaned Holly her cell phone so she could call home. They had also questioned Pedro Salas at the Family Dollar store, and had been unable to find two of the three men who had appeared in the footage. They had spoken with the older man that lived in Aguila and had attempted to interview the elderly Hispanic woman but, unfortunately, her family reported that Aleta Gomez had suffered a stroke and was unavailable for an interview. I wrote down the contact information for all three people. Right now, this case appeared cold as dry ice. Not looking good. Holly was the proverbial needle, and the haystack looked to be the entire state of Arizona and possibly beyond. She literally could be anywhere.

The back door slammed so hard, the floor vibrated. I looked around and saw Julie heading for her desk. I smiled and waved to her as she tamped down her tousled hair and remarked breathlessly, "Morning! Boy, it's blowing like crazy out there today." As if to demonstrate just that, Marshall burst in the front door accompanied by the remains of a dust devil, scattering papers all over the room.

"Man oh man alive!" he boomed, clutching his white Stetson in one hand while strong-arming the door shut with his elbow, "if I'd been on a sailboat, that wind would have blown me into the next county!"

"Yeah," Duane commented, now ensconced back at his desk, "it's a bitch today." As he bent down to retrieve papers, his lightning-quick eye movement in my direction communicated to me that he wasn't just referring to the wind. If I dared laugh aloud, I would have. Obviously, I'd severely wounded his manhood and I knew from past experience that he'd sulk awhile before he got his second wind.

Running a hand over his ruffled snow-white hair, Marshall shot me a cheerful smile as he hung his hat on the wall peg beside his desk. "You're up bright and early, Kendall."

I returned his grin. "Yeah. The early bird, worm and all that."

"What can I help you with today?" He rolled out his worn chair and settled his bulk into it with a short grunt.

I tapped the file. "Lucinda asked me to look into her sister's disappearance and I wanted to ask you a few questions if you have time."

His eyes narrowed critically and he studied me in thoughtful silence for measured seconds while he smoothed his handlebar mustache. "So, I'm guessing she's not too happy that we've found nothing substantial since the last time she called, which was just a couple of days ago. We can only work with what we've got and I know you know that."

I always had to tread carefully at this point. I needed his cooperation and didn't want to convey the impression that I intended to encroach on his territory or insinuate that he wasn't doing his job. "I sure do." I turned one palm upward and issued him an apologetic smile. "Maybe she's thinking I'll be a pair of fresh eyes. I can see you don't have a lot to go on."

"No, we don't."

I glanced down at the page, which corroborated just about everything Lucinda had told me and that I'd read online. "Was the clerk at the Family Dollar store able to add anything of significance that might explain what happened to her?"

"Everything we know is right in front of you except now I have surveillance footage I can show you."

I glanced over at Duane. He quickly avoided my eyes, pretending to intently study something on his desk. So, he'd made an exception just for me, had he? Turd. I decided to let it slide. No reason to burn this useful bridge. "Duane was kind enough to let me see the footage earlier."

"Good," Marshall remarked, squeezing out an indulgent smile. "You probably already know this young woman has been in trouble since she was a juvenile and has been incarcerated numerous times in the past five years."

"I did read that."

"And," he continued, shuffling papers on his desk, "that she's pulled this disappearing act before."

"So I understand. Has Lucinda seen the footage?"

Marshall fired a questioning glance at Duane. "I don't think so. Has she?"

Duane looked up at us. "I don't believe so."

Incredulous, I turned back to Marshall. "Why not?"

He glared at Duane. "I told you to get hold of her."

"I did," he protested, grimacing. "I left her a message."

"Didn't you follow up?" Marshall persisted sternly.

Looking sheepish, he replied, "Not yet."

I glanced back and forth between them. "That footage is two and a half months old."

Marshall's white brows dipped into a scowl and he shifted in his chair. I interpreted his hangdog expression as being defensive. "Look, apparently, the new manager at the Dollar Store was unfamiliar with the surveillance system when we first questioned him. He thought it only maintained footage for a month. Lucky for us, their system actually saves footage for ninety days, but we've only had a short time to follow up since viewing it ourselves."

"I see. By the way, I didn't see any exterior footage."

Marshall pursed his lips tightly. "Yeah. The guy told us they'd been having technical trouble and the cameras facing the parking lot were not working. Because of the holiday, they didn't get fixed 'til the following week." He turned to Duane. "Call Lucy right now. Tell her to get in here pronto and view it so we can release the video to the public."

I nodded. "Send me the link. We'll post it on our website ASAP and hope someone out there knows something." I rose from the table, closed the file and shouldered my purse as I walked to Marshall's desk and handed him the files. "What can you tell me about Holly Mason's husband?"

He grimaced. "Let's just say he's been less than helpful so far."

"Why's that?"

"Because, he is one pissed-off guy. Said he's done with her. Done with her irresponsible behavior and what it was doing to him and their kids and he didn't really give a shit if she came back this time, pardon my French."

His statement further stirred my suspicions. "So he doesn't have any idea how she managed to remove the ankle monitor?"

"He says no. He told us he came home from work at the mine and the GPS monitor was in their bed under the covers." A look of disgust etching his ruddy features, he growled, "She'd left those two little girls alone in the house and split."

"I did a little research and I'm sure you already know it's nearly impossible to remove those monitors."

Marshall puffed out an extended sigh. "That's true in most cases."

"So how'd she do it?"

"Apparently butter was involved."

I drew back and stared at him. "Butter?"

"Yeah. From what we can tell, she used something to heat the plastic so it would weaken, then she rubbed butter all over her foot and, poof, off she came."

I couldn't help but nod appreciatively. "Well, that took some ingenuity."

Marshall shook his head. "Nah. She probably saw it on YouTube."

"So, you think she did this all by herself with no help from hubby." I stared down at him. "Really? That story sounds somewhat fishy, don't you think?"

Marshall hitched his shoulders. "We've got nothing

to tie him to her disappearance…right now."

I caught his inference. At the very least, Lynnis Mason could be considered a person of interest, so a trip to Bagdad was now in the cards, along with the truck stop near Kingman. According to what Marshall had written, the waitress who had loaned Holly her cell phone that November night had not been able to provide him with anything substantial in the way of clues, other than Holly appeared distraught and anxious to get home to her kids.

"One more thing," I ventured, maintaining eye contact with Marshall. "I'm assuming you've questioned Nelson Trotter."

"First thing we did," he acknowledged dryly. "With him being a registered sex offender, we check on him pretty often, but that night he had an airtight alibi. His sister and her kin swear he was home sick and, so far, we haven't been able to prove otherwise."

I flicked a glance at my phone. I had more than an hour to kill before the library opened. I entertained the idea of stopping into work for a few minutes, but quickly dismissed it, knowing I'd be caught up in whatever the crisis of the day was and my plans would go down the drain. "Thanks for the update on everything," I said, giving a general wave to everyone as I grasped the doorknob. "I'll keep you posted."

Marshall hunched forward and used his body and outstretched arms to shield all the papers on his desk in preparation for my exit. "Make sure you do." He pinned me with a warning glance. "I'm going hunting this weekend up near the Grand Canyon. Cell service is pretty shitty there so if you come up with anything significant you think I oughta know about, do not try to tackle it yourself this time, okay?

Call Duane."

I didn't miss the egotistical glint of triumph in Duane's eyes and decided that was the last thing I would do, but nevertheless said, "Roger that." I reached for the door handle, but hesitated, turning back. "One more thing. Do you have access to old records kept by Jack Hughes? I heard he was the sheriff here forty years ago."

Marshall pursed his lips and nodded. "I think they're in a storage unit at that facility over on Smoke Tree. Why?"

"I'm working on another assignment for Thena regarding the old church on the Double G Ranch and I need to verify an incident that took place out there regarding Glendine Higgins."

"Huh? Julie can probably help you out with that."

I checked the time. "Not today, but I'll check back with her. Thanks." I pulled the door open and the howling wind rushed in, causing an explosion of papers. Shouting, "Sorry!" I yanked the door shut behind me.

Rather than waste the next hour sitting in the library parking lot, I decided to use the free time to check out Youth Oasis. Before my hiatus from work, I had driven by the old American Legion Hall, curious to see what progress had occurred to revamp the run-down, shoebox-shaped building. Still under construction at the time, I hadn't really gotten a good sense of the finished product and because checking the place out was now part of my assignment, I was anxious to see the renovation and get a few exterior photos. I remembered from my conversation with Ginger that the clinic didn't open until...was it eleven or twelve? Either way, I'd have to call later to set up an appointment for interior shots and hopefully arrange for an interview with Dr. Mallick as well.

It was uncanny. As if Ginger had picked up vibes that I was thinking about her, my phone rang. "Hey, girlfriend! How did your visit go at Youth Oasis?"

"Wait 'til you see how they've gussied up the place. All us girls wuz blown six ways from Sunday."

"Really? Well, I'm actually on my way there right now."

"I don't think they're open yet."

"I know. I'm just going to grab some exterior shots."

"Well, that's gonna blow you away too," she crowed. "You remember what the building looked like, right?"

"Yeah," I answered, eyeing the street signs, "pretty plain."

"Well, it ain't now."

"So, did you buy anything?"

"Did I buy anything?" As always, her infectious laughter delighted me. "Dumplin', let's jest say I may have to ask you for an itty bitty raise 'cause I pert near spent half my paycheck there last night."

"Are you serious? Why would you do that?"

"Scoff if ya like," she retorted airily. "You shoulda seen the before and after pictures they showed us. I'll tell you what, if these beauty products work like they say, I'm gonna be as purty as a pie supper in two shakes of a dog's tail."

"Ginger, you crack me up." How lucky was I to have this adorable person in my life? "We still on for breakfast tomorrow morning?"

"I'll be there with bells on!"

Ten minutes later, I swung onto Buckskin Trail and drove west along the quiet, winding street lined with mature ironwood and mesquite trees, now whipping back and forth in the fierce wind. I passed by several ranch-style homes sitting on multi-acre lots, some with stables and small horse corrals while others accommodated both horses and peacefully grazing cattle in fenced pastures. Backyard ranches, Tally liked to call them.

I rounded the corner, rumbled over the narrow bridge spanning Date Creek and felt a little zing of surprise when I spotted the muted-earth-tone adobe structure nestled beneath a grove of cottonwood trees. What an astounding transformation from the stark white building to this pueblo-style structure complete with thick round-edged walls, dark brown wooden protruding roof beams and graced with an arched door and small, inset, square windows. The three-tiered stone fountain occupying the entrance to a flower-festooned courtyard projected an aura of supreme tranquility.

I pulled my Jeep alongside the road, parked and surveyed the property for a few seconds. Yep. The wide shots would be better without my vehicle showing in the pictures. I zipped my coat, picked up my Nikon—which in my opinion still produced better photos than any smartphone—slung the strap over my head and wound an elastic band around my long curls, capturing them in a ponytail. Outside once again, the strong wind gusts at my back felt like an insistent hand pushing me across the narrow street towards the pink-graveled parking area. My boots made a muted crunching sound as I moved from place to place, snapping photos. Occasionally when the wind gusts died down, I enjoyed the lively chirping of birds in the surrounding trees. As I hoped, the early-morning sun, broken by a procession of swift-moving clouds, provided ideally soft lighting as I photographed the building from various angles. Hands down, this was truly the nicest building in Castle Valley. Kudos to the architect. I wondered fleetingly if it was our architect, Neil. I'd have to ask him next time I saw him.

The landscaper deserved credit as well for the careful design and placement of the flowerbeds—a little slice of paradise bursting with colorful blooms. I paused a moment, listening to the frantic melody of wind chimes while admiring the placement of whimsical metal sculptures of deer, bunnies and squirrels. In addition, an eye-catching cinnamon-tinted, stone Buddha beckoned from the center of the garden, instilling a feeling of sublime inner peace.

Strolling along to the front entrance, I took several photos of the intricately-carved wooden door flanked by wrought iron benches and bronze wall hangings of smiling sun gods. A small plaque announced the Youth Oasis Medi-Spa and their hours. I couldn't help but admire the fact that someone had put a great deal of planning, thought and money into the dramatic renovation. I wondered if Dr. Craig was the brainchild behind the creation of such a bucolic atmosphere. I was anxious to meet this talented, innovative man and thank him for spearheading this unexpected gift to the citizens of Castle Valley, and vicariously, the newspaper. A gut feeling told me that Youth Oasis was going to have a far bigger impact on Castle Valley than anyone could predict.

I was kneeling beside the fountain lining up a great shot when I heard what sounded like a door slamming. Startled, I looked behind me, thinking it might have been a car door but my lime-green Jeep sat alone across the street and the nearest house had to be at least a quarter of a mile away. I stood up listening intently, but heard nothing but the moan of the wind around my ears. Had I imagined it? I snapped a few more pictures and was poised to leave when I again heard a resounding thump that sounded like it came from behind the building. Was anybody supposed to be here this early? I could have just ignored it, but as usual, my curiosity got the best of me. Deciding to check it out, I convinced myself that I wasn't really trespassing, as the clinic would be open to the public in a few hours. Anyway, that's what investigative reporters do. They investigate.

The constant rattle of the cottonwood leaves camouflaged the sound of my footsteps as I followed the flagstone walkway around the side of the structure and came face-to-face with an impressive wooden gate with a sign reading PRIVATE. There was a padlock on the latch, but on closer inspection, I realized that it was just hanging there, invitingly unlocked. I reached out my hand but hesitated. Should I open it, or just be on my way?

My pulse spiked when I heard subdued voices on the far side of the wall. Ultra quietly, I lifted the latch and cracked the gate open just in time to see a slim, dark-skinned man with a well-trimmed beard and mustache, along with a heavyset blonde female, both in light blue scrubs, pushing a slender woman in a wheelchair towards a shiny, black SUV with dark-tinted windows. The woman wore oversized sunglasses and a big floppy hat, so I could not really see her face. The man helped her gently into the back seat, and then leaned in and said something I could not hear before shutting the door. Because he looked to be East Indian, I assumed the man must be Dr. Raju Mallick. He gave a hand signal to the driver who made a wide U-turn and then cruised past me. I only caught a fleeting glimpse of the driver's silhouette before the person accelerated through an electric gate that closed slowly as the vehicle turned onto Buckskin Trail heading towards town.

I turned back and watched the doctor's assistant push the wheelchair through a double door and it dawned on me that I'd probably just observed one of the rich and famous celebrities Thena had referred to, taking full advantage of the freedom to maintain a low profile totally out of the public eye following whatever medical procedure she'd had performed.

The man stayed outside, his attention focused on tapping out a message on his cell phone. I debated retreating for a few seconds, but why should I pass up this perfect opportunity to grab an interview? I opened the gate a little further and called out, "Dr. Mallick?"

His head shot up and his mouth fell open. Ebony eyes reflecting shock, he finally croaked out, "Who are you? What are you doing here? This…this is a private…" he hesitated, apparently searching for the right word, concluding with, "location." He spoke with a heavy East Indian accent, his words strung together in a singsong cadence. "You should not be here," he went on, his tone turning suspicious. "No one is allowed except patients, so you must go now."

Slightly disconcerted by his brusque behavior, I ignored his request and advanced towards him, treating him to a full-toothed smile as he continued to scrutinize me warily. I dug a business card from my back pocket and extended it to him. "Kendall O'Dell. I'm a reporter for the *Castle Valley Sun*. I'm writing a piece on Youth Oasis and wanted to ask you a few questions."

He continued to blink and stare at me as if I had just landed in a spaceship. What in the hell was wrong with him? I gently cleared my throat. "I've heard a lot of good things about your and Dr. Craig's work from Thena—"

As if he had not heard me, he interrupted, pointing towards my chest. "What are you doing with that?"

"This?" I asked, touching the camera hanging on the strap around my neck. "Ah…taking pictures?"

"No, no! That is strictly forbidden," he harangued me, wagging an accusatory finger in my face. "Our patients are guaranteed complete privacy."

His stiff unflinching demeanor broadcast clearly that he did not want me there, for whatever reason I could not fathom, but I forged ahead employing a soothing tone. "Not to worry! I didn't take any pictures beyond the gate, just the gardens and the front of your beautiful clinic…or spa. Do you prefer that I refer to it as a medical spa or a medical clinic? With your permission, I'd like to take some interior shots now and also get a few quotes about all the services you offer and some background information on yourself."

Beneath protruding eyelids that reminded me of a praying mantis, his beady eyes darted about as if he were trying to gather his thoughts and, even though it was anything but hot, I could swear I saw beads of sweat glistening on his forehead. If I was reading his tortured body language correctly, he seemed petrified.

He glanced at his phone and announced firmly, "You will please come another time. I have another patient waiting." He hurried past me, held the gate open and gestured for me to leave. "You will go now. Goodbye."

Even though I was accustomed to being rebuffed by people reluctant to answer my questions, nevertheless I was seething inside as I took my time sauntering through the gate. However, never one to give up easily, I turned back and suggested cordially, "I can certainly come back at a time more convenient for—" Abruptly, he closed the gate in my face. Stung by his rude, unprofessional behavior, I stood there a moment debating my next move. Should I present myself at the front door of the facility or wait and come back later after they opened? Or, should I admit I'd lost this round and just pack it in?

A quick look at my phone answered the question. I stomped towards the Jeep, still seething with irritation. No question the man had blown me off. But why? Okay, so maybe he was pissed because he suspected I was from one of those celebrity-stalking tabloids or perhaps the explanation was that I'd simply taken him by surprise. Was I wrong or did it appear that Dr. Mallick was trying to conceal something? I had no clue as to what that could possibly be, but his surreptitious behavior had definitely tweaked my interest. I'd make it a point to check out his medical credentials soon.

I turned the key and was about to pull onto the road when I noticed a white pickup truck approaching from behind in my side view mirror. I waited until the truck pulling a big trailer had passed by before making a U-turn. It was close to 9:30. Time to get going to the library. I don't know why I glanced again in my mirror but when I did, I noticed something so peculiar that I braked to a stop in the middle of the road. Was I seeing correctly? Wasn't that the same pickup I'd seen yesterday at the Starfire now turning into the driveway at Youth Oasis? What had Jake called the company? The Last Roundup? My thoughts whirled crazily. What business would someone who disposed of dead animal carcasses have at Youth Oasis?

I drove ahead until I found a place to make a second U-turn and cruised back along the street, slowing at the mouth of the driveway. Well, what do you know? None other than Dr. Mallick stood at the electric gate. What was this all about? So much for him hurrying off to attend to another patient.

Walking swiftly towards the truck, he said something I could not hear to the driver and then appeared to hand something through the open window. When he stepped back, his head suddenly jerked towards me. He stared at me and then turned back and mouthed something to the driver who craned his neck sideways in my direction. Before I could deduce anything at all about such a perplexing connection, Dr Mallick pointed across the street. Seconds later the truck and trailer began backing out of the driveway. Forced to move out of the way, I drove a few hundred feet and doubled back, once again traveling slowly past the rear entrance to the clinic. This time Dr. Mallick was nowhere to be seen. I switched my attention back to the street in time to see the pickup turn left onto a nearby ranch road and stop at the gate. Mildly disappointed, I had to admit my reporter's intuition was dead wrong and that there was no sinister activity involved after all. Apparently the driver had merely gone to the wrong address.

"Trying to turn nothing into something again," I admonished myself, feeling deflated. What a waste of precious time. Driving past, I glanced again towards the pickup and made eye contact with the driver. Chilled by his malevolent scowl and his close-set eyes that appeared to reflect recognition, I was shocked when he very prominently extended his middle finger towards me. What?

Mystified, I turned my attention back to the road. Had my eyes deceived me or did the man look an awful lot like Nelson Trotter?

CHAPTER 8

As I drove on towards town rehashing the odd incident, the disconcerting sensation persisted. Even though I'd only gotten a fleeting glimpse of the driver, I was fairly certain it was the same guy. Random thoughts, none of which made any sense at all, cartwheeled in my head like blowing tumbleweeds. Was I allowing my imagination to run wild, or should I accept the grim reality that it *was* Nelson Trotter and he appeared to know exactly who I was? And if he did, that meant Dr. Mallick had to have told him. Why he would do that, I had not the slightest idea.

Perhaps my initial impression that the two men were acquainted was not a mistake after all. But then, what interaction could this guy possibly have with a doctor who had only been in Castle Valley mere weeks? While Dr. Mallick had seemed nervous and agitated by my presence, Trotter's menacing behavior was downright scary. It occurred to me at that moment that my new assignment on the Double G Ranch increased the odds tremendously that I would run into him again soon, intensifying my feelings of discomfort. Since childhood, I'd always relied on my intuition and it was always a mistake if I chose to ignore that unique sense of "knowing" that vibrated deep in my psyche.

I pulled into the library parking lot at 9:40. Clara Whitlow's old, blue Ford sedan was nowhere in sight, so I sat there drumming my fingers on the steering wheel while admiring the graceful lines of the historical stone house cozily tucked among a stand of waving tamarisk trees. Why not make good use of the time?

I dug out my phone and dialed Wanda Trotter Keating's number. Voicemail picked up after the fifth ring. A guttural female voice barked, "*Leave a message. I'll call you back.*" Okay. Succinct and to the point. I left a message stating my name, vocation, my association with Thena, my phone number and that I planned to be in her area later today and would like to get interior photos of the church if possible. Beyond that, I had not had time to formulate any kind of plan to broach the subject of her selling the property. I certainly did not want to spook her right out of the starting gate.

Next, I searched for information on The Last Roundup since I knew next to nothing about the livestock disposal business. The webpage listed the owner's name as Candice Pomeroy and a phone number. The mission statement read: WE ARE HERE TO HELP YOU NAVIGATE THROUGH THIS DIFFICULT AND EMOTIONAL TIME FOR YOU AND YOUR BELOVED ANIMAL COMPANION. Very empathetic sentiment, I thought.

Next came the list of their fully licensed services, which included working with veterinarians to handle the end-of-life needs, followed by their professional, respectful, benevolent 24/7 removal of large deceased animals such as horses, cows and donkeys from home or ranch. The Last Roundup provided the disposal method chosen by the owner, which ranged from burial or cremation to transportation to a rendering facility or university. There were several photos of horses and cows grazing in fields but the last one featuring the silhouettes of a cowboy astride a horse leading another horse across the desert towards a ruby sunset brought a lump to my throat. I looked up and stared out the windshield, imagining how stressful it would be to deal with death on a daily basis as well as consoling the grieving owners. I tried to picture myself in that role and failed. No way could I do something like that but I felt overwhelming admiration for those who could. That thought circled back to Nelson Trotter, a man who struck me as anything but compassionate. Why would a person with his background be working in this sensitive business? But then, how easy could it be to find people willing to do this type of work on a daily basis? It would require someone with a strong constitution and stomach.

I swiped to my phone book and dialed Ronda's number. Two rings later, I heard her usual low-key monotone, "Hullo?"

"Hey, Ronda, it's Kendall. How are things going there?"

"Wilson brothers just got here from Colorado. Couple big buyers from California are already looking too."

"Good. Well, listen, I know you guys are super busy, but can you spare a couple of minutes to talk?"

"Yeah."

"What can you tell me about The Last Roundup?"

No response for long seconds and then, "You mean

other than they pick up dead animals?"

"Yes. Do you know Candice Pomeroy? How long have they been in business?"

"Uh…well…let's see. Candice and her husband bought the business from a guy named Clyde Benson maybe ten years ago. She retired last year after her husband died and she turned the business over to her daughter, Marita. Nice girl. Been working with her mom since high school."

"So the daughter handles the business all by herself?"

"Nah. Her husband was helping her out, but he's been sick and was recently diagnosed with MS so I'm guessing he's out of the picture for a while."

"That's too bad. So, she picked up the cows and Dolly yesterday?"

"Nope. Wish she had. Marita is kind and considerate because she has horses and cattle of her own, so after the vet administers the shot and they…you know, go down, she's real considerate and throws a sheet over their heads. Then she'll cut off a section of their tail or mane and even braid it for people to have as a keepsake."

Thinking of poor, old Dolly, my throat closed with emotion and I could not speak for measured seconds. "That's really nice. So, what happens next?"

"After she collects the fee, she asks us to leave while the…body is loaded into the trailer. She's knows that's a real traumatic moment and she's always respectful of our feelings, unlike the guy who was here yesterday."

That's what I was waiting to hear. "Tell me about him."

"Name's Nelson Trotter."

A little gut stab. So I was right. "Uh-huh," I

murmured softly. "Thought so."

"You know him?" she asked, sounding surprised.

"Not personally, but I saw him delivering materials at the construction site yesterday and also read about his criminal background online."

"Yeah, he's a troublemaker from way back."

"I noticed he has a juvenile record, but most of the time they're sealed. Do you know anything about his past offenses when he was younger?"

"A little. I heard he was in and out of detention facilities a couple of times."

"For what?" I asked, reaching for my notepad.

"Um…vandalism, I think…driving drunk…um…I think he got suspended in high school for fighting with a teacher." She said nothing for extended seconds. "Wait! The thing most people remember is he stalked a girl named Darla Hunt to the point that her dad threatened to kill him if he didn't leave her alone. The family ended up leaving town in the middle of the night to get away from him."

"Anything else?"

"Both of his ex-wives claimed he beat the ever lovin' shit out of them."

I contemplated the disturbing details momentarily before Ronda added in an ominous tone, "I'm guessing you read about that girl he kidnapped last year."

"I did." Just thinking about the sinister look he'd skewered me with earlier made my skin crawl. Ginger was right. I'd best watch my heinie when I visited the Double G Ranch. And, that sparked another uncomfortable realization. This sicko knew what my vehicle looked like. Tally had given me no end of grief regarding my impulsive decision to buy the new Jeep last fall. I'd been super proud of myself for negotiating a smoking deal on it, but now it galled me to admit that his cautionary words might be right. How smart was it for someone in my profession to be driving a bright, lime-green Jeep?

Ronda's next words cut into my thoughts. "Besides being a creepy pervert," she stated with an undertone of disgust, "he was a real asshole about handling…poor Dolly."

"How so?"

"Not a kind word, no sympathy at all. He just threw those cow carcasses into the trailer, didn't bother with the sheet over Dolly's head and just winched her in on top of the chewed-up, bloody mess right in front of me. It was awful."

Sounded stomach-churning to me. "I'm really sorry."

"Yeah, me too." Her voice faltered slightly, so I waited several seconds before asking, "How long has he been working for The Last Roundup?"

"I dunno. On and off this past year."

"He sure gets around. One minute he's on top of Sidewinder Hill and two hours later he's picking up dead animals. Busy guy."

"He used to make a butt-load of money working for some big trucking company," Ronda said, "but I don't think anyone wants to hire him now, so he takes whatever jobs he can get. I heard he does all sorts of freelance delivery work and somebody told me he bought his own rig not too long ago so he can haul independently."

I paused to digest the additional information. "Considering his criminal background, I'm wondering why Marita would hire someone like him."

"Probably because he's her husband's uncle."

My head spun in confusion. "Wait, what? Who's her husband?"

"Wanda Keating's son, Grayson."

Wow. I had not seen that coming, but it explained a lot.

"What's this all about?" Ronda pressed.

"Just curious. I saw him driving the truck and trailer early this morning over on Buckskin Trail."

"There are some mini-ranches out there. He was probably making a pick up."

"Okay, but can you think of any reason he'd be going to Youth Oasis?"

"That new beauty clinic?" she mused, sounding puzzled. "No, but I'm guessing he was headed for the bone yard."

That got my attention. "The bone yard? What's that?"

"It's a big sinkhole on the north end of their ranch, about a mile past the old Gold Queen mansion, not too far from the mine. Ranchers around here have been dumping dead cattle and horses there forever. No permits required. Fastest way there from town is Buckskin. It turns into a dirt road just around the corner from the clinic."

The mental image of a hole filled with rotting carcasses and sun-bleached animal bones was disturbing, yet oddly intriguing. "Wait a minute. I just read online that remains are transported to the county landfill."

"They're supposed to be," she grumbled, "but he's a lazy-assed son-of-a-bitch. We pay a hundred extra for that service, but I suspect he's dumping 'em out there 'cause he doesn't have to drive very far and he can pocket the extra cash he'd otherwise have to fork over to the county. I imagine he's probably cleaning up big time now."

"Why do you say that?"

"He gated the road and neighboring ranches aren't allowed to use the bone yard anymore."

"Why do you think that is?"

"Because, they're damn money grubbers. The Last Roundup is the only game in town now unless you want to haul the remains to the landfill yourself and most people just don't have the time or inclination to mess with it. I know I don't."

"Well…thanks for your time, Ronda."

"No problem." Dead air then, "These questions you're asking about Nelson Trotter, are you thinking maybe he had something to do with Holly's disappearance?"

I hesitated. Did I? The man obviously had serious issues with women and the circumstances surrounding the two cases seemed alarmingly similar. Both had been picked up at a truck stop, each had eventually vanished. Being an investigative journalist, I could surmise all day long, but at this moment in time, neither the sheriff nor I had definitive proof to connect him to either disappearance. However, I intended to go look for it. I couched my answer carefully. "I don't know. I just came from the Sheriff's Office and to be honest, there's not a whole hell of a lot to go on right now."

Silence again, then, "Anything you can find is better than nothing. No matter what the outcome," she added morosely. "Hey, thanks again for doing this. I gotta go now. Tally's waiting on me."

"Just one more thing."

"What's that?" she asked.

"How would you like to trade cars for a couple of days?"

CHAPTER 9

Stay cool, I admonished myself eyeing the time on my phone again while fighting a growing sense of agitation. Along with having a hair-trigger temper and occasionally being overly impulsive, patience was another positive character trait I sorely lacked. I was working on it, but could feel it slipping away as the minutes ticked by and there was no sign of Clara Whitlow.

My schedule was tight as it was and now I had to factor in at least an hour to switch vehicles with Ronda. Just sitting there watching the feathery, gray clouds roll past while strong wind gusts rocked my Jeep like a small boat in rough waters was not part of my plan. I sighed aloud. Go figure. Yesterday had been sunny and warm, today just the opposite. Arizona winters were fickle, to say the least.

As a precaution, I hopped online and checked the weather. Continued high winds, some gusting up to forty miles per hour would prevail today, but no rain predicted until later this evening. Remembering the scarlet dawn sky sent a flash of uncertainty through me as I glanced out the windshield again at the bank of leaden clouds gathering over the northern peaks. Nature's weather clues were a safer bet than any predictions made by man, and to me, rain looked imminent. Not exactly what I was hoping for traveling to unfamiliar places, but since I'd made a promise to Thena and the fate of the newspaper was now tied to my efforts, I felt compelled to jump-start my assignment.

Unrelated to the history of a rundown old church and highlighting its possibilities as a commercial venture, my mind drifted back to the sequence of events this morning. I'd ferreted out some damning information about Nelson Trotter's background, but his association with Dr. Mallick really puzzled me. I typed the doctor's name into my search engine. Fifteen minutes later, after following link after link, I had been unable to find out a single thing about him. He appeared to have no social media presence. It was almost as if he did not exist. I wondered what Thena would think about him rudely evicting me from the clinic and made a mental note to call her as soon as possible.

When my phone chimed, it took me a couple of seconds to recognize Wanda Keating's number. "This is Kendall O'Dell."

"You leave me a message earlier?" a woman stated bluntly.

"Yes."

"We got real shitty cell service out here, so I couldn't make out much of what you said. Who are you and waadaya want?"

She sounded gruff and none too friendly. Her mug shot came to mind and I thought it interesting that she sounded just like she looked. Rough around the edges—totally unlike any nurse I'd ever met. Keeping my tone upbeat, I explained why I had called and her response was swift and firm. "Oh, so Thena Rodenborn put you up to this. Well, you're wasting your time. I already told her I can't sell it to her any more than I can sell it to some guy from a California winery who has been bugging me for months. Believe me, I would if I could, but it ain't all my decision."

She would if she could. Now that was revealing. She didn't sound as adamantly against the idea as Thena had indicated. I sensed the opening and took it. "No worries! That's a subject for another day. Right now, I'm mainly interested in getting some exterior and interior shots for my article. I'll be in your area this afternoon and I thought you might have some interesting stories to share about your family, why you decided to buy the church and your possible plans for—"

"I can't really talk about this now," she snapped. "My son ain't feelin' good and I'm driving him to the doctor in Scottsdale now. Most likely I'll lose you in a few minutes anyhow, so talk fast."

I assumed she was talking about her adult son, Grayson, the one suffering from MS. "Sorry to hear that," I responded in a soothing tone, but pressed my case. "I could meet you at the church this afternoon. What time works for you?"

"I dunno. I'm just goin' with the flow…what the hell!" she shouted unexpectedly and then growled, "Hang on a minute." Unintelligible sounds in the background, then I heard her screech, "Can't you dumb shits read the signs? It says, no trespassing! Get it? *No trespassing!* It meant no trespassing last week and it means no trespassing now."

It was faint, but I thought I heard someone shout back, "Pastor Gates was okay with it!"

"I don't give a flyin' shit what Pastor Gates told you! He don't own this property anymore, so get your bony asses out of here before I call the sheriff…or maybe I'll just shoot you myself! Grayson, hand me my shotgun!" Garbled voices, doors slamming and then the roar of a car engine followed by Wanda's cackling laughter that ended with a coughing fit. She finally came back on the line. "Sorry about that," she huffed, annoyance still edging her words. "Asinine hikers and cavers. Seems like I have to chase them off every other day."

"Cavers?" I inquired with interest.

"Yeah. You know, young numskulls traipsing around our property hunting for hidden caves."

"I see." Sounded fascinating and I wished I'd had time to explore the subject further, but I steered her back to the matter at hand. "So, ah…would you be able to meet me at the church at say…four o'clock?"

"I can't promise anything. I'm not sure how long we'll be at the doctor's office."

"Well…is there anyone else who could let me inside?"

After an extended hesitation, she announced, "I… uh…we can't let you go inside at all."

"Why not?"

"Because, lightning hit the bell tower in that big storm we had a couple weeks back. Blew a hole in the roof. The rain put the fire out but there's a lot of water damage to the ceiling and a whole section of the wood floor is collapsing into the basement. It's gonna to have to be shored up 'cause it's too dangerous to have anybody wandering around in there now."

Unwilling to retreat, I pressed, "Well, I thought if you..."

As if I hadn't spoken, she talked over me. "My brother delivered all the materials to fix the place, but you're gonna have to wait until he gets it repaired enough to be safe...if Mr. Procrastination ever gets around to it." The tinge of doubt in her tone reinforced Ronda's assertion that Nelson Trotter was lazy.

"I'd be happy to sign a waiver if you could just allow me to—"

"News flash for you. I'm afraid the building is in a lot worse shape than when Miz. Rodenborn saw it last December. But, hey, knock yourself out taking pictures of the outside 'cause we ain't takin' a chance on you or anybody else getting hurt on our property and suing our asses off! I got enough trouble..." I heard a few more garbled words and then the connection evaporated. I immediately called her back, but it went straight to voicemail. Must be the shitty cell service she had mentioned.

"Crap!" Okay. Okay. So I would make do with exteriors and whatever information I could glean from Clara...if she ever got here.

Jittery and growing more frustrated with each passing minute, I tapped in Thena's number. When she answered, I described my altercation earlier at Youth Oasis. In a bewildered tone, she murmured, "Well, that doesn't sound like Dr. Mallick." Silence, then, "Perhaps you caught him at a bad time. He's always been very courteous and helpful."

"Not to me," I answered dryly, deciding not to

mention the inexplicable incident with Nelson Trotter.

"Not to worry," she said solicitously, "as luck would have it I spoke with Dr. Craig last evening. He and his staff are probably in Arizona by now. If you like, I can call him back and arrange for you to meet him at the clinic after hours."

"What time would that be?"

"I believe they close at five today, but I'll let you know if that doesn't work for him."

Damn. That kind of blew a hole in my plans for the remainder of the day but...bird in hand. "Okay, sounds good."

I ended the call, jumped back online and typed the address for the Double G Ranch in my map app. Travel time was only twenty-five minutes. I was poised to close the screen when I noticed the name of the neighboring town. Aguila. "Holeee shit!" I whispered. What were the odds that the last known sighting of Holly Mason placed her within six miles of the ranch?

Next, I checked the driving distance from Castle Valley to Aguila. 31 miles. I leaned back against the headrest. This unexpected discovery presented a whole host of new possibilities. Like a pinwheel in a stiff breeze, my thoughts spun out in different directions. What if the truck driver Holly had hitched a ride with *was* Nelson Trotter? Had he kidnapped her in the same manner as the first girl, Krystal Lampton? Was it far-fetched to imagine that a registered sex offender had committed the unthinkable? Horrifying and bizarre stories of missing young women who eventually turned up dead seemed to be in the news unnervingly often nowadays.

I thought again about the surveillance footage. Holly had appeared somewhat edgy, but not frightened. There had been plenty of time for her to alert the clerk if she believed she was in danger. Or, I mused, had she hitched a ride with someone else and headed for Castle Valley instead? It would make sense, since she had family here. But, if that had been the case, wouldn't she have called Lucinda instead of her husband? No. A confirming twinge in my gut told me she had exhibited expectations of reuniting with her children. Why else would she have impulsively bought toys and clothing that night?

My suspicions about Nelson Trotter intensified even though he appeared to have an airtight alibi. But, could his family be trusted? After all, his sister had been charged with murder, and even though she had been exonerated, how good was her word? I pressed fingers to my throbbing temples. I was giving myself a headache cooking up "what ifs". One thing was sure. Since I would be so close today, it would be convenient to pop over there and question the clerk at the Family Dollar store if I had the time.

A powerful wind gust slammed into my Jeep and jolted me back to the present. I eyed the time. Clara Whitlow was now over an hour late and suddenly concern for her welfare overrode my restiveness. Where could she be? The frail, blue-haired octogenarian, a much-beloved and respected fixture of the community, was highly regarded as a former teacher-turned-librarian and town historian. She also had a reputation for being prompt.

Her continuing absence seemed totally out of character and galvanized me to action. I looked up her home number and dialed. No answer. Something had to be wrong. I didn't have her cell number so I decided my next move would be to drive to her house and see if she was okay.

Apprehensive, I started the engine and was poised to shift into reverse just as Clara's car rolled to a stop at the north end of the parking area. Instant relief washed over me as I strong-armed my Jeep door open against the unrelenting wind. Cold air blasted my face. Holy cow! It felt like the temperature had dropped at least ten degrees as I jogged across the parking lot towards her car.

"Goodness gracious!" she exclaimed wide-eyed, as I opened her car door and leaned my full weight against it. "Sorry to be so late!" She reached beside her on the passenger seat and handed me a folder. I quickly tucked it securely inside my jacket as I extended her a helping hand and shouted back at her, "I'm just happy you're all right."

"I'm fine, but my beautiful old ironwood tree bit the dust and blocked my driveway," she yelled back, her coat billowing out behind her like a wind sock. "I had to wait for my neighbors to push it out of the way."

Hunched over, she clung to my arm as we fought our way to the library steps and I couldn't help but think how much younger and more vibrant Thena appeared when compared to Clara, who couldn't be more than a few years her senior. Maybe the secret anti-aging formula was no joke after all.

It seemed to take forever for Clara to find the key. My long curls whipped wildly around my face, slapping my cheeks as she rummaged through her purse and finally unlocked the front door. We hurried inside, relieved to escape the cold, screaming wind. "Lordy, it feels much better in here," she remarked as she removed her coat, flipped on lights and patted her wispy curls back into place. "I know it's impossible to have a hurricane in Arizona, but it sure feels like it today." She stepped into a narrow hallway, tapped the thermostat button and increased the heat.

"It does," I agreed, shedding my jacket. "Driving in these weather conditions is going to be a real bi... *challenge* today."

"I can attest to that." She turned towards me with a knowing smile. "So, Kendall, Thena tells me you're off on a new and exciting assignment."

"I'm not sure exciting is the right word," I answered with a wry smile, "but I am looking forward to hearing more details about the old church and the people who now own it."

"Well, you've come to the right place." She set her purse on the desk, pulled a gray sweater from the back of her worn armchair and shot me an appraising look. "An interesting family history there."

"So I've heard."

"Give me a few minutes to get things set up for the day," she said, shrugging into her sweater. "I'll meet you in the back room shortly."

I immediately felt a sense of profound tranquility as I stepped into the spacious room lined with floor-to-ceiling bookcases on both sides. I laid the folder, my purse, phone and notepad on the scarred mahogany table and stood for a moment inhaling the pleasing aroma of old books that permeated the air while listening to the muted ticking of an ancient wall clock situated between two tall windows.

From the time I had learned to read at age four, I had fallen in love with books. Libraries rated among my favorite places on earth. I wondered now, as I strolled around the cozy room turning on the table lamps, if these peaceful storehouses of knowledge and entertainment would one day be on life support like print newspapers and magazines. It was a sobering thought.

"Here you go!" Clara declared enthusiastically, depositing an armload of books on the table. "These will give you a small taste of the rich history of the Catholic Church's influence on the native population of Arizona beginning with the introduction of the Spanish missionaries in 1629, to the arrival of Father Kino around 1691. He established some of our most illustrious missions including Tumacacori and San Xavier del Bac near Tucson."

I could tell by her animated expression and flushed complexion that she was in her element. I didn't have the heart to tell her that she'd brought way more information than I would ever have time to read or use for my articles, but said nothing. I took copious notes as she regaled me with fact upon fact, including a sobering chronology of Apache Indian raids on the missions and surrounding settlements where priests and hundreds of families had all met a gruesome fate. Clara Whitlow possessed a truly astounding wealth of knowledge regarding the history and unique architectural enhancements incorporated into designs of Catholic churches.

She placed her hands reverently on one volume. "Did you know that Our Lady of the Desert is among only a handful of churches remaining in this state that contain a priest hole *and* a crypt?"

Now *that* was interesting. "I did not."

"Very few people know about either, but Thena and I are quite familiar with the layout of Our Lady since we used to attend Mass there years ago. Since you'll be visiting the church today, I'll share with you the secret of how to find the priest hole." Her eyes searched mine. "Do you know what that is?"

"I'm guessing a place to hide."

"That's correct! These tiny, cleverly-concealed rooms originated around the 16th century in England at a time when priests were routinely hunted down by Protestants and then executed. There are still a number of them scattered throughout England in what they called 'safe houses'. However, here in Arizona, there were no safe houses, so these hidden chambers were incorporated into the designs of the missions for the specific purpose of providing a hiding place in case of Indian raids. The tiny rooms were hidden behind false walls, staircases, chimneys and sometimes there was a second concealed area within that room. At Our Lady, the priest hole is located behind the pulpit in the sacristy." Her eyes sparkled with excitement as she revealed in a hushed tone, "The entrance is cleverly secreted behind wood paneling in the closet where the priest's robes used to hang. Unfortunately, the downside is that in many cases, the priests had to hide in them so long that a large percentage of them starved to death or died of suffocation."

Her vivid description caused a faint shiver, reminding me again of childhood explorations of my grandmother's old house. The dank, shadowy basement rooms had been particularly captivating and intimidating to us kids as we prowled the dim corners conjuring up visions of ghosts and monsters that surely lurked behind the mountains of ancient, discarded furniture and crumbling boxes of family treasures. "I'd be all over that one except Wanda told me she can't let me inside."

Clara pushed her glasses higher on her pointed nose and blinked at me slowly like an owl. "Really? What reason did she give?"

I repeated the woman's claims of interior storm damage to the building and then added with a disappointed sigh, "I would have loved to explore that crypt as well."

She expressed surprise and then informed me that she and Thena had once ventured into the crypt many years earlier. "It's accessible only from the outside like a storm cellar." Her gaze grew distant as if she were reliving the memory before she reconnected with me. "It was like visiting an ancient cemetery, except it was dark and dirty and we both felt a profound sense of sadness for the poor lonesome souls down there neglected and for the most part forgotten. It was a deeply touching, yet sobering experience. We were both supremely glad to walk out into the sunshine afterwards." Faint frown lines etched her forehead as she intoned philosophically, "I think the phrase etched on one of the vaults sums it up best: ***We were what you are; and what we are, you will be.***"

We both sat staring in solemn silence listening to the rhythmic ticking of the old clock, until I remarked with an impish grin, "Sounds totally intriguing to me."

Her eyes twinkled with mischief. "You're quite the adventurer, aren't you?"

"Part of my job."

She leaned forward, resting her elbows on the table. "It's so heartwarming to have a young person interested in history. So many youngsters these days have no interest whatsoever and yet history defines the future."

I pointed to the pile of books. "This will all provide great background information for my articles."

Her face lit up. "There's one more thing you may

find of interest."

"What's that?"

"There have been whispered stories handed down through the years that somewhere in the crypt is a hidden door that leads to an underground passage where many a monk and priest made his escape from savage Indian tribes."

That gave me a little chill. "Sounds like something out of an Edgar Allen Poe novel...or maybe Nancy Drew."

She nodded in obvious delight. "It does, doesn't it?"

"And in all these years, no one has ever discovered it?"

"Not to my knowledge."

"Thena told me that the Higgins family has always had a close connection with the church, that one of the uncles was a priest, correct?"

Her eyes softened. "Oh, yes. Everyone loved Father Kerrigan. He was a wonderful, spiritual man and we were all crushed when he was transferred to another diocese. But, listen to this," she announced, her voice rising slightly. "After speaking with Thena last evening, I put in a call to my friend, Jane Freemen. She's been with the State Historic Preservation Office in Phoenix for many years. I shared Thena's plans for the church with her and she told me they recently came across several boxes that contained some of the original architectural plans for Our Lady. There may be some truth to these rumors of a hidden passageway."

I gawked at her. "You're kidding!"

"I'm not. She promised she'll get back to me if she discovers anything of importance."

"Wow! I hope you'll share that news with me."

Her cheeks flushed bright pink. "Of course, my dear."

I consulted my notes and one particular comment

jumped out at me. "Thena also said something about there being logistical impediments to overcome in order for this project to be successful," I said, crooking my fingers in air quotes. "Now that you've told me about the crypt, I'm wondering…is she referring to the remains?"

A shadow of doubt clouded her eyes. "More than likely. I've talked with her at length about that delicate situation and there is no easy solution." One wispy brow arched drolly, she deadpanned, "If she succeeds in converting Our Lady into a recovery facility, no doubt some guests might feel…shall we say, a little uncomfortable sleeping over what is essentially an indoor graveyard."

"Is it possible to move the remains and ashes somewhere else?"

"Oh, yes. But, it's going to require a substantial amount of money. Certain permits would have to be approved along with the permission from family members to relocate them to another site."

I shook my head wistfully. "I was really looking forward to photographing the church, but exploring the crypt sounds even more captivating."

"Well, my dear, I'm not sure it would have been possible for you to go down there in any case."

"Why not?"

"Didn't Thena mention that the family installed a padlock on the door last year?"

"No. For what reason?"

She eyed me shrewdly. "I guess Wanda didn't tell you that Glendine insisted that her ashes be stored down there."

"No." I leaned forward, addressing her earnestly. "I've only heard bits and pieces about the Higgins family, but since her name keeps popping up in conversation, I'm gathering that Glendine was a pivotal figure."

"She certainly was."

"I also understand that your cousin was the housekeeper on the ranch."

"For many years."

"And I'm assuming you knew Glendine personally?"

"I did."

I jotted a few more notes and then looked up at her. "So, what's so special about the old church that she didn't want to be parted from it…even after death?"

"It's a rather long, sad story. How much time do you have?"

I looked up at the clock. I was anxious to be on my way, but at the same time, curiosity kept me glued to the chair. Understanding the motivation behind Glendine's deathbed request might help me nudge Wanda in Thena's direction. "At least another hour, but I don't want to monopolize your time."

She arched a look toward the front door just as another blast of wind rattled the windows. "Since we're the only two people here, I don't think that will be a problem unless someone is in dire need of a book. I doubt many people will venture out in this weather."

I grinned at her. "Except for me."

"Brave girl," she murmured lacing her hands together on the table. "So, let me tell you about Glendine Higgins. She and her sister Gwyn were the daughters of Glen and his lovely wife Anna Marie Kerrigan and yes," she inserted, holding up one finger for emphasis, "her Uncle Robert was the priest I referred to earlier. Anyway, the girls were not identical, but fraternal twins. Gwyn had dark hair like her father and Glendine was fair like her mother. They were two of the prettiest children you'd ever meet and totally devoted to each other."

"Just as a point of interest," I interjected gently, "Ginger mentioned something about there being a family curse and she wasn't joking. Do you know what she's talking about?"

She pinned me with a questioning frown. "I don't know if I'd label it a curse,maybe very bad luck, but, to your point, there did seem to be an inordinate number of tragedies that occurred after the birth of Gwyn and Glendine, beginning with the death of Anna Marie when they were both toddlers."

"What happened to her?"

"She was struck by a hay truck out on the highway, not two miles from the ranch, on her way to the church. She was killed instantly. Her sudden death devastated Glen Higgins. Following the funeral, he fell into a deep depression. It wasn't six months later that his twin brother Gary died."

I shook my head in wonder. "And what happened to him?"

"The story goes he was chasing down some strays when a rattlesnake spooked his horse. It bolted and Gary was unseated. Sadly, one boot got hung up in the stirrup and by the time the horse arrived back at the ranch...well, Gary had been dragged to death."

Grimacing, I murmured, "Ouch. That must have been an awful sight."

"Undoubtedly. After the second funeral in less than a year, Glen became withdrawn and bitter. My cousin,

Nelda, said he worked the ranch from dawn until dark, keeping mostly to himself. She practically raised those poor little girls." For prolonged seconds, her eyes glazed with introspection and then she continued with, "Later on when they blossomed into beautiful young women, Glen seemed to come out of his shell. He hadn't really paid much attention to them for years and then all of a sudden he grew very protective and decided to assume his role as a parent. Nelda told me he became a strict disciplinarian and could be heavy-handed at times. He was also a devout Catholic and insisted Glendine and Gwyn attend Mass every day…and that proved to be a deadly decision for everyone."

"Meaning…?"

She didn't answer immediately. Instead, she sat in silence for measured seconds. When we made eye contact again a little shock buzzed through me at the look of profound sadness clouding her blue eyes. "At the tender age of fifteen, Glendine fell madly in love…with the handsome new priest…and he with her."

"Uh-oh," I whispered, dread hollowing out my belly.

"They became lovers and met in secret at Our Lady of the Desert. Glendine was sixteen when she became pregnant. She confessed to Gwyn, of course, and later shared the news with Nelda. After a few months, there was no hiding her condition and she was terrified. Nelda told me that Glendine confided to her one night that she and the young man, who planned to abandon the priesthood, were going to run away together. My cousin advised her that she was too immature to make such a rash decision and that she must confess the situation to her father, that he would understand." Clara rolled her eyes, muttering, "And that also proved to be a dreadful mistake."

"How so?"

"In those days, having a child out of wedlock was not as acceptable as in today's world. Glen Higgins went stark-raving mad. He stormed to the church and confronted the priest, whose name was Father Dominic, and beat him half to death. Then he went home and beat Glendine within an inch of her life and forbid her from ever seeing him again." She hunched forward, announcing in a subdued tone, "The young man hung himself in the bell tower that very night."

"Oh, my God."

"And he's buried in the crypt beneath the church."

I nodded understanding. "Of course. That explains it. So, now they're together for eternity."

Clara went on to tell me that the tragedy did not end there. To save face with the tight-knit community, Glen Higgins forced a deeply mourning Glendine into an arranged, loveless marriage with neighboring rancher, Hudson Foley, almost forty years her senior. Just the thought gave me one of those lightning-quick internal shivers. "That must have been a nightmare for her."

"Yes and no. Nelda said Hudson had been a lonesome widower for many years and acted very kindly towards her, even though Glendine greatly resented him and her father for controlling her life. I think Glen thought he was making it up to her when he decided to spend an enormous amount of money renovating the old Gold Queen mansion for them as a wedding present."

"Oh, yes," I murmured under my breath, "the Shut-away house."

Her eyes widened with surprise. "Oh? You know

about that."

"Tally told me a little about it last night, but I'm anxious to hear more details."

She lifted one bony shoulder. "I can only share what I've heard secondhand but, according to Nelda, the newlyweds moved into the mansion the following spring and shortly thereafter, she gave birth to a little girl." I didn't miss the shadow that passed behind her eyes and braced myself for more bad news. "That dear baby provided the only happy time in Glendine's life and for a while Nelda said she seemed content with her situation. Unfortunately, it was very short-lived."

"Oh no. Please don't tell me the baby died."

"Three months old," she reported, her compressed lips turning downward. "The doctors attributed it to a rare birth defect, something to do with her heart. Little Grace Irene Foley is also buried in the crypt." She reached for the folder and opened it. "Would you like to see a picture of Glendine?"

"Yes, I would."

She sifted through the contents, pulling out old newspaper clippings and finally a dog-eared photo. Silently, she set it in front of me. I stared with interest at the faded likeness of a young, fair-haired woman with a strikingly beautiful oval-shaped face—full rosebud-shaped lips, wide-set green eyes and a pert, slightly turned-up nose. "Wow," I breathed appreciatively, "she was gorgeous."

"Indeed she was," Clara concurred with a forlorn smile. "Every man who met Glendine fell in love with her, but I think she was only in love with the memory of her first true love, the young priest."

"How sad."

"Yes, she had a very sad life." We both sat again in reverent silence, listening to the sound of the wind whistling outside the windows until she said crisply, "Since you've been denied access to the church, I have some interior photos if you are interested in seeing them as well. The stained glass windows are some of the most beautiful I've ever seen."

"I...am," I answered in a distracted tone, continuing to study the photo. All at once, the strangest feeling washed over me. I felt it in my bone marrow. Something wasn't right. Based on nothing more than intuition and the odd sensation of uncertainty locked in my stomach, I glanced up at Clara and voiced my suspicions. "I know this is going to sound weird, but from what you've told me, I get the impression that even though Glendine made some really disastrous decisions, it sounds to me like she was a genuinely nice person."

"She was a lovely woman with a good heart who, unfortunately, went astray more than once and it ruined her life."

I mulled over her remark. "That's what's puzzling me. Her children seem nothing like how you describe her. I've seen Nelson Trotter in person and a picture of his sister. Neither of them looks anything at all like her."

Her steady gaze reflected shrewd admiration. "Ah, so you guessed."

"Guessed what?"

"That Glendine was not their mother."

CHAPTER 10

Finally out on the open road, I drank in the unfamiliar scenery as the majestic mountains and cactus-decorated vistas of the Sonoran desert opened up before me, filling my senses with the spirit of the Wild West. The longer I lived in this magnificent state, the more I explored its ever-changing beauty, the more I loved it. I stepped hard on the accelerator, relishing the invigorating rush that always gripped me at the dawn of a new assignment, especially one with multiple layers like this one—compelling details of historical significance brought forward and intermingled with a cast of living characters.

I had stayed much longer at the library than planned, and by the time I'd traded my Jeep for Ronda's dented, scratched, dirt-caked brown one, I was running a full two hours behind my self-imposed schedule. I didn't regret it, however. The treasure trove of information I had gleaned on the old church, combined with background information on the Higgins family, was well worth the time.

As I'd expected, the Starfire Ranch was choked with dozens of people milling about along with a caravan of pickup trucks hauling horse trailers. While it would have been fun to stop and visit with Tally, I knew he'd be up to his neck in alligators and decided I really only had time to make the switch with Ronda. She had tried to talk me out of it, explaining that the old family Jeep was usually only used to drive around the ranch property. It did not have all the modern bells and whistles like mine, had not been serviced for a long time and the gas gauge was broken. *"Better fill it up before you take off,"* she had advised me when I handed her my key fob and she dropped a conventional car key in my hand. *"I haven't had it out on the highway for a long time either, so take it easy, okay?"*

Being fifteen model years old, it certainly didn't have the impressive horsepower of my Jeep and the suspension wasn't all that great, but considering that my destination could conceivably involve me running into Nelson Trotter, it would achieve my objective of staying under the radar far better than driving my neon-lime-green Jeep.

Forceful wind gusts were definitely a factor and as I glanced westward at the ominous-looking thunderheads approaching the ragged spine of the distant Harquahala range, odds were good that I was going to see rain in the next few hours. As a precaution, I tested the windshield wipers. Dry and crumbly, they practically disintegrated, screeching loudly against the glass. I pushed the windshield washer button. Nope, no fluid either. "Good job!" I grumbled, chastising myself for making another impulsive decision, but quickly shrugged it off. I'd just have to deal with it. No turning back now.

Traffic was light as I traveled northwest, thinking about the rest of the tragic stories Clara had shared with me. Even though I'd been half-expecting it, the revelation that Glendine was not Nelson and Wanda's mother had startled me nonetheless. I learned that after the death of her infant daughter, Glendine had gone a little "haywire" as Clara had phrased it. Hysterical and inconsolable, she had fallen into deep despair, refused to eat or speak to anyone except her sister, and was finally placed under the care of a psychiatrist and medicated. *"Nelda said she didn't pull out of it for a year and when she finally recovered from her loss, she raged about the injustice of the arranged marriage and rebelled."* Clara had gone on to say that Glendine had insisted on separate sleeping arrangements and when she was twenty-one, took a job in town at one of the bars. Nelda knew she was seeing other men behind her husband's back and cautioned her to stop, go back to church and ask God for forgiveness.

Hudson Foley, distraught and angered by his young wife's wanton behavior, moved out of the mansion and returned to his ranch where he suffered a fatal stroke a few months later. Glendine's father, disgusted by his daughter's activities, stopped communicating with her even though the family ranch home was only two miles from the mansion. As Clara told it, that arrangement was just fine with Glendine who had never forgiven her father for "wrecking her life". The following year, she took the family surname back.

While all that drama was unfolding, her twin sister, Gwyn, had met and married a geologist named Elvin Trotter and then given birth to Nelson. Less than a year later, Wanda had been born. Because her husband's job required him to travel to foreign countries for months at a time, Gwyn had moved into the mansion with Glendine, who doted on her babies. She appeared to come to her senses and seemed relatively happy again. Responding to her sister's ardent requests, she agreed to clean up her act, began accompanying Gwyn to church again and finally seemed content enough with her life to forgive and reconcile with her father.

Tragedy struck again, when Gwyn contracted pancreatic cancer. She died within the year. Per her request, Gwyn's body was interred close to home beneath the old church. Heartbroken, Glendine struggled mightily with depression again, lamenting that God was punishing her for her sins. Somehow, she managed to keep it together enough to fulfill her promise to Gwyn and care for her sister's children.

Elvin Trotter arrived home in time for the funeral, but soon realized he was in no position to raise two babies and decided they were better off with Glendine. Barely two years old when Gwyn died, Nelson and Wanda believed Glendine was their biological mother until she finally told them the truth when they reached their early teens. *"Nelda said they were both shocked and suffered severe emotional trauma,"* Clara had conveyed to me in a somber tone. *"And then, a year later, the family learned that Elvin Trotter had been murdered somewhere in Colombia by leftist rebels. A few months after that, Glen Higgins was struck by lightning herding cattle out on the range. He died instantly and so did his horse."* She had shared several obituary clippings and I had the opportunity to study the photos of Gwyn Trotter—who wasn't nearly as attractive as her sister—as well as her husband and her father, Glen Higgins. And then she shared two photos given to her by her cousin. One pictured Nelda and her daughter Rachel with Wanda and Nelson as small children, but the second photo she set in front of me really caught my interest. It looked like a typical picture of a family dressed in swimwear enjoying a sunlit day at the lake. She pointed out a smiling Glendine along with the sullen-faced Trotter twins, now teenagers, but did not identify the dark-haired man with his arm draped around her shoulders or the unsmiling young blonde boy standing behind them.

"Can you identify these two people?" I asked Clara.

She stared at the photo a long time before commenting, "I don't recognize the man she's with. Glendine…dated quite a few as I understood it, but…the boy looks slightly familiar."

"Really? Do you remember anything about him?"

She looked at me with a faraway sheen glazing her eyes. "To be honest, I don't. He may have been in one of my classes."

I tapped the photo. "Tally told me the story of her inviting her abusive boyfriend and his kid to live with her at the ranch. Do you think it's possible this might be him and his son?"

She adjusted her glasses and studied the photo again. "I'm pretty good at remembering my students, and I've kept in touch with many of them, but…it's been over forty years and I'm afraid I don't recall this boy's name. Is it very important to you?" she asked, edging me a questioning look.

I grinned at her. "I find this whole story intriguing. It's got everything. Family drama, illicit love affairs, infidelity, suicide, attempted murder, pathos, and a ton of unanswered questions, just the kind of thing that rings my bell."

A broad smile lit her face. "I guess that's why you do what you do. How about this?" she proposed, folding her hands in front of her. "It may take me several days to locate my collection of yearbooks during that particular time period, but I'll be happy to go through them and see if I can find him."

I waved away her offer. "Please don't go to any extra trouble."

"I'm delighted to share whatever information I can."

I thanked her profusely and took a few minutes to record the photos on my phone. She had already given me a lot to absorb, and as I added to my notes, I contemplated the magnitude of the tragedies that had befallen Glendine and her family. No wonder Thena had referred to her *'poor, suffering soul.'* The grim reaper really did seem to stalk the Higgins family then and now.

Clara was poised to launch into what she remembered of the final chapter—the violent altercation between Glendine and the man who had mutilated her face, the one I was most anxious to hear more specifies about, when several people walked—or rather blew in—the front door. She had excused herself to assist them and minutes later several other patrons struggled inside so I decided it was time to go. I gathered up all my material and we agreed to meet again, but until that time, I decided I'd pick Ginger's brain at breakfast tomorrow and find out if she could fill in more of the blanks.

The myriad of facts I'd learned was still bouncing around in my head when I realized I was only a few miles away from the Double G. Good thing. The sky was now a quilted river of fast-moving gray clouds with flashes of weak sunlight peering through intermittent patches of blue. My window of opportunity to get any decent photos of Our Lady of the Desert was quickly closing.

Ahead to my left, I noticed an abandoned gas station

and close by what looked like the crumbling remains of an old motel. Sections of the dilapidated building's roof flapped wildly in the incessant wind. Probably because of the childhood fascination with my grandmother's house, I loved the essence of old houses, old buildings, old cemeteries. Each one had a story to tell about its past and sometimes when photographing them, on some inexplicable level, I could feel a certain aura surrounding them, almost as if they were still imbued with the spirits and memories of their former occupants. Tally always teased me about being fanciful, but I'd been aware of my "sixth" sense from an early age. My wise grandmother urged me to embrace the gift of precognition and heed it. Most of the time, I did, but on occasion I'd ignored it, usually to my peril.

I checked my odometer. I'd come twenty-five miles, which meant the church should be around the next curve. Yep. There it was—easily recognizable from Clara's photos. The graceful, cream-colored structure sat at least a half a mile off the highway, flanked on three sides by tall cypress trees. Lovely setting. But my attention was instantly refocused on the cluster of black, weirdly-shaped, volcanic rock piles rising in sharp contrast to the flat, sage-and-mesquite-covered landscape. Having never seen anything quite like them, I stared in amazement, entranced by the jagged, perpendicular cones. I wondered if the hot springs Thena had mentioned lay hidden from view behind a series of gentle hills peppered with swaying cottonwood trees. It looked like a real desert oasis. I had to admit Thena was right. It was indeed a unique property.

Then something extraordinary happened. Mother Nature provided me with an once-in-a-lifetime visual gift when all at once a brilliant beam of sunlight sliced through the fast-moving clouds illuminating the church, and only the church, in an ethereal golden glow. Talk about a breathtaking photo!

I fumbled for my camera, hoping to capture the unbelievable image, but then another cloud snuffed out the luminescent shaft of light as quickly as it had appeared. What were the odds that I would happen along at that exact moment? Maybe it was a good omen. I hoped so as I turned right and bounced along uneven ground until I came to a fork in the road. A cracked, sun-bleached sign marked the entrance to the Double G Ranch. Ahead, the wrinkled, brown road snaked eastward into rolling hills where a small herd of cattle grazed near a stock tank adjacent to a briskly spinning windmill. PRIVATE PROPERTY and TRESPASSERS WILL BE PROSECUTED signs were posted on the metal gate and along the fence line, including one boldly stating, IF YOU DON'T BELIEVE IN LIFE AFTER DEATH, TRESPASS HERE AND FIND OUT FOR SURE, which clearly conveyed its pithy message.

I turned left, traveling another quarter of a mile and parked the Jeep beneath a desert willow tree on the far side of a clearing, which I surmised had once been the parking area. When I opened the door, the cold wind slammed it shut again. Damn! The weather was definitely not cooperating.

For a few seconds I considered just staying put, but was I going to let a little wind deter me? I pocketed my cell phone, snapped the camera into the waterproof case and slipped the .38 into my jacket. My propensity for charging into dicey situations had not been lost on Tally. So, when he insisted that I learn how to handle and shoot a firearm, I had taken his advice. That training had certainly come in handy the last time I'd found myself out on assignment alone in the middle of nowhere.

It was a struggle to keep the door open, but I was finally able to slide out. I pushed my way through the thrashing willow boughs and began snapping a panorama of photos. I wanted to see it all—the hot springs, the church and the old mansion—but by the looks of the lightning-charged clouds forming overhead followed by the rumbles of thunder, I doubted that was going to happen today.

Our Lady of the Desert rose up before me, far larger than I had imagined. The picturesque structure, even with the sprays of graffiti and sections of peeling stucco, presented an awe-inspiring sight, gracefully displaying her arched corridors, curved gables and wide, projecting eaves. The eye-catching copper-domed bell tower, which amazingly still housed a rusted bell and was topped by an ornate cross, tilted slightly toward the northern mountains. A dark scar ran along one side where I presumed lightning had struck. A blue tarp, whipping in the wind, cascaded down one side of the roof, anchored by several boards and concrete blocks. At the base of the old structure were other signs that repair was imminent—bundles of lumber, buckets of roofing tar, ladders, and pallets piled with rolls of tar paper. Groves of mature acacia trees encircled the perimeter of the property while additional NO TRESPASSING and KEEP OUT signs hung prominently on a wooden fence.

With only the keening wind as my companion, I ignored the signs and slid over the barrier. If anyone tried to stop me, I could always say Wanda had given me permission and that I would be meeting up with her later, which might actually be true. I wandered about capturing a series of images, including the crumbling marble-inlaid stairs that lead to the boarded-up front door that must have stood fifteen feet high. Above it, the darkening sky created a dramatic backdrop for the bell tower as I snapped a succession of photos. My close-up shots revealed a small flock of mourning doves huddled together for warmth in the opening beneath the bell. I could not help but think of the story Clara had told me. Imagine the horror of discovering the body of the young priest hanging from this ancient structure. Tragic.

As I walked around the periphery, wading through knee-high weeds and taking note of the shuttered arched windows, an overwhelming sense of melancholy suddenly gripped me. Was it the fact that I was now privy to the sad history of this abandoned house of worship? I must admit, when I reached the rear of the church and spotted the padlocked entrance to the crypt, a pervasive atmosphere of danger stopped me dead in my tracks. I spun around, searching for the reason for my acute discomfort. My intuition was rarely wrong, but there did not appear to be another soul around. Not a live one anyway. A macabre thought.

Nevertheless, details of Glendine's tragic tale continued to parade through my mind. Was I picking up vibes from the crypt? "Cut it out," I chided myself severely. More than likely it was merely the lonesome setting combined with the wind and impending storm—a perfect setting for a ghost story.

The first drops of rain splattered on my face as I continued towards a small stone structure that housed a well pump. Just beyond it, behind a rusted fence, lay a sadly neglected graveyard. Pots of plastic and what looked to be wilted fresh flowers adorned tumbledown gravestones almost hidden in the overgrown grass and weeds. It looked like another great place to explore, but that would take more time than I had today. I moved on to the remains of the rectory.

Just as Thena had described, there was ample evidence of a fire—charred timbers were strewn about, one graffiti-stained wall had partially fallen away while fragments of roofing shingles flapped noisily in the rising wind. The remnants of several Adirondack chairs littered a small yard along with scattered toys and broken beer bottles. A toppled concrete birdbath added to the air of desolation.

I stepped over a pile of rubble and gingerly poked my head through a doorway. The murky light made it difficult to see, so I fished my small LED flashlight from my pocket and shined it around the room. Of course, I searched around for signs of live spider activity, but saw only shredded cobwebs waving in the breeze. I moved about the debris-littered floor while photographing the blackened interior of a room easily identifiable as a kitchen. The appliances were either gone or vandalized. Pipes stuck out of the wall beneath a yawning window where the sink had once stood. Had the fire originated here?

Intermittent flashes of lightning helped brighten the way as I picked my way around pieces of discarded furniture, assorted garbage and clothing remnants, accompanied by the shrill whine of the wind whistling through cracks in the walls and broken window panes. Paw prints and piles of animal droppings everywhere, including what looked like bat guano, gave ample evidence that the desert creatures had taken up residence in the absence of humans. The dilapidated rectory was obviously unlivable now and probably needed to be demolished. I thought it odd that the Trotter family had done nothing to improve the property in a year's time and was curious to find out what they planned to do with it if they didn't sell to Thena.

I could definitely see possibilities for the church, but if the interior damage was as severe as Wanda indicated, the amount of money it would take to refurbish it would be truly staggering. Thena would need outside help and that brought to mind my interview with Dr. Craig. If I was going to be on time, I'd best complete my exploration of the property and get back to town.

Once outside, I flinched violently when an ear-splitting clap of thunder announced the arrival of the storm. An upward glance at the now-black, low-hanging clouds confirmed that I'd probably waited too long. I broke into a run and made it about halfway towards the clearing when the sky opened up.

Clara was right. There are no hurricanes in Arizona, but there are microbursts and the occasional tornado. I didn't know which this was, but the screaming wind tore at my hair and within seconds the rain turned to hailstones, painfully pummeling my face. Bombarded by the volley of ice pellets, there was little I could do to protect myself from the onslaught. I started towards the Jeep, but my footsteps faltered when I heard the faint roar of a car engine. My vision blurred by the torrential rain, I squinted ahead at two approaching vehicles. What looked to be a silver-colored SUV peeled away onto the Double G Ranch road while the second one headed right towards me. Disbelieving, I blinked rapidly and stared aghast. No way! It couldn't be. The shock of seeing the familiar white pickup and trailer made my stomach plunge. Oh, shit! The memory of Nelson Trotter's menacing behavior flashing through my mind raised the question: did I want to be caught out here alone with this known sexual predator who had already advanced a veiled threat? I had to make a decision. And fast. There was zero chance I could make it across the clearing to the Jeep before he arrived, and if I did make a run for it, more than likely he would see me.

Instinctively, I spun around and sprinted towards the church. Blinded by the maelstrom, I ducked behind a row of cypress trees and dove behind the air-conditioning unit. I slid along the slushy ground, wincing aloud as my palms scraped across sharp stones and then felt a searing pain beneath my chin before slamming my cheek into the rough exterior wall. Dizzy and slightly nauseated, I folded myself into an alcove like a hermit crab, only slightly protected from the storm.

Carefully, I touched my aching cheek and then cupped a hand beneath my chin. My pulse surged in horror at the sight of all the blood on my fingers, which quickly mingled with raindrops, spilling a dark pink river onto my clothes. What a mess! All I could do was press my coat sleeve hard against the wound and hope it would stem the flow of blood.

Panic locked my throat, as the distinctive whiny clatter of the diesel truck grew closer. Huddled in the corner, thunder crackling overhead, pounded relentlessly by rain and hail, all I could do was pray he did not discover me. The irony of that act—praying against the *outside* walls of the church—was not lost on me. I thought my heart would explode when the pickup stopped not twenty feet from me.

Soaked to the bone, barely breathing, I peered

through the downpour and watched Nelson Trotter jump from the driver's side, trot around the truck's grill and yank the passenger door open. Astonished, I stared through the curtain of rain into the interior of his pickup. Was I hallucinating, or did the cab appear to be overflowing with pink flowers? He reached inside and grasped a bunch along with a plastic garbage bag. When he dragged out a cooler bag and slung it over his shoulder, I noticed something fall to the ground before he slammed the door and loped out of sight.

My mind swimming with confusion, I cautiously peeked around the corner in time to see him kneeling on the ground, unlocking the door to the crypt. Transfixed, I watched him tug the door open, then pick up the flowers and bags. He descended a few steps down before turning to pull the door shut behind him.

CHAPTER 11

Crouched in the corner, wet and freezing, the palm of my left hand, cheekbone and chin throbbing painfully, I muttered under my breath, "O'Dell, you're a first-class idiot." How had I managed to trap myself in such a stupid situation? Wondering what in the world Nelson Totter could possibly be doing, I waited for what seemed like an hour for him to reemerge from the crypt. Finally, my patience ran out. It was time to extricate myself from this awful predicament and get the hell out of there. Thank heavens the punishing hail had finally stopped. The whirlwind had died down and the rain had slowed to a drizzle as the purple-tinged storm clouds churned south towards Castle Valley, eerily illuminated with strobe-like lightning flashes followed by diminishing grumbles of thunder.

Ready. Set. Go. I struggled to my feet and immediately collapsed from the agonizing cramps in my calves. Suppressing the urge to scream, I rubbed and massaged my legs vigorously until the stinging pain subsided.

Then, primed to make a mad dash towards the front of the church, I rose again only to succumb to my unquenchable curiosity. What had he dropped near his truck? As much as my whole being yearned to escape, I peered around the corner of the church and, still seeing no sign of him, darted past the cypress tree and splashed through muddy puddles while glancing anxiously over my shoulder. When I reached the truck I peered through the window, again struck by the astonishing sight of the flower-filled cab.

Intermittently looking back at the church, I quickly searched the area near the passenger door, unearthing a small white box half-buried in mud. Impulsively, I shoved it into my coat pocket before turning to run in the opposite direction. Panting hard, I stopped near the front door of the church, listened closely for a few seconds and then bolted across the open space towards the Jeep. Heart hammering madly, I ducked beneath the sagging, dripping boughs of the willow tree, vaulted inside and collapsed in the driver's seat, amazed that I had arrived undetected.

Unable to stop shaking, my teeth clattering from the cold, I fumbled for the key. Poised to start the engine, out of the corner of my eye I noticed movement near the rear of the church. Startled, I watched Nelson Trotter emerge from the crypt, minus the flowers and cooler bag, but hauling a now-bulging plastic bag. He squatted down, secured the padlock, hurried to his truck and then proceeded to drive straight in my direction. OMG! He appeared to be looking right at me! Cold dread shrinking my insides, heart frozen in my throat, I inched down in the seat and held my breath as he slowly cruised by.

Relief flooding my body, I exhaled a thankful sigh

and watched him turn onto the Double G Ranch road. As a precaution, I forced myself to wait several minutes before starting the engine and congratulated myself on making at least one good decision today. While Ronda's mud-brown, nondescript Jeep blended into the background, my iridescent green one would have captured Nelson Trotter's attention immediately.

All at once, my stomach felt hollow. Extreme weakness flowed over me as my adrenaline levels plummeted. I closed my eyes for a few seconds, and then remembered the little box in my coat pocket. I pulled it out and wiped the mud off with my sleeve. What had possessed me to take it? There was really no way to know if it had fallen from the truck or been lying there for weeks. I wrestled with myself. I really should put it back…but as long as I was now in possession, why not check out the contents? I opened the flap on the box and three small glass bottles rolled into my palm. One by one, I turned them and read the labels: Oil of Lavender, Oil of Chamomile and Phenoxyethanol. What in the world was Phenoxyethanol? Puzzled, I took a photo of each label, and was in the process of returning the bottles to the box when drops of blood appeared on my hand.

Dismayed, I positioned the mirror on the visor. Son-of-a-bitch! It looked like I'd been in a knife fight! There appeared to be about a two-inch gash in the soft flesh beneath my chin. Had I slammed into a sharp rock? A broken beer bottle? Whatever, I reached over, opened the glove compartment and my heart sank. I had not transferred my first aid kit to Ronda's Jeep. Totally deflated, I wondered if the day could get any worse.

Oh well, I'd just have to make do with what I had. I

pulled a wad of tissues from my purse and pressed them firmly against my chin. Ouch! Lamenting that it was probably too late to have it checked out by Dr. Garcia, I suddenly remembered my appointment to interview Dr. Craig at Youth Oasis. Should I call to reschedule or show up looking like I'd been living under a bridge for a week? I reached for my phone only to see the "no service" message displayed on the screen. Great. Just great. All I really wanted to do was go home, soak in a hot bath, savor a steaming bowl of soup and crawl into a warm bed with my cats. None of those wishes appeared plausible at this point. But, luckily I had packed some provisions for the trip.

After wolfing down a protein bar and half a bottle of water, I felt marginally recharged. The still-cloudy sky was in the process of ushering in an early twilight, so I turned the key and pulled cautiously from my leafy hiding place. The coast looked clear, so I navigated my way though deep puddles, rocking back and forth towards the main road, all the while struggling to make sense of the entire crazy escapade.

What exactly had I just witnessed? Was there a logical explanation for Nelson Trotter's odd visitation? Was he simply honoring Glendine's memory by bringing flowers to her ashen remains stored somewhere beneath the old church? Touching indeed, but what would be the urgency to complete that task in the middle of a thunderstorm? What little I knew about him made me question his display of apparent grief. He appeared to be anything but sensitive. What had the plastic bag and cooler contained? Moreover, where was he going afterwards with the cab of his pickup jam-packed to the ceiling with all those flowers? I could think of no plausible explanation for any of my questions.

I caught up with the storm again about ten minutes from the clinic and had a devil of a time trying to see out the smeary, rain-drenched windshield using the dried-up, practically useless wiper blades. A trip to the auto parts store sometime tomorrow was a definite must.

Thankfully, I made it to Youth Oasis about fifteen minutes before five. There were still two cars in the parking lot and I had zero desire for anyone I knew to see me in my present disheveled state. I could only imagine what Dr. Craig's initial reaction would be. I could not help but think of the old adage, *"There's no second chance for a first impression."*

I decided to trade my sodden, filthy, bloodied coat for the beige windbreaker I'd thankfully transferred to Ronda's Jeep at the last minute and made a valiant attempt to fluff out my damp curls. I viewed my sorry reflection in the mirror again and dabbed at my chin. The damn cut would not stop bleeding.

A fiery bolt of lightning lit up the clinic's exterior just as a small, tan pickup pulled in. A young man jumped out carrying two white plastic bags, sprinted towards the front door and disappeared inside. Within a minute, he reappeared, ran to the truck and as he drove past me, the little triangle signboard on his vehicle identified his mission: Fazio's Pizza. My stomach rumbled noisily. Hot pizza sounded awesome.

Now it was my turn to face the steady downpour—pretty much the last thing I wanted to do, but since I had no idea how long the storm would continue, I secured my Nikon underneath the windbreaker, zipped it up to my chin in hopes of hiding the unsightly gash, and once again, stepped into the freezing rain. I made a beeline for the entrance, thinking that I'd be lucky if I didn't contract a serious cold by the time this fiasco ended.

When I stepped inside the waiting area, I paused, marveling at the stunning transformation of the old American Legion Hall. Ginger was right on the money. The renovation was breathtaking. Gone was the dark wood paneling, replaced by textured walls painted a delicate rose-colored shade. Recessed lighting illuminated the spacious room in soothing lavender tones and the once-scarred concrete floor was now pink and gray marble. Scattered about the room sat a half a dozen plush white chairs accented by slim, silver vases, each containing a single long-stemmed red rose. An impressive driftwood coffee table commanded attention as the room's centerpiece and pastel watercolors featuring Arizona landscapes adorned the walls on either side of a natural stone fireplace. Wow. Hats off to the interior designer.

Feeling like a dirty, shabby interloper, I ambled towards the half-moon, glass-enclosed reception desk, my shoes emitting a slushy, squeaking sound. The young, platinum blonde glanced up at me and performed a classic double take. Visibly recoiling, her critical glance swept over my dripping hair and soiled clothing. She reached up and slid the panel open a few inches asking warily, "Is there something…we can do for you?"

"You can tell Dr. Craig that Kendall O'Dell is here and direct me to the ladies' room." I managed to muster up a tight smile that did nothing to thaw her condescending demeanor.

Still appearing doubtful, she dragged her eyes away from me and typed something into her computer. After a minute or so, she turned back to me. "I'm sorry, I don't see you name here and we are booked solid for the next...two months."

In my present physical and mental state, I had no tolerance for Miss Perfect Skin, Hair, Makeup and Nails's snarky attitude. "He's expecting me," I said tersely. "And the ladies' room is where?"

Wordlessly, she pointed to my left.

"Thanks." I tried to maintain some modicum of dignity as I sloshed my way along the hallway. I could feel her eyes boring into my back and fired a glance in her direction as I pushed the door open. Sure enough, she hurriedly withdrew behind the partition. "Bitch," I whispered uncharitably under my breath.

Even the bathroom was impressive. The cozy anteroom boasted a gold couch with black pillows flanked by two black chairs with gold pillows and a round glass coffee table. A small chandelier sparkled from the ceiling enhancing the sheen of the gold fixtures on the four hand-painted sinks. All around scented candles burned. Pots of green plants and more vases of fresh flowers completed the decor. I could live here, I thought dreamily, pumping creamy soap from a mother-of-pearl-encrusted container.

Once I got the dirt washed off, the cut on my palm didn't look too bad and my right cheekbone had only a minor scrape, but even with the soft glow of flattering pink lighting, my scruffy reflection in the gilded mirror was unsettling. No wonder the receptionist had stared at me. I looked like a homeless person with my lank, wet hair and soggy clothing. And, there was no way she hadn't seen the blood on the collar of my nice beige jacket. Crap! I wet one of the neatly rolled washcloths and attempted to scrub the collar to no avail.

Well, this jacket was probably toast. Next, I pressed damp paper towels under my chin and it occurred to me that I was certainly in the right place to find a couple of Band-Aids. I did the best I could to make myself look more presentable and then squeaked my way back towards the reception desk.

"If you'd care to wait, Dr. Craig will be with you in a few minutes," the Barbie look-alike announced, her tone cordial even though her porcelain expression remained skeptical.

I nodded and returned to the waiting area. I would have dearly loved to sit down in one of those gorgeous, comfortable-looking chairs, but didn't dare take a chance on soiling them. Instead, I strolled around the room listening to the lilting strains of New Age music and stood warming myself in front of the fireplace until I heard the text signal from my purse.

I scooped out my phone and read Tally's text. HOW WAS YOUR DAY? GOOD, I HOPE. SLAMMED WITH BUYERS. TALK SOON. He ended it with one smiley face and two hearts. I was in the process of texting him back when I heard a mellifluous voice behind me ask, "Miss O'Dell?"

I swung around and immediately recognized the silver-haired man from the photo I'd seen online yesterday. He was far better-looking in person. As his searching gaze skimmed over me, I could tell by the host of question marks glazing his midnight-blue eyes that he hadn't missed the fact that I looked like a wet dog. Did I smell like one too? "Dr. Craig." I mustered up a friendly smile, dug a business card from my purse and handed it to him. "Thena Rodenborn speaks very highly of you. Thanks for taking the time to see me on such short notice."

"Of course," he murmured, accepting the card while continuing to study me with a puzzled frown. "Is… everything all right?"

"What do you mean?"

"Well, you appear to be rather…damp and there is blood on your collar."

My hand flew to my chin. "Oh, that. I…ah…was out on assignment earlier and…did kind of a face plant during that hailstorm. I'm sure it'll be fine." I babbled on, sounding inane to myself when I suggested hopefully, "Perhaps I could borrow a couple of Band-Aids from you."

His eyes darkening with concern, he digested my self-diagnosis before asking quietly, "Would you mind if I take a look?"

Self-consciously, I replied, "Um…no, I guess not."

Being slightly taller than I was, he reached out and gently tilted my chin upwards. "Oh my. This needs some attention. Why don't you come to my office where the light is better?"

"All right, but would you mind if I take a few quick shots of the reception area? This is the first time I've seen the building since the renovation."

"Not a bit. Thena told me you'd be wanting photos to accompany your article." Smiling, he tilted his head slightly, inquiring, "What do you think?"

"It's…stunning…elegant…awesome, just awesome. Can I assume that you had something to do with the exterior design and interior furnishings?"

His face flushing, he responded modestly, "A little."

"I can tell you for a fact that there is nothing nicer in Castle Valley."

"I'm glad you like it," he said, treating me to an engaging grin. "And just so you know, Thena had many complimentary things to say about you."

"Awww. She's a sweetheart. I don't know what we'd do without her."

"Feel free to photograph whatever you like. My office is the second door on the right along that hallway," he said, pointing beyond the reception desk. "I'll be expecting you shortly."

"Thank you." What a nice surprise. His ultra-pleasant bedside manner was the polar opposite to Dr. Mallick's rude behavior towards me this morning. "I'll just be a few minutes."

"Take your time." When he swiveled around, I couldn't help but notice the crisp cut of his gray suit, which looked super-expensive, and the way the heels of his polished loafers clicked smartly on the marble floor. Not bad-looking for an older guy, not at all. While I pulled out my Nikon and adjusted the aperture and shutter speed for indoor lighting, he stopped at the desk and chatted quietly with the receptionist who was slipping on a black coat and shutting off lights. A second woman clad in scrubs that I recognized from this morning hurried to his side and spoke to him briefly in low tones as she, too, pulled on a jacket and stocking cap. He accompanied both women to the front door, opened it and then locked it behind them. I decided it was very generous of him to not only offer a medical opinion, but to stay late for my benefit. He appeared to be a real gentleman. A rarity nowadays.

I took several wide shots of the waiting area and then moved towards his office. Dr. Craig had removed his suit jacket and slipped on a white coat by the time I walked through the door. "You can set your things there." He pointed to a narrow table. "And then," he invited, gesturing towards the surgical chair, "have a seat here."

I did as he suggested and after I settled into a reclining position, I inquired, "Okay if I ask you a few questions?"

Eyes shimmering with humor, he gave me an astute grin. "Thena warned me about your attributes as a tenacious reporter and that you'd have a million of them, but, seeing as I'm now your doctor, at least for the next half hour or so, I need you to not move your jaw while I examine you, all right?"

"I guess I can be quiet for a minute…or two anyway," I joked, returning his tight-lipped smile. "I really appreciate your concern. This certainly isn't the introduction I had planned."

His demeanor turning professional, he turned on a bright light above me and slipped a paper drape around my neck. "Things happen in life that we don't expect," he murmured, scrutinizing my chin. "If you don't mind, I'd like to clean this area first."

"Okay."

He snapped on gloves, slipped on a mask, opened a sealed container and dabbed at the scrape on my cheek before moving beneath my chin where he blotted and then proceeded to scrub. It stung like crazy. "Owww!" I finally squeaked.

Observing my distress, he pulled back. "Sorry, but I have to remove the dirt and grass. You're lucky though," he tacked on, "the good news is the tear is smooth, almost as if it were sliced with a sharp knife, but it's deep enough that it needs to be sutured. You okay with me doing that?"

"I guess I have to be."

"Good. Otherwise, you'll probably have a very noticeable scar and I don't think you want that."

"No, I don't."

"And you're okay with signing a release giving me permission to treat you?"

"Sure."

He ran practiced fingers along my jawline. I couldn't see his face but his critical gaze reflected admiration. "In case no one has ever told you before, you have great cheekbone structure and extraordinarily healthy, beautiful skin."

"Really?"

"Really. It's smooth, supple and elastic. May I ask your age?"

"Sneaking up on thirty in August."

His eyes registered surprise. "Well, your skin certainly doesn't show it. Most women would kill to have such a flawless complexion."

"Perhaps it's because I'm a recent transplant from cool, damp Pennsylvania."

"Possible."

"Or, maybe I just inherited good genes."

"Very likely." He took my blood pressure, then moved to the counter where he discarded the gloves and pulled supplies out of several drawers. "I hope you drink lots of water and use moisturizers and sunscreen, especially here in Arizona where the sunlight is so intense."

"I do."

"Excellent. Over the years, I've dealt with a substantial number of women and some men who are sun worshippers. After they've baked their skin for many years, they come to me, very unhappy campers, and expect me to perform miracles."

I grinned. "Well, if Thena's remarkable transformation is any indication, I would say you are a miracle worker."

His eyes glowed with pleasure. "Thank you very much, but I'm afraid I can only take part of the credit."

"Why do you say that?"

"Because my main contribution is financing Dr. Mallick's research. He's the brains behind this ground-breaking venture. He's responsible for the years of tedious clinical trials and this is only the first phase. As with all scientists, he's optimistic about future discoveries and we're all very excited about the initial results of this latest rejuvenation treatment." Eyes alight, his pleasant baritone voice rang with enthusiasm as he continued. "What we've been able to accomplish to this point is just the beginning of what we all believe will be revolutionary breakthroughs in the arena of gene manipulation and applying that technology in conjunction with our anti-aging injections."

"What do you think about all the TV, Internet and magazine ads out there touting eternal youth with supposed breakthroughs in HGH and BHRT research? Looks like you have a lot of competition."

Nodding agreement, his expressive eyes held a glint of reservation. "That's how it appears to the general public, but these other products that promise the sun, moon and stars produce only a targeted, temporary approach. We are working on something more permanent, much bolder and far beyond human growth hormone injections or bio-identical hormone replacement therapy. We believe that ours is... unique in the marketplace."

"In what way?"

"I can't get into specific details, but our bio-research team has discovered a revolutionary combination of techniques that appear to assist the body in significantly slowing the aging process and, who knows," he posited with a slight shrug, "possibly at some point in time actually reversing it."

I stared at him skeptically. "Sounds futuristic. You really are searching for the Fountain of Youth."

He gave me a probing look. "Isn't everybody?"

"I guess so."

"Look at it this way, a hundred years ago, who would have thought technology would have advanced to this level, so think about the innovations that will be made in science and medicine in the next hundred years. Imagine the possibilities."

"So, can you share just one salient fact regarding these injections that I can pass on to my readers?"

"You're very persistent."

"So I've been told."

Appearing introspective, he paused for a few seconds. "I can tell you this much. According to our studies, our exclusive formula significantly improves DNA repair and actually helps trigger the body's natural production of youth hormones that help rejuvenate the skin by replenishing collagen and elastin, which diminish as we age. And," he added with a secretive twinkle entering his eyes, "early results show our process does appear to produce more permanent, lasting effects in the majority of our patients."

"Awesome. So, I'm curious how you met Dr. Mallick and can you divulge any details regarding his initial research? Why did you decide to open a clinic here in Castle

Valley and…"

Chuckling, he held up a hand. "For the next several minutes, I'll need you to stay still and quiet while I close this wound. After that, I'll be more than happy to answer more of your questions." He snapped on another pair of gloves. "You okay with that?"

"Sure."

"I'm going to numb this area with Lidocaine before I begin." He picked up a syringe and leaned in close. "Little poke here."

The needle stung and I tried not to flinch as he carefully injected the medication several places and then pulled back. "That'll take effect in just a minute."

Genuine gratitude filled me. "Thank you. I appreciate this more than you know."

"Don't mention it. This is what I do." Pride shone in his intent gaze. "One of the most satisfying aspects of my profession is to witness patients' positive responses to my efforts and feel good about themselves again." His pleasant voice charged with enthusiastic sincerity, he added, "I am able to give those desiring it a new lease on life by improving where nature fell short, or give hope to the person who is suffering from an unfortunate life event such as a birth defect or a debilitating accident. It's exacting and tedious work, but more gratifying than people will ever know."

I stared up at his beaming eyes, remembering how my mother used to grumble about some of her doctors having a "God complex" but decided that Dr. Craig had probably earned the right to be a bit full of himself. At the same time I felt thankful to have someone with his skill sets addressing my immediate problem. "That will be a perfect quote for my initial piece," I remarked with an appreciative smile. "Thank you for sharing your insight."

"It is my passion in life."

Unfortunately, at that exact moment, my empty stomach protested, squealing loudly, like someone slowly releasing air from a balloon. I clamped a hand tightly over my midsection, unable to suppress a giggle. "Sorry."

"Don't apologize," he admonished me lightly, his observant eyes narrowing. "When was the last time you ate?"

"I had a protein bar hours ago, but apparently that wasn't a sufficient lunch."

He was silent for long seconds. "How about this? When we finish here, why don't you join me in the break room? I had pizza and salad delivered a short time ago, and I'd be happy to share while we talk."

"Are you sure? I don't want to take too much of your time."

"I do have work to catch up on later this evening since I've been gone for two weeks, but hey, I have to eat too."

Was this guy nice or what? Both Tally and Ginger constantly teased me about my insatiable appetite and his kind offer literally made my mouth water. "You're on."

He worked swiftly and efficiently. My stomach continued to emit embarrassing sounds and I had to fight to keep from bursting into gales of laughter. Because of the mask, I could not discern his facial expression, but I could tell by the mirth reflected in his eyes that he clearly heard my stomach's uproarious symphony.

"My goodness," he finally remarked. "You really are hungry."

Shrugging, I smiled sheepishly.

"Hang on, I won't be much longer." Within twenty minutes, he gave me a hand mirror so I could view the six neat stitches beneath my chin. Then he applied a light bandage, which he advised me to leave on the laceration for 24 to 48 hours. After that, I should apply a topical antibiotic cream for several more days to avoid infection. "You'll need to have the stitches removed in about five to seven days," he informed me with a professional smile after pulling off his gloves and mask. "If I'm not available, your family doctor can take them out." He stepped back and removed the white coat. "I'd also suggest you use Vitamin E, cocoa butter cream or a scar-reducing product which you can find at any drug store."

"Boy, this day sure didn't turn out anything like the way I planned. I can't thank you enough," I remarked with sincerity while he removed the paper bib.

As I sat upright and swung my legs towards the floor, he held out a hand to me. "You feel okay to walk? Not light-headed?"

"I feel good. Just starving." I could understand now why Thena had a crush on this man. Not only was he an altruistic and highly-skilled surgeon, but also super personable as well.

"I think I can remedy that." He gave me a little wink. "Follow me."

CHAPTER 12

In the neat, compact break room, finally feeling warm and relatively dry again, I signed the necessary paperwork and then proceeded to pepper Dr. Craig with a barrage of questions. I jotted notes between bites of Caesar salad and the best pepperoni pizza I'd ever tasted in my life. In response to my request for a short biography, he told me how, as a young man, he had chosen the medical field because of a close friend who had sustained a debilitating, life-altering injury. He had practiced first as a family physician and then decided to specialize in cosmetic surgery. Later he had studied abroad for a number of years before moving to New York where he practiced for several more years before settling in Beverly Hills. Over time, he had grown his business by garnering a loyal following and favorable reputation among celebrities. "Good word of mouth in that community is like pure gold."

I finished the remainder of my salad. "More important than ever in today's world. A couple of bad reviews online can ruin a lifetime of good work."

"Unfortunately, that's true," he intoned, pouring himself a soft drink.

I eyed the remaining slices of pizza. "Do you want these last three pieces?"

His good-natured laugh filled the room. Gesturing towards the box he insisted, "Please, feel free."

I scooped up a slice and then paused. "Are you sure? I didn't know if you wanted to save this for Dr. Mallick. Is he here now?"

"No. He drove to Phoenix earlier for supplies that aren't available here." He tapped his cell phone. "He sent me a text right after you arrived saying he won't be back until tomorrow."

"That's too bad. Okay, well, how did you two meet and become business partners?" When he hesitated, I added with a wry smile, "I'm not asking you to give away any trade secrets."

His circumspect gaze turned cautiously indulgent. "That's good, because I'm not at liberty to divulge any for your article." He sat forward; his expression earnest as he rested folded hands on the table. "What I can tell you is that I first met Raju…Dr. Mallick at a medical symposium in Mumbai. It was there that I learned about the biomedical research company he and a colleague had founded. As a matter of reference for your readers, doctors and researchers in foreign countries are not subject to the same rigid rules, regulations and government oversight as the United States, so in many ways, their research is light-years ahead of us. But, that is finally beginning to change. Long story short, I ended up staying in India for more than a year. I practiced cutting-edge surgical procedures, while also studying the results of his anti-aging skin rejuvenation treatments, which seemed at the time like a futuristic study of cellular regeneration. Of course since then, more and more researchers are studying actual age reversal and, in a few trials the results have been promising."

"Impressive. So, you encouraged him to bring that expertise to this country?"

"I did. It took a few years to convince him, but he finally agreed and you are now witnessing the outcomes of many, many years of tedious experimentation and exhaustive clinical trials."

I flipped to a new page in my notebook. "Okay. I'm really looking forward to getting additional background information from him for my article." I looked up and squeezed out a sheepish grin. "I hope he isn't still upset with me."

Dr. Craig raised a curious brow. "What…ah…what do you mean?"

"I saw him briefly this morning, but he was rather testy with me, to say the least."

"I don't understand," he said, now looking thoroughly confused. "This morning? I thought you said this was your first visit to Youth Oasis."

"Second actually." I popped a stray piece of pepperoni into my mouth. "I ran into Dr. Mallick while I was taking photos of the grounds and the building. I introduced myself and requested an interview." Making a little face, I added ruefully, "Apparently, I said or did something to irritate him. Didn't he tell you?"

"He did not." An emotion I could not quite discern flashed across his face. "Sorry about that." Sighing heavily, he swiped a hand through his thick, wavy hair. "You'll have to excuse Dr. Mallick. He is a brilliant man, but sometimes comes off as being…um…short with people. Truthfully, I think he'd rather be in the lab conducting experiments than dealing with the public. It's just his style, which can be off-putting to some. I'm sure he meant no offense, but I will definitely speak with him and arrange an interview for you."

Was I imagining or did he sound slightly pissed? I waved off his apologetic explanation. "No worries. Thena mentioned that protecting patient privacy is of utmost importance and I totally get that." I pointed to my Nikon. "He probably thought I was the paparazzi or something."

He opened his mouth to say something but I interjected, "And speaking of privacy, Thena mentioned that you don't seem particularly keen on her proposal of renovating Our Lady of the Desert church into a secluded spa or getaway or whatever you want to call it."

Appearing taken aback, he remarked softly, "I wasn't aware that she'd shared that information with you."

"Just yesterday. She is adamant about securing the property and wants you on board in the worst way." I lowered my voice to a confidential tone. "To be honest, I can understand her point of view, but also your objections now that I've seen the condition of the place." I grinned at him. "It's going to cost a few bucks to restore it, but she is right about the setting. The surrounding scenery is out of this world. I've never seen anything quite like it before. It's spectacularly beautiful."

He observed me with an unreadable expression in his eyes before commenting. "So, if you just learned about this yesterday, when did you visit the church?"

"Today." I explained Thena's request for a series

of articles focusing on the community benefits of the clinic in tandem with the prospect of acquiring the old church for her commercial aspirations while maintaining the historic preservation designation.

"Oh, I see. You were on assignment out there when you had your accident."

"Yep. Trying to escape the storm." It fleetingly crossed my mind to mention Nelson Trotter's odd visit to the crypt, but I decided it wasn't germane to the subject matter and what could he possibly know about it? "I was really disappointed that I couldn't get inside. It's truly a magnificent structure but looks really sad all boarded-up. However, I understand that Thena was able to show you the interior at some point. When was that?"

Forehead crinkled in thought, he closed his eyes momentarily as if trying to recall. "Let's see. I think it was some time last November, perhaps December during the renovation at this facility. No question it's a unique setting and I agree with Thena in regards to the property itself." A shadow of uncertainty crossed his face. "What I really question is her theory of altering the character of the building to serve as a recovery facility. I'm not convinced that the interior is suitably large enough to incorporate the number of rooms we'd need to make this venture viable."

It didn't sound to me like he was sold on the idea at all. Perhaps this whole conception was solely a pipe dream in Thena's mind. I turned to another page, still scribbling copious notes. "I understand what you are saying, but it would be an amazing windfall for this area. If it does come to fruition, it would do wonders to revitalize and benefit the economy of all the surrounding communities."

"Please don't assume anything, but for the short term, I'd prefer any comments on my possible involvement with this project be off the record, at least until I've had more time to study the feasibility of this endeavor. Our attorneys are in the beginning phase of negotiations and I don't yet know what my final answer will be." Apparently, I must have looked disheartened because he flashed me an encouraging smile. "I don't want to get Thena's hopes up or lose any leverage with the property owners during negotiations. You do understand that, I hope."

"Of course. Have you already met the ranch owners?"

"Briefly. A woman named Wanda...Keating I believe her name is, let me tour the interior of the church with Thena a few months back, as I mentioned before."

"You're lucky," I remarked, chewing on the remaining pizza crust, "she wouldn't permit me to go inside."

Tiny frown lines crinkled his forehead. "Why not?"

I repeated my conversation with her and his eyes reflected a mixture of surprised concern and disappointment. "Huh. Well. Thena didn't tell me about the storm damage. That surely means an additional layer of expense to any planned renovations."

My spirits tumbled. Oh, crap. For Thena's sake, for everyone's sake, I'd best shut my big mouth now. Everything I said seemed to push him further away from any participation in the project. I beamed him a sunny smile. "On the bright side, I just happened to read an article online a few weeks ago describing how many churches around the country have closed only to be reborn as other successful businesses, like day care facilities, art galleries, wine-tasting rooms, restaurants, B&B's and even bookstores."

His eyes glowed with approval. "You are an excellent ambassador for Castle Valley, Miss O'Dell. And to be frank, all of your aforementioned suggestions sound more feasible than Thena's…shall we say…unique conception." He must have noticed my downcast expression because he hastily added, "But, don't panic. I haven't taken anything off the table yet."

I felt the tension seeping from my shoulders. "Well, that's a relief." I glanced down at my notebook once again. "I am curious about something Thena mentioned."

"What's that?"

"She said you've maintained a residence in this area for some time, but what made you choose our little town to open Youth Oasis? I mean, why Arizona at all?"

"It seemed like a good fit. I travel here at least twice a month to…decompress, and to be honest, it's more cost effective to do business. Real estate prices are quite reasonable compared to California, taxes are lower, operating expenses are less and for the time being, several staff members from my Beverly Hills office are helping me out until we can hire qualified full-time personnel here."

"Yes, Thena did mention that, so…is your home located near Castle Valley?"

"Aguila, to be exact."

I looked up and stared. "Aguila?"

Looking perplexed, he drew back slightly. "Yes. Is that surprising?"

"To be honest, I didn't even know Aguila existed until yesterday. From what little I've read, it's just a wide spot in the road. So, what is the attraction there for you? I would think you'd feel more at home somewhere like

Sedona. They have a cool little airport there located on top of a mesa, not to mention the fabulous views, hotels, spas, restaurants, palatial homes and what I imagine is a perfect built-in clientele for your type of business."

An acquiescent smile etched his aristocratic features. "They do indeed, and I did consider it, but a good friend of mine put me onto the Eagle Roost Airpark in Aguila years ago."

"Define airpark."

"It's a secure gated community designed exclusively for pilots. There are several others, but we have the option of using a private runway and all the homes in the development have hangars to park the planes."

"That's cool. What kind of plane do you fly?"

"A Cessna 206."

"Does your family come with you?"

A cagey little smile played around his lips. "Are you asking me if I'm married?"

I smiled back. "Yes. I'm sure many of my readers will be interested in a little more background on you, like where you were born, where you went to medical school and if you have a family."

He seemed to be considering my questions for long seconds before he answered. "I'm afraid my personal life isn't all that interesting. I was born in Albuquerque, New Mexico, I went to the University of Colorado, I'm divorced, and have no children. I enjoy flying and playing golf occasionally, but I'm mainly focused on my work." He palmed his hands upward. "I hope that's enough for your readers because that's all I've got. Pretty boring, huh?"

"Not at all. I read some of the glowing testimonials

posted and I'd say you are contributing a lot to the good of mankind, or womankind."

His eyes lit up. "It's a deep source of pleasure for me to possess the skills necessary to help people feel the best they possibly can about themselves no matter what the circumstances."

"That's admirable," I murmured, penning more notes before looking up to meet his gaze. "So, I'm curious about your first name."

Smiling, he narrowed one eye at me. "Why?"

I lifted one shoulder. "I've never heard it before. Is it a family name?"

"Sort of," he answered after a slight hesitation. "Anything else?"

I edged him a mischievous grin. "Oh, I never run out of questions."

"And I'm sure that's why you're good at what you do."

"I stay busy and, except for things like this," I said, touching the bandage on my chin, "I love it when my assignments take me out of the office and into the wide open spaces where I can explore new places."

"More stimulating for you, I gather."

"I'll say. In fact, I'm already planning another trip in a day or two."

I'm pretty sure he was feigning interest when he asked politely, "Oh? Where to?"

"Aguila. And I'll definitely be checking out that airpark. Sounds interesting."

He shot me an inquisitive look. "As part of your assignment?"

I paused. "Maybe indirectly." I really didn't want

to get into the real reason for my visit, but a few paragraphs about the airpark and a few photos would be a noteworthy addendum to my article.

He rose and poured himself another soda from the refrigerator. "Getting back to your question as to why I didn't choose Sedona, there is a simple, practical answer. I don't have to contend with winter flying conditions in Aguila. It's a quick, straight shot from LA, the air is crisp and clear, it's quiet and extremely private, which is the major draw for a lot of people. His eyes alight with secretive mischief, he leaned in, whispering conspiratorially, "You'd be surprised to learn the number of Hollywood stars and industry executives who own a home there."

I nodded sagely. "I get it. They can swoop in, under the radar so to speak, in the dead of night, fly out again and no one even knows they were there, right?"

"Right."

"I see. It makes more sense to me now why Thena is interested in renovating the church. She's thinking the close proximity to the airpark would make it more convenient for people to maintain their privacy."

"I'm sure that's true. And given her track record of past successes, there's no doubt she has an uncanny instinct for buying real estate in the right places at the right time…"

"And having the foresight to invest in new businesses such as Youth Oasis."

He pinned me with a look of candid appraisal. "You point is not lost on me, Miss O'Dell. I'm well aware that Thena is expecting a reciprocal agreement on my part, but, as I said, I'm still on the fence about that particular location. However," he continued, shooting me a smile of encouragement. "I will be making a final decision soon."

"Well, she'll be happy to hear that." His phone buzzed and when he picked it up and tapped out a response, I noted the time on mine. Yikes! I hadn't realized it was almost eight o'clock. I closed my notebook, stifling a yawn. "Good grief. I've taken up way too much of your time." I stood up and grinned at him. "I mean, how lucky can a girl get? Medical aid, pizza, an exclusive interview and a full-page ad in our newspaper. I'd say I hit the jackpot!"

"It was my pleasure to meet you and be able to help." He rose to assist me with my windbreaker and then accompanied me to the door. "If all goes as planned, we'll be buying more ad space very soon."

I was pleased to see the rain had abated, but the cold wind chilled my face like a splash of ice water.

"Doctor's orders," he urged in a light, compassionate tone as we stepped outside. "Go straight home, take Advil or Tylenol and get a good night's sleep. You've had a strenuous day."

I turned and held out my hand. "I intend to do just that. Dr. Craig, thank you for everything. Really."

"You are quite welcome." He grasped my hand in both of his. "Listen, we're having a little grand opening celebration Saturday afternoon starting at four. I know that's probably early, but I'm attending a charity golf tournament at Pebble Beach on Sunday, so I have to fly out around seven."

"That's actually perfect for Castle Valley. Except for the bars, the sidewalks roll up by eight o'clock."

"Is Saturday a work day for you?"

"Most of the time."

"Well, I hope you'll make time to drop by for at least

a few minutes."

For a nanosecond, I thought I saw some emotion behind his eyes other than the pure professionalism he had exhibited. He wasn't coming on to me, was he? I touched the bandage on my chin. "That will be day five. Maybe you can take these stitches out."

"I can assess your situation and if it's time, I will."

"In that case, I'll definitely be here. Casual or dressy?"

Mischief danced in his eyes. "I was thinking about wearing my tux. Too pretentious for Castle Valley?"

"Perhaps a little, but hey, this is a pretty big deal for us and we don't have that many opportunities to get dressed up. In addition," I added with a hopeful grin, "I wouldn't be surprised if your ad doesn't generate interest from other surrounding communities like Prescott, Scottsdale and Phoenix."

"All right then." Looking pleased, he swiveled around and then turned back. "Oh, and I promise a more elegant menu than this evening's fare."

"I don't know," I responded lightheartedly, shouldering my purse. "It's going to be hard to top that pizza." We both laughed, waved goodnight and I heard the door close behind me as I reached the Jeep. The steady wind had blown the storm clouds away revealing a bright crescent moon and a dazzling sea of starlight. Sitting behind the wheel, I waited a few minutes for the engine to warm up, then turned on the heat.

When I picked up my phone, I realized I had never returned Tally's text. I dialed his number and he answered after the first ring. "Hey, are you home? You didn't answer my text. Is everything okay?"

"I'm on my way there now. I did get your text and everything's...pretty much okay...now."

A heavy silence and then, in a voice tinged with suspicion, he quietly asked, "Pretty much okay? What does that mean?"

Oh boy. Here we go. As much as I loved this rugged, intelligent, industrious man, it seemed that we always arrived at the same fiery impasse when it came to me pursuing my passion of becoming the preeminent investigative reporter in the country. I knew he had my best interests at heart, but it irked me nonetheless that he made no secret of the fact that he profoundly disapproved of my propensity for jumping headlong into dicey assignments. I reluctantly had to admit that some of the outcomes had ended up being far more dangerous than I bargained for, but of course, I had no way of *knowing* that I should have been earning hazardous duty pay when I undertook them. Nonetheless, over the past year, we'd had numerous verbal altercations where each of us had stubbornly stood our ground. Bracing for his critical response, I gave him a quick overview of the day's events, and even though I tried to gloss over my injury, the depths of his censure came through loud and clear.

"Are you kidding? First day out of the gate and you're injured already? God damn it, Kendall, you're lucky it wasn't worse!" he griped, not bothering to conceal his displeasure. "Would it be too much to ask to have my bride present and in one piece on our wedding day?"

"Tally..."

"I hate the idea of you being out alone in the middle of nowhere with someone like Nelson Trotter. What were you thinking?"

I bristled. I was not in the mood to have to defend my actions, but also didn't feel like getting lured into yet another dead-end argument. "Believe me," I said in a placating tone, "I did not plan on that happening."

"You never do."

Instant irritation heated my cheeks, but instead of taking the bait as I usually did and firing back with a snippy retort, I responded calmly. "Just so you know, I'm going to be safely in the office all day tomorrow. Here is my itinerary for Thursday and Friday. My plan is to visit the Roadrunner Truck Stop stop near Kingman, then drive to Bagdad to interview Holly Mason's husband and if there is time, I'll pop over to the Family Dollar store in Aguila. Otherwise, I'll do that on Friday and then I'm hoping to interview Wanda Keating at the Double G Ranch later in the afternoon. Yes, I'll have my gun, my knife and my flashlight with me. Does that make you feel better?"

"Somewhat."

"Good."

More dead air, then, "Um…listen, I'm sorry about your accident. You gonna be okay?"

"I will. Dr. Craig did a great job on the stitches and Tally…?"

"Yep?"

"You're more than welcome to come along if it makes you feel better. In fact," I tacked on, "I'd love having your company."

Silence. "You know I can't this week."

"Tally?"

"Yep?"

"Do you recall me showing you how to track my

cell phone?"

"I…I'm not sure I remember how to do it," he grumbled lamely.

I rolled my eyes. Even though Tally was only six years older than me, he was admittedly old-school and everyone teased him about his resistance to embrace modern technology. I'm pretty sure he had been one of the last people on earth to finally own a cell phone, which I had persuaded him to do, and he still vehemently refused to join any social media sites, citing ongoing privacy violations. He contended that it was a waste of time and energy. At my insistence, he'd agreed to learn how to text and finally admitted it was easy and convenient. "Well, you can. I'll send you the link again. Just follow the prompts. Will that help put your mind at ease?"

"I suppose."

"Good. So, I'm heading home right now. I hope your day went well and I'll talk to you tomorrow if you have two minutes to spare." Ending on a high note, I said, "I miss you, I love you and I really do appreciate you worrying about me, but I'll be fine, okay?" I left out saying, "*Please, just let me do my job!*" At some point, after we were married and decided to start a family I knew my stimulating career would end, or at least be on hold for many years. It was daunting to think about, although I knew it would make him "happier than a clam" as Ginger would often say.

"Love you too. Night." While sounding slightly more conciliatory, there was still an edge to his voice.

I tapped the phone, lamenting softly, "I can't win," then slid the cell phone into my purse and turned towards the road in time to see a light-colored SUV illuminated in my headlights. It sped past only to immediately slow and turn into the clinic's private driveway. As the electric gate opened, motion sensor lights flashed on and I could have sworn I recognized the silhouette of Dr. Mallick sitting behind the wheel. I hit the brakes. What? Hadn't Dr. Craig said he was not expected to return until tomorrow? So, what was he doing here now? Was I reading too much into it or did it seem a strange coincidence that he would drive in just as I was driving out?

I clenched my jaw. Was he deliberately avoiding me? But...why, and how would he know I was here? Had Dr. Craig told him? But, why would he do that? I ran a hand over my forehead, suddenly feeling fatigued. The obstinate half of me wanted to march right back into the clinic and confront the irascible doctor while the other half, the fatigued half, wanted nothing more than to get home and relax in a hot bath.

Torn, I sat there wrestling with myself for another minute until common sense won out. What would it gain to antagonize Dr. Mallick further? Considering that it was actually my fault that we'd gotten off on the wrong foot, wouldn't it be better to wait and let Dr. Craig smooth the way for me? Yep. The interview would just have to wait until another day.

Satisfied with my decision, I headed towards home and fifteen minutes later I was sailing along Lost Canyon Road still chastising myself for trying to make something sinister out of what was obviously nothing.

CHAPTER 13

As usual, the Iron Skillet was jam-packed with diners when I arrived the following morning at seven in hopes of speaking with Lucinda before Ginger arrived. Listening to the babble of conversation and laughter overlaid by the clanking of silverware and dishes, I inhaled the mouthwatering aroma of frying bacon and freshly brewed coffee. I wove my way between the tables smiling and waving at people's friendly greetings and responding to their curious inquiries about my bandaged chin, before heading to the counter where Lucinda chatted amiably with customers while she topped off their coffee cups.

"Do you have a minute to talk?" I asked when she finally glanced in my direction.

"Hang on," she said, her brown eyes reflecting curiosity tinged with a quick flash of concern.

Hastily, she scribbled several orders on a pad, then swung around and handed the sheets through the window to her Aunt Polly who hollered, "Hey, Kendall! How you doin' today?"

"Fine! And you?"

A wink and a smile. "Always glad to be on the sunny side of the dirt," she cackled in her raspy cigarette-singed voice.

I laughed. "Amen to that."

Lucinda beckoned me with one finger and I followed her through the swinging door into the kitchen and then to a quiet corner near the rear exit. She whirled around, her expression anxious. "You got news about Holly?"

"Not yet."

Her shoulders drooped. "Oh. Well, then, what's up?"

I leveled her a critical look. "Why didn't you tell me your sister was under house arrest and had removed her GPS monitor?"

A trace of uncertainty crossed her face. "Does it matter?"

"Yeah, it might," I cut in more harshly than I'd planned. "Has it occurred to you that she may not be missing at all but simply decided she didn't want to face the consequences of her incriminating behavior?"

"No." Apprehension filled her eyes. "Why? What will happen to her?"

"Who knows? She could face a variety of charges and most likely she'll have to make restitution for breaking the monitor, which could cost her up to $2000."

She clapped a hand over her mouth and murmured, "Will she have to go back to jail?"

"Possibly." I stared at her intently. "Did you think I wouldn't find out?"

"No." She squirmed uncomfortably, looking at

everything in the kitchen but me. "I knew you would... eventually."

I glared at her until she met my eyes and mumbled contritely, "Okay. To be honest, I didn't want to tell you because I was afraid you wouldn't try to find her if you knew."

She appeared suitably chastened, so I said, "It's a moot point anyway. Here's the deal. I talked to Marshall yesterday. He said Duane called you about coming in to view surveillance video of Holly, which I've already seen. Why haven't you done that yet?"

Chewing her top lip, she lowered her eyes. "I guess I've been putting it off because, because...I'm afraid it might be...well, the last time I ever see her." Her dark eyes sparkled with tears as she broke eye contact with me.

A morbid thought, even though I suspected she could be right. "We don't know that, so let's try to stay positive, okay. Look, it's important for someone who knows her well to look at it. I need you to tell me if you detect anything out of the ordinary, anything noticeably different about her appearance or her actions that might yield a clue as to her whereabouts. So, can you get over to the Sheriff's Office today?"

She nodded sheepishly. "I'll go as soon as I can." Then she frowned and pointed at my chin. "What happened to you?"

"Oh, it's nothing. I took a little spill in that storm yesterday." I knew this latest inquiry was among many I'd be hearing all day. "Call me after you view the footage. And you'll need to watch it several times."

"Okay. You staying for breakfast?"

"Yeah. I'm meeting Ginger in a few minutes."

Totally out of character, I got a rare smile brimming with gratitude. "Thank you, Kendall. I'll be right there."

I nodded, still unaccustomed to receiving anything even close to civil treatment from her and then repeated what I'd told Tally about my plans for traveling on Thursday and possibly Friday. "And text me your brother-in-law's address in Bagdad and a phone number, please." She brandished a thumbs-up, so I pushed through the door and slid into our usual booth just seconds before Ginger arrived all bundled up in her coat, scarf and gloves.

"Wooeee! It's colder 'n a frosted frog out there this mornin'!" She wriggled out of her coat, plopped onto the red vinyl seat, unwound her scarf and pulled off her gloves. "This is definitely a day for some scaldin' hot chocolate," she announced, perusing the specials page on the menu. "What do ya think, sugar? Maybe a bowl of hot oatmeal with nuts and raisins, or…" she suggested, squinting at the possibilities, "a big 'ol stack of buttermilk pancakes an' a side o' bacon?"

"Everything always looks good to me," I replied, tickled that her enthusiasm for food equaled mine, although I didn't have to worry about gaining weight while she constantly complained about hers.

She finally dragged her eyes from the menu, looked straight at me and, of course, noticed the bandage. "What in the Sam Hill happened to your chin?" she gasped.

I opened my mouth to tell her at the same instant Lucinda arrived at the table. "Well, goooood morning, girls!" She turned our coffee cups upright and filled them to the brim. "Kendall, what can I get for you?" She set the pot on the table, whipped out her pad and beamed me a megawatt smile. "We've got fresh baked cranberry muffins, eggs Benedict is on special today, or I could bring you a large stack with bacon or ham. What'll it be?"

Out of the corner of my eye I noted Ginger's face register shock as her eyes darted back and forth between us. "I'll go for the pancakes and bacon."

"Perfect," she chirped, scribbling my order on the pad. "And," she added with a conspiratorial wink, "I'll make sure to slip in a few more slices of bacon for you. Blueberry or maple syrup?"

"Maple."

"Got it. And how about you, sweetie?"

I had to suppress a giggle watching Ginger's bewildered expression. "Uh…I'll take one o' them muffins, hot chocolate and the eggs Benedict."

"Comin' right up!" She flashed me another vivacious smile before she headed towards the kitchen, her substantial backside swinging like a pendulum in the tight pink uniform.

I turned back to see Ginger staring at me goggle-eyed. "Well, butter my butt an' call me a biscuit! Did I just see Lucy bein' nice to you?" She lowered her high-pitched inquiry to a loud whisper and locked eyes with me. "What is goin' on here?"

I grinned at her. "I kept trying to tell you on the phone yesterday, but I couldn't get a word in edgewise. Didn't you read the article I posted yesterday?"

Slight chagrin. "Um, I ain't had time yet."

It took me less than five minutes to fill her in on what I'd learned about Holly's inexplicable disappearance. With interest, I watched a mosaic of emotions—cool perception, mild concern and what looked like a hint of reproach—parade across her expressive face. "Well, that's a dang shame," she intoned sagely, "an' we can only pray that she's okay, but this ain't a whoppin' surprise seein' how she never did follow the straight and narrow. She got herself hog-tied in all manner of troubles in school. She ran with a bad group of kids, got into drugs and other unlawful crazy stuff, you name it." She added several sugar packets and cream to her coffee, stirred thoughtfully then continued with, "God gifted that girl with the face of an angel, but the devil led her astray. She was loose as ashes in the wind."

Chuckling, I shook my head in amazement. "I swear you come up with some of the most original and descriptive phrases I've ever heard."

Her face flushed pink. "Thank you, darlin'," but then her expression turned serious. "So…why are ya doin' this for Lucy after she's been mean as a mama wasp to you since day one?"

"It's as much for Ronda and Tally as for her." I defensively hitched one shoulder. "You know, keep peace in the family and all that. Plus, I have to admit that it's a genuinely intriguing story."

A slight frown. "I thought you wuz workin' on somethin' special for Thena."

"I am. And on that subject, I was scoping out the old church on the Double G yesterday and I'd like to pick your brain about that family curse you started to tell me about, especially everything you've heard about Glendine Higgins."

Ginger scrunched a puzzled face. "Why do you wanna know about her? That is ancient history. I wuz thinkin' you'd be more interested in all the shenanigans them Trotter twins got themselves into."

"That too. I actually talked to Wanda on the phone and I'm trying to arrange a meeting."

"I see. Well, ya can't look at her an' not believe there might jest be a little somethin' to that curse," she said with wide-eyed sincerity. "She had herself a fine-lookin' husband, two darlin' little boys and a good payin' job at the hospital before the ax fell on her."

"Yeah, I read her file over at Marshall's office."

"Half the town thinks she's guiltier 'n all git out and the other half don't. Whatever, her whole life went in the shitter." She leaned forward, her tone confidential. "I heard tell from Doreen down at the beauty shop that she never did git to live the life she wanted. First gittin' two-timed by her husband an' after they yanked her nursin' license and pretty much losin' one of her sons, she got lower 'n a gopher in a hole. Doreen said her hair wuz all fallin' out and turned gray, she got real bitter and let herself go to pot."

"That's a pretty sad story."

She leveled me a contemplative look. "What about her depraved brother? You laid eyes on him yet? I'll tell ya, that man was born sorry."

I couldn't help smiling at her never-ending inventory of entertaining colloquialisms. I went on to tell her about Nelson Trotter's baffling appearance at Youth Oasis, his brazen gesture towards me afterwards, and when I mentioned his peculiar visit to the old church, Ginger's lips puckered with concern. "Good Lord, sugar! Runnin' into the likes of him alone in the middle o' the boonies would make me dampen my drawers for sure. Ya did the right thing hidin' from that ol'crap weasel! He's rotten down to the core."

I laughed aloud. "Crap weasel? I love it!"

She took a sip of coffee and then mused aloud, " Why would that pervert be takin' flowers down into the crypt of that ol' closed-up place? It don't make a lick a sense."

I repeated Clara's story regarding Glendine's wish to have her ashes interred beneath the old church. "There were wilted flowers strewn around some of the gravestones at the cemetery, but he didn't leave the fresh ones there. He drove off with the bulk of them stuffed inside his pickup."

Ginger pondered that briefly. "That does seem mighty strange. I heard he does a passel of odd jobs to make ends meet. Maybe he's makin' an extra buck deliverin' flowers now?" She waved away her own hypothesis. "Anyway, let's git back to Clara's story. Yours don't match the one I heard about Glendine."

That prodded my interest. "Oh? What did you hear?"

"I'm purty sure I remember hearin' that Doreen's middle daughter who went to school with Nelda's girl overheard Glendine saying that she wanted her body donated to science."

I stared at her doubtfully and did a quick mental calculation. Her version was way beyond secondhand; it was more like fourth-hand. "So, there was no funeral service, celebration of life, nothing?"

Ginger sat in silence, her frown introspective for long seconds. "Honest to Pete, I cain't remember."

"Maybe I can get the straight skinny when I meet up with Wanda Keating." I added some sweetener to my coffee and stirred absently. "You know, the more I learn about Glendine, the more it appears that she played a pivotal role in the family history."

"So, you got the whole scoop on her already."

"I know some. I spent almost two hours with Clara at the library yesterday." I hesitated, gathering my thoughts. "I can't put my finger on it exactly, but in an odd way, the aftermath of Glendine's shattered legacy seems to be influencing the actions of her heirs and vicariously through Thena's association, it's affecting the future of the *Sun* and all of us as well."

The look of startled bewilderment on Ginger's face was priceless. "Whatever you jest said went flyin' over my head. Your momma would be proud."

Ginger was forever teasing me about using what she termed my "million-dollar words". My mother, who still taught college-level English, had always been a hard taskmaster when it came to my brothers and me using correct grammar and advancing our vocabulary. Grinning, I waved away her comment. "That's okay. Listen, I got quite a bit of background information on her, but there are still important pieces missing, so anything you can add to her story will be a real bonus for my article and help satisfy my own curiosity."

"Sure thing, sugar pie. Fire away. I'll tell you all I know, but first explain to me what happened to you." She twirled her forefinger beneath her chin.

I gave her a quick overview of my pratfall and my subsequent medical attention from Dr. Craig.

Her face brightened with admiration. "Well, smack my bottom! If you ain't the lucky one. He sounds like a dreamboat. And was I not right?" she announced, her self-important smile laced with mischief. "Was that not the most amazin' makeover you ever seen in your entire life? Some serious bucks went into that place."

"I agree. And, I was very impressed with Dr. Craig.

He's informative, professional and not bad-looking for an older guy."

Eyes twinkling, she leaned in whispering, "I won't tell Tally you said that."

"Thanks. Anyway, Tally told me a little bit about the night Glendine was attacked by her boyfriend, but I didn't get to hear Clara's version so I'm interested to hear whatever you can fill in."

She wrapped her hands around the cup and took another long gulp. "Well, you gotta keep in mind this all happened forty some years ago an' it's the second or third tellin', so the truth can git a tad fuzzy…" She paused when Lucinda set our plates in front of us and refilled my coffee.

"Anything else I can get you girls?" she inquired, her pleasant smile supplanting her usual dour expression.

I looked at my tower of pancakes and overflowing plate of bacon. "No, I guess not. Just the bill."

"It's on the house," she announced, her tone exultant. "Enjoy!"

Before I could respond, she sauntered away. Ginger eyed her retreating figure with suspicion and then fired a warning glance at me as she sliced into her eggs Benedict. "She loves you now, but I sure hope you find out somethin' about Holly soon or she's gonna turn on you like a cross-eyed snake."

"You're probably right. Anyway, you were saying."

"Yeah. Here goes." She drew in a deep breath. "From what I been told, after all the terrible things that happened to Glendine, she got her act together an' did a real good thing raisin' her dead sister's kids. Durin' the day she took care of those two like they wuz her own, and at night,

Nelda's daughter, Rachel, stayed with 'em while she was workin' over yonder at the Rattlesnake Saloon." A look of bemusement filled her eyes. "Why they both turned out so dang messed-up is a real mystery, but most folks think it had a lot to do with her hookin' up with that drunken trucker fella one night."

"How old were the kids when that happened?"

She took a big bite of her eggs and chewed thoughtfully. "Mmmm, I'm not sure, twelve, thirteen, maybe fourteen."

"What was the guy's name?"

Frowning, she shook her head reflectively. "I think it wuz Dillon somethin' or other. I never did catch his last name," she lamented with an apologetic shrug. "But, any hoot, I guess Clara told you that Glendine kinda flipped out after her sister and daddy died."

I nodded. "Apparently, she suffered a nervous breakdown. Tally said she was lonesome and not too selective about the caliber of men she got involved with."

"I'll say not," she concurred, nibbling on the muffin. "Accordin' to what Nona said she—"

"Wait! Your grandmother knew her?"

"Oh, yeah. From church. You gotta remember that a whole passel of folks from 'round here drove out there for Sunday services back then, an' of course, she'd run into her in town sometimes. Nona told me she seemed friendly enough but said she always got the impression Glendine acted preoccupied like she wuz thinkin' about somethin' else."

While Ginger ate and chattered away, I took my first bite of fluffy, buttermilk pancakes drenched in syrup followed by a slice of crisp bacon, and practically swooned.

Man, oh man. Sheer heaven!

"Did Clara tell you she was a real purty gal?"

"I saw her picture. She definitely was."

"That's what Nona said, but she also told me that Glendine wuz maybe not the sharpest tool in the shed," she offered dryly, sipping hot chocolate. "Supposedly, this Dillon character gave her a sob story which she fell for hook, line and sinker."

"Let's hear it."

"Scuttlebutt was he had himself a good-lookin' wife who earned herself a nice chunk of change when he was away on the road for two or three weeks by…shall we say, entertaining other guys, if you git my drift," she stated, arching her brows expressively.

"I do. And I'm guessing the shit hit the fan when he found out."

"Big time. Rumor is he wasn't no saint either."

"Meaning?"

"Word was he didn't turn down the affections offered by some of the ladies who hung out at the truck stops," she stated with a naughty grin before turning serious again. "Any hoot, when he found out about his wife's little money makin' operation, he walloped her within an inch of her life. Then he packed up an' took his kid on the road with him."

I stopped mid-chew. "Tally mentioned that. Boy or girl?"

"Boy."

"Great role models," I commented wryly. "That must have left some lasting psychological scars. What happened next?"

"She moved on to Phoenix where business was better

and he stayed out on the road for months, dragging that poor kid everywhere, until he decided to bring his ass back to town." She paused to finish her hot chocolate and eat the last few morsels of the muffin before setting the cup down with a satisfied sigh. "Dang, that was lip-smackin' good. And free to boot!"

I grinned agreement. "Want some of mine? It's delish, but I don't think I can finish eight pancakes and a pound of bacon."

She waved away my offer. "Naw. I'm good."

I glanced at my phone. Crap. In order to make it to the office by eight, I needed to leave in ten minutes and then I'd just barely have time to drop my coats at the dry cleaner's and run by the auto supply store to buy new windshield wipers, although, with no rain in the forecast today, that could probably wait until tomorrow. "Go ahead and finish the story. Remember, Tugg's not coming in today and I'm running out of time."

"Oh, flapdoodle! That's right! Well, let's see, where wuz I?"

"Dillon came back after his wife left town."

"Oh, yeah. So, that's supposedly when Glendine met him at the bar boo hooin' about his ex. She must've felt real sorry for him 'cause purty soon they hooked up an' before you know it he wuz spendin' the night at the ranch with her. After a couple o' months, he and his boy moved in. She ended up takin' care of all three kids while he wuz on the road." With a disdainful sniff, she added, "If you ask me, he got the best part of that arrangement. I guess it worked out okay at first, but then things started to go south."

"Let's get to the night in question."

"Keep in mind that I been told a couple o' different versions of what happened so some of it might be true an' some might jest be back-fence talk."

Eager to finally hear details of the story, I laid my notepad on the table. "Shoot."

With gusto, she launched into the tragic tale. According to Clara's cousin, Nelda, Dillon was a heavy drinker and soon became abusive to the Trotter kids. They hated him and the feeling was mutual. When the fighting escalated from verbal to physical abuse, things quickly deteriorated. Following a loud and violent altercation, Glendine warned Dillon before he left for a three-week road trip that if things didn't change, she intended to end the relationship. While he was gone, the rumor mill churned out a story that she had fallen into a depressed state of mind and found solace with one of the young ranch hands. "Now, there ain't ever been no proof that anything ever happened between them two, but the story is Dillon came home a couple of days early from his trip and caught the feller in the house with her."

I interrupted her. "Just in the house or in her bed?"

"Nobody knows for sure, or they ain't tellin', whatever, he wuz drunk as a skunk and all hell broke loose. He accused Glendine of doin' the same thing his wife had done an' proceeded to beat the snot out of her. The cowboy tried to stop him and the Trotter kids too. I guess it was a purty awful scene. Anyway, supposedly, they all joined forces an' threw his fanny out, but he came back later that night an' locked Glendine in her bedroom where he…and this is the really bad part, " she reported ominously with melodramatic flare. "That wicked jackass broke a beer bottle and proceeded to cut up that poor woman's face, yellin' like a banshee that he'd fix it so nobody would ever want to look at her again. Then, he took his kid and hightailed it out east and nobody's seen hide nor hair of him since."

My appetite evaporated, I set my fork down. "Yeah, that matches the version Tally told me." I sat back, shaking my head in dismay. "Wow. The whole thing sounds like a plot for a book or a movie."

She nodded solemnly. "It sure does—a real sad one."

I repeated the story Tally had told me about his Halloween night adventure with school friends to the old mansion and Ginger nodded morosely. "I heard tell she went to a bunch a doctors, even had a couple o' surgeries someplace in Europe, but then I'm guessin' they weren't all that successful 'cause she locked herself away in that big ol' house. Folks in town still call it the 'Shut-away' house."

"Tally told me that too." I pushed my plate aside. "I'm hoping when I finally meet up with Wanda that she'll at least give me permission to tour the place."

She eyed me expectantly. "I guess nobody told you about the fire."

I drew back. "What fire?"

"At the mansion."

My heart fell. "Oh no! I was looking forward to exploring it."

"The story about the candlelight is true," she confirmed. "Supposedly, Glendine ordered everybody to keep the curtains closed up tight during the day, at night no lights got turned on. Oh! And she insisted all the mirrors be taken away. Nelda said she never went out during the day and only wanted the soft light of candles so…I'm thinkin' it was maybe three years ago, she supposedly tried to end it all by settin' fire to the house."

"Are you serious?"

Wide-eyed, she stated emphatically, "I am! Half the place burned down and she ended up livin' the last years of her life in the part that wasn't. It's all deserted now with a big ol' fence around it to keep out vandals and other folks. Kinda like the old church."

Disappointment snaked through me. "Ronda told me they fenced off the back entrance to the ranch last year."

Ginger reached for her coat. "They probably don't want nobody gettin' hurt an' suin' their butts off."

I stood and shrugged into mine. "Thanks a bunch. That was very enlightening."

"Glad to help," she said, pulling on her gloves. "So, look real close. Do you notice any difference in my complexion?" Preening, she turned her face from side to side. "I used a smidgen of my two hundred dollar serum last night."

"Two-hundred-dollars!"

"Yes, ma'am, and it's an itty-bitty jar to boot." She caressed her cheek. "I sure hope this stuff is for real. It sure woulda been nice to have a bottle of their foundation too. It feels like liquid silk." She sighed wistfully. "I'd love to have them injections like Thena, but I cain't afford 'em."

We moved towards the door and as I pushed it open, I tossed her a sidelong glance. "You don't need them."

"Good thing," she muttered as we stepped outside into the wind. "The lady at Youth Oasis told us gals that just one costs almost two thousand bucks!"

"Whoa! That's definitely not in my budget either," I said, part of me shocked by the large dollar amount, but yet not totally surprised considering the generous amounts of money invested in research and development of these so-called miracle drugs. I grinned playfully at her as she slid into her car. "Just think, your little contribution to Youth Oasis helps pay for Dr. Craig's travel expenses from here to Beverly Hills in his private plane."

"I guess it does. See ya in a few!"

I dropped both jackets and a few other clothing items at the dry cleaner's in record time and was at my desk a few minutes after eight ready to tackle the day's workload. After explaining my injury to everyone, as expected, I caught up on emails, returned phone calls, held an editorial meeting with Jim and Walter, consulted with Rick and signed off on website upgrades. It was a usual crazy workday and it was after one o'clock before I had a chance to check my text messages. Good to her word, Lucinda had sent me Lynnis Mason's phone number and address in Bagdad, including her mother's name as well, so I picked up the desk phone and dialed.

Four rings later, a woman answered "Hullo?" amid the sound of a children screeching in the background.

"Hi, is this Roberta Shaffer?"

"Yeah."

"Is Lynnis Mason available?"

"Who is this?" came her wary response.

I explained who I was and why I was calling.

"Hang on a second." I heard her set the phone down and say in an irritable tone, "Grandma's trying to talk on the phone. Quiet down and I'll turn on cartoons, okay?" It seemed like an hour, but actually only four minutes passed before her weary sigh hissed in my ear. "Lynnis is not available right now. He's on night shift rotation this week and I'm trying to keep these girls quiet so he can sleep."

"I'm planning to come your way tomorrow. What would be the best time to meet with him?"

I heard nothing but the sound of the TV in the background for long seconds, before she said, "I don't know. Sometime later in the afternoon, I guess." Then she hastily added, "But I doubt he's going to want to talk to you."

Her unexpected declaration threw me a curve. "Why not?"

She lowered her voice. "Look, I think overall Lynnis is a decent guy, but my daughter's irresponsible, inexcusable behavior pushed him to the limits. These past few months have been hard on everyone. I don't agree with his latest decision because he's still married, but he's moving on with his life."

"Moving on how?"

Dead air and then, "He is seeing other women."

That sparked my suspicions about him big time. He was acting like a man who didn't expect his wife to return.

"And if I even so much as mention Holly's name," she continued in a dejected voice, "he flies into a rage, so I don't talk about her in front of him anymore. Don't get me wrong, I love her and I want her back…terribly, but he swears he's done with her forever, so I don't know what will happen if you do find her."

"It's important…"

"My whole life has been turned upside down over this awful situation, and I'm working my tail off trying to create a stable home life for these two little girls," she interjected, sounding utterly forlorn. "So…can't you just interview him over the phone?"

Fair question. I could, but in my experience, personal interviews always proved to be far more effective. My dad, a veteran of the newspaper business for over forty years, had taught me well, always emphasizing, *"Remember, the eyes are the windows of the soul."* And he was so right. There was far less of a chance for a person to evade tough questions, tell bald-faced lies or simply terminate the conversation. Because I had not answered her question, she continued to press her point. "It sounds like Lucy has told you pretty much everything. What else do you need to know?"

Best mollify her, or I had a feeling there would be no interview. "Well, for starters, I'm pursuing this story at your daughter's request and I promised her I'd do everything in my power to locate Holly."

"I…see."

She sounded only slightly more convinced, so I followed up with, "It's possible there may be some minute detail that may have been overlooked. Or perhaps a seemingly unimportant conversation your son-in-law may have had with Holly in the days leading up to her leaving last fall. Even her exact wording in the phone call the night before Thanksgiving might contain some clue and be of help finding her…" I paused when Ginger suddenly appeared in the doorway. Puzzled that she would interrupt me in the middle of a call, I murmured, "Ah…can you hold on a minute?" then placed my hand over the receiver and whispered loudly, "What?"

"You're gonna want to take this other call." The compelling message reflected in her wide-eyed stare made my pulse rate surge.

I issued her a quick a thumbs-up and said to Roberta, "I'm sorry. I have to take an urgent call. Expect me tomorrow between three and four o'clock." Hurriedly, I gave her my cell number, thanked her for her time and punched the extension button. "This is Kendall O'Dell."

"Hi. I…um…read your article online yesterday and felt I should contact you." There was an undertone of quiet urgency in the woman's voice.

"Which article?"

"The one about the young woman who vanished last November."

My stomach chilled with anticipation and a slight whisper of dread. "And who am I speaking with?"

"My name is Patty Cole. I live in Lake Havasu."

My pulse rate ramped up. "You have information about Holly Mason."

No answer and then, "Possibly."

"Okay, I'm listening."

"Three weeks ago my stepdaughter also went missing from a truck stop."

CHAPTER 14

It happened far sooner than I'd imagined. While the phone call didn't directly concern Holly, it solidified my growing suspicion that hers was not an isolated incident. I kept the woman on the line for half an hour and learned that her twenty-two-year-old stepdaughter, Lindsay Cole, who had been staying with friends and working in California for the past year, had texted her from Tom's Truck Center near Vicksburg. Her message indicated that she had snagged a ride with a trucker and expected to be home in mere hours. That was the last communication she had received from her. The details sounded so eerily similar to those of Lucinda's sister and the missing sixteen-year-old Krystal Lampton, it made my scalp prickle. "What was she doing at that particular truck stop in the first place?" I asked, jotting down her information. "How did she get there?"

"She stopped for dinner. She had phoned my husband a few days earlier to say she intended to catch a ride with an acquaintance who was driving to Tucson."

"The exact time of the text?"

"Just a second, I'll check." Silence for a minute and then, "6:10 pm. When she didn't arrive by eight, we tried calling and texting, but she didn't respond."

"What do you know about the person she was traveling with from California?"

Patty Cole cleared her throat gently. "She told her father she'd be riding with a young man she'd met at a sports bar several weeks earlier. She'd said he seemed nice enough, he had family in Tucson and had accepted her offer to pay for gas."

"Did she mention his name?"

"Apparently she did, but my husband couldn't remember it and we didn't find out for another week."

I scribbled as fast as I could while she explained that the man, identified as Daniel Hertzberg, had contacted them after he had seen Lindsay's picture posted by them on several social media sites. He denied knowing her whereabouts, explained that she had met a trucker in the parking lot while having a cigarette and decided to accept the man's offer to drive her to Lake Havasu. Daniel hadn't thought too much about it and admitted to being relieved, since the detour would have been out of his way and added another three hours to his trip. Patty had notified law enforcement, and sheriff's deputies from La Paz County had grilled him for hours only to come away with no evidence that he'd had anything to do with Lindsay's disappearance.

"I assume there is surveillance video from the truck stop."

"Yes, but it doesn't show us much. She was too far away from the cameras and we couldn't clearly see who she was talking to. We did see her go back inside and talk to Daniel Hertzberg, where she presumably told him that she was hitching a ride with this… stranger. She walked out the door and no one has seen her since."

"Was that unusual behavior for her?"

A little groan of frustration reached my ears. "Not completely. She's always been a free spirit, very trusting of people and… doesn't always use good judgment."

"Meaning…?"

"Poor decisions about men, drugs and other problems. She seemed to be getting her act together when she decided to attend college, but then she and her father had a terrible fight when she dropped out unexpectedly and announced she was moving to Los Angeles. They didn't speak for six months."

"What was she doing in California?"

A protracted sigh. "Following her dream of becoming a famous actress, like a lot of foolish young people."

"I gather her dream didn't work out."

"She got a few minor roles in a couple of low budget films and did some modeling, but pretty much ended up waiting tables and walking people's dogs. After a year of living hand-to-mouth, she decided that maybe her father was right after all about her finishing college." She stayed quiet for several seconds before remarking softly, "So, tell me. Don't you think the circumstances parallel those of the young woman in your article?"

I hated to add to her distress, but the bleak sensation that fell over me confirmed that she could very well be right. The coincidences in the two cases were alarming, undeniable, and my suspicions about Nelson Trotter's possible involvement mushroomed exponentially. I'd have to double-check, but hadn't sixteen-year-old Krystal Lampton reported that he'd picked her up at a truck stop near Quartzite? That meant he had most likely been traveling from California to Arizona. I quickly looked up the mileage between Quartzite and Vicksburg. Bingo. Only thirty miles apart. "Unfortunately, yes," I answered succinctly. "When was her last social media post?"

"That same evening. She posted a photo of herself on Instagram."

"Text it to me, please."

"Well, it's not a good likeness of her. It's a selfie with her tongue stuck out."

Not a big fan of selfies, I could not fathom why people felt compelled to post distorted, unflattering pictures of themselves that would live forever on the Internet. "Send it along anyway with the most recent good likeness you have of her."

"Of course."

I urged her to contact me if she learned anything new and hung up. Fueled by the expectation of establishing a solid connection among the three missing women, I eagerly flipped to a new sheet and began to list the facts, as I knew them. While only anecdotal evidence at this point, I drew a circle on the page and wrote in my prime suspect's name: Nelson Trotter, truck driver, registered sex offender and all-around creepy guy. Then I drew lines outward forming bicycle spokes where I listed, Krystal Lampton, Holly Mason and Lindsay Cole. Several common denominators were at play. All three led troubled, freewheeling lifestyles, all three had recklessly accepted rides from strangers at truck stops and all three had vanished without a trace—the only exception being Krystal Lampton, who had eventually escaped to tell about her two weeks of captivity. The mystifying part, the part that did not fit into my developing hypothesis, was the fact that Nelson Trotter was in jail at the time the first girl vanished, which let him off the hook. So, then, what happened to her? Obviously, her testimony at Nelson Trotter's trial could have been damaging enough to lead to a conviction, so that meant someone else had to be responsible for her sudden disappearance. It seemed an outrageous leap to think that Wanda Keating might somehow be involved, but then, maybe not considering her own disturbing background and the secretive, reclusive nature of the Higgins clan. Would she have arranged for the girl to disappear to protect her brother? Of course, the other possibility was the Lampton girl had chosen to resume living life on the streets somewhere doing drugs and God knows what else.

My thoughts flitting about like hungry hummingbirds, I contemplated the countless possibilities as I drew another spoke on my fact wheel. Each missing woman had left a digital footprint by communicating via cell phone before disappearing. Of course, in Holly's case, she had borrowed one, but what happened to the phones belonging to Krystal and Lindsay? Everyone knew that technology made it possible to track someone virtually anywhere because even if GPS and location services were turned off, the phone could still be tracked via the last ping to the closest cell tower. That led me to believe that the abductor had immediately disabled each phone by removing the battery, completely destroying it, or perhaps had done something as simple as wrapping the phone in aluminum foil to block the satellite signal.

I rocked back in my chair, pondering the monumental task before me. Thanks to continuous advances in crime detection, law enforcement now possessed a quiver full of powerful tools at their disposal, making it harder than ever for would-be criminals to pull off a foolproof crime. However, also thanks to the Internet, savvy crooks were privy to the same technologies. The bad guys knew how to more cleverly cover their tracks, making the job harder for law enforcement and for people in my profession.

In the commission of whatever crime, criminals were keenly aware of leaving any DNA material at the crime scene now. They wore gloves, shaved their heads, wore hats, and covered their clothing and shoes to prevent forensics specialists from discovering even the tiniest trace of fibers, skin, blood or any other substances that could lead to their capture. They were careful to avoid surveillance cameras or, if that was unavoidable, they concealed their identity by wearing masks or other face coverings.

Another troubling trend that had emerged in the past several years involved the act of not only disposing of a murder victim's body in unique ways, but of completely dissolving it with acid or chemicals. Without a corpse, which usually contains a treasure trove of evidence, the killer's conviction becomes far more difficult for prosecutors.

With the number of obstacles looming ahead of me, it was obvious the assignment I had so hastily accepted was developing into something far more complex than just a missing person story. By the time two o'clock rolled around, a little headache tapped at my temples and my chin throbbed with each heartbeat. I had no one to blame but myself.

Best follow Dr. Craig's suggestion, I thought ruefully, rummaging in my desk drawer for the Advil bottle. I'd no sooner swallowed the two capsules than I heard my phone chime. I scrolled to the message from Patty Cole and stared in awe at the striking face of her platinum-blonde, blue-eyed stepdaughter. As I studied the young woman's perfect oval face, I felt overcome with the innate sense that something dark and frightening was happening, but I could not seem to grasp the significance.

I rested my head in my hands, struggling to formulate a logical theory. Okay. I knew this much. Missing persons websites displayed hundreds, if not thousands of photos of people—from all fifty states, all walks of life, all genders, all ages. Were these three women merely statistics or was there something exceptional about these particular cases?

Exasperated, I opened the photo app on my computer and lined up the pictures side-by side. Each had a hauntingly beautiful face—not average, not simply pretty, but striking. I looked up and stared vacantly, waiting for some hint of enlightenment to wash over me. What was I not getting? Come on! Think. Think!

I stood and paced impatiently around the room, trying to arrange the puzzle pieces into a coherent picture. But, after fifteen minutes of sorting though my notes and digesting every detail, my mind was still a muddled mess. "Damn it," I grumbled in frustration, "what am I missing?" I collapsed into my chair and stared vacantly at the ceiling fan slowly rotating until all at once, a lightning bolt of comprehension illuminated my tangled thoughts, funneling them into an astounding revelation. "Holy shit!" I gasped, sitting upright.

Who was in a more perfect position to operate a sex-trafficking ring than Nelson Trotter? That would explain where the money came from to hire the super-expensive attorney and buy the church and surrounding acreage. And even though Ronda claimed that, due to his criminal record, he was no longer being hired by reputable trucking companies, that didn't prevent him from freelancing and hanging out at truck stops on his own scoping out victims. Could there be a better place to pick up these vulnerable young women and transport them who knows where?

Gripped by a blend of excitement and dread, I let my imagination take flight. Could it be that each of them had been carefully targeted because their outstanding beauty would fetch a higher price? A bone-chilling thought, but sadly, because of Arizona's porous border, it would not be a big stretch of the imagination for this idea to be a real possibility.

The ruthless, depraved Mexican cartels that ran these diabolical, insidious, modern day slave-trading operations, possessed no scruples nor did they think twice about brutally murdering anyone who got in their way. If I was right, jumping into the middle of this could be far dicier than any of my previous assignments. Did I really want to pursue something this perilous? If I did choose to continue, no way could I share my ideas with Tally, especially after his forceful reaction yesterday to a simple cut on my chin. He'd blow his stack and probably call off the wedding. But, I cautioned myself, what if none of what I'd theorized was true and I'd just "what if'd" myself into a fabricated tizzy? I had not one ounce of proof to present to anyone.

On impulse, I called Marshall and laid out my hypothesis. At first, he seemed dubious, but as I pressed further and possibly, to mollify me, he offered to contact an ICE agent he knew at the field office in Phoenix and find out if they had any active cases in this area. Before hanging up, he cautioned me to be careful and notify him immediately if I learned anything of substance during my next few days of investigating Holly's disappearance. I agreed and hung up, feeling more confident about continuing to search for answers.

With difficulty, I refocused my attention to the remainder of mundane work projects I needed to complete before leaving today. I fielded several phone calls, one from Carlos at the dry cleaner's informing me that they'd found a small, white box in the pocket of my jacket and that they would set it aside for me. Good grief, I'd totally spaced and forgotten about it.

My curiosity rekindled, I located the photos of the small bottles on my phone and typed the word Phenoxyethanol into my search engine. I read with interest that Phenoxyethanol (ethylene glycol monophenyl-ether) is a bactericide that functions as a disinfectant, antiseptic or antibiotic that is primarily used as a preservative in cosmetic products and as a stabilizer and fragrance additive in perfumes and soaps. Other examples listed were moisturizers, eye shadow, foundation, sunscreen, shampoo, lip-gloss, lotion, nail polish, shaving cream, deodorant, hair spray and a host of other products.

How bizarre was this? I re-read the paragraph several times and grew increasingly puzzled. What would bottles containing, oil of lavender, oil of chamomile and most especially Phenoxyethanol be doing half-buried in the mud near the old church? Again, I questioned my memory. Yes, it had been hard to see clearly during the violent downpour yesterday but I was almost positive the box had fallen out of Nelson Trotter's truck. Why would one or any of these items be in his possession? But, if I was mistaken and he hadn't dropped them, how and why would they be there? How long had they been there? It made absolutely no sense.

Before I knew it, late afternoon sunlight was streaming through the windows and I could hear the mourning doves in the big mesquite tree cooing as they prepared to roost for the night. I was in the middle of proofing Walter's piece on the groundbreaking ceremony for a new senior center when the intercom buzzed. "Hey, sugar," Ginger called out with a mischievous lilt, "your new best girlfriend is on the line."

Pulling a blank, I asked, "Who?"

"Why, Lucy o' course."

"Very funny," I responded with a forced laugh, picking up the phone again, half of me curious, the other half rebelling that I had to talk to her at all for any reason. "What's up?"

Without pretense, she launched into me. "I hope you're happy now. I did like you asked and watched the video a couple of times over at the Sheriff's Office." Lucinda's tone sounded charged with repressed outrage, but also thick and nasally as if she'd been weeping.

"And?"

"It made me cry my freakin' ass off, that's what!" Erratic breathing. "Marshall said he's going to release it to the public now and it's going to kill Ma when she sees it," she shrieked in my ear. "I wish to hell I hadn't seen it."

It didn't take much to ignite my short temper and Lucinda had mastered that tactic. I had to refrain from snapping, *Well, then go bust your buns and find her yourself,* and dig down deep to find a few grains of sympathy before saying, "I'm sorry. I figured it wouldn't be easy, but it's necessary. You know her, I don't. What's your takeaway? Did you notice anything unusual about her behavior, anything different about her appearance?"

"I don't know," she griped. "Maybe she seemed a little thinner, but generally okay. At the start, she looked like she was in hog heaven picking out all those toys 'n shit for my nieces, but then it just tore me up inside to see her turn so sad, and having to borrow money from some shit-heel to pay for everything. It was totally depressing and I can't get her out of my mind." I could hear her sniffling. "What if I'm right? What if that was the last time I ever see her?" Without waiting for my response, she tacked on, "I have a really bad feeling about what might have happened."

I said nothing for a moment. Now that I knew more about the other two missing women, her worst fears were probably justified. "Anything else?"

She blew her nose noisily in my ear. "Do you remember the last time she came back inside with her clothes all wet?"

"Yes."

"I thought she seemed…well, kind of frantic and maybe a little bit pissed off."

"Yeah. I picked up on that too." I cautioned her not to jump to conclusions too soon, that I had more leads to explore in the next few days and that I'd let her know if I came across anything noteworthy.

She thanked me and I was prepared to end the conversation when she added, "Um…there might be one more thing."

"What?"

"I...don't know if this is important, but did you notice that she bought a pack of cigarettes?"

"I did."

"She doesn't smoke." She cleared her throat nervously. "Did you see the brand?"

The odd undertone in her voice put me on alert. "I'm afraid I didn't. And your point is?"

"They were Kingstons," she croaked so low I could barely hear her.

I sat there with my pen poised above my notebook, trying to absorb her inference. "And that's significant why?"

"God, I hate to even put it out there, but...that's the same brand my brother-in-law smokes."

Her dramatic, yet cautionary admission sent my blood pressure soaring. I knew it. This duplicitous woman was withholding information. At that moment, I wanted nothing more than to back out of my promise to her and Ronda and forget the whole thing. Breathe deeply, I cautioned myself. Breathe deeply. Finally, I remarked in a controlled voice, "Lucinda, are you suggesting that your brother-in-law had something to do with Holly's disappearance?"

"No, I'm not saying that," came her swift, petulant response. "I'm sure lots of people smoke that brand."

"Then what *are* you saying?" When she remained silent, I inquired firmly, "Have you left out any other key details that I should know about?"

"Maybe a few," she admitted, sounding defensive.

Seriously? Perhaps it was the fact that I already had a lot of time and effort invested in this assignment, or maybe it was simply my unquenchable curiosity, but I was not ready to throw in the towel yet. "I'd like to hear them."

"Lynnis and her were always fighting."

"About what?"

My hand was tired from taking notes by the time Lucinda finished telling me the disturbing tale of the young couple's contentious relationship—total opposites as she described them. Holly's unexpected pregnancy set off a chain of unfortunate events beginning with a hastily arranged marriage, rejected at first by Holly, but steadfastly urged by Lynnis Mason and what Lucinda described as his ultra-traditional parents who insisted it was the right thing to legally tie the knot for the sake of the baby. Holly's pattern of disappearing for days and weeks at a time began after the birth of their daughter two months later, supposedly spawned by a severe case of postpartum depression, which she used as an excuse to justify her increasing drug use.

"She was a hot mess, crying all the time," Lucinda explained morosely. "She hated that she'd gained weight, hated the baby crying all the time, hated being a housewife, so one night she took off and left Lilly alone while Lynnis was at work. It was only a few hours, but the shit hit the fan when he found out about it later from one of his friends who saw her out partying while he was busting his ass on a twelve-hour shift at the mine. They ended up having a knock-down, drag-out fight and Lynnis came close to kicking her out, but she pleaded with him to let her stay and she promised she'd try harder to be a good mother."

"And was she?"

"For a while. She was always bugging Mom to drive over from Flagstaff so she could have more 'me' time and go out with her girlfriends," she informed me, sounding glum and a tad irritated. "She said she felt trapped. Anyway, things seemed okay, but the next thing you know she's pregnant again and now she's got two babies to take care of."

"How'd that work out?"

"Not good. She had a major meltdown one afternoon and took off again, this time for a couple of days. When she came home, Lynnis was fit to be tied, but there wasn't much he could do to control her. Mom and me and Aunt Polly, we all read her the riot act and she straightened up until last summer when she got mixed up with that scary dude in Tucson. Next thing you know she's busted and then under house arrest."

"So, let me get this straight. The last time she ran off was early November, right?"

"Yeah."

I paused to digest everything she'd told me before venturing, "She had to know she'd be in deep shit if she removed the GPS monitor. What happened to precipitate that? Another fight? And I want the truth. All of it."

An extra-long hesitation followed by a lot of throat clearing. "I…uh…look, we…I didn't tell you because we don't want everybody to know about this." Another pause and deep sigh of frustration. "If I tell you, it has to be…what do you call it, off the record? You can't put this in the paper."

I chewed on that for a few seconds, before making my decision. "Agreed. Off the record."

"I don't know why for sure…but last summer Lynnis sent away for one of those DNA test kits…" Based on what I already knew about Holly's wild behavior, I felt only mild surprise when she concluded with, "The results showed that Lilly's little sister, Emily, isn't his kid."

"And when he confronted her with this information?"

"He punched her lights out. She told my mom it was the worst fight ever and that he said some really shitty things to her."

"Shitty enough for her to pull that Houdini stunt with the GPS monitor."

"I guess."

"Anything else?" I figured I'd finally gotten to the crux of the story when only silence met my ears. "Lucinda, you still there?"

"Yeah."

"So, let's get back to your original assertion that Lynnis might be involved in her disappearance. What makes you think that?"

Her voice barely above a whisper, she admitted, "He told my mom that if he ever laid eyes on her again, he'd kill her."

CHAPTER 15

It was five-thirty by the time I left the office, totally fried and far from being finished with my "to do" list, which seemed to expand by the minute. Even so, I decided to run by the cleaner's and retrieve the white box. I didn't know if it held any significance or not, but considering the perplexing contents and weird location, combined with the possible connection to Nelson Trotter, I felt better having it back in my possession.

Afterwards, just to be safe, I stopped by the auto parts store and bought new windshield wipers, which the young salesperson was kind enough to install for me. The ever-changing weather forecast now predicted a forty percent chance of rain during the next few days, which meant it might actually rain or we might not get a drop. Either way, I didn't want to take a chance getting caught on the road again with non-working wipers.

Then I gassed up the Jeep and headed for the grocery store. I was close to completing my shopping when I received a text from Tally. HAVING DINNER @ TATE'S BBQ WITH 2 COUPLES FROM HIGH WIND RANCH IN WYOMING. WANT TO JOIN US?

Did I? Wavering, I stood in the frozen food section considering his last-minute invitation. As much as I wanted to see him, it was now totally inconvenient and most likely, he would be preoccupied with the buyers anyway. A slight prickle of irritation swept over me. Why hadn't he let me know sooner? I could have altered my plans. I fired back a text. THANK U! WISH I COULD, BUT ON MY WAY HOME W/ GROCERIES. RAIN CHK? ☺

His response was swift. FINE. I caught the subliminal sarcasm. With a despondent sigh, I slipped the phone into my purse and pushed the cart forward while fighting off a twinge of regret. As much as I loved this fiercely independent, yet sometimes dogmatic man, at some point in our relationship he had to accept the fact that I sometimes had my own agenda. I knew it sounded selfish, but right now all I wanted was to go home, eat and get comfortable. Oh well, I counseled myself; the days would fly by, his buyers would leave and we'd be together again soon. For the next couple of nights, it would be just the cats and me. That thought led me to the pet food section where I stocked up on their favorite food, treats and a new container of catnip, which they both loved.

It was closing in on seven-thirty as I zoomed along Lost Canyon Road, feeling physically and mentally drained. Lucinda's shocking suggestion that her brother-in-law might have had something to do with her sister's disappearance had thrown a giant monkey wrench into my carefully constructed theory singling out Nelson Trotter as my main culprit. Now, I wasn't sure what to think. Hadn't Marshall said that he had not ruled out Lynnis Mason as a person of interest? It appeared from what Lucinda had conveyed that he certainly had the motive, means and opportunity to have arranged for her 'vanishing'. Had he lied to his family and authorities on the details of his phone conversation with her? Had she really hitched a ride with a trucker that night or had Lynnis been the one who had picked her up? However, if that were true, why would he detour to Aguila? Alternatively, if she had hitched a ride with someone else, had Lynnis been lying in wait for her when she arrived home? Then what? Had he refused to allow her inside to see her children? Had they fought again, forcing Holly to run away, or had something more sinister occurred?

The multitude of unconnected thoughts flitting about in my head like fireflies made it difficult for me to focus, so I gave up trying to make sense of it. I turned up the radio, blasted upbeat music and sang at the top of my lungs to drown out the mental bedlam until I pulled into the driveway.

Shivering slightly in the biting wind, I gathered the grocery bags from the Jeep and made my way in semi-darkness along the gravel path towards my front door, thankful that I'd forgotten to turn off the porch light this morning. As always, I marveled at the serene stillness of the desert disturbed only by owls faintly hooting somewhere high in one of the four stately saguaros standing guard like shadowy sentinels over the small ranch house. I glanced above the roofline and drew in a sharp breath. The awesome sight of the Milky Way forging a glittery swath across the ebony sky infused me with fierce joy, cementing the innate knowledge that I would never tire of the solitude and beauty of this magnificent place I now called home. I must have stood there in the cold night wind at least another five minutes watching shooting stars streak across the sky until my empty stomach reminded me that I'd not yet had dinner.

Once inside the house, I snapped on lights and answered the complaining meows from both Marmalade and Fiona. "I'm sorry, girls," I sighed, depositing the bags on the kitchen counter. "I'm starving too, but you'll have to wait a minute." However, cats being cats, they didn't care one bit about me needing to start laundry or unload groceries. They just wanted to be fed and insisted on staying underfoot, curling around my ankles until I gave up and opened a can of tuna, which I helped them eat while my microwave dinner heated.

An hour later, I shut off the kitchen light, thinking how nice it would be to head directly to bed, but decided I'd better confirm tomorrow's interview with the waitress at the Roadrunner Truck Stop. In addition, I needed to connect again with Wanda Keating in hopes of arranging a visit with her sometime on Friday if Tugg didn't need me in the office all day. The call to Kelly Simms went unanswered, but I left her a message stating my estimated arrival time and to look for a redhead wearing a green turtleneck sweater. Then I dialed Wanda's number. She answered after the third ring. "Yeah? Who's this?"

"Kendall O'Dell."

"Who?"

"Kendall O'Dell? We talked yesterday." Silence. "About photographing your church," I pressed. "I'm the reporter."

"Oh, yeah, yeah. You get all the pictures you wanted?"

"I did, but if there's some way you could show me the inside, I'd still love to see it," I coaxed brightly, hoping perhaps she might have changed her mind.

"Like I told you yesterday, that ain't happening until it's fixed up and safe to go in."

My throat tightened with irritation. It was on the tip of my tongue to remark sarcastically, *Really? It seemed safe enough for your creepy brother* but instead I conceded, "I plan to be in your area again on Friday. If possible, I'd like to stop by and get some additional information on Our Lady of the Desert for my article, a little background information on your ranch, and I also have a few other subjects I'd like to chat with you about." She didn't need to know how much I already knew about the church's history and that of her family.

"If you wanna talk, you'll have to come here to the house 'cause I'm babysitting my grandson all day," she informed me gruffly. "And it will have to be later in the afternoon, maybe around four after his nap."

"That's perfect." If everything went well, I'd have plenty of time for the interview and hopefully get permission to at least photograph the old mansion.

"I'll leave the main gate open. Keep driving 'til you come to a fork in the road. There's a stock tank on the right where you'll turn left and my house is about a mile from there."

I thanked her, ended the call, started a load of laundry and then allowed myself a few moments to enjoy the hilarious antics of my cats getting high on catnip. While the clothes were drying, I jumped online to confirm the route and mileage to the truck stop and then, from there to Bagdad. If everything went as planned, I should be back home by dinnertime tomorrow. On impulse, I clicked on Google

Earth to examine the layout of the Double G Ranch again before my visit.

My first virtual visit had been cursory, but now I took the time to go over the area more carefully, this time noticing how extensive the ranch property really was with its interconnecting web of roads, plus the surprising number of fixed structures along with several mobile homes. I zoomed in on the extreme eastern boundary, for the first time noticing the shadowy openings in the hillsides. Nearby, skeletal remnants of what appeared to be pieces of old mining equipment were scattered about, leading me to assume that I was looking at the old Gold Queen mine. From there, probably not more than a mile south, I zoomed in on the old mansion. It was hard to make out much detail other than yawning rows of arched windows since the bulk of it abutted the side of the rocky foothills. Now that I knew the backstory of the Shut-away house, I was anxious to explore it and held out high hopes that Wanda would permit me to photograph the exterior and perhaps to tour the interior as well.

By the time I finished folding laundry, it was a struggle to keep my eyes open. After a quick shower, I examined the stitches on my chin. They were starting to itch, which was a good sign. I applied antibiotic cream, a wide Band-Aid and collapsed into bed. Within minutes, the cats were snuggled close, purring up a storm. Somewhere in the distance, a pack of coyotes yipped and howled at the night sky. Burrowing under the blankets, I sighed with contentment thinking that I had all the ingredients needed for a restful night's sleep, but that proved elusive as the events of the past two days replayed endlessly in my mind.

Lucinda's startling revelation that Lynnis Mason

was not the father of Holly's youngest daughter was a real bombshell and awarded him equal footing with Nelson Trotter on my list of prime suspects. I wondered why Holly's mother, Roberta, had left out that all-important detail during our phone conversation, but perhaps she'd planned to tell me when I'd cut her off to take the call from Patty Cole. That thought sent my mind spinning off into all directions again, but as always returning to the suspicious coincidences surrounding the disappearance of the three young women. And that inevitably led me back to Nelson Trotter. The most vexing aspects centered on his odd interaction with Dr. Mallick at Youth Oasis, his intimidating behavior directed at me, the flower-filled truck and his perplexing visit to the crypt. I tried approaching the riddle from every conceivable angle, but could make no sense of it. Two hours later, a bright half-moon sat poised above the western peaks and I finally forced myself to blank out all thoughts.

I had just slipped into that blissful twilight stage between consciousness and the soft precipice of sleep when one piece of the mystifying brainteaser suddenly presented itself. My eyes flew open as I whispered, "Oh, my God!" Of course. Why had this not occurred to me before? I could think of no other person in the town of Castle Valley who could have any possible use for the contents of the little white box—oil of lavender, oil of chamomile and Phonoxethanol—other than Dr. Raju Mallick. It had to have something to do with the ingredients in the beauty products created and sold by Youth Oasis. But, my elation at reaching that conclusion led me once again to confusion as I continued my midnight musings. If I had indeed witnessed him handing the little box through the truck window to Nelson Trotter yesterday, the big question was why? What possible purpose could Nelson Trotter have for fragrant oils and a cosmetic preservative? The whole scenario seemed insane and no logical answer presented itself.

I thumped the pillow and turned it over. One thing I did know for sure. Up to that point, I hadn't decided whether I would attend the open house at Youth Oasis on Saturday. Now I most definitely would. And, my mission would be to corner the disagreeable Dr. Mallick, quiz him about the uses for Phenoxyethanol and hopefully dig further into his background. That decision made, I finally drifted off into dreamless slumber until the annoying, repetitive buzz of the alarm clock woke me at six.

After a forty-five minute jog in the brisk morning air, I felt energized and ready to take on the day. I fed the cats, packed up the Jeep and headed for the office where I dove into the daily routine. The first email I checked was from Marshall. The surveillance footage of Holly would be provided to all media outlets on Friday. I felt a rush of gratitude that he, or most likely Julie, had included a link to the video so that the *Sun* could release it first. I did just that and linked it to my article.

By late morning, I'd completed most of my other work and decided to spend a few minutes scrolling through the digital archives, hoping to find some gem pertaining to the events surrounding Glendine Higgins, but there was only a short mention of her in the obituaries. That seemed odd. To me, the woman who had led a fascinating, if troubled life, should have garnered more than a few sterile statistics at the end. I had my work cut out for me if I wanted to research the past forty years to find out more about her. That would mean spending hours at the library pouring through old microfilm. Fat chance of that happening.

As part of my homework to prepare for the upcoming meeting with Wanda Keating, I looked up what it would take for her to have her nursing license reinstated. After I'd finished reading all of the requirements, which were lengthy, and added in the steep attorney's fees, it seemed as if an act of God might be more in order. According to the website, it could be done, but what were the odds that she could come up with between ten and fifteen thousand dollars to hire a good attorney? I looked up and drummed my fingers on the desk. Unless…unless she sold the old church. Then she'd have more than enough.

Good to his word, Tugg breezed in the office door just before noon. I had calculated a two-hour drive to the truck stop near Kingman, so I gathered my things while he hung up his coat and settled into the chair behind his desk. "Everything go okay at the dentist?"

"Yep! Like my new pearly whites?" he inquired with a mile-wide grin, pointing to his upper teeth.

"Yeah! They look super. How much did that set you back?"

Wincing, he announced, "Twenty-five hundred bucks."

"Yikes."

"Tell me about it." He squinted hard at me and drew back wearing a look of concerned puzzlement. "Hey, what's with the Band-Aid under your chin?"

It took a few minutes to explain what had happened and tell him where I was going. He cautioned me to be careful, and after receiving the same advice from Ginger, I climbed into the Jeep, eager to explore new territory and hopeful that my interviews would provide some tangible information.

I made great time, even though traffic was heavy on SR 93, the main artery between Phoenix and Las Vegas. My mind busy formulating questions, I cruised along beneath a sapphire sky populated with puffy thunderheads, and wound through cactus-studded valleys surrounded by rolling hills and distant mountain ranges. A thrill of pure delight surged through me as the road rose in elevation revealing new and picturesque scenery, most noticeably when stands of spike-leafed Joshua trees appeared and totally transformed the landscape. I'd read that these sometimes forty-foot-tall evergreens, a member of the yucca family, grew nowhere else in the world besides the Mojave Desert.

Enthralled by the mesmerizing scenery, I almost missed the turnoff. Hastily, I swung onto the exit and pulled into the Roadrunner Truck Stop, passing row after row of parked eighteen-wheelers while others sat idling or roared past me on both sides. Wow! This was a happening place. The parking area adjacent to the restaurant was choked with cars, many bearing out of state license plates, which was not surprising since it was the height of tourist or "snowbird" season in Arizona. After driving around for what seemed like an hour, I finally snagged a spot. Strong afternoon sunlight warmed my face as I walked towards the café, impressed by the range of amenities offered—showers, truck wash, gift shop, a Native American trading post, convenience store and scores of gas pumps.

Once inside the noisy café, I zigzagged my way through throngs of people waiting for tables and asked the frazzled hostess where I could find Kelly Simms. Wordlessly, she pointed to the dining area to my left. Again, I weaved my way through the crush of humanity and stood in the doorway for several minutes watching the wait staff scurry from table to table until a fortyish-looking blonde woman wearing dark-rimmed glasses focused her attention on me. Her expression conveying uncertainty, she tentatively waved. I waved back and she rushed up to me carrying several plates. "Are you Kendall O'Connor?" she asked, sounding out of breath.

"It's O'Dell. You're Kelly?"

"Yeah, hey listen, we're really short-handed today so I don't get a break 'til two-thirty and then I'll only have about fifteen minutes."

Fifteen minutes? Not much time. I tamped down my disappointment. "That'll work. Where can we talk?"

"There's a couple of picnic tables outside on the south side of the building. I can meet you there."

"Sounds good."

Her tone apologetic, she added with a sheepish smile, "Sorry about that. Hey, if you haven't had lunch yet, you ought to try a hamburger, fries and one of our famous chocolate milkshakes. I can have Josie bring 'em out to you in five minutes flat."

Never one to pass up food, I happily accepted, then pushed my way past the crowd and out the door, glad to escape the bedlam. Lucky for me, I found a vacant table under a soaring Aleppo pine filled with merrily chirping birds and snagged it. Good to her word, within ten minutes the back door to the café opened and a heavy-set Native American woman wearing a hairnet deposited my lunch in front of me. I thanked her and held out twenty dollars, which she eagerly pocketed with a cheerful smile. "Thanks, sweetie! You enjoy!" she called out before vanishing through the kitchen door.

And boy, did I. One bite of the succulent burger and crispy French fries confirmed why the café was so busy. Scrumptious! While happily munching fries, I listened to the dynamic sounds of the place—the constant growl of diesel engines and whoosh of airbrakes as scores of eighteen-wheelers entered and exited the parking area along with a steady stream of passenger vehicles. I was finishing the last bite of the burger when Kelly Simms came trotting around the corner and plopped onto the opposite bench. "Whew! It's crazy here today."

I grinned at her. "I can understand why. That burger was awesome!"

"Glad you liked it." She pulled an e-cigarette from her pocket and inhaled so deeply her cheeks caved in. "What can I help you with?" she inquired, exhaling a long stream of vapor. The breeze caught it and blew it over her shoulder. I gave her a quick summary and scrolled to Holly's picture on my phone. "Is this the girl?"

After studying it for a few seconds, she murmured, "Yeah, that looks like her." She pushed steel-rimmed glasses higher on her nose. "That's a real nice picture. She didn't look half that good when I saw her. What's her name again?"

"Holly Mason. Do you remember approximately what time you first saw her on Wednesday, November 25th?"

Her powder-blue eyes widened expressively. "When I started my shift at eleven she was already at a table. One of the other girls said she'd been here since early morning hanging around the gift shop, the trading post and outside bummin' cigarettes from some of the truckers."

"Was she carrying any belongings?"

"She had a backpack and get this," she said with an undertone of confidentiality. "One of the customers told me she about freaked out when she took her daughter to the ladies' room. She swore to God she saw Holly in there buck naked takin' a bath in the sink." Her eyes mirroring disbelief, she added, "I've seen and heard a lot of peculiar things over the years, but that one takes the cake."

I made notes, silently agreeing with her assessment and then asked, "How would you describe her overall demeanor?"

She pursed her lips and scowled. "If you ask me, I'd say she was on something."

Interesting that she'd reached the same conclusion as me. "What makes you say that?"

"I dunno. She was…all over the place, you know, kind of edgy, fidgety, flighty, talking people's ears off if they'd care to listen."

"Did you happen to overhear any of the conversations?" I asked, sipping the remainder of the luscious chocolate shake.

"Oh, yeah! She was tellin' everybody she'd been away on a trip and was going home to see her baby girls for Thanksgiving. I heard her asking a couple of truckers if she could hitch a ride, but they all turned her down because, you know, that's strictly forbidden by the major companies now."

"Really? Why?"

She tossed me a perceptive look. "Because nowadays, the driver would get canned. The reason I know that is because my husband, Roger, has been a long-haul trucker for over thirty years. Things are way different now from when he was working freelance with his old Peterbilt. Back then you could pick up a hitchhiker, but not now."

"Why's that?"

A nonchalant shrug. "A lot of new rules. Most companies prohibit it. Roger says practically every move drivers make can be tracked; you know everything is computerized—dispatch, fuel stops, speed, destinations. He says it's not nearly as much fun now. He misses the freedom and independence. Big Brother watching you and all that." With a sad, little smirk, she added, "The old-timers call these newbies 'steering wheel holders' 'cause that's really all they have to do."

I hadn't really planned to get a dissertation on the trucking business, but took notes anyway, not wanting to stop her train of thought. "Interesting," I finally remarked, pulling her back to the subject at hand. "Holly hitched a ride here with somebody, we know that much."

"We get lots of runaways hanging around here selling drugs and entertaining the truckers," she said with a disdainful sniff. "We call 'em lot lizards."

I raised a curious brow. "Lot lizards?"

"Yeah." The naughty glint in her eyes matched her smile. "You know…hookers."

"So, this activity takes place in their trucks?"

She nodded. "Most of 'em have sleepers nowadays."

"You mean the compartment behind the cab."

"Uh-huh. Makes it private and real convenient for both parties."

A twinge of discomfort stirred inside me. "So, if she was hidden in someone's sleeper, no one would know."

"That's right." A trace of sorrow swept across the

woman's angular features. "I got three kids and I felt real bad when the sheriff told me she never made it home. That's a damn shame. I mean, when she talked about those little girls, her face just lit up. She seemed real determined to see them." She leveled me a somber look. "So...it's been almost three months now. What do you suppose happened to her?"

"Nobody knows, but that's why I'm here. Anything you can tell me about her actions or activities that day could be helpful." I glanced at my notebook. "What did she do after she got turned down for a ride?"

"She started bugging Mel, my manager, to let her use the phone in his office."

"And did he?"

"Yeah, but, he didn't expect her to camp out at his desk all afternoon."

I leveled her a questioning look. "What was she doing?"

"Mel overheard her leaving messages for someone to come and get her and then she just sat there waiting by the phone."

"Did he say who it was?"

"He thought maybe her husband."

That was interesting and appeared to reinforce Marshall's sobering declaration that Lynnis Mason might be involved. I scribbled a few more notes. "Did anyone call her back?"

"I don't think so. Mel finally got pissed off and hauled her butt out of there. She started bawlin' her head off and caused such a ruckus, he threatened to call the cops if she didn't leave the building."

"Is that when she asked to borrow *your* cell phone?"

The tip of the e-cigarette glowed emerald green as she drew in more vapor. "That wasn't 'til a lot later."

"Do you remember what time?"

"My shift ended at six and when I stepped outside it was raining like hell. If I hadn't been messing with my umbrella, I might've not noticed her standing over in the corner by the ice machine. She looked like a drowned cat. When she saw me looking at her, she came running up to me, begging to use my phone. She sounded desperate and told me she had to get hold of her husband and that he might answer if he didn't recognize the phone number. I couldn't help but feel sorry for her, standing there shivering in the cold and here I am on my way to a nice warm house looking forward to being with my family on Thanksgiving, so I let her use it."

I perked up. "Were you able to catch any of her conversation?"

She inhaled more vapor and shook her head. "Bits and pieces. She moved away from me, the rain was coming down in sheets and of course, there's this constant traffic noise," she said, flicking a hand in the direction of two big rigs throttling down at the end of the parking area. "But even with all that, I could hear her screaming and cussing up a storm loud enough to make a sailor blush."

My suspicions about Lynnis Mason's possible involvement in her disappearance resurfaced with a vengeance. "What were the bits and pieces?"

"Oh, I dunno," she remarked, her eyes taking on a faraway look. "Stuff about her kids needing their mother and that she was coming home no matter what. She was damn near hysterical when she came back. It was pitiful." Sorrow clouding her face, she lamented, "I offered to let her spend the night at my house, but she told me she'd wait a few more hours and if he didn't show up, she'd hitch a ride with someone else. I gave her thirty bucks of my tip money, went on home and didn't think another thing about it 'til the sheriff came by a couple months back." In the same breath, she asked, "What time is it?"

When I told her, she shoved the vape pen into her pocket and stood up. "Sorry. I gotta get back to work now."

"Hey, thanks for meeting me." I stood, reached across the table to shake her hand and then gathered my things.

"No problem," she said with a faint smile before turning away to stride towards the café. "I hope you find her."

"Yes. Oh! One more thing…" I called out, sprinting to catch up with her. When I reached her side, I scrolled to the mug shot of Nelson Trotter. "Have you ever seen this guy before?"

She stared at the screen, her lips twisting with distaste. "Yeah. I have."

CHAPTER 16

A sense of foreboding accompanied me during the entire hour's drive to Bagdad as well as an odd feeling of isolation when I realized there was no cell service. Winding upward through pristine desert and mountainous terrain, my mind churned through the new and unsettling information shared by Kelly Simms. It turned out that Nelson Trotter's infamous reputation as a womanizer was well known to a majority of the other truckers who had crossed paths with him, including Kelly's husband. Up until his arrest, Nelson Trotter had worked for McKay Enterprises, a large, nationwide trucking company, but he was now freelancing.

Kelly also told me that she had experienced numerous uncomfortable interactions with him in the café and described him as obnoxious, lewd and a lousy tipper. "None of the other girls wanted to wait on him, and the way he'd stare at young girls who walked by his table bothered all of us, but that's not against the law, so there was nothing we could do about it."

She admitted that none of the wait staff was surprised by his arrest after hearing of Krystal Lampton's disturbing allegations and everyone hoped he'd be in jail for a long time to come. "Imagine our disappointment when he showed up six months later driving his own spankin' new purple rig with naked girls painted on the door. Barf!"

How interesting to hear yet another account of the supposedly financially-strapped Trotters seemingly awash in cash. She had then gone on to say that his disgusting behavior hadn't stopped the "lot lizards" from visiting his truck. "No question he had to buy sex," she'd groused disdainfully, "no self-respecting woman would go near that pervert, so do I think he's the one who offered Holly a ride and had something to do with her disappearance? It's certainly possible, but who knows?"

I was still mulling over her disturbing description of Holly's tearful phone conversation when the first structures in the small town of Bagdad materialized. As I coasted past modest homes, one-story buildings and several churches, my Google Maps alerted me to turn right, then left and the house would be on my left. I followed the directions uphill and within a minute I spotted a plain-looking white house with a small weed-infested yard populated with children's play equipment and toys. In fact, as I looked around the hilltop neighborhood, most of the structures looked pretty much the same, indicating typical look-alike company housing provided for mine employees.

When I stepped out of the Jeep, mild surprise swept over me. Wow! The temperature had plummeted and the wind had risen. The mass of ominous gray clouds rapidly obscuring the pale blue sky foretold a rainy trip home. Guess

I'd get to try out the new wipers.

Walking along the crumbling, grass-choked sidewalk, I passed by a white SUV marred with dents and scratches. A dusty black pickup with oversized tires that most likely belonged to Lynnis Mason sat next to it. To my left, a large, yellow lab ambled across the yard towards me; tail wagging as he barked a short greeting. "Hey, there, fella," I said, reaching over the fence to scratch his head before continuing towards the house.

Faded letters on the torn slip of paper taped to the scarred front door announced that the doorbell was broken. I knocked twice before the door cracked open to reveal a tall woman about my height who looked like a much older version of Lucinda. "Roberta Shaffer?"

"Yes."

"Kendall O'Dell. We spoke on the phone yesterday." I handed my card to her through the narrow opening. "Is your son-in-law available to talk?"

"Oh. I was hoping you'd change your mind about coming." Her drawn, pinched face and the stone-cold glint of resentment reflected in her dark eyes mirrored her words. She darted a baleful glance to her right and just stood there frozen, looking uncertain. Behind her, over the din of raucous crowd noise that sounded like a sporting event, an irritated male voice shouted, "Whatcha ya doin', Berta? Either shit or get off the pot!"

Oh boy. Bet she hadn't told Lynnis I was coming today.

She leaned into my face, whispering harshly, "Things are difficult enough around here so do me a favor and don't piss him off. Okay? The last thing I need is for him to fly off the handle and take it out on the girls and me. Got it?"

Slightly taken aback by her abrasive attitude, I murmured, "I'll do my best."

She swung the door open wide. "Lynnis, there's a lady here to see you." She tossed me a final sidelong glance before disappearing into a small kitchen. Based on her agitated demeanor, I wasn't sure what to expect when a slender, young man with unkempt brown hair, a wispy mustache and sunken blue eyes appeared in the doorway dressed sloppily in faded jeans and a loose flannel shirt. Clutching a beer bottle, he looked intently at me, his expression reflecting surprise with a hint of puzzlement. "Somethin' I can do for you, miss?"

I smiled and held out my card. "Kendall O'Dell. I'm a reporter with the *Castle Valley Sun.* If you have a minute, I'd like to ask you a few questions."

His careless glance skimmed over me as he took a long pull from the bottle and then eyed the card. "Castle Valley's kind of a long jump from here. Questions about what?"

I kept my expression bland. "Your wife, Holly."

His entire body stiffened. "What about her?"

"According to the information I have, you were the last person to hear from her before she went missing. Do you have any idea where she is?"

A look of guarded suspicion gathering in his eyes, he glared at me hard and unblinking for several seconds before responding with a spiteful, "Lucinda put you up to this, right?"

He didn't need to know that so I answered with a generic, "A lot of people are concerned about her whereabouts."

"Well, I'm not." His jaw muscles tightening, he growled, "I don't want to talk about that bitch, I don't want to think about that bitch, I don't want to hear nuthin' about that bitch, I don't give a rat's ass what happened to that bitch. Does that answer your questions, *Red*?"

Unperturbed by his insolent show of belligerence, I pulled out my notepad. Keeping my tone composed, I said coolly, "FYI, Mr. Mason, the sheriff is investigating your possible involvement in her disappearance and I thought you might like to tell your side of the story."

"*My* side of the story!" he exploded, his face contorting in anger. "I already told the sheriff everything I know and he doesn't have a smidgen of proof to say otherwise."

His brash statement belied the sheen of apprehension glazing his eyes and confirmed that I'd planted seeds of uncertainty. "I wouldn't be so sure. I've looked through your report and..." I clicked my tongue and shook my head doubtfully. "Do you know a good lawyer?"

Eyes bulging, he swallowed convulsively, insisting in a defensive tone, "Listen, if that effin' drug-addled slut went and got herself offed, it didn't have nuthin' to do with me. I gave her plenty of chances to do right by me and the girls but, no, she couldn't stay away from the meth and all the other shit she smoked, sniffed, injected or shoved down her throat."

"Did that situation improve during the time she was under house arrest?"

An exaggerated skyward eye roll. "Not that I could tell. All she had to do was call one of her lowlife girlfriends or maybe one of her chicken-shit, dealer boyfriends and have the stuff delivered here when I was at work. She could be real clever when she wanted something bad enough."

"Like removing her GPS monitor."

"Yeah. Like that."

"So, you have no concerns whatsoever about the fact that she hasn't been seen for almost three months?" I asked, locking eyes with him.

Smirking, he lifted one pale brow. "I'd be lyin' if I said I did."

"And you're saying that you had nothing to do with assisting her escape."

"Damn straight that's what I'm saying," he bellowed, thrusting his jaw forward. "I was working all night and I can prove it!" Chest heaving with emotion, he stepped to within a foot of me and slapped my notepad so hard I almost dropped it. "You want a story for your stupid paper? I'll give you a story!" He stepped back and started pacing from side to side, swigging beer before he whirled around to face me again. "Broken promises!" he fumed, wagging a finger at me. "Write that down! That's what Holly was all about. After all the broken promises, after all the hell she put me through, I gave her one last chance. And what does she do?" He threw his hands high. "I drag my ass home after a twelve-hour shift and find out that conniving, scheming, bitch…I swear I don't how she did it, but the ankle bracelet was on our bed and…she's nowhere." Fury smoldered in his eyes. "You know what else? Every penny…every god dammed penny I had saved is gone and then she goes and leaves the babies here alone all night. Two little babies! What kind of a person does that? What if the house had burned down?"

He took another mouthful of beer and angrily hurled the bottle into the yard before stabbing his finger in my direction again. "I'll tell you what, if they handed out awards for the worst wife and mother *ever*, she'd win."

I penned copious notes wondering whether his righteous indignation was genuine or if he deserved his own award for acting. "So, moving forward, tell me about her phone call to you on the night of November 25th."

He closed his eyes and took a few calming breaths. "I'm guessing you already read about it from the police report. Or, maybe my smart-assed sister-in-law told you."

Keeping my voice composed, I answered, "Something like that. But, I'd like to hear your version."

He fished a lighter and cigarettes from his shirt pocket, pounded one out and jammed it in his mouth. I noted the brand, Kingstons, just as Lucinda had told me. As he fought with erratic wind gusts while attempting to light his cigarette between cupped hands, I glanced at my cell phone, noting that a voicemail from Thena had arrived after restored cell service. It would have to wait.

"Okay," he exclaimed, exhaling a stream of smoke. "Here's the deal. She called me, I dunno, around six, boo-hooing about missing me and her precious baby girls. Then she lied her ass off about how much she loved all of us and how she couldn't wait to get home and celebrate Thanksgiving with everybody."

"And what was your response?"

A sarcastic chuckle. "I don't know what in the hell she expected me to say. Oh sure, I forgive you for all the crap you put us through." He shook his head slowly. "That woman can't open her mouth without lying, so I told her, 'Not this time, babe. I'll do whatever it takes to keep you from coming anywhere near Lilly or Emily ever again.'"

It must have dawned on him how incriminating his statement sounded, because, in a more tempered tone, he quickly followed up with, "Of course, I know that would be up to the courts after I divorce her ass. But, I've watched a lot of those TV shows about lawyers. When the judge sees her track record, I'm gonna get full custody and she'll have nuthin' to say about it." He puffed on the cigarette and the noxious fumes blew away in the wind. "But, I don't trust her. The woman is bat-shit crazy and I know she'll try to cast her evil spell on me all over again. You watch! She'll come crashing into our lives and then disappear without a second thought as to how it affects me or the kids or anyone else." His eyes widening expressively, his lips curled in a malevolent sneer that kind of creeped me out. "She Devil. That's what she is, a doll-faced She Devil."

"You've made no secret of how you feel about her. I understand she called and asked you to pick her up at the Roadrunner Truck Stop. Is that correct?"

The vengeful light in his eyes shone brighter. "Yeah, and I told her to go to hell."

"And what was her response?"

"She called me every name in the book, said she had rights and that I couldn't do anything to stop her and that she'd hitch a ride and be here in a couple of hours."

"I guess you know that she was spotted on surveillance video at the Family Dollar store in Aguila."

"The sheriff told me."

"And have you watched it?"

His exaggerated yawn accompanied by a negative headshake answered my question.

I frowned at him. "So…you're not the least bit

curious to see it?"

"Not even a little."

"And you don't have any idea why she would have gone there?"

"Not a clue."

The urge to punch him in the face was so overwhelming, I had trouble taking a full breath. He definitely personified the word insensitive. Fighting to hide my disgust, I cautioned myself to remain professional. "I posted the video on our website if you'd like to view it. Perhaps you'll be able to provide me or law enforcement with some significant insight that might help us locate her."

He fixed me with an arctic glare that gave me goose bumps. "If you do, don't bring her here."

We had one of those classic eye duels for long seconds before I ventured, "So, what exactly did you plan to do when she showed up?"

He gently shook his head as if I was an imbecile. "She might've been here." His spiteful smirk chilled me.

Caught off guard, I struggled to conceal my surprise. "What do you mean?"

"Guess you didn't do your homework. The kids weren't even here that night."

"I'm…not sure I'm following you."

"They were with my folks. Been there with my mom for two weeks."

Chagrined, I felt like kicking my own butt. I should have done my homework better. I'd made the mistaken assumption that the family had all been together in Bagdad.

Wearing a self-important grin, he lifted his chin and announced loftily, "You wanna know what I did after I finished talking to my piece-of-shit wife?"

Of course, I had to ask. "What?"

"I jumped in my truck and headed out to my folks' ranch to celebrate Thanksgiving dinner with them and my kids."

As his sanctimonious statement sunk in, anger ballooned in my chest. What a heartless asshole! What a filthy rotten thing to do to another human being. It took every grain of willpower I possessed to stifle the torrent of caustic remarks I yearned to shout at him. Okay, I got it. Holly was never going to win a mother-of-the-year trophy, but his vindictive actions, apparently spawned by years of pent-up rage and resentment, still struck me as incredibly cruel when I thought about the young woman's dogged determination to get home to her children that stormy night. "I'm assuming Holly knows where they live."

"Yeah." He kept his eyes fixed on me as if he were anticipating my next question.

"So, assuming she actually arrived here and discovered the place empty, would she have tried to follow you?"

"Maybe." His eyes glittered with secretive malice.

The vile creature was baiting me. "And where exactly is your parents' ranch located?"

"About thirty miles outside of Kingman."

CHAPTER 17

Friday morning at the office passed quickly in a blur of editorial and management decisions. I intended to leave before noon, but it was twelve-thirty before I raced out the door, hopped in Ronda's mud-streaked Jeep and headed out on the now familiar road towards Aguila. Earlier I had taken a few minutes to research the tiny community—not an incorporated town, but simply known as a "census-designated place" in far northwestern Maricopa County, boasting a population of 1,066. Aguila meant "eagle" in Spanish and its claim to fame was being one of the largest melon-producing areas in the world. Who knew? Because of time constraints, my plans to have a sneak preview of the area on Google Earth never materialized, but it didn't matter. I'd pulled up the street map online and still relished the adventure of exploring new places sight unseen.

Windows wide open, I inhaled the sweet, rain-washed air as I cruised along the scenic, winding highway. In the distance, the rumpled spine of the Harquahala Mountains rose majestically from the desert floor, cutting a serrated pattern against a cobalt sky sprinkled with feathery clouds. As always, breaking free from the daily office routine to plunge knee-deep into a challenging assignment improved my outlook on life. When I passed the entrance to the Double G Ranch and saw Our Lady of the Desert and the eye-catching, black lava rock formations, it reawakened a surge of urgency. The pressure to make sure the meeting with Wanda this afternoon produced positive results weighed heavily on my mind.

Pressing harder on the accelerator, I calculated that I'd have almost three hours to scope out everything in Aguila. In addition to questioning Pedro Salas at the Family Dollar store, Dr. Craig's description of the private airpark had tweaked my curiosity. I planned to check that out as well before backtracking to the ranch.

Crunching on an apple, I thought about my disturbing interview yesterday with Lynnis Mason, which had ended abruptly when his cell phone rang. He'd scooped it from his back pocket, glanced at the screen and caustically declared, "Lady, I'm done answering your questions." Before I could say another word, he disappeared inside the house.

Even though it was my job to report the facts and remain objective, sometimes that proved to be a difficult task. To me, the man had come across as belligerent, snarky and pitiless. It occurred to me numerous times, as I stared into his soulless eyes, that I might be standing face-to-face with Holly's cold-blooded murderer. On the other hand, his callous actions could just as easily be dismissed as the vengeful ravings of a man stretched to his breaking point. After all, he was the wronged husband, which to some might provide justification for his abrasive demeanor. The only good attribute he had going for him was his decision to raise a child who had no genetic connection to him whatsoever.

After returning to the Jeep to start the drive home from Bagdad, I took advantage of the time and cell service to return Thena's call inquiring about my visit to Youth Oasis. I told her how impressed I was with the clinic and that I had spoken to Dr. Craig. I didn't mention my injury or his skepticism concerning her pet project, but assured her that he was seriously considering the proposal and that he planned to make his decision soon. She sounded pleased and when I reminded her of my upcoming meeting with Wanda Keating, she reiterated again, how much she was depending on my success and wished me luck.

Frustrated, knowing what I did about Wanda's troubling background, I had a feeling I was going to need more than just luck in my toolbox. Might as well be honest with her. But at the same time, with the fate of the newspaper being so uncertain, I'd best not say something I'd regret later. Choosing my words carefully, I began, "Thena, is there a good reason you didn't explain *how* Wanda lost her nursing license?"

Following a few seconds of silence, she answered in a wary tone, "I didn't think it was important. Her previous…situation has nothing to do with her agreeing to sell me the property."

"It's kind of an important piece of information, don't you think?"

"Not really. I knew you would do your usual excellent research and reach the same conclusion I have."

"Which would be?"

"That what happened was not her fault. It was an unfortunate accident; she was exonerated and has paid a heavy price. I happen to believe that people deserve a second chance in life, don't you?"

Careful! Careful! "I…suppose so."

"Good. I'm counting on you to come up with just the right words to convince her to sell."

"You do know you've got competition, right?"

Dead air, then, "Whatever do you mean?" she inquired, her voice edged with uneasiness.

"Wanda told me there's a California winery interested in the property as well."

An audible gasp. "Oh dear. That does complicate things, doesn't it?"

"Possibly, or maybe not."

"What does that mean? We have no way of paying more than I've already offered."

"I have an idea, but I'm going to need your help to make this work."

She cleared her throat. "What do you have in mind?"

"The last time I spoke with Wanda, she was still adamant about not selling the property to anyone, but…if you're willing, I think you can provide her an incentive for something she desperately wants."

"I'm listening."

"Okay. If I'm going to have any chance at all of convincing her to change her mind, I have to offer something more substantial than a vague suggestion of possible employment sometime in the future."

"And what exactly would that be?" she asked, sounding dubious, but curious.

"We're going to have to sweeten the pot." I repeated Ginger's account of how Wanda's life had fallen apart following her arrest. I outlined the woman's despair over the loss of her RN license, her marriage, one of her sons and the subsequent financial difficulties that followed. Then I told her about the time I'd spent online researching the arduous process of getting a nursing license reinstated. "It's lengthy and expensive," I explained, "but here's my proposal. What would you think about offering to pay for an attorney to help her through the process in exchange for selling you the property, and the promise of employment at either the clinic or the recovery spa?"

Another hesitation. "How much are we talking about?"

"Ten to fifteen thousand dollars. Possibly a bit more."

"Kendall, that is a brilliant idea! I'm going to think of it as an investment in her and the new facility."

Having received her blessing to proceed and promising to see her at the grand opening of Youth Oasis, I ended the call feeling a lot more confident about approaching Wanda. Large drops of rain had begun to splatter on the windshield as I put the Jeep in gear and headed down the mountain.

Yesterday's late afternoon thunderstorm had deposited an additional two inches of welcome rain, but made the drive home especially dicey. Even with the new windshield wipers whipping back and forth like an out-of-control metronome, the wind was so fierce and the downpour so heavy, they couldn't keep up and I had to pull off onto a side road. While I waited for the storm to abate, I studied my information and added several new spokes to my suspect wheel. Lynnis Mason's damning revelation that he had deliberately driven right past the Roadrunner Truck Stop the night of Holly's mysterious disappearance was a stunning admission. It had reignited my misgivings about his involvement, but most importantly, shattered my carefully constructed theory branding Nelson Trotter as my number one suspect.

Within twenty minutes, I was back on the highway again and had regained cell service. I immediately contacted Marshall to share what I had learned. He confirmed that Lynnis Mason was on his radar, but as of now they had no evidence to tie him to Holly's disappearance. Yes, he had interviewed him and his parents, who verified that their son had arrived later than expected sometime during the night in question. Since they had gone to bed early, however, they were unable to confirm exactly when. Lynnis had claimed that, due to a horrific accident on Highway 93, it had taken him five hours to complete the journey. Marshall confirmed there had been a seven-car pileup with multiple fatalities and traffic had been at a standstill for hours. However, the knot of suspicion in my stomach tightened even further when Marshall advised me that, because Lynnis had left his cell phone at home in Bagdad, they had been unable to track his whereabouts that night. How convenient. Did that mean Lynnis was careless or perhaps more clever than he appeared?

While driving, I pondered possible scenarios. Lynnis Mason made no bones about his all-consuming hatred for Holly. And, by "forgetting" his cell phone, he had created the perfect alibi. How easy would it have been drive to the truck stop, pick up Holly, take her to some desolate spot, kill her, and dispose of the body? His claim that she planned to hitch a ride with someone else could be bogus. But, the burning question was why would he have driven her to Aguila first?

That thought and a thousand others were still spiraling in my head when my chiming cell phone brought me back to the present. One hand on the wheel, sorely missing the hands-free convenience of my own Jeep, I fished it from my purse and saw that it was Tally. My pulse spiked. Oh boy. We had not spoken since our verbal spat. Was he still pissed at me? I pressed the speaker button and set the phone in my lap. "Hey, there, cowboy. How's everything going?"

"Busy."

"Busy is good."

"Yep." Nothing for measured seconds, then in his easy-going manner he said, "Been thinking about you. Been meaning to call all day. Just wondering how you were doing with your sore chin and everything."

Warm waves of delight rolled through me. Tally was a man of few words, but the ones he used were just fine by me. "Thank you for checking on me. I'm okay, but these stitches are itching like crazy, so I think they'll need to come out soon."

"Hmmm. So, where are you?"

"About five minutes out from Aguila. I'm interviewing the manager at the Family Dollar store and when I'm finished there, I'm going to the Double G Ranch, and then I plan to meet up with the gang at Buster's to celebrate Thena's decision to keep us afloat at least for awhile."

"So, the pressure is on you."

"Big time."

After another short silence, he said, "Kendall, I was thinking…"

"Yes?"

"That I'm not happy about waiting until next week to see you."

My heart contracted with fierce joy. I knew him well enough now to realize that this was Tally's way of sneaking up on an apology without actually having to express it. "I was thinking the same thing," I replied lightly, tingling with happiness. "Can you break away from your guests long enough to come over later? I should be home by eight-thirty or nine."

"Um…well, I can't tonight, but…you're not working Sunday, I hope?"

Hearing the expectant, yet doubtful inference in his voice, I answered cheerfully, "I am not. I was actually planning to bring Ronda's Jeep back, reclaim mine and hopefully catch a little glimpse of you."

"I think I can provide a little more than that. Do you have time to hang around for the barbeque dinner?"

"Are you kidding? Do I ever pass up food?"

He chuckled. "I was hoping you'd say that."

"Ten thousand wild horses couldn't keep me away."

"Oh, uh…one more thing. Afterwards, what would you think about me heading over to your place?" Lowering his tone to a suggestive growl, he added, "Your bed to be exact."

His alluring proposition infused me with pleasurable exhilaration. We ended our conversation echoing, "I love you," to each other and I let out an audible sigh. What a welcome surprise. Such a great guy. What a hunk! Blissfully, I envisioned Sunday night when we'd be wrapped in each other's arms again. Preoccupied by my romantic fantasy, imagining his lithe, muscular body pressed against mine, I almost missed the sign alerting me that Aguila was only two miles ahead. Reluctantly, I refocused my attention.

After rounding a series of gentle hills dotted with cattle peacefully feasting on deep-green winter grass, I headed down into a wide, flat valley. To my surprise, large swaths of land stripped of all vegetation appeared on both sides of the road. What was this? The fallow fields of dirt stretched outward to the surrounding foothills as far as the eye could see. Holy cow! There had to be thousands of acres. Busy gawking at the amazing transformation, it took me a few seconds to realize I had entered the small farming community of Aguila.

After reading what little I could find of the area's history online, I guess I expected a more prosperous place, but instead the town looked mostly deserted. Slowing to study my new surroundings, I noted a fair number of abandoned and boarded-up buildings, some crumbling beyond repair. Beyond them to the south, narrow side streets boasted rows of shabby houses and rusted mobile homes. Further ahead, encouraging signs of life appeared—a restaurant, food market and my ultimate goal, the Family Dollar store on the opposite side of the road. I continued on just to scope things out and passed by a gas station, post office, a tiny library, hardware store, several churches and a series of one-story buildings that appeared to be occupied. Before I knew it, I had traveled through the entire town and once again, vast acres of vacant fields appeared. I passed a sign announcing Martori Farms and gathered it was the company growing the melons. But, where were the melons?

It finally occurred to me that it must be too early in the season for planting, which probably accounted for the fact that the town seemed so dead. I made a U-turn and drove back more puzzled than ever. My expectations of finding some connection to Holly had dwindled. For the life of me, I could not fathom why she would have ended up here on that stormy Thanksgiving Eve. That thought had no sooner crossed my mind than the answer came to me. Of course, whoever she was with had been detoured off the main highway because of the traffic accident. That had to be it. Now all I had to do was tie her disappearance to either Nathan Trotter or Lynnis Mason.

Encouraged by my hypothesis, I cruised back through the quiet community, taking note of an abandoned motel and RV park before I turned right and headed south towards the saw-toothed mountain known as Eagle Eye. The closer I got, the more I appreciated how it had earned its name. From my vantage point, the impressive, crescent-shaped archway at the summit sure did look like an eagle's eye. Never one to miss a good photo, I pulled over and stood in the quickening afternoon breeze recording various shots of the distinctive landmark. Then I continued to meander along roughly paved roads flanked with aging wooden, adobe and slump-block houses. Sprinkled in between them were small groups of sun-faded mobile homes, all sporting satellite dishes. A few of the dwellings appeared to be well cared for, but most looked dilapidated and cluttered with rusted old cars, overgrown weeds, neglected cactus gardens and assorted junk piles.

I parked on the side of the road and climbed out again. To the melodic strains of energetic Mexican music blasting from one of the houses, I tapped out several more photos—a spindly leafless tree adorned with Christmas bulbs, a goat standing on top of a car and wooden animal carvings interwoven into a chain-link fence. Such a quirky little town, but interesting.

When I resumed driving further south, more modern, spacious homes—some with horses grazing in the front yards and many boasting airplane hangars—become visible. Definitely two distinct socio-economic levels living just blocks apart. It made me wonder why a wealthy, sophisticated surgeon like Dr. Asher Craig would pick such a funky place for a second home. From what I had seen, there were few amenities, certainly nothing to attract a man of his stature. However, it was secluded and very, very quiet—a perfect hideaway for celebrities, just as Dr. Craig had suggested.

No sooner had the thought crossed my mind than I heard the drone of a single engine plane. I squinted into the bright sunlight and seconds later it touched down on a dirt runway just beyond a sign that read: SAMPLEY AIRPORT. It taxied across the road to one of the houses and parked adjacent to the front door. Cool beans! Now that was the way to travel.

A minute later, I spotted another sign reading: EAGLE ROOST AIRPARK. So, this was the place where the rich and famous came to get away from it all. I slowed and strained to get a clear glimpse of some of the homes, but it was difficult to really see much of anything because they were set back from the road or hidden behind tall, mature trees. A substantial-looking barbed wire fence surrounding the complex made it impossible to get any closer.

It seemed I'd driven at least another mile before I reached the entrance. A prominent sign on the imposing white gate warned: NO TRESPASSING! $5000 FINE.

Wow. Five thousand dollars? No question the residents of the airpark were dead serious about protecting their privacy.

My curiosity about the place partially satisfied, I made my way back to the Family Dollar store and parked in the nearly empty lot. After noting the locations of the outside security cameras, I pushed inside the glass doors and asked the middle-aged woman at the checkout counter where I could find Pedro Salas. She directed me to the manager's office and I tapped lightly on the door. A male voice called out, "Yeah, I'm here," so I pushed the door open and immediately recognized the young Hispanic man from the surveillance tape. A gleam of surprise entered his dark eyes as he rose from the cluttered desk. I introduced myself and we shook hands before he pulled over a chair for me. "What can I help you with, miss?" he asked, returning to his seat.

He listened intently while I explained the reason for my visit. But, I could tell by his impassive expression that he might not have any meaningful information to share. "Sorry I can't really help you out more. Like I told the sheriff, we'd only been open a couple of days and only the interior cameras were in working order that night."

Disappointed, I asked, "Were you the only one on duty?"

His full-lipped smile revealed super-white teeth. "I gave everybody else the night off. It wasn't busy anyway with the storm and all."

"Had you ever seen Holly Mason before that night?"

"No. Lots of people come in here every day and I can't always remember their faces, but I do remember her." His eyes sparkling with ribald mischief, he tacked on, "I was thinking she was pretty hot until she started busting my ass."

"I noticed that," I responded, nodding. "On the video, I saw you talking to an older guy with gray hair quite a while. Does he live around here?"

"Yeah. He comes in here a couple of times a week."

"So, I imagine you know most of the locals, right?"

A slight shrug. "Well…yes and no. Some are tourists or truckers just passing through and some live and work here year-round, but many of them are seasonal workers. They come and go with planting and harvesting. Then we get the rich folks flying in and out from who knows where."

"Right." I flipped my notepad open. "Can you think of anything else noteworthy about Holly?" I paused. "Other than the fact that she seemed agitated about not having enough money for her purchases."

He thought for a moment. "At first she was running her mouth about how much she missed her kids and how she wished she could buy the whole store for them and nonsense like that. But, when she came up short on cash, she went ballistic, started crying like a baby and calling me a f…" he glanced away, his eyes darting uncomfortably around the room before fixing me with a sheepish look. "Let's just say, she called me some things I don't think you can print in your paper." The chair groaned loudly as he shifted his weight. "When she came running back in the second time and I told her she still didn't have enough for everything, she went total bitch-crazy on me. She screamed something about…'cause I wouldn't just give her the rest of the stuff for free, that I was going to be responsible if she had to…ah…put out for this dude she was riding with."

That perked me up. "Did she say anything else about the guy or if that's where she got the extra money?"

"No."

Crap. Every time I thought I was onto something, it evaporated. Frustration gripped me. My high expectations of finding even one simple lead that would shine a light on the mystery of why Holly was even in this out-of-the-way place plummeted. Sighing inwardly, I ventured, "Okay. New subject. What can you tell me about Aleta Gomez? The sheriff identified her as one of the shoppers here that night."

He leaned forward with a look of sad recognition lighting his eyes. "She's a real nice lady. She's been around town forever, you know." He held up three fingers. "Her and her whole family have worked in the fields and other jobs for the produce company three generations."

"The sheriff said she had a stroke and was unable to talk."

An affirmative nod. "The day after Thanksgiving. Elisa says she's having a lot of trouble walking, but I guess she can talk a little now."

I sat up straight. Now that was news. "And who is Elisa?"

"Her daughter."

I mentioned to him that I had studied the footage numerous times and noticed that when Aleta left the store, she had stood in the rain staring ahead into the parking area at something or someone for at least a minute before her ride had shown up. Did he have any idea what she might have been looking at?

Looking slightly bewildered, he ventured, "She told me her granddaughter, Tina, was coming to drive her home. She was probably looking for her, but I don't know how she could see anything real clear the way it was coming down that night."

On impulse I asked, "I wonder if there's a way I could get in touch with her? Could you tell me where they live? If she can talk now, I'd like to ask her a few questions."

He frowned. "I don't know. Even if she can talk a little now, she doesn't speak much English. But," he added, brightening, "everybody else in the family does and one of them is with her all the time, so somebody can translate for her."

"Any information she might have is better than none."

He wrote something on a Post-it note. "The Moreno house is on Ray Street, two blocks over," he said, thumbing over his shoulder. "Look for the pink house. And watch out," he warned, "she's got a cranky old rooster guarding her hens and he'll peck your eyes out if you give him half a chance."

I got up and smiled. "I'll be on the alert. Thank you for your time."

Hopeful that I might get the unexpected opportunity to question the woman, I hurried to my car. Pedro was right; it took me all of three minutes to find the house nestled beneath a canopy of mature ironwood trees. I parked and walked to the gate, noting at least twenty brown and black hens milling about pecking at the ground beside a fluted, stone fountain flanked with two colorfully painted ceramic donkeys. I pulled up the gate latch, which emitted a loud squeak as I pushed it open. I stopped to look around for the "guard rooster" Pedro had warned me about. Sure enough, rounding the corner of the house came the biggest red rooster I'd ever seen. Eyeing me warily, showing me clearly that he was the boss, he strutted his stuff across the dirt yard strewn with children's toys and parked himself between the porch and me. I nudged the gate a little further and he bobbed his head up and down, performing a peculiar little dance. I'm not sure, but I think he was warning me to stay out. I froze in place. Oh boy. Now what? Was I going to permit this feisty rooster to get the best of me?

We had a stare-off for what seemed like five minutes and I was trying to decide what to do when the front door opened and a short, stocky Latina woman stuck her head out. "Who are you looking for?"

"Elisa Moreno?"

"Who wants to know?" Her thick, black brows gathered in an inquisitive frown as she clapped her hands and moved towards the rooster. "Don't look at him," she ordered me firmly. *"Adelmo! Vete!* Someday, I will cook you for Sunday dinner," she shouted with a slight Hispanic accent, advancing towards the bird. He stood his ground until she strode back and grabbed a broom from the porch. Squawking loudly, he retreated to the company of the hens, throwing me a last look of contempt. Really? Had a bird just bested me?

She leaned the broom against the fence and turned back to face me. "Sorry. You are a stranger, so he is protecting his flock." She surveyed me critically. "If you have something you are selling, I am not interested."

Flushed with embarrassment, struggling to regain my self-esteem, I handed her my card, gave her my name and explained why I was there.

A look of doubt ruling her blunt features, she cautioned, "My mother is a little better, but she is still not well. Her right side is useless and I must warn you her eyesight is not very good, so you are probably wasting my time and yours."

Oh no, please! Not another dead end. Doggedly, I pushed ahead. "Was her eyesight always bad or just affected by the stroke?"

"It was a little better before, but not much. She has macular degeneration."

Still standing behind the gate, I quickly pulled out my phone and showed her the photo of Holly. "I appreciate the situation, but if I could just have five minutes of her time it might make all the difference to this girl's mother," I implored earnestly. "She may have seen something that night that will help save this young woman's life, or, worst-case scenario, she may very well be the last person to have seen her alive."

When she continued to hesitate, I added, "Any information would be helpful. I'm sure you can understand how important this is to her family."

Hands on hips, Elisa glared at me, her generous lips pressed into a taut, straight line. I'd all but decided that the interview wasn't happening when I noticed her shoulders relax. That subtle action ignited a tiny spark of encouragement. "My mother does not speak much English." She waved me through the gate. "But, I will translate for you."

"Thank you."

She put up a hand. "This is my rule. If I see that she is tired or upset, we will stop. Do you agree?"

I quickly agreed and followed her inside a small, but immaculately kept living room where a tousle-haired young woman lounged on a chair, her nose buried in her phone. "Tina, come help me with *abuelita*," she commanded sharply, disappearing along a short hallway.

Tina jumped up, pocketed her phone and tossed me an enquiring, but friendly, smile as she breezed past me. "Hi! Whoever you are."

She was gone before I could introduce myself, so I took a quick look around, noting that the furniture and rugs looked worn and the walls were adorned with crosses and religious paintings. The dog in the corner must have been old or disinterested, because its tail thumped on the floor but it didn't bother to get up or even open its eyes. Then I peeked my head around the corner into one of the tiniest kitchens I have ever seen. It was then that the tantalizing aroma hit me. "Yum," I whispered aloud, my belly rumbling like a freight train. Homemade Mexican food!

I turned at the sound of footsteps. "She's ready to see you now," said Elisa, beckoning to me. I walked into a tiny bedroom containing only a hospital bed, a chest of drawers and two chairs. Sitting in a wheelchair near the window, I recognized Aleta Gomez, although she now looked much thinner than she had on the surveillance footage. Speaking in rapid Spanish, Elisa introduced me to her and she nodded slightly, returning my smile with her crooked one as she squinted at me with deep-set eyes dark as black marbles. Tina offered me one of the chairs and I sat down in front of Aleta. The first thing I did was to enlarge the photo of Holly and hold it up close to her face. I spoke in short sentences that Elisa immediately interpreted. The elderly woman stared at my phone, blinking slowly. As I kept talking, she lifted one gnarled hand and rubbed her chin thoughtfully, the vacant expression in her eyes gradually lighting with recognition.

She looked up from the screen and nodded. My breath caught. Was I about to get the break I'd been hoping for? My pulse rate accelerated with expectation as she began to speak in a faint, halting voice. Yes, she did remember that night and Holly. She had felt sorry for the poor girl not having enough money to buy the gifts for her children. Yes, it had been raining heavily, but she was sure she had seen two vehicles and two men standing with Holly, their faces and voices angry as if they were arguing.

Eagerly, I sat forward and asked if she could describe the vehicles. After Elisa had translated, the older woman's brows dipped into a deep frown. Her eyelids closed slowly and she just sat there for long seconds until Elisa signaled me with one finger that it was time to leave. "My mother is getting tired now."

"Of course." I felt sure she had more to say and now I'd never know. Fighting to suppress the crushing disappointment, I whispered, "Thank you very much and please thank your mother for me when she wakes up." I started towards the door and then heard Aleta murmur something. I turned to see Elisa leaning close to her mother listening intently before she made eye contact with me again. "My mother says there was a white or maybe silver SUV, she is not sure."

"And does she remember anything about the other vehicle?"

While she spoke, I waited impatiently until Elisa said, "She says it was a big truck."

My heart started to thump like a kettledrum. "Could you ask her if she remembers what the men looked like?"

Elisa nodded and as she talked, the furrows on Aleta's forehead deepened and her eyes glazed over. Finally, she pushed her thick glasses higher on her nose and answered her daughter in a firm tone.

Elisa turned to me. "She says that one of the men was wearing a coat with a hood so she did not see his face. She felt in here," she intoned, pressing hands to her abdomen, "that something was not right when the other man started pulling the girl towards his truck."

Gripped by excitement, I could hardly formulate the next question. Did she remember what the second man looked like? I waited with bated breath for Elisa to interpret, and when she did, her face reflected profound uncertainty. "I do not know how much of what she is saying that you can believe. Her memory was affected by the stroke too."

"Well, what did she say?"

A shrug and eye roll. "My mother says the man had a face like an angry bulldog."

Bingo! I held up a finger. "One more question and I promise I'll go. Was your mother able to make out the color of the truck cab?"

Elisa frowned at me, then spoke to Aleta who answered immediately, *"Púpura."*

"Which means?"

"Purple."

CHAPTER 18

I came away from the interview energized and cautiously optimistic. Okay, the tiny clue was not much and tenuous at best, but it was something. Back in the Jeep again, I sat there sipping water and chewing on a protein bar, still totally preoccupied with Aleta's revelation that, unfortunately, confirmed my worst fears about Holly. I wanted to share the news with Marshall, but I hesitated calling. After all, my star witness was an 88-year-old stroke victim with failing eyesight and a faulty memory who had been standing in the middle of a downpour at night. Her version of the events would most likely be considered circumstantial at best. I doubted that would that be enough to convince him to get a search warrant.

Minutes later, I was back out on the highway thinking that my next challenge was to somehow ferret out indisputable evidence at the Double G Ranch. But, how was I going to prove that the purple truck Aleta had described belonged to Nelson Trotter and how did the second man factor into the equation? Who was he and why had the two men been arguing? Was it a coincidence that Lynnis Mason owned a white SUV and his exact whereabouts for five hours that night were still unknown? If it had been Lynnis, what possible connection could he have to Nelson Trotter?

Less than ten minutes later, I swung onto Dry Gulch Road. As I passed by the ancient church, the sun suddenly ducked behind a cloud, shrouding the deserted old building in deep shadows. How odd. Just the opposite from the first time I'd delighted in seeing it bathed in brilliant sunlight. This time I drove through the main gate where I got a different perspective of the black, lava rocks and wished I had time to stop and explore them and the hot springs. Oh, well. Another time. Casting a final backward glance at the damaged bell tower, I headed east, once again picturing Nelson Trotter's descent into the crypt bearing the pink roses—an action that still puzzled me greatly. That thought provoked an uncomfortable gut swoop when a new and monstrous theory shoved its way to the front of my mind.

What if...what if the flowers were not meant to honor the memory of Glendine at all? What if he had kidnapped Holly and was keeping her imprisoned as his sex slave? Why else would he be taking a cooler bag down into the crypt? It seemed a highly suspicious place to have a picnic alone. What was in the plastic bag he had brought out? And, hadn't I just read about a similar scenario several weeks earlier where some perverted sicko had kidnapped a young woman, kept her locked in his basement for years and brought her gifts to salve his guilty conscience? Since Nelson Trotter had already been accused of that very crime, it seemed like a logical theory. But, why would he bring his victim flowers, and where had he taken the rest of them after he left the church? If I was remembering correctly, he did not travel back towards the highway, but had driven through the gate to his own ranch as I had just done. My overloaded mind went blank for a few seconds before the grim realization struck me. Was I being fanciful or did it seem that my two assignments had now officially converged? The only way to find out if my theory held water was to somehow get inside the crypt. And just how was I going to arrange that, I pondered, absently noting that I'd just passed by a small herd of cows grazing beside the stock tank and windmill Wanda had described.

I continued along the meandering dirt road for at least another mile until I finally spotted a white, one-story ranch house ahead nestled beneath two tall Cottonwood trees. When I passed beneath the wooden archway announcing the Double G Ranch, the first thing that jumped out at me was the purple truck cab parked adjacent to a tumbledown shed. The mere sight of it infused me with foreboding. More than likely, I would finally meet in person the man I'd been speculating about for the past five days. I suspected he would be less than happy to see me, although I still had no idea why he had exhibited such animosity towards me. Could I be reading too much into the incident? Was it possible he had simply mistaken me for someone else?

Approaching the rambling L-shaped ranch house, I took note of the other structures on the property, which I had seen from the satellite photos. There was a large red barn with adjacent corrals containing numerous horses, and several goats roamed nearby. I counted four outbuildings, numerous stock pens, three mobile homes, two adobe bunkhouses and, perhaps a quarter of a mile away another house that looked like a residence. As I rolled past a rickety-looking carport, I noticed a beat-up orange pickup, an ATV and a dirty, white Suburban. I did a quick double take. What? Another white SUV? I stared at it hard for a few seconds, but decided not to read too much into it. White vehicles in Arizona were a dime a dozen.

Squinting into the softening afternoon sunlight, I parked, slipped on my jacket and placed the notebook and camera into my shoulder bag. When I stepped from the Jeep, a high-pitched cry caught my attention. I turned and walked towards the expansive front porch, zeroing in on Wanda Keating seated in a rocking chair cradling a baby on one shoulder. We made eye contact as I walked up the steps. Until that moment, I had always thought of mug shots as akin to passport photos, which were always awful and rarely a good likeness of the person. In this case, however, she looked exactly like hers—a raw-boned, square-jawed woman with thin graying blonde hair, a splotchy complexion and yeah, she had a mustache.

"You the reporter? O'Dell, right?" she called out in a raspy voice, shifting the fussing infant to her other shoulder.

"Nice to finally meet you, Mrs. Keating." I placed my card on the small table beside her, noticing the beer can, empty baby bottle, a lighter and a pack of Kingstons cigarettes sitting next to an overflowing ashtray. It took a few seconds for the name of the cigarettes to fully register. It was the same brand Holly had purchased at the Family Dollar store and used by her husband. I pointed to an adjacent chair. "Mind if I sit here?"

She studied me wordlessly for several seconds before

inclining her head. I swiped dirt and a couple of leaves from the threadbare cushion, sat down and pulled out my notebook. "How old is your grandson?" I inquired, breaking the ice with a friendly smile.

The baby was still whimpering, so she rocked faster and pounded the little guy harder on the back. "I'm changin' my name," she announced abruptly.

I hesitated, and then said, "Ah…I'm not following you."

"For the story in your paper. I decided I ain't using that goddamn, cheating asshole's name anymore. The sunuvabitch ruined my life and my reputation and stole my other son away." She shook her forefinger in my direction. "Go ahead, write that down. From now on, refer to me as Wanda Kay Trotter. I'm takin' my maiden name back again, yes sirree Bob. Or," she pondered aloud. "Maybe I'll change it to Higgins, in honor of my late moth…aunt."

Ginger was right. She did have a potty mouth. Careful to show no emotion, I said amiably, "I'll list it however you like."

She squeezed out a self-satisfied smile. "Good. And little Henry here is four months old, thank you very much." Her harsh features softened as she stroked the now quiet baby's head and back.

"Is your brother here?"

"I think he's off somewhere makin' a delivery. Why?"

Masking my intense relief, I stated nonchalantly, "Oh, nothing. Just thought he might want to contribute some of his own recollections to the article."

A dubious frown. "Humph. I doubt it. Let's get

on with this. I gotta get dinner goin' soon and go check on my boy," she stated brusquely, jerking her chin towards the smaller house, "so get to the point. What d'ya wanna talk about? My screwed up family history or why I can't sell Miz. Rodenborn our church?"

"Both." Her use of the word "can't" instead of "won't" reaffirmed the challenge that lay ahead of me. "Let's start with your family's long association with Our Lady of the Desert. I understand that one of your uncles served as a parish priest for a number of years."

"Yep."

"Do you have any photos of him?"

Appearing thoughtful, she said, "Yeah, I think there's a couple in some albums around here someplace."

"That would be helpful and really enhance my article..." My mind went blank when I noticed a gigantic speckled spider crawling up the side of the house behind her head and only inches from the baby. Frozen in place, unable to take my eyes off it, I gasped aloud and pointed. "Look out! There's a...there's a...gigantic s...spider on the wall behind you!"

Wanda looked casually over her shoulder and then back at me, her expression amused. "What? You're scared of this little spider?"

Scared? Hell, no. Was I petrified? Definitely! Embarrassed, I began to blabber, "Well...maybe a little. I'm not crazy about...It might be poisonous and...and...you don't know what...I mean...you've got the baby right there and..."

"Oh, for pity's sake," she huffed, reaching up with her free hand to pluck it off the wall. I knew how completely illogical and silly it might seem to a person who does not suffer from arachnophobia, but I shrank back in my chair, staring in fascinated horror. "What are you…going to do with it?"

She rocked back and then propelled forward to her feet. "I'm gonna give it to my brother for his collection."

"He collects spiders?" The guy was even weirder than I thought.

She showed me a mouthful of discolored teeth when she burst out in a guttural laugh. "Just yankin' yer chain," she said, shaking her head at me as if I were the imbecile I felt like. Still holding the baby on her shoulder, she shuffled to the far end of the porch and flipped the creature into a bush. Then she calmly returned to the rocking chair and sat down with a grunt. "Spiders don't scare me none. They're part of the environment out here. They do good work getting rid of pesky insects. Hell's bells, my brother and me collected a shitload of all different colors and sizes one year for our science fair. Piece a cake."

Still preoccupied with the irrational fear that the spider would somehow leap onto the porch, crawl back and find me, I flinched at the sound of a vehicle approaching. I looked over my shoulder as a dilapidated pickup rumbled by. Two Hispanic men inside the cab and one in the bed of the truck waved and grinned at Wanda. She issued a tight smile, waved back and I watched the pickup turn along the road leading to the bunkhouses. "Your ranch hands, I assume," I said to Wanda, trying to corral my distracted thoughts back to the interview.

"Yeah. This batch is pretty dependable. It's tough finding people who don't mind hard work nowadays." When she reached for the cigarette pack, she deftly pulled one out with her teeth, lit it with her free hand and then launched into her family story. I already knew most of the names and listened politely, but my interest level spiked when she arrived at the night of Glendine's attack. At first she tried to gloss over it, insisting that she didn't want to talk or even think about it, but after I assured her that the salacious details could be off the record, she finally agreed and spoke forcefully about the "bastard" who had disfigured her beautiful aunt. Her mottled face flushed brick red and her voice turned bitter as she described how the horrifying assault had affected her and her brother's lives emotionally, financially and how nothing was ever the same again after that night. They had reported the unspeakable crime to the local authorities, but the man she knew only as Dillon and his son were never seen again.

"How old were you when this happened?"

"Fourteen."

I shook my head sympathetically. "That must have been really traumatic."

"Tell me about it. Just a couple of months before her face got sliced to ribbons we got knocked on our asses by her confession that she wasn't...really our mother." Her face contorted, she puffed furiously on the cigarette. "After she came home from the hospital, we had to get our shit together and deal with all her medical and emotional problems. I'll tell you what," she said, her tone somber, "it was a bitch trying to handle schoolwork and keep the ranch running. If it hadn't been for Ruben I don't know what we would have done."

She went on to explain that their longtime foreman and two ranch hands had single-handedly saved the Double G, while Clara's cousin, Nelda, and her daughter, Rachel, had stepped in to help care for them and Glendine while she recovered from a string of difficult and painful surgeries. "Nelda died when I was eighteen and then Rachel got married and moved to North Dakota."

"So, the responsibility of Glendine fell to you and your brother."

The corner of her mouth lifted in a sardonic grimace. "Mostly me." She glanced over and tenderly adjusted the blanket around Henry before remarking wistfully, "Caring for her was one of the reasons I became a nurse." Drawing deeply on the cigarette again, she blew out another long column of smoke. I wanted so badly to remind her how dangerous secondhand smoke could be for a baby. Hadn't she learned that in her nursing classes? But, I bit my tongue. Eyeing me perceptively she stated with assurance, "Seeing how you're a reporter and all, I'd bet my last dollar that you already know all about my past legal troubles, don't cha?"

No point in denying it. "Yes."

She rolled her eyes in disgust. "And my brother's too?"

"Yes."

"Thought so." She poked an accusing finger in my direction. "Don't be too quick to judge us. We're both victims of circumstances…we can't control."

As I glanced over at the west wing of the house, I wondered which room Nelson had imprisoned Krystal Lambert in. I didn't want to piss her off but could not help saying, "So, you think your brother's childhood trauma is a good excuse for confining a young woman against her will?"

Bristling, she grumbled, "Did you bother to read the facts in both of our cases?"

"I did."

"Then you know that slut didn't stick around because she was lying through her teeth. My brother wasn't guilty of anything other than being a goddamned asshole." She sat scowling for several seconds before she exclaimed, "That's what everybody thinks about me too, am I right?"

"I'm…not quite following you."

"Do you know what it's like to feel like you got a shadow hangin' over you all the time?"

"No."

"Nobody, I mean *nobody* will ever know or care how much I loved my work…how much I loved helping my patients. I didn't deserve the shit storm that came down on me," she fumed, her face growing scarlet. "All people will ever remember about Wanda Keating is that she wasted her husband's girlfriend." Her green eyes burning with indignation, she commanded, "Write this down. I want everyone to know something. I was a damn good nurse!" For emphasis, she stabbed her forefinger into her bosom twice. "Damn good. Oh, don't get me wrong. I'm not sorry that whore my ex was screwing is pushin' up daisies, but her dyin' like that wasn't my fault. It was a stupid-assed mistake, an accident."

"That's what I read." I studied her distraught expression and body language carefully, wondering if the rage underscored in her vehement denial was sincere or meant to hide genuine guilt. As with Lynnis Mason, I could not tell.

"My life went in the shitter after that and you know what? They yanked my license away, but I'm still a nurse right here," she proclaimed proudly, thumping her fist against her heart. "I sacrificed the best years of my life taking care of Glendine holed up over there in that dark, drafty, old house.

I tended to all her medical needs, cooked her meals, washed her clothes and cleaned both houses when I had two babies of my own. I put up with her tantrums and her criticism and all her bat-shit crazy demands." For emphasis, she smashed her cigarette in the ashtray. "But, she was totally absorbed in her own wacky delusions."

"Which were?"

"Oh, you know, some doctor somewhere in the world was gonna discover a new miracle technique that would turn back time and make her beautiful again," she sneered, baring her teeth. "I wish to hell he'd never put those ideas..." Sudden alarm blazing behind her eyes, Wanda snapped her mouth shut, then quickly interjected, "In the end, no matter how much we tried to make her happy, Glendine turned into a selfish, miserable old bitch bawlin' about the past. It was all about her. She didn't give a shit about me having to deal with my son being so sick or my daughter-in-law being pregnant with Henry."

As I penned more notes, I could not help but zero in on one particular detail of her diatribe. Her veiled reference to "he" intrigued me, along with the fact that she'd aborted the last part of her thought. Was she talking about her brother feeding Glendine's wild fantasies? My instincts told me she would most likely not answer if I probed too much. Instead, I asked, "Had your aunt given you any indication of her deathbed request regarding the church prior to her passing?"

"No. Never. In fact, I wasn't even here the night she died, just Nelson."

That captured my attention. "Really? Did that fact surprise you?"

"I couldn't believe it. I told him it was bullshit, that

we needed the money to pay the taxes on this place and God knows, I could have used it to help pay medical bills, but no, he insisted that we honor her final wish, so what choice did I have?"

She glared at me as if I had the answers. Well… maybe I did. "Mrs. Rodenborn has a proposal you may want to consider."

Her mouth twisted in disgust. "You mean her lame offer to work at the clinic? Doing what? Scrubbing toilets?"

"Far better than that."

She sat rocking as I delivered Thena's offer to help restore her nursing license and the promise of employment in one of the two facilities for her and other family members. In exchange, Wanda and Nelson must agree to sell the church to the Historical Society at a greatly reduced price. When I finished, she had stopped rocking and sat stone-still in the chair, her mouth agape and a storm of emotions roiling in her eyes. "You're not shittin' me, are ya?" she asked with a noticeable catch in her voice. "She'd be…she'd be willing to do that for me?"

"Yes." I mentally crossed my fingers. If I were any judge of human nature at all, she was going to bite.

She swallowed hard and, with brows knotted, she stared off into the distance, apparently deep in thought before turning back to me. "When is Miz. Rodenborn expecting an answer?"

"She'd like to get the ball rolling as soon as possible."

"Sunuvabitch," she whispered, her emerald eyes glimmering with anxious expectancy. "I…I got to run this by my brother, but if it was just up to me…I'd say yes right now."

Hot damn! I could not believe my good fortune.

"When do you think you might be able to speak with him about this?" It was an effort to suppress the surge of elation rising in my throat.

"Soon. As soon as I think the time is right."

"All right," I said, dropping the notebook in my bag. "I think we're done here. I'll write up a draft of my article this weekend and if you can find those photos of your uncle, I'd really appreciate it." I stood and checked the time. The distinct pre-dusk chill in the air and lengthening afternoon shadows creeping across the desert floor confirmed that I had approximately an hour and a half of daylight remaining.

Still cuddling the baby on her shoulder, Wanda rocked forward and rose to her feet. "I'll look for 'em as soon as I put Henry here in his swing." She reached for the door. "You wanna come in and wait?"

"Um…actually, I'd rather use the time to get a few shots of the mansion, if you don't mind." I beamed her an upbeat smile, hoping to piggyback on her compliant mood. "The lighting is perfect," I said, gesturing towards saffron-colored cloud castles gathering above the southeastern mountains, "and Thena would be super-pleased since, you know, she's anxious to obtain historical designation for it as well."

She paused and pinned me with an unfathomable stare. "I…don't…know about that." Her stilted delivery sounded wary. "It's just that…well, my brother says the place is in piss-poor shape so he's got the area all fenced off while he's fixin' things up."

"No problem." I patted my bag. "I've got a camera with a great telephoto lens."

Still, she hesitated, her mouth set in a straight line, her despondent gaze broadcasting some inner turmoil. "Nelson don't want nobody snoopin' around over there. He says it's too dangerous."

Puzzled by her sudden reticence, I inquired, "Why would it be dangerous?"

Wanda's face registered instant irritation. "I don't know, I guess some parts of it are real unstable."

"Just like the church?"

"Yeah, I guess so."

Her excuse sounded lame and insincere. "So…you haven't been there to judge for yourself?"

Her eyes shifted away and then back to me. "I don't like goin' over there. That place holds nothing but bad memories for me. I wish the rest of it would burn down. It don't make one bit of sense to spend another penny on that rundown old place. If Thena wants it, she can have it too as far as I'm concerned, but it ain't up to just me."

"Well, perhaps if I spoke to your brother—"

"No! Don't do that. He's…real stubborn about… change."

Unwilling to give up, I wondered how many other chances I would have to nail down both structures for historical designation. If I were able to arrange that, Thena would be ecstatic and the *Sun's* future would be stable, at least in the short term. Might as well use the ammunition I had. I gave her a reassuring smile. "I'm sure your cooperation today will be greatly appreciated and with Thena's help you'll have your nursing license back before you know it."

Still appearing indecisive, she looked away, chewing her lip before finally saying, "Fine. As long as you promise not to get too close."

Flushed with triumph, I exclaimed, "Deal!"

CHAPTER 19

Under a time crunch as usual, I secured directions and hotfooted it to the Jeep. Within minutes, a plume of yellow dust rose behind me as I tooled along the dirt road, marveling at the unique landscape. In addition to mounds of gigantic Stonehenge-type formations comprised of crimson, brown and gold perpendicular boulders, there were also impressive stands of cottonwood and tamarisk trees that indicated abundant ground water. The Double G Ranch really was a stunning and unique piece of property. I slowed to rumble across a cattle guard and then pulled to a stop, scooped up my camera and stood outside for a few minutes snapping a panorama of photos before continuing my drive.

Approaching the mountainous terrain bordering the eastern section of the ranch, I finally arrived at the "T" in the road Wanda had described. I glanced down at my phone, dismayed to see that I had only one bar displayed—not super-great, but better than no cell service at all. When I looked up and out the windshield again, I noticed an unusual number of ravens and hawks imprinted against the broad, blue sky, circling and diving towards the ground probably less than a mile away. Something was dead—and judging by the sheer number of them, most likely something big. I watched the macabre aerial ballet for another minute when it finally dawned on me. If my calculations were correct, the ravens were feasting at the animal dumping spot Ronda had called the "bone yard".

Stalled by indecision, I absently tapped on the steering wheel. If I turned right, I'd be at the mansion within minutes, but if I changed course and went left instead, I'd have perhaps my one-and-only opportunity to check out the bone-filled sinkhole. As usual, overcome by unquenchable curiosity, I slid the Jeep into drive and turned towards the bone yard.

If I spent thirty minutes or less checking it out, I'd still have enough daylight to get decent shots of the old mansion. In fact, closer to dusk—well-known to photographers and cinematographers alike as "magic hour"—would be a perfect time to highlight the distinctive architecture of the old structure I'd viewed earlier on Google Earth. What an unexpected bonus!

After traveling the sandy, dirt track another mile or so, I rounded a curve and stared ahead at what looked like a grayish-tan bush ahead of me in the middle of the road. Intrigued, I slowed to a crawl and then flinched when five coyotes raised their heads and stared back at me with piercing, yellow eyes. I braked and just sat there, thinking that these particular coyotes, normally skittish around humans, did not move. Should I blow the horn and chase them off? On closer inspection, my suspicions became clear. While similar in coloring to the coyote's mottled gold, brown and gray fur, these animals looked heavier, their fur thicker, and their heads wider. These must be the endangered Mexican gray wolves Jake had mentioned. The standoff continued and I had just made the decision to turn around when the pack suddenly slinked away and disappeared into the brush.

Relieved, I waited a minute to see if they'd return and when they didn't I moved forward, interested to see what they'd been feasting on. The sight of a partially chewed hind leg of a horse made me feel slightly queasy. I don't know why, but it really bothered me to see the horseshoe still attached to the hoof. Intellectually, I knew I had just witnessed a perfectly natural event, but it still unnerved me. I accelerated and continued another quarter of a mile before the road widened into a small clearing, so I figured I'd reached my destination. After parking in the shade of a spreading palo verde tree, I slid out, immediately aware of a faint, unpleasant odor. When I started walking, the source of the smell became obvious. Bones. There were bones of every size and shape scattered everywhere. I picked my way around countless skeletal fragments; some bleached white and clean with age, while others had hair and pieces of flesh still attached. All the while, I kept glancing around, jittery and worried that the wolf pack might be hiding nearby watching me.

I walked on, stopping to snap multiple shots of ravens, turkey vultures and hawks, some continuing to pick at the bones while others flapped away, their wings whipping the cool evening air, their screeching cries breaking the utter silence. Alerted by the mounting and putrid stench of rotting flesh, I knew I was getting close to the actual bone pit itself.

I clambered up a gentle rise and, without any warning sign, the ground suddenly fell away, sloping downward at roughly a forty-five-degree angle. "Holy cow," I whispered in awe, standing on the ledge of an enormous steep-sided, rock-rimmed crater that looked to be at least a hundred feet across and perhaps thirty feet deep. I don't know what I expected, but the ghastly sight of countless bloated horse and cow carcasses in various stages of decomposition strewn on top of a gigantic mountain of bones sent shockwaves surging through me. My insides churning uncomfortably, it took me several seconds to realize the high-pitched humming sound I kept hearing was flies, millions and millions of flies.

My immediate instinct was to get out of there, but instead I steeled myself and moved gingerly around the perimeter of the basin, taking a series of photos, noting that the gentler incline on the side closest to the clearing permitted easy access for the dead animals to be dumped from trucks or trailers. It also allowed coyotes, wolves and other predators to drag pieces of their treasure to the top, which is probably where the horse leg had come from. I scanned the morbid sight through the telephoto lens and it occurred to me that, by the sheer magnitude of the pile, ranchers had probably been discarding dead animals here for many years. Panning the camera over the bodies of horses and a few cattle scattered on the slope roughly fifteen or twenty feet below me, I zeroed in on something that made me flinch. I zoomed in further. When I focused clearly, my heart faltered and hot tears stung my eyes. Oh no! Was I looking at the partially eaten body of Dolly, the beloved Starfire donkey?

So, Ronda had been right. Nelson Trotter *was*

skimming the hundred-dollar fee that should have paid for the sweet donkey to at least be buried. Granted, being unceremoniously discarded at the county dump along with other animals was hardly a dignified send-off, but it sure beat being tossed into this hellish hole to rot in the sun and be torn to pieces by scavengers.

Hot with fury and without really thinking it through, I half-slid, half-climbed down the slope until I reached her remains. *Eeewwwww!* Her body was covered with flies, ants and fast-moving, little brown beetles. Bitter bile rose in my throat. I swallowed hard, fighting back nausea and murmured, “Poor, sweet Dolly,” while I swatted at the insects swarming around her head.

Acting on impulse, I dug out my pocketknife and sawed off a few inches of coarse hair from the end of her tail. I used my sleeve to slap away the bugs and wipe off dirt before stuffing the wad of hair into my pocket. It wouldn’t be much, I thought, struggling back to the top, but at least Ronda would have the keepsake she hadn’t gotten from Nelson Trotter, the selfish, callous, greedy, loathsome, odious degenerate.

By the time I got to the Jeep, I’d run out of unflattering adjectives to apply to the sleazeball. I gunned it out of there almost sorry I’d come because it was a scene that would be branded in my memory forever. I’d stayed longer than planned and was now chasing the light as the sun forged its fiery path towards the western peaks.

In less than ten minutes, I arrived at the fenced-off ruins of what must have once been a grand architectural achievement, considering where it was located. Staring up at the remains of the stately Gold Queen mansion, it occurred to me that transporting all the workers and building materials to such a remote location in the 1800s must have been a bitch. And why, I wondered, studying the graceful arched windows, thick rock walls and carved-stone balcony, would someone build such an elaborate dwelling so far out in the boonies to begin with? Although Clara had given me quite a bit of background information already, I looked forward to gathering additional details for my article.

I slid from the Jeep and trudged up the gentle incline, noting the time and then the NO SERVICE message on my phone. I walked on and one bar appeared, but in the next few steps it vanished again. Just as Wanda had warned, cell service was spotty. I don't know why, but I was suddenly apprehensive knowing that I was out of communication in this desolate spot. I shook away the uneasiness. With daylight fading fast, I had no time for fanciful musings.

As the buttery hues of the setting sun illuminated the lush, desert foliage in a bright, golden glow, I moved around hurriedly photographing the mansion from different angles using both my Nikon and cell phone camera. For the burned-out portion, I switched to stark black and white, which helped accentuate the forlorn, yet deliciously eerie quality of the antiquated mansion. Standing there looking up at the shuttered windows, my emotions morphed from wonder to mild depression, similar to what I'd felt when viewing the old church. Was I picking up vibes from this derelict old place based on my knowledge of Glendine Higgins's tragic history? Visualizing the poor woman roaming the darkened rooms of her self-imposed prison like a damaged Rapunzel, never to be seen again in public, was profoundly sobering. "The Shut-away house," I murmured, fervently wishing there was some way I could sneak inside to get some interior shots. Sighing with disappointment, I moved on, passing by crumbling stone walls and piles of burnt rubble. I snapped a few more photos and then walked beside the imposing chain-link fence plastered with DANGER, KEEP OUT and NO TRESPASSING signs until I came to a padlocked gate.

Several stacks of fresh lumber, bags of concrete, ladders, plastic paint buckets and other building supplies stood inside the enclosure adjacent to the house. If repairs were underway, I could see no evidence of them and considering that both old structures on the ranch had been functional for well over a century, it seemed peculiar that within a year each had deteriorated to the point of being uninhabitable.

I continued walking, troubled by one of those niggling, inexplicable feelings that there was something important I was supposed to remember. I plumbed the depths of my memory, but for the life of me, I could not think of what it could be. Then a strange sound interrupted my thoughts. I stopped and stood there straining my ears, but could not determine the origin of a constant humming sound. My head cocked to one side I focused on the whirring noise and followed it around to the south side of the house.

The foliage was so high I could barely make out the remains of a stone staircase that must have once led to the landing on the second floor, but now ended halfway up the side of the house. Crap. There was no way to get over or around the fence perched atop on old retaining wall, so I high-stepped my way through tall grass past piles of splintery old boards, rusted appliances and other mounds of junk, until I was finally able reach the rocky hillside behind the house.

After an arduous ten minute hike, pushing my way through dense underbrush and overgrown trees, I was high enough to have a better view of the backside of the mansion.

Pushing aside the branches of a scrub oak tree, I arched upward as far as I could, screwed on the telephoto lens again and zoomed in on the upper floor. All four east-facing windows were hidden behind blackout curtains or blinds and protected by thick iron bars. Two of the windows had an air-conditioning unit attached. Another larger unit, barely visible through a thick clump of salt cedar trees, sat on the ground. Nearby, a ladder leaned against the wall surrounded by a jumble of paint cans. Interesting. As far as I could tell, no new paint had been applied to the exterior, so I could only assume Nelson Trotter was painting the interior. But, now that I'd discovered the source of the humming sound, I was totally bewildered. Even if he were painting the inside, why would the house need to be air-conditioned in the middle of February? Wouldn't it make more sense to air out the fumes by leaving the windows open?

Still peering through the telephoto lens, I swung the camera to the north. In the side of a rocky knoll wearing a jagged crown of limestone, I could make out the yawning black opening of the old Gold Queen mine. Above it, smaller cavities with dark mine tailings littered the cliff face. I panned around to the south and zoomed in on a grove of trees encircling a small body of water. Beautiful!

When I moved slightly to the southeast, the camera caught the dying rays of sunlight reflecting off a formidable metal gate. I assumed that it was the second entrance Ronda had mentioned—the one that now closed off access for other ranchers to use the bone yard. Why, I wondered. I looked beyond the gate at a wide dirt road snaking into the distance and deduced that it had to be the extension of Buckskin Trail that passed by Youth Oasis. That thought reminded me of Nelson Trotter conversing with Dr. Mallick. Now that I knew more about him and the fact that the same road led right to the Double G Ranch, it seemed incongruous that he had turned into Youth Oasis accidentally to ask for directions. No question he was intimately familiar with the area and once again it raised the question: why would Dr. Mallick, a supposedly highly regarded and successful dermatologist/ research scientist from California, be associating with the likes of Nelson Trotter?

More perplexed than ever, I snapped a few more photos just before the sun winked out behind the mountains. Time to go. I slid the camera into my shoulder bag and started downhill only to stop dead in my tracks when I heard a menacing growl. Icy dread piercing my abdomen, I slowly turned and spotted a pair of Mexican gray wolves not ten feet from me. Holeeee shit! Should I run or remain perfectly still? Cognizant of the steep, rocky terrain and deepening shadows, I felt certain I'd take a serious header if I made a run for it, so I opted to stay put. Both animals were staring a hole through me, so I decided it would be less intimidating if I broke eye contact with them. They probably feared me as much as I did them.

Doing my best not to panic, I looked away. No sooner had I done that than one of them moved. Out of the corner of my eye, I saw the wolf snatch something from the ground. I glanced back and caught sight of something clenched in its teeth just before both animals vanished into the brush. Were my eyes playing tricks on me or had I seen what appeared to be the fragmented skeleton of a human arm with finger bones attached?

So freaked out I could barely think, I forced myself to wait measured seconds before willing my legs into action. My pulse racing erratically, I scurried down the hillside, stumbling on rocks and roots and slipping on gravel as I tried to digest the horrifying implications of what I'd just witnessed. I'd seen a lot of bones in the past hour but nothing shaped quite like that.

Panting hard, my heart knocking painfully against my chest, I reached the bottom of the hill and made a beeline for the Jeep. The further I walked, the more I began to doubt my eyesight. Had I made a mistake? Could it have been a tree branch or perhaps the arm bone of some other animal like a bear or a raccoon? Raccoons have hands. But, what if I had not been mistaken? Had the wolf carried it from the bone yard? If so, did that mean the rest of the body was there? That alarming thought sent a barrage of goose bumps skimming along the nape of my neck. Could it be that my macabre theory about Holly's kidnapping and murder was a reality after all? My suspicions about Nelson Trotter's involvement skyrocketed. It was time to get the sheriff involved, time for a search warrant. However, the fact that I had no physical evidence, the light had been sketchy, and I had been scared shitless presented a credibility problem. I wished I'd had the wherewithal to take a photo.

Chilled by the evening breeze, I quickened my pace, still intermittently looking over my shoulder. Tally was right. The old mansion did seem creepier at twilight, but probably more so because my nerves were still frazzled from my encounter with the wolves and whatever strange cargo the one had carried off.

Speaking of frazzled nerves, I nearly jumped out of my skin when I spied an unfamiliar pickup ahead with its headlights aimed directly at my Jeep. I stopped in my tracks and stared ahead in disbelief. Straddling the hood of the Jeep in an obvious show of dominance, Nelson Trotter sat cradling a rifle on his lap.

CHAPTER 20

"Well, well, well," he announced in a distinctively mocking tone, as I walked up, uncertain and wary. "Whoever you are, I'm guessing you can't read."

I glared at him, feeling a hot flash of annoyance. Who did this snarky dude think he was he fooling? I suspected he knew exactly who I was. Stay calm. Stay alert. Be smart. "You would be wrong about that."

His eyes narrowing with displeasure, he slid off the hood, stepped towards me and poked the rifle muzzle into my rib cage. "Oh yeah? Well, how about this? *You* are trespassing on my private property. So, I got a right to shoot your ass." His lips twisted in a snide grin. "Got any last words?"

I had no way of knowing whether he was bluffing or dead serious, but I felt a palpable sense of danger, far more than I had with the wolves. Deep in my psyche, I sensed the malevolent aura surrounding this man and instinctively knew that I dare not exhibit even the slightest sign of weakness or I'd be in grave danger. Returning his hostile glare, I mustered enough courage to make a bold decision. My last words on this earth would not be pleading for my life. I reached out and pushed the barrel away. "Actually, I do."

He appeared momentarily taken aback, but then taunted, "Better make 'em good, cupcake, and real convincing."

"How about this? I am not trespassing," I stated succinctly with bold assurance. "So, unless you intend to shoot me, I suggest you stick that where the sun doesn't shine."

His nostrils flared while contempt glittered in his ice-blue eyes. He thrust his substantial chin forward in an angry scowl. "You got yourself a real smart mouth, lady. Didn't your momma ever teach you no manners?"

"She taught me not to use double negatives."

At that moment, in those circumstances, it seemed insane, but I struggled to keep from laughing at his profound look of confusion. Then, like quicksilver, he bared his teeth in a cynical smile and fingered the rifle. At the same time, I ran my hand over the .38 tucked in my pocket. No way was I going down without a fight. "I know you're accustomed to bullying women, Mr. Trotter," I said coolly, "but that's not happening with me. Call your sister."

His eyes widened. "What?"

"Call your sister. She gave me permission to photograph the house."

His first reaction appeared to be shock, but then he leveled me the evil eye. "You're lying. She wouldn't do that."

"Call her and find out." Never in a million years would he ever know how much my insides were trembling and that I was close to peeing my pants.

With a slight glimmer of doubt reflected in his

intimidating glare, he lowered the muzzle towards the ground and dug out his phone. As he dialed the number, a warm river of relief streamed through my entire body. I thanked God for that one tiny bar of cell coverage or who knows what would have happened next.

"Hey, it's me," he barked into the phone, never taking his eyes off me. "I just found some redhead snoopin' around over here by the big house. She says you gave her permission." His dark brows fused together in a perturbed frown as he listened intently, before shouting, "Are you *nuts*? You know damn well he don't want nobody..." he bit back the remains of his sentence, listening again. "What pictures?" More silence, then, "Shitfire, Wanda, you got no right blabbin' our private family business to some goddamned reporter...what? No, you shut up! I'm bringin' her back right now." Chest heaving, he pocketed his phone and barked through gritted teeth, "Get your ass in the Jeep. I'll be right behind you."

The mulish side of me ached to challenge him, but fortunately, the logical side prevailed. Best get out of this hairy situation right now. Leveling him a final look of disdain, I wordlessly climbed into the Jeep. As promised, he followed me back to the ranch house, staying dangerously close to my bumper, blinding me with his headlights. "Asshole," I muttered, relieved to see the outline of the house ahead and seconds later, I spotted Wanda on the porch, backlit by a dim, yellow bulb. Determined to finish what I'd come for, I jumped out and raced up the steps, keenly aware that Nelson would be on my tail within a minute. "Did you find those photos?"

"Yeah, these two." She hastily extended them to me,

and then hurled a look of worried defiance over my shoulder before muttering, "Tell Miz. Rodenborn that I'm gonna make this thing happen…somehow."

Nodding, I absorbed her meaningful glance just as he pushed between us and roughly grasped her arm. "You oughta know better." To me he commanded harshly, "You get the hell out of here."

"Leave her alone!" Wanda whined. "I told her it was okay to take a few pictures. What's the big deal anyway?"

"Don't shit in your own nest, Wanda." His tone carried a veiled threat. "Be real careful here."

"You know what?" she snapped back, yanking her arm from his grasp. "I'm sick to death of taking orders from both you and…that…that pompous asshole."

"Shut up!" he roared, curling his fists.

She thrust her chin out. "I won't. I'm tired of doin' all the work around this place and spending half my life in the kitchen being a frikkin' scullery maid. This place is half mine. It's long past time I started living my life the way I want for a change," she huffed, thumbing her chest.

I glanced at her sharply. Pompous asshole? Who was she referring to?

He skewered her with a searing glare. "Like hell you do. You're skating on thin ice as it is. We both are." With that, he roughly shoved her towards the front door, wrenched it open, and as she tried to slap his hand away, he pushed her inside. I traded one last look of trepidation with Wanda before he slammed the door in her face and swung around towards me. "Don't even think about snoopin' around my ranch again. You got that, bitch?"

I knew I should not say anything but could not stop

myself. My face burning with fury, I seethed, "Apparently abusing women is your specialty."

He bared irregular teeth. "This is between me and her. It's none of your goddamn business." Still glowering, he crooked a finger in my direction. "Gimme."

"What?"

"Your phone."

I glared back at him. "No. Why should I?"

"I got a right to see the pictures you took of my house."

My insides went numb. "And if I refuse?"

"I hope my poor sister won't have to suffer later because you refused to cooperate. And, when I call the sheriff on you for trespassing, it would be too bad for you if she somehow forgot she gave you permission." His wily grin matched the malicious glint in his eyes.

Repulsive troll. Cheeks on fire, I fought to control my volcanic temper. Then, the idea came to me in a flash. This moron didn't know about my Nikon or that it contained ninety-nine percent of the pictures. There were only a few on my phone camera and those did not include the last few I'd taken right before the wolves appeared. Why pass up this golden opportunity? Mr. Nelson Trotter may have just outsmarted himself.

"All right." Surprise dominated his features when I stepped closer to him and, without relinquishing my phone, held it up, and slowly scrolled through the mansion photos. "Satisfied?"

His eyes still tinged with suspicion, he grunted, "These all of 'em?"

"Yes." I took a step back and feigned innocence. "Oh, wait a minute. I forgot to show you one." I swiped to the photo of Holly Mason then shoved it in his face. "Does she look familiar?"

He drew back and stared in stone-faced silence for several seconds before glancing back at me. "Why are you showing me this?"

"It's my job."

The tiniest flicker of apprehension appeared behind his deep-set eyes. "Whadaya mean?"

"Her name is Holly Mason. She has been missing for three months and I'm asking people if they might know of her whereabouts. Do you?"

"Never seen her before."

"You're positive?" I challenged, eyeing him doubtfully. Was I wrong or was his left eyelid twitching ever so slightly?

"Positive."

I pocketed my phone and he pointed to the Jeep. "You got one minute to get off my ranch. And you can tell that Rodenborn woman that thanks to *you,* she can forget about us selling her the church and you can also tell her that I'll tear the whole goddamned place down before I'd let her get her mitts on it."

Realizing it was time to pack it in, I turned and left, grappling with the uneasy feeling that Wanda was probably going to pay dearly for her generosity towards me. No question that Nelson held the upper hand in what appeared to be a volatile sibling relationship. As I drove along the deserted, dirt road, the unsettling events kept replaying in my head—the haunting vision of the bone yard, the wolves, the bony hand, and some vague memory about the old mansion kept bothering me.

As far as Nelson Trotter was concerned, I wasn't sure what to think of his aggressive behavior towards his sister and me. What did he mean they were both skating on thin ice? Was I reading too much into it or did his threats convey some underlying significance? In fact, in retrospect, it sounded to me as if each of them had deliberately tempered their words. Even more puzzling was the fact that the siblings had referred to an unnamed third person before aborting their sentences. Who was the mysterious "he" they had both mentioned? I thought back to the man in the hooded coat Aleta Gomez claimed to have seen the night Holly vanished. Could it have been Lynnis Mason? But, how would he and Nelson Trotter even know each other? If they did, had he conspired with Nelson to "disappear" his wife? But, how would that involve Wanda? I had no substantive answers to my list of unending questions. I blew out a sigh of pure exasperation. It seemed as if the entire day had been a bizarre waste of time and netted me nothing.

At least the sunset was noteworthy. Waning shades of soft violet streaked with crimson clouds hugged the horizon as I sped along the main road, feeling smothered by a severe case of the doldrums. All of the pent-up rage in my system had seeped away, leaving me feeling as boneless as a jellyfish. And I felt abnormally cold and unusually tired. I fumbled to find the knob for the heat and wondered if I should just head home, or put in an appearance at Buster's with Tugg and the rest of the gang? Even though my stomach rolled with hunger at the promise of one of their famous barbequed pork sandwiches and crispy fries, I wasn't in the right state of mind to make small talk the rest of the evening. All I really craved was a quiet meal and about twelve hours of sleep. At the same instant, I also felt an urgent need to disclose my information with Marshall as soon as possible. I would call him first thing tomorrow…oh wait. My mood darkened, when I remembered he had gone hunting. Did I really want to share my suspicions with Duane? No, but then Marshall had urged me to do so in his absence. Not a happy thought.

And, it was painful to admit how much the surprise encounter with Nelson Trotter had shaken me. I dared not admit to Tally that I'd gotten myself into yet another situation that could have led to calamitous consequences. He would be light-years beyond pissed. He'd be apoplectic and his list of "I told you so's" would be unending.

However, it was even more than that. I was sorely disappointed in my own performance as an investigative journalist. What did I have to show for all the hours I'd devoted to these two assignments the past five days? A big, fat, depressing zero.

All the good will I'd worked to build up with Wanda had been trashed and burned by her paranoid brother in a matter of minutes. So, what was I left with? A gazillion unanswered questions. Oh, I had a boatload of theories about Holly, but no way to prove any of them. The only concrete evidence available was the surveillance footage confirming she had been in Aguila. And that's where the story ended. It was time to admit that why she'd been there and what happened to her afterwards were questions that might never be answered. Thoroughly disheartened, I admonished myself severely. I'd let Ronda down, and what little faith Lucinda had in my sleuthing abilities would be shattered. But the thing that really irked me was the fact that, as usual, I had let my impetuous nature and sarcastic tongue rule the day. Confronting Nelson Trotter's abusive conduct towards his sister had been a fleeting triumph, but the disastrous results meant no historical designation for the church, which meant no more capital investments from Thena to keep the *Sun* afloat. Translation? I'd managed to ruin everything for everyone. "Priceless, O'Dell," I complained, trying to swallow past the lump of misery clogging my throat. "Just priceless."

I reached the edge of town and found myself in a quandary. What to do? Turn tail and run or face the music? The fact that I knew everyone would be expecting me to join in the celebration drove my decision. I could certainly use a drink and Tugg was the next best person to Marshall to confide in, so—onward to Buster's.

The parking lot was jammed and it took me five minutes of circling to find a spot. As I trudged towards the door, I heard the sound of air brakes and glanced over at a big rig turning into the driveway. I did a neck-cracking double take and my jaw sagged as I watched an eighteen-wheeler rumble past me. What were the odds that there was a second purple truck in Castle Valley? Just when I'd convinced myself that it could not possibly have been anyone other than Nelson Trotter at the Family Dollar store that night, now this. Just to be sure my eyes were not deceiving me, I stayed put until a muscle-bound guy with a short beard and a thick neck emerged from the cab. My carefully constructed hypothesis crashed and burned. From a distance, he looked a lot like Nelson Trotter.

The timing of this coincidence was not lost on me. It tainted my reliance on Aleta's eyewitness description of Holly's alleged abductor and knocked the underpinnings out from my carefully constructed scenario. "Crap on a cracker," I muttered. There was no way Marshall would agree to issue a search warrant now, so why even bother to ask him? I was back to square one.

Steeped in frustration and more dejected than ever, I plodded towards the brightly lit, barn-like building trying to get myself pumped up. The front door swung open and the lively strains of country-western music met my ears as a laughing foursome pushed past me. Once inside, the tantalizing aroma of grilling steaks and burgers reminded me how hungry I was. Threading my way among the crowded tables, I finally noticed Ginger and Tugg waving at me from the far corner of the room.

"Here she is!" Ginger announced enthusiastically, clapping her hands as I approached the table. "Kudos to our superstar!" Listening to their raucous cheers, applause, and seeing the happy, expectant looks on their faces, my heart shrank into a painful ball. I managed a forced smile. Jim and Walter, who appeared to be already half in the bag, whistled and performed vigorous fist pumps while Harry, Al, Rick and Tugg all wore ear-to-ear grins. How was I going to break the news that I'd let them all down?

Ginger invited me to sit between her and Tugg, while Jim shoved plates containing picked-over potato skins and onion rings in front of me. Wearing what Ginger would call a "shit-eatin" grin, he shouted, "We waited for you like one pig waits for another!" and then toasted me with his glass as everyone else chimed in with wild cheers of appreciation. The more fuss they made, the worse I felt and for once I was at a loss for words. Smiling, I nibbled on a potato skin while the server took our dinner orders.

"How'd everything go today?" Tugg inquired cheerfully over the din.

I met his inquisitive eyes. "Well…it was…an experience."

"Did you make some headway with the Trotter woman?"

"Yes…and no."

He arched one fuzzy brow. It was hard to fool him. "Anything you need tell me?"

"Yes, but let's talk after dinner," I answered, leaning close to his ear. He turned and locked eyes with me. Then, apparently reading the distress signal in mine, he nodded and changed the subject.

After downing a giant margarita, I began to relax and feel halfway normal again. I didn't think anyone but Tugg guessed there was anything wrong, even though Ginger gave me a soul-searching look and finally asked, "What's goin' on, dumplin'? Cat got your tongue? Ya seem mighty quiet tonight."

"Just tired and hungry."

Skepticism brimming in her eyes, she reached into her purse and handed me an envelope. "I found a couple more places you and Tally can think about for the weddin'."

"You are the absolute best," I said, squeezing her hand. "We'll look at them on Sunday and I promise to have an answer for you soon."

There were more drinks all around, a scrumptious dinner and after the second margarita, I found myself laughing at Jim and Walter's hilarious jokes. Tugg picked up the tab just as he had promised and the party broke up around nine o'clock.

After everyone else had left, Tugg ordered coffee and it was time to fill him in on everything that had transpired. I had so many details marinating in my brain, I hardly knew where to begin and so I just launched. As the long list of facts, figures, locations and suspicions poured out, I could tell by his confused expression that he was overwhelmed.

"Whoa, whoa, whoa! Kendall, slow down. There's a lot of stuff going on here. I agree that Trotter's behavior is suspect, but without at least one piece of solid evidence, it's going to be hard for Marshall to get a search warrant."

"I feel like I'm forgetting some important piece of the puzzle. Let me start over."

Tugg put up a protesting hand. "Go home and get some rest. You had a pretty traumatic afternoon."

"Dammit! I practically had Wanda signing on the dotted line, but because I cannot keep my big…mouth…shut they're never going to agree to Thena's terms now." I exhaled a glum sigh. "I single-handedly deep-sixed the paper."

"Come on, Kendall, that's horseshit and you know it. Your efforts alone have kept us afloat longer than expected, so don't beat yourself up," he advised me sagely, pushing aside his empty coffee cup. "Buck up. You win some, you lose some."

"I prefer winning."

"I know you do," he said with a compassionate grin. "Look, if Youth Oasis takes off, we can survive on increased ad revenue and Thena's additional capital until we can bump up our online subscriptions. As far as Holly's whereabouts are concerned, Marshall may decide there is enough circumstantial evidence to pull Trotter in for more questioning. In the meantime, the video is posted, we'll run her photo in the next couple of print editions and you can keep working on this story when you have extra time. Sound good?"

"Yeah."

He rose from his chair. "Things will look better in the morning."

As we walked toward the Jeep together, Tugg remarked ruefully, "I wish I could help you out tomorrow at the office, but Mary's got big plans for me this weekend."

"Going somewhere fun?"

He chuckled. "No. Painting the family room."

"Don't worry about it. I appreciate you coming in on your week off so I could go on this wild goose chase. I'll see you Monday unless you're going to the grand opening at Youth Oasis tomorrow afternoon. I know Thena is planning to attend. Sounds like it's going to be a pretty ritzy affair."

He rolled his eyes. "That's not my bag or Mary's. Enjoy yourself."

I climbed into the Jeep. "Thanks for treating everyone to such a great evening."

"Don't mention it," he called, waving good night as he ambled towards his car. I started the engine and headed home. Skimming along Lost Canyon Road beneath the silvery light of the moon, I continued to torture myself. Unless I was dealing with a case of alien abduction, Holly Mason had to be somewhere, or her body. People did not just vanish off the face of the earth.

Grimly, I reminded myself that I was not dealing with just one missing person, but three. Tugg was right. This really was a complex assignment. The labyrinth of events and facts I'd harvested the past week orbited endlessly in my head, but above all the thing that bothered me the most was the haunting vision of the human hand bones in the wolf's mouth. I could not purge it from my mind.

The beginning of a headache pulsed behind my eyes as I pulled into the driveway and parked. For a while, I just sat there in the stillness of the open desert waiting for some miraculous revelation to occur. The answer had to be right in front of me, but I could not retrieve it.

Well, this wasn't accomplishing anything. I slid out into the gentle night breeze and hurried to the front door mindful that I was probably suffering from information overload. What I needed to do was to stop thinking about it for a while and let my feverish thoughts cool down.

When I hung my coat on the peg by the door, I remembered that Dolly's tail hair was in the pocket. I pulled out the tangled clump and stared sadly before stuffing it into a plastic bag. I would give it to Ronda on Sunday.

I fed the cats and then plugged my almost-dead phone into the charger before listening to three voicemails. The first was from Neil, asking me to call him regarding questions on roofing materials, and the second one was from Clara Whitlow. She'd heard back from her historian friend and had some astounding news for me. I debated calling her, but stopped myself. She may have already retired for the night. The third message was from Thena. She was anxious to know how my visit had gone with Wanda. What was I going to tell her? That I'd blown any chance of her getting the church because I'd pissed off Nelson Trotter? Nope. I wasn't calling anybody back tonight. I did send a LOVE U & MISS U text to Tally, but everything else could wait until tomorrow.

It was late when I finally slipped into a hot bath and felt myself beginning to relax. I closed my eyes and let my mind drift, thinking mostly of Tally and how much fun we'd had together during my hiatus from work—our romantic walks on the beach, candlelit dinners, exciting conversations about our wedding and the new house—and how much I looked forward to being with him again on Sunday.

I collapsed into bed with both cats pressed against me and slept soundly until the wee hours of the morning. Rejuvenated, I lay there watching the waning moon disappear behind the western mountains while listening to cheerful birdcalls. Probably because my brain was now uncluttered, the elusive fact that I struggled to remember yesterday suddenly came to mind. I sat bolt upright, startling the cats. If I had bothered to consult my notes, I would have found it last night. It was one of those minor details easy to overlook. The startling answer was buried in Krystal Lampton's allegation. Hadn't her statement read that she had escaped from Nelson Trotter by jumping from a *second-story* window? Now that I knew the family ranch house was only single level, it meant my hypothesis about the old church was wrong. Krystal must have been held captive inside the Gold Queen mansion. It was the only two-story structure on the property.

I threw off the covers, leaped out of bed and ran barefoot to the kitchen. I located my Nikon and scrolled through the photos—the chain-link fence, the blackout curtains on the windows, the A/C units running, and the imposing gate. The clues were all there. And when I added in Nelson Trotter's threatening demeanor and terse ultimatum to stay away from the Gold Queen mansion I wondered why

I hadn't guessed the answer sooner. I had no evidence, so it was pure speculation on my part, but what if he *was* part of a human-trafficking ring? Was it possible that he was holding Holly Mason and Lindsay Cole hostage inside the old house at this very moment?

CHAPTER 21

Two hours later, I was at my desk staring at the computer screen. Even though it was quiet as a morgue with the staff gone on Saturday, I fidgeted in my chair, stewing internally, unable to concentrate on the work I needed to complete before Rick showed up at nine. My mind a million miles away, I finally gave up and stared blankly out the window, watching a couple of ground squirrels chasing each other around a prickly pear cactus.

The fact that Marshall had removed himself from any form of communication at this critical juncture in my investigation left me hugely frustrated. If I relied on my instincts as a reporter combined with the damning facts I had gathered, it meant something horrible was going on at the Double G. The pervasive feeling that someone needed to take action now gnawed at me. However, I still lacked the most important thing—evidence. It would be risky as hell, but in order to validate my hunch there was only one answer; somehow, I had to get inside the old house. How exactly did I plan to pull that off? No way was Nelson Trotter going to greet me with open arms and invite me in, so that meant I would have to deliberately trespass. Was I prepared for the consequences of such actions? And, what were the ramifications if I was wrong? Then what? The fact that I was even asking myself these questions surprised me. A year ago, I wouldn't have hesitated, but could it be that, since my last harrowing episode, I'd grown more cautious, not quite as eager to charge headlong into danger?

A safer route would be to bring reinforcements. Should I ask Tally to be my wingman? I envisioned myself suggesting it to him and shook my head. No way was that happening. He had no idea how deeply I was already involved in this story as it was. Okay, perhaps I could convince Tugg to ride shotgun. However, considering his age and health issues, that seemed like a remote possibility at best. My mind searched for solutions. Wait a minute! How about Jim or Walter, or Jim *and* Walter? It was one thing to get myself in hot water, but quite another to involve someone else in one of my harebrained schemes. My thoughts flitted about and after contemplating every imaginable scenario, I dialed the one person on earth I could always count on to give me sound advice—the man I'd idolized all my life, my mentor, my hero.

"Pumpkin!"

"Hey, Dad, how are you doing?"

"Great to hear from you! Everything's fine here. What's up?"

Because my father had been an award-winning photojournalist for twenty-five years and now owned and operated my hometown newspaper in Spring Hill,

Pennsylvania, where I'd cut my teeth as a cub reporter, I felt certain he would steer me in the right direction. "I need to bounce a few things off you concerning a couple of assignments I've been working on. Do you have a few minutes?"

No immediate answer, then in a hushed tone he said, "I've got about ten minutes before your mother drags me downtown to another one of her tedious fundraising events."

"I'll make it quick." Talking at lightning speed, I gave him a loose outline of everything I'd been working on the past week. "So, what would you do if you were in my shoes?" I asked breathlessly.

"Are you sure you want my advice?"

My heart fluttered with uncertainty. I could tell by the hesitant reservation in his voice that he might not support my idea of storming the gates of the castle.

"I do."

"First, let me say that these two stories sound really intriguing. I'd sure as hell jump on both of them and you're right, they do seem to be strangely intertwined. You've certainly done your legwork and have a lot of balls in the air…but, before I say anything else let me ask you a couple of questions, okay?"

Buoyed by his words of approval, I eagerly answered, "Shoot."

"Do you have any rock-solid evidence that this Trotter character is involved in a sex-trafficking ring?"

"No."

"While you were on the property, did you find any physical evidence to back up your supposition that he might be holding these two women, or perhaps others, captive inside that house?"

"No."

"So…this is just a gut feeling."

"You're the one who always told me to follow my instincts."

"True, but—"

I cut in, "Considering everything I've told you, doesn't it make sense to you?"

"It seems plausible," he answered cautiously, "but on the other hand, considering the amount of time that has passed, what makes you think that either of these women are even still alive?"

"Well…I…don't know that."

A poorly disguised sigh met my ears. "Okay. In order to break this story, are you willing to accept the consequences of getting caught alone by this known sexual predator and possibly becoming his fourth victim?"

My skin crawled and stomach quaked at the thought. "No…I'm not."

"I didn't think so."

I paused as his remark sunk in. Incredulous, I stated sharply, "Wow. It sounds like you're trying to talk me out of this assignment."

"I've never been able to talk you out of anything," he said with a trace of wry humor before continuing more firmly, "Look, I used to be where you are…fire in the belly and all that. Just like you, I wasn't afraid to take all kinds of crazy chances to snag that all-important scoop. Believe me, I understand your ambition and your passion, I really do. You are tenacious, adventurous and unbelievably strong-willed." His low chuckle met my ears. "You are a true redhead. Since the day you were born, your mother and I always insisted you came with a warning label and could 'out-stubborn' a mule."

He was just like Tally, comparing me to a mule. "Thanks a lot, Dad."

"Don't get me wrong! Your determination to see the bad guys taken down and justice served is truly admirable, but can you give me one good reason you can't take your foot off the accelerator and wait on this one aspect of the story until your sheriff returns on Monday?"

Crap. Why did he have to be so damn logical?

"Really, Dad? That's your answer."

"Think of it this way. If you're right, you're still gonna get to break the story wide open. You're just gonna have to wait forty-eight hours and let law enforcement take the risk instead of putting yourself in harm's way."

"What if he doesn't believe me? What if he doesn't think there's enough here to obtain a search warrant?"

"Kendall," he said softly, "You asked me what I would do, right?"

"Yeah, I did."

"In my opinion, this would be the wisest course of action."

When I said nothing, he added with an encouraging note, "Nothing is stopping you from working on the church assignment for Thena. To me, it sounds like that one is more important to the future of the business anyway."

"You're starting to sound like Tally," I grumbled, hating myself for sounding so petulant. "You're both no fun."

"Come on, kiddo, you know I'm your biggest fan," he went on, his tone warm with compassion. "I couldn't be prouder of the way you've handled yourself, laying your life on the line to break those other stories, but this time I hope you'll slow down a little bit and think this through. I mean, look what happened just two months ago. Yeah, you got the scoop all right, but you also got your arm broken and damn near got yourself killed right in front of us. I'm not too excited about that happening again to my only daughter."

"I didn't plan it that way. Sean was in danger if you will recall. I had no choice."

"Okay. Okay. You're right. No one is questioning your motivation and we're all grateful that you intervened, but now…things are different."

"How?"

"You don't *need* to do this. You've already proven to the world that you're one hell of a gutsy reporter. This could be a turning point in your life."

Frustration ruled my senses. "What does that mean?"

"Come on, Pumpkin. Open your eyes! You've finally found yourself a great guy, you've got a wedding to plan, a house being built…. and maybe you'll start thinking about starting a family soon. You have a great, big, beautiful life out there ahead of you so you need to ask yourself, is it worth taking this kind of a risk at this point in time?"

"Dad! I've invested a lot of sweat equity in this story already…"

"Don't misunderstand me," he interrupted. "I'm not suggesting that you give up on this assignment entirely. Hell, I wouldn't either! This is such a multi-layered story going off in so many different directions…you've got lots of avenues to follow other than taking on this one aspect by yourself. That's all I'm saying."

His response left me feeling impotent, aggravated

and glum, but in my heart of hearts, I knew he was right. "Thanks for the long distance ass-kicking, Dad."

His robust laugh exploded in my ear. "Don't be so fatalistic. Subconsciously, you must have felt you needed it or you wouldn't have called me, am I right?"

I exhaled a resigned sigh. "I guess so."

"I love you, Pumpkin."

"I love you too, Dad."

"And, puhleeeeez do me a favor," he added, a beseeching note entering his voice.

"What?"

"Make a decision soon about the location for your wedding. Your mother is driving me nuts wondering what you're going to be wearing, what she's going to be wearing and all the other rigmarole that you gals need to figure out."

Oh, my. Even though my mother wasn't completely thrilled about my decision to marry an Arizona rancher, once she'd accepted that our impending marriage was a reality, she had not stopped obsessing about the wedding for one day. To appease her, I'd asked Ginger to keep her in the loop and include her as much as possible. "I promise to make all those decisions soon, although it's definitely not at the top of my most important things-in-life-to-do list at the moment."

"Well, this time, you might want to bump it ahead of this assignment."

I hung up, deflated by his common-sense lecture and forced myself to accept the unhappy conclusion that, just this once, it might be best to follow his sage advice. Instead of running off "half cocked" as Tally always reminded me, the sensible thing to do was report my suspicions to Duane as Marshall had requested. At least when Marshall returned on Monday, he would have the facts in hand and could then decide if there was sufficient cause to get a search warrant. Being pragmatic would be safe but definitely not exciting. In the meantime, I would forge ahead with my planned interview of Dr. Mallick this afternoon. I must remember to bring the little white box to the clinic in hopes he could enlighten me on the intriguing contents.

Feeling somewhat content with my decision, I picked up the phone again and dealt with Neil's questions regarding roof tiles for the new house before dialing Clara's number. She answered on the fourth ring. "Oh, Kendall," she exclaimed, "I'm so glad you called. I have some fascinating information to share."

"I'm all ears," I answered, trying to muster up a modicum of enthusiasm.

"You remember me telling you about my friend, Jane, who works with the Historic Preservation Office in Phoenix?"

"Yes."

"Well, she and several other volunteers have been going through some of the original architectural plans for Our Lady of the Desert, and guess what?"

Dutifully, I asked, "What?"

"They have confirmed the existence of a hidden passageway!"

Her news reawakened my interest in the story. "No kidding?"

"And get this," Clara continued with a tone of restrained excitement, "she also tracked down a man at an assisted-living facility who once worked as a custodian at the church many years ago. He told her that one particular priest, who was quite elderly, showed him how to access the entrance."

"From the priest hole you told me about."

"No! From inside the crypt."

I sat up a little straighter. "Tell me more."

"I will, but this is not for publication. In fact, Jane swore me to secrecy and you must do the same. She's afraid Our Lady will be inundated with adventure-seekers and the crypt will be vandalized."

"Unfortunately, that's probably true."

"Anyway," she continued in a confidential tone, "apparently, it's been a tightly kept secret all these years, with each priest showing only his successor how to find it. Nothing was ever written down and the location has only been handed down by word of mouth for centuries. According to Jane, the gentleman, who is now blind and in failing health, told her he learned of the existence of the passageway about seventy years ago when he was just a young man. He said the priest had fallen gravely ill and wanted to make certain he passed on the secret to someone who could inform the new priest, should he pass away during the night."

My attention fully engaged, I eagerly took notes thinking that it was more crucial than ever that the church gain protected status. And that brought up an interesting thought. "So…when Father Dominic hung himself in the bell tower, does that mean the incoming priest was not made aware of the passageway?"

An extended hesitation. "That's a good question."

"I wonder if he shared the secret with Glendine?" I mused, almost to myself. "And if so, did she tell anyone else in her family?"

"I don't know, but I see what you mean. It is fortuitous that Jane was granted access to the plans and that she was able to track the man down before he died or this information might have been lost forever." She squealed with delight. "Isn't this thrilling? It's like participating in a great adventure or perhaps a mystery novel."

I had to admit she was right. "So, where is the entrance to this secret passageway?"

"Oh! That's the most intriguing information of all," she squealed. "On the west end of the crypt, there is an altar where one may light a candle and recite a prayer for the deceased. Mounted on the wall above it is the magnificent statue of St. Barbara. I remember seeing it when we were down there and thought at the time it seemed an unusual place to hide such an impressive work of art. She stands about four feet high and holds the key to accessing the hidden door. Do you know who she was?"

"No."

"Her tomb is said to be the site of many miracles. Now, in the Catholic Church, there are many Patron saints, but she in particular is known as the Patron saint of those at risk of sudden or violent death...hold on just a moment, dear." I could hear paper rattling in the background then, "Here it is. St. Barbara holds a golden cross that must be rotated three full turns to the right and then two full turns to the left in order to open the door to the passageway."

"Kind of like a safe combination?" I ventured.

"That's what it sounds like."

Her statement reinforced my continuing fascination with old buildings. "You're right. This does sound like something from an Edgar Allen Poe mystery novel."

Clara laughed. "Indeed! Thena is going to be ecstatic when she hears this news. In fact, I'm going to see her later today at the grand opening for Youth Oasis."

That brought me back to reality. Oh boy. How was I going to explain that I had totally botched her plans to buy the church? Would she then pull her support for the *Sun*? Perhaps this afternoon would not be the right venue to confess my sins. "I'll be there as well, covering the event for the paper, so I'll probably see you later."

"That would be lovely."

I hung up and dialed the sheriff's office. When Julie answered I asked for Duane, but she informed me that he was on another call. I asked her to tell him that I had new information on the Holly Mason case and that I'd stop in around one. I cradled the phone just as Rick rapped on the doorframe. "Hey, boss! Ready to rock an' roll?"

"Yep. Be right there." We worked in his office updating the website for the next four hours until my eyes ached from staring at the screen. I pulled back. "This is great stuff, Rick and I know we should keep going, but what do you say we call it a day? I have other things to do and I know you probably do too. We'll pick this up again on Monday."

He flashed me a grateful grin. "Fine by me." He was out the door before I got all the lights shut off. I locked up, climbed in the Jeep and steeled myself for the meeting with Duane, which I dreaded with every bone in my body.

When I drove into the parking lot, I realized I was about fifteen minutes early, but doubted he would care. I was mildly surprised to see his wife's pea-green minivan parked beside his patrol car. Well, this could be interesting.

I could hear the kids laughing and squealing as I pushed the door open. If I had not already had personal experience dealing with the fact that he was such a smarmy, deceitful lecher, I might have been touched by the warm, fuzzy portrayal of Duane, the devoted husband and father, clutching his squirming twin boys on his lap. Beside him, his ten-year-old daughter, Trish, stood leaning her head on his shoulder while Ada sat in front of his desk, cuddling their six-month-old baby girl. Paper plates, straws, napkins and cups littered the desk and floor.

The look of raw discomfort on Duane's face when he saw me was priceless. Here I was, the woman he lusted after every chance he got, standing in the same room with his plump, beleaguered wife. Unceremoniously, he jumped to his feet, dumping the kids onto the floor. "Ken…I mean… Miss O'Dell, I wasn't expecting you until one o'clock," he gulped, his eyes ping-ponging nervously back and forth between his wife and me. Was he afraid I was going to unmask his piggish, raunchy, predictably macho behavior in front of her and the children?

"Sorry, I'm a little early. Hi, Ada!" I called out cheerily, "I didn't mean to interrupt your family lunch."

"Oh, that's all right, Kendall. We thought it would be a nice surprise to have a little indoor picnic with it being Saturday and all, and knowing he couldn't get away with Marshall out of town this weekend." Swiping a lock of limp, blonde hair from her forehead, she rose, transferred the baby to her hip and shouted, "You kids help me get this mess cleaned up. Daddy has to get back to work now."

Trish was really the only one that helped, while the two rambunctious boys giggled and chased each other around the room. The baby started to fuss as Ada finally corralled the screeching twins and herded them towards the door like baby quail. It was then I noticed Trish surreptitiously side-glancing at me while tugging at her mom's sleeve. Ada leveled her a look of exasperation and yelled, "You boys settle down! I can't even hear myself think," while barking at her daughter, "what are you trying to tell me, Trish?"

Her daughter stood on tiptoe, whispered something in her ear and Ada's face immediately softened. "Well, why don't you ask Miss O'Dell yourself, sweetie?"

Trish looked up at me shyly with luminous brown eyes. "Um…my friend, Carly…well, she's got cancer and… um…our church is selling tickets for a pancake breakfast next Saturday to raise money for her. Would you like to buy a ticket?"

"Absolutely." I pulled my wallet from my purse without a second thought. "How much for one?"

"Five dollars."

Her eyes widened with amazement when I handed her two twenty-dollar bills. She threw a questioning glance at her mother and squealed. "Mom! Look at this!"

Ada frowned at me. "Oh, Kendall, are you sure? Eight tickets?"

"Positive. You'd be surprised at how many pancakes I can eat when I'm hungry."

Ada got my joke and winked at me, but Trish looked genuinely bewildered. Nevertheless, after she counted out the tickets in my hand, I stuffed them in my back pocket and then locked eyes with Ada. "We'd be happy to write a feature article on Carly that might generate even more interest, if it's agreeable to her family."

"I think that would be wonderful." I handed her my business card and she made eye contact with her daughter. "Go on. Tell Miss O'Dell thank you."

She did and thanked me twice more afterwards. Ada waved goodbye to Duane and the family trailed out the door. In the ensuing awkward silence, I turned to Duane, who gave me a searching look before muttering, "That was a real nice thing you did."

"It's for a good cause."

"That's a side of you I've never seen before," he remarked, fingering his thin mustache. "You're usually... all business, you know, balls-to-the-wall chasing down the bad guys."

Balls to the wall? Not altogether sure it was a compliment, I thought it was an interesting expression to apply to a woman. Raising one brow, I countered, "Seeing you interact with your kids is a side of *you* I've never seen before." He had no response, except to shrug and gesture to the chair in front of the desk. "Julie said you had something important to tell me."

I sat down and leafed though my notes. "I have what I feel is significant information on Holly Mason and another missing woman that you can pass on to Marshall. Hopefully, he'll follow up with a search warrant as soon as possible."

His eyes hardened as he leaned back in the chair, his chest puffing up like a toad. "Well, Marshall's not here, so that means I make the determination as to how significant I think it is."

Okay. Duane was back to the normal assclown I knew and disliked—arrogant, smug, patronizing, and officious. Part of me wanted to throw the notebook in his face, but I decided not to react. Instead, I laid out all the facts, finishing up with my uncorroborated sighting of the skeleton hand carried in the wolf's mouth, which brought a smirk to his lips. "A hand? Really?" He shook his head doubtfully before cracking a disparaging smile. "Sounds to me like you've been binge-watching too many horror movies."

"Hardly."

His elongated shrug reached his ears. "A judge is never going to issue a search warrant based on something that far-fetched." He leaned forward, hands folded on the desk, his pointed gaze dubious. "You're positive it wasn't just a stick or something like that?"

It irked me to admit, "I'm not positive, but my gut feeling when I add everything together…"

"A gut feeling isn't gonna cut it. I need actual evidence to present to the judge."

"I have a pretty good track record going, Duane, don't you agree?"

"Doesn't matter. It's still conjecture."

I stared at him intently. Was he blowing me off? "Whatever. Look," I said more forcefully, "I've got a really bad feeling about Nelson Trotter. He could be holding Holly Mason and perhaps Lindsay Cole against their will as we speak."

He didn't bother to disguise his cynicism. "I can see your headline now," he said, arcing his hand in the air. "Missing Girls Shut Away In Shut-away House." He laughed heartily at his own joke.

"You think this is funny, Duane? Have you considered the possibility that he might be involved in one of these human trafficking rings…or…that he may have murdered these two women and hidden their bodies somewhere in the house?"

Deep frown lines appeared on his forehead as his thin

brows meshed together. "That's pretty serious accusation to make with no proof."

"I'm not making it lightly." I closed my notebook. "So, you're not the least bit curious about my supposition?"

He blinked at me. "Your what?"

"My theory about Holly Mason."

"Look, I know you're real good at what you do, but part of my job is to check on this guy every couple of months, you know, because he's a felon and registered sex offender and all. But, I've been out there to the Double G a bunch of times and, so far, he's been nuthin' but cooperative. He seems to be working hard and keeping his nose clean as far as we can tell, so don't you think he'd be kinda stupid to do something like that right under our noses?"

"I'm just giving you my takeaway, Duane. I think there's something weird going on out there."

"Well, I need to have probable cause, so maybe I'd better take a drive out there and check things out for myself."

"If you do, it might be wise to get that search warrant first and wait for Marshall to get back."

He fixed me with a look of derisive resentment. "You think I can't handle this myself?"

Good thing he couldn't read my mind. "I didn't say that."

"Yeah, you did," he bristled, his complexion reddening substantially. "I know you think you're pretty hot stuff, grabbing the headlines for yourself all the time, but this time I suggest you let me do my job, okay?"

Whoa! Taken aback, I stared at him. It had not occurred to me until that moment that he might be jealous of the fact that I had broken five complex cases this past year and he had not. "Take it easy, Duane. I'm just saying that from what I've observed, Nelson Trotter strikes me as a loose cannon. You can laugh if you want, but I get the innate sense that he's a seriously dangerous guy."

"Thanks for the heads-up. I'll take it from here."

Had I just been summarily dismissed? Apparently, I must have offended his masculine sensibilities, or perhaps this was his way of getting back at me for spurning his constant advances. I refrained from making a face. "You're welcome." I rose and could feel his angry gaze burning into my back as I walked towards the door. With a sense of relief, I stepped outside, whispering, "Insufferable asshole."

Striding towards the Jeep, I donned my jacket and climbed into the driver's seat taking note of the dark clouds gathering over the mountains to the northwest. Seriously? More bad weather?

With a slight headache pulsing at my temples, I sped home to change clothes for the Youth Oasis event mired in mixed emotions. I hated to admit that my dad was probably right. On the one hand, it was a relief to have removed myself from what could have been a perilous confrontation with Nelson Trotter, but on the other I felt dejected at having taken myself out of the game. It was sobering to realize that my days of pursuing these types of intriguing stories, especially the ones that got my blood running wildly, were winding down and might soon be in my rear-view mirror when I started my new life at the Starfire in just a few short months. I chastised myself. If Tally had any inkling of the trouble I'd already gotten myself into this past week he'd be spitting mad, to put it mildly. I hated keeping secrets from him, but was well aware of how he felt about my obsession with super-challenging assignments. "Farewell, intrepid reporter, Kendall Shannon O'Dell," I murmured morosely. "Hello, unadventurous, totally boring, totally uninteresting ranch wife, Mrs. Bradley James Talverson."

Hot tears pooled behind my eyes as another insightful phrase uttered by my grandmother echoed in my head: "*It's fun to dream but they can be as elusive as trying to catch a cloud.*"

CHAPTER 22

Late. I hated to be late. If I had not fallen asleep on the couch, I would have made it to Youth Oasis with time to spare. Prickly with irritation, my frustration mounted as I searched in vain for a parking spot. Unbelievable. Not only was the parking area packed to overflowing, Buckskin Trail was also choked with vehicles parked in both directions. Crap! Apparently Dr. Craig's full-page ad in the *Sun* had been hugely successful, as word of the clinic's miraculous, age-defying products had spread like wildfire throughout the community.

My short patience fuse ignited. I stomped on the accelerator, blasted past the clinic's private entrance and drove around the east side of the hill where the pavement ended. Traveling beneath an ever-darkening overcast sky that milked the color from the desert landscape, I finally found a spot on the far side of a cattle guard. Could I be any further away?

Sighing, I shouldered my purse and when I slid

outside into the blustery wind, I shivered violently. How weird. It didn't seem *that* cold. Stepping gingerly across the metal grid, trying to avoid twisting my ankles, I headed towards the clinic. Had I known I would have to hike a quarter of a mile crunching through rocks and loose gravel, I certainly wouldn't have worn four-inch heels or dressed for the gala event in my new black-and-white suit. The quickening wind blew my carefully arranged curls into a spinning haystack as large raindrops began to pelt my face.

Come on! Was I going to arrive at Youth Oasis for the second time looking disheveled and soaking wet? Moreover, it would really suck if Thena had already left, ruining my plan to snag photos of her and other prominent citizens of Castle Valley with Dr. Craig.

Earlier, as I'd rushed around getting dressed for the event, I had to admit that I didn't feel well. Looking back, I wondered how had I overlooked the first sign that something was amiss. Even though I had skipped lunch, I'd had no appetite when I'd arrived home. It hadn't been a stretch to reach the conclusion that the hour I had spent huddled in the freezing rain at the church last Tuesday was most likely the culprit. In hindsight, that folly had netted me nothing but an injured chin and now a cold.

Mind over matter, I had told myself. Mind over matter. There was no time in my busy schedule for illness. I finished brushing the cats and topping off their food bowls. They ate and then lay sprawled on the floor while I sat down at my computer. I had high hopes of ferreting out at least one salient fact about Dr. Mallick before interviewing him at Youth Oasis. After spending an aggravating hour online, almost dozing off at times, I had come away empty-handed. Considering that just about everyone in the world was mentioned by someone, somewhere, at least once on the Internet, especially when there is a business involved, it seemed more peculiar than ever that I could find no mention of him other than he worked with Dr. Asher Craig. Finally, I had shut my laptop, taken two Advil to stem the burgeoning headache and curled up on the couch under a blanket.

And now, as needle-like raindrops stung my face, I mentally berated myself for falling into the comatose-like sleep and waking more than two hours later feeling lethargic, out of sorts and super-late for the grand opening.

Relieved when I finally reached the pavement and moments later the parking area, my steps faltered when I reached the front door. What if I was contagious? I certainly didn't want to infect anyone, but then, I thought with a twinge of dismay, staring back at the road, traipsing back to the Jeep in the pouring rain was equally unappealing. While I mentally pledged to distance myself from people so as not to infect them, I acknowledged the low likelihood of that occurring as I was there for the express purpose of gathering information.

I'd no sooner stepped inside than Ginger rushed to my side. She wrapped her arm around my waist and stared up at me. "Where in the heehaw have ya been?" Her golden eyes reflected concern and puzzlement. "I been tryin' to git hold o' ya for the last hour."

"You have?" I reached into my purse and retrieved my phone. Sure enough, there were four voicemail messages. Three from her and one from Tally. "Sorry about that. Looks like the sound got turned down somehow."

"How come you're so late? You're missin' all the excitement! They been givin' away door prizes an' Doreen won a two hundred dollar coupon for beauty products. There's live music and wait 'til you see…" She stopped and searched my face. "You okay, sugar?"

"Yeah…I fell asleep on the couch…"

"You look whiter n' a barn owl."

"I think I'm coming down with a cold so you might want to keep your distance," I advised her gravely, disengaging from her embrace and taking a step back.

"Oh, flapdoodle," she scoffed, reaching to hook her arm through mine. "That don't worry me none. Let's gitcha a glass o' champagne. That'll make ya feel a whole lot better…an' wait 'til you see the fancy spread Dr. Craig has laid out. Talk about puttin' on the feedbag. Mercy me, there's a fella in there carvin' up a big ol' juicy prime rib and makin' sandwiches on these itty bitty buns that melt in your mouth like butter. I swear, I have never in my life tasted anything so slurpin' good!"

While she prattled on about the mounds of caviar, smoked salmon, cheeses, vegetables, dips, fifteen different kinds of crackers, fruit, cakes and cookies, I looked around, surprised by the sheer number of smartly-dressed women crammed into the waiting room and foyer, laughing and talking in animated tones. There appeared to be a handful of younger faces, but the majority were older women, apparently all there in search of the miracle of restored youth. Soft guitar music played in the background and, in keeping with Dr. Craig's promise, he had provided an elegant catered event far beyond the level of most gatherings in Castle Valley.

"Here you go, dumplin'." Ginger snagged two glasses from a young man wearing a crisp, white shirt and red bow tie as he deftly weaved his way through the crowd bearing a tray loaded with flutes of champagne. She clinked glasses with me. "Come on now. Down the hatch!"

The champagne went right to my head and gave me a delicious buzz, making me feel better, at least temporarily. Chattering away, Ginger led me to several draped, flower-decorated tables overflowing with the beautifully prepared dishes that would have normally made me swoon, but my appetite appeared to have vanished. At Ginger's insistence I nibbled on a prime rib sandwich and drank a second glass of champagne.

"Ya see that tall, blonde gal over there?" she asked, tilting her head to my right.

I turned slightly and saw Dr. Craig's receptionist wearing a tight-fitting, scarlet dress that hugged her perfect Barbie-like figure. "Yeah, what about her?"

"Betcha can't guess how old she is."

I really didn't feel like playing her guessing game, but to placate her I offered, "I dunno. Twenty-five?"

Dramatically, she clamped a hand on my arm. "Forty-five."

I studied the woman's youthful appearance in disbelief. "No way."

"It's true. Mabel wuz yakkin' with her earlier and she's one o' them volunteers who's been gittin' them miracle shots just like Thena. She's a walkin' advertisement for the stuff."

"Kendall, there you are!" As if she'd heard us talking about her, I swung around to see Thena smiling and waving at me from across the room. She separated from the gaggle of women and as she moved towards me, I could not help but notice how radiant she looked in her flowered, floor-length dress. Recalling some of what Dr. Craig had shared with me regarding the age-defying, possibly age-reversing injections I decided she should be the poster girl for the remarkable product. At that moment, she looked younger than I felt. "I was beginning to think you weren't coming," she exclaimed, her expression slightly bemused.

"I'm sorry. I…got held up," I replied lamely. "But, I'm here now." I handed off my plate and empty glass to another member of the catering staff and reached for my Nikon. Thena leaned in, whispering in my ear, "I'm dying to hear all the details regarding your interview with Wanda."

My stomach contracting, I chose my words carefully. "I thought our discussion went pretty well." True statement. "And, as far as I could tell, she is blown away by your offer and seems open to the idea of selling the church." Also true. I simply left out my troubling encounter with Nelson Trotter that had effectively cancelled out his sister's positive response.

Her eyes glowing with gratitude, she clasped her hands together. "This news makes me so happy. I'm feeling far more optimistic about this venture now."

Thankful that I was off the hook, at least for now, I mustered a feeble grin, "Me too." As I watched her glide away, I felt terrible knowing that I would have to face the consequences of my flippant remarks towards Nelson Trotter. But, that wasn't all. I'd also neglected to tell her about Dr. Craig's lukewarm reaction to her proposal, which may have been partially provoked by my leading questions. The double whammy would pretty much shatter her plans for the old church. I dreaded my next conversation with her, which I feared would be an unmitigated disaster.

Fighting off several waves of dizziness along with intermittent bouts of cold sweats, I spent the best part of an hour photographing Thena and other well-known members of the community while gathering quotes for my article. Then I wandered about, chatting with some of the small business owners, who clutched brochures that outlined surgical procedures, a list of age-defying skin products offered and the astronomical prices that accompanied them. I found it astounding that, to a person, they all seemed prepared to go into debt to obtain the promise of reinstated youth and vitality. I wondered if I'd feel the same way in twenty or thirty years.

Perhaps because I was feeling punk and somewhat fuzzy-headed, it didn't dawn on me until I glanced at the time that I had not yet seen Dr. Craig. I searched the room wondering if I'd missed him. It was imperative for the success of the article that the founder of Youth Oasis and host of this lavish event appear in photographs with Thena. I remembered him telling me his plan to fly out to California for a charity golf tournament in the morning. Crap on a cracker. My impromptu nap had screwed up everything.

I busied myself organizing quotes and photos for my article when I sensed a subtle change sweep over the room. I looked up as every woman's head turned towards the doorway. The decibel level of the conversation decreased and there seemed to be collective indrawn breaths when Dr. Craig appeared in the doorway looking like ten million bucks in his black tuxedo.

The sexual electricity in the room was palpable as he moved among the crowd, smiling, talking and shaking hands. I could not suppress a certain degree of empathy at the myriad of expressions flashing across the women's faces—adulation, yearning, reverence and hope. There he was, the man of the hour, a godlike creature who possessed what every woman in the room desired—the ticket to Shangri-la, the key to immortality, a last grasp at restoring the venerated, celebrated vitality of youth.

Our eyes met. He raised a hand in greeting and favored me with a disarming smile. Even though he had to be close to thirty years my senior, it was hard to deny the fact that he looked pretty hot. Again, there was a collective turn of heads, but now curiously aimed at me as he strode purposefully in my direction. "Miss O'Dell," he crooned, "I am delighted you were able to make it." Preening like a peacock with tail feathers fanned out, he gestured towards the food-laden buffet tables. "Be honest. This is far better than pizza, right?"

The euphoric effects of the champagne had worn off and I was beginning to feel really crappy. Nevertheless, I rustled up a sunny grin. "Everything is truly amazing."

"Thank you," he replied, returning my smile before his appreciative gaze roamed around the room. "Like I told you, it's my goal in life to fulfill expectations and make people happy."

I glanced again at the sea of reverent faces and nodded. "I'd say you're off to a good start."

At that second, Thena arrived at my side. "Dr. Craig, you *must* share the name of your caterer. The food and presentation is divine!"

"Of course." He stepped closer and stated in a confidential tone, "These people are very popular. It wasn't easy to get them on short notice. Are you planning a special event soon?"

Her expression turning sly, she pinned him with a coy but meaningful look. "I certainly hope I'll soon have a reason to celebrate."

It wasn't hard to figure out that she was referring to a handsome return on her planned investment in Youth Oasis along with her anticipated, triumphant acquisition of the church, and I'm sure he realized it. Thena reached out and laid one hand on my arm. "I'm sure Kendall would love to have the name of your caterer as well."

Dr. Craig issued me a pleasant, but quizzical stare. "Oh? Something important to celebrate on the horizon?"

"Her upcoming wedding!" Thena volunteered with a benevolent smile.

His eyes strayed to my left hand and I thought it odd that he hadn't noticed my engagement ring earlier in the week when I'd been sitting right under his nose. "Well, congratulations are in order then," he said in a jovial tone, motioning to another member of the catering staff. A pretty, young Hispanic woman dutifully stopped in front of us with another tray of filled champagne flutes. "Please." He gestured to Thena and me as he plucked one for himself.

Thena happily accepted his offer, but I put up a hand. "Thank you, but I think two drinks are enough for me today."

His hazel eyes alight with good humor, he cajoled, "I'm sure another sip or two to toast your impending nuptials won't hurt you." He winked. "Doctor's orders."

No question. The man simply oozed charm. To please him and because I owed him big-time, I accepted a glass and smiled my appreciation as he and Thena raised theirs. I thought it curious that he took only one tiny sip, but then realized why. "What time do you fly out this evening?"

His eyes strayed to the wall clock. "I actually have to leave here in about thirty minutes."

Thena wore an anxious frown. "Are you sure it's safe to fly in this storm?"

"Thank you for your concern," he responded solemnly. "Don't worry. I've been monitoring weather conditions for several hours. According to the National Weather Service there are a series of Pacific storms moving in, so I only have a short window of time after this one passes to make my flight before the next one moves in." He turned his attention back to me. "I know we talked about me removing your stitches, so if you want to meet in my office, I'll say my goodbyes to the guests and stop by in a few minutes to take a look."

"I'd love that. They're itching like crazy." I zigzagged my way through the now-thinning crowd and headed along the hallway towards his office. Much to my surprise, I almost collided with Dr. Mallick when I rounded the doorway. He jumped back like a startled kitten, so I said quickly, "Hello, Dr. Mallick." I pointed to myself. "Remember me? Kendall O'Dell, *Castle Valley Sun.* I'm so glad I ran into you again, pardon the pun." I gave him an impish smile, but when he didn't respond in kind, I figured he didn't get my little joke. "Um...did Dr. Craig mention that I'd like to get a little background information on you for our readers?"

"Yes, yes, he did." Appearing deferential this time, he bowed his head subserviently in my direction. "And please accept my apology for offending you the other day. It was not my intention."

Huh? Nice about-face in behavior. "No problem." When he glanced up, I thought I deciphered a gleam of apprehension in his eyes. If I didn't know better, I'd think he was afraid of me. "Do you have time now?" I whipped out my notebook. "I'm especially interested in what sparked your interest in moving from the practice of medicine to founding the bioresearch company with your brother in your home country. Our readers will be interested in how you came to focus on the study of aging, the results of your initial clinical trials, how you met Dr. Craig and made the decision to emigrate from India to the United States and perhaps some details outlining your current research. By the way, what's the name of your company?"

He stood frozen in place, continuing to stare at me in boggle-eyed silence before reaching in his pocket to extract his cell phone. He glanced at it and announced with a strained smile, "Forgive me. I must take this call."

Funny, I hadn't heard a sound, but then he could have set it to vibrate only. "I'll wait. We can talk after you've finished."

"I cannot promise for tonight as I must depart soon for another…engagement."

Well. Now I knew for sure. Dr. Mallick was trying to avoid answering my questions. Perhaps because I was feeling worse by the minute, what little patience I had evaporated. "Oh, really? How convenient."

Ignoring my sarcasm, he made a move for the doorway. "Next week will be much better. You must excuse me, please."

Unwilling to be deterred a second time, I stepped

sideways and blocked his exit. "Wait just a second!" I fished the little white box from my bag. "Before you rush off..." I pulled out the little bottle of Phenoxyethanol and held it in front of him. "Do you use this substance in your anti-aging products?"

He stared at it, blinking rapidly. Was I mistaken or was there now a hint of alarm in his hooded eyes? "Where... where did you get this?" he finally asked, his lips pinched in a straight line.

"Near an old church miles from here. Do you have any idea how it might have gotten there?"

"I...I do not know..."

At that moment footsteps sounded behind me and I turned when Dr. Craig breezed though the doorway and graced me with his amiable smile. "Ah, I see you've found Dr. Mallick. Raju, were you able to answer Miss O'Dell's questions?" He strode past us into the room, removed his tuxedo jacket and slipped on the white coat. "Have a seat," he invited, glancing over his shoulder at me as he washed his hands in the sink. His gaze rested briefly on Dr. Mallick. "Everything good, Raju?"

"I will need to consult with you on several important matters before you leave."

"You'll have to make it quick," Dr. Craig said lightly, drying his hands as he turned to face us. "As soon as I'm finished examining Miss O'Dell, I'm gone."

Dr. Mallick glanced at me surreptitiously before focusing again on Dr. Craig. It seemed obvious he didn't want to talk about whatever the important matters were in front of me. Apparently neither did Dr. Craig because his face darkened with concern. "Does this have to do with one of our patients?"

"Yes. One in particular." With that, he tossed me an inscrutable look and made his escape. My insides roiling with agitation that he'd managed to evade my questions again, I watched him scurry out of sight. What was it about me that made him so jumpy?

I sat down on the reclining chair as Dr. Craig approached, snapping on gloves and inquiring pleasantly, "So, did you get the information you needed from Dr. Mallick?"

"Not really."

He drew back slightly. "Oh? Why not?"

"Because I can't seem to get him to stand still long enough to ask him anything. Both times now, he has acted… spooked, like he can hardly wait to get away from me. Am I that intimidating?"

His eyes shimmered with humor. "Since our first meeting, I've read more about some of your past escapades. Very impressive detective work."

I arched him a droll glance. "Escapades?"

"I think we've established that you possess a rather bold nature, so perhaps he may find your…approach a bit daunting. However," he quickly interjected, "as I mentioned before, Dr. Mallick is one of those people, brilliant as he is, that prefers his own company. You weren't here earlier, but shortly after I introduced him to our guests, he withdrew to his office, so I wouldn't take it personally."

"How does he manage to work one-on-one with patients?"

A little shrug. "He tolerates them," he replied with a rueful smile. "Dr. Mallick is only helping me out here until I can get permanent staff on board, as I know he's anxious to return to his work in the laboratory."

I leveled him a probing look. "Well, his bedside manner…" I paused, wanting to say "sucks", but I didn't really know Dr. Craig that well so I murmured, "leaves a lot to be desired."

A soft chuckle. "I know. He's just not a terribly social being." Changing topics, he said in a more professional tone, "Now, I'm going to lay you back in the chair." He donned a mask and clicked on the light above me before lowering it. He moved closer to me and then stopped. "Your face is quite flushed. Are you feeling all right?"

I sighed. "Not really. I think I'm coming down with the creeping crud, most likely a result of freezing my ass off earlier this week. Oh! And speaking of that…" I held up the bottle of Phenoxyethanol. "Do you happen to know what this is?"

He took it and studied the label for a number of seconds. "Phenoxyethanol?" When we made eye contact again, his eyes reflected genuine puzzlement. "I've met a fair number of women in my life, but you definitely take the cake."

"Why's that?"

"Who walks around with something like this in her possession? Where did you get it?"

I explained where I'd found it and he shook his head in amazement. "That is bizarre. This is a common chemical with many uses, but I can't think of any reason it would be found in such an odd location."

"Is it an ingredient used in your line of cosmetics and lotions?"

He handed the bottle back to me. "It's possible. But, that would be Dr. Mallick's bailiwick. I imagine he could tell you for certain, but right now," he said, tipping my chin towards him, "I need you to stay still for a minute." He examined the area gently and soon made the disappointing pronouncement that I needed to wait at least another two days. "I could remove them now, but I don't think you'd be happy with the results. I'd suggest you wait until Monday or Tuesday," he said, pulling back. "Just a moment before you go." He rummaged in a drawer, came back with a thermometer, and ran it across my forehead. "I can feel the heat of your skin through my gloves." He glanced at the thermometer and both brows shot up. "Hmm. 102.6. I'd recommend that you go home and get some bed rest for a few days. Tylenol or Advil, plenty of fluids, and be prepared to have someone drive you to urgent care if your fever goes higher. Doctor's orders."

"There isn't any urgent care in Castle Valley. I'd have to drive to Prescott or Phoenix."

"Nevertheless, if your fever persists, I suggest you see your family doctor on Monday." He removed the mask and gloves. "Are you feeling light-headed? Do you need someone to drive you home?"

"No. I'm okay." I allowed him to assist me to a sitting position, where a wave of dizziness swept over me. Perhaps he was right. I felt like Typhoid Mary and cringed at the thought that I'd probably infected everyone at the party. Disappointment filled me. Even if I felt like going tomorrow, if I was still running a fever, I should do the right thing and cancel my trip to the Starfire barbeque. Nothing was going as planned.

Aware that Dr. Craig was in a hurry to leave, I thanked him, left his office and made a quick stop in the ladies' room.

Moments later, as I walked towards the reception area, I glanced back and saw Dr. Craig and Dr. Mallick standing near the rear entrance conversing in hushed tones, their faces somber. Part of me would have loved to stop and eavesdrop on their conversation, but all I could think about was getting home as quickly as possible and lying down.

A few people remained in the reception area talking to the guitar player while the catering staff busily worked to dismantle the tables. When I stepped outside, almost all of the cars were gone from the parking area and along the road. It was no fun at all trekking along in the dark using my cell phone flashlight while the wind sliced through me like a cold knife. At least it was a beautiful night. The moon intermittently peeked through the ragged clouds and if I hadn't felt like death warmed over, I would have enjoyed the solitary walk. As it was, my nose was beginning to drip like crazy and I coughed repeatedly. A chest cold. I must have contracted a lousy, miserable chest cold.

After what seemed like an hour, I finally reached the Jeep waiting alone by the side of the road. Sighing with relief, I slid inside and shut the door. Unfortunately, when I set my bag on the passenger seat, I accidentally dropped the ignition key onto the floor. "Oh, good grief," I muttered, leaning down to feel along the dark floorboard. All at once, the interior lit up enough for me to see the key's reflection when a vehicle roared past. I picked it up and glanced out the window in time to see taillights vanishing around the bend. Someone was in a big hurry. As far as I knew, Buckskin Trail dead-ended at only one other ranch beyond the Double G.

I coughed and sneezed all the way home and by the time I pulled into the driveway, I didn't even feel like talking to Tally. I was in no mood to listen to him tell me "I told you so", even if he didn't use those exact words. Instead, I sent him a text. SO SORRY! RUNNING A FEVER & FEELING CRAPPY. PROBABLY CONTAGIOUS. CALL U TOMORROW! IF FEVER IS GONE, I'LL BE THERE! LOVE U! GOING STRAIGHT TO BED NOW! ☹ I also sent a text to Ronda informing her of my illness, and that if I didn't see her tomorrow it would be Monday.

To say it was not a good night would be a major understatement. Alternately freezing and burning up, my chest felt weighted down, as if both cats were sitting on it. I finally fell into a fitful sleep and tossed and turned, beset by nightmares. In one, I was being held hostage inside the Gold Queen mansion, locked in a hot, windowless room. Gigantic spiders lurked in every corner and I clawed helplessly at a giant, wooden door, screaming my lungs out. I awoke from that one, having saturated the sheets with sweat. Delirious with fever, I managed to swallow two more Advil, along with a 12 oz. bottle of water. Then I lay in bed sweating, throwing off the covers one minute and then grabbing for them the next as my teeth chattered with the cold.

To fend off further nightmares, I struggled to stay awake and study my assignment notes, but finally gave up, unable to concentrate. Following what seemed like a thousand hours of suffering through the never-ending night, I finally drifted into a fitful sleep and dreamed that Nelson Trotter was dragging me up steep stone steps to the bell tower in the old church. Waiting for me at the top, his face partially shrouded in dim candlelight, stood Dr. Mallick dressed in a monk's robe, his dark eyes glowing with evil intent. I fought with every ounce of strength I possessed, but could do nothing as Nelson Trotter wound a rope around my neck. His malicious laughter echoing in my ears, he and Dr. Mallick pushed me through the arched opening. My stomach dropped in hollow horror as I felt myself falling, falling, falling until my own shout of fright awakened me with a violent start. I sat up in bed, gasping for air, coughing and struggling to banish the tendrils of the dream still lingering in my memory. I decided, as the gray light of dawn tinged the horizon, that I would not go back to sleep and take a chance of the nightmares resuming.

The cats, no doubt disturbed by my nocturnal tumbling, had left the room. Even though I still felt terribly ill, I was relieved to be awake. And alive. Wobbly-kneed, I made my way to the bathroom where I caught sight of my ghost-white reflection in the mirror. Good God! There was no way on earth I was going to Tally's barbeque looking like this! I rummaged around in drawers until I found my thermometer and ran it across my forehead. Dismayed to see my temperature was now 103, I took more Advil and stumbled back to bed. Even though I'd vowed not to, I fell asleep again and tossed restlessly while an annoying little song played repeatedly in my head until it finally punctured my fuzzy brain that it was my phone ringtone.

Barely able to open my eyes, I felt around for my cellphone and croaked, "Hello?"

"Kendall?"

"Yes?" I didn't recognize the voice. "Who is this?"

"It's Ada."

My mind swam with confusion. Ada? Ada who? Oh! Ada Potts? Why would she be calling me on a Sunday morning? Why would she be calling me at all?

"I'm sorry to bother you so early," she stated in a faltering tone, "but I didn't know who else to call."

"What do you mean?" I responded groggily.

"I'm worried out of my mind! I've been trying to get hold of Marshall but my calls just go to voicemail, so I phoned Julie, but she didn't know anything and then... and then I called Marshall's wife, Karen," she wailed, "and I asked her if there was any other way to reach him but she wasn't any help, so..."

I could hear the tinge of hysteria in her tone and sat up, fighting to clear my foggy brain. "Ada, what's this all about?"

"It's Duane," she sobbed. "He didn't come home last night."

CHAPTER 23

Oh no. No, no, no. Had he been foolish enough to try and check out the Gold Queen mansion by himself?

"After we left the office yesterday, he phoned to say he was driving to Congress to handle a domestic complaint, but he didn't give me any other details." I could hear her blowing her nose. "He's been late before," she went on, snuffling. "Sometimes he doesn't come home until three or four in the morning, but he always calls to tell me what's happening and where he is going. This time he's not answering his phone. What should I do?"

Consumed with burgeoning remorse, I prayed that he *had* gone to Congress. I told Ada about our conversation. "It's possible he was following up on information I gave him about Nelson Trotter, so I'd suggest calling the Department of Public Safety. I can't think of anyone else who might have jurisdiction in this area. Find out if they'll send a patrol officer to look for him."

"I'll do that right away," she responded, her voice

quavering. "Are you all right? You don't sound like yourself."

"I'm flat on my back in bed with a bad cold."

"Oh! I am so sorry I bothered you. I just...couldn't think of anyone else to call."

"Marshall told me he'd be back in town tonight, so he's going to get your messages. Try to stay positive and keep your phone with you."

"I will. Thank you, Kendall."

"And please call me if you hear from Duane."

"I will."

When she hung up, I suffered another violent coughing spell and blew my nose until it was raw before collapsing back on the pillow. All I really wanted to do was sleep, but could not relax as my mind swirled with possibilities regarding Duane's disappearance. The most logical explanation was the one I really did not want to contemplate—that to prove me wrong, to grab a headline for himself for once, he'd brashly driven out to the Double G without a search warrant, tried to be the big, bad cop and confronted Nelson Trotter. It probably didn't go well. Nelson could very well have beaten the crap out of him and left him lying in a ditch. I should have just kept my mouth shut and waited until Marshall returned. Now, grinding guilt gnawed at my insides, along with the high fever.

I tapped out Tally's number and he answered immediately. "Hey, babe, I've been thinkin' about you. You doing okay?"

"No."

"You still in bed?"

"Yeah. I'm not feeling great," I said, stifling a yawn.

"Well, I'm coming over."

"No! No, you're not. You can't afford to get whatever this is with your busy week ahead. I'll be okay. I'm just going to get up and feed the cats and then I plan to spend the day in bed sleeping. I didn't get much last night."

"Sounds like a good plan." A long silence, then, "I'll miss you today."

"I'll miss you too. I was so looking forward to going to your barbeque."

"I don't know…" he said, sounding hesitant. "I still don't feel right about you being there alone and sick…"

"Tally, I'm not dying. I've got a bad cold or something. If I don't feel better by tomorrow, I'll go see Dr. Garcia."

"Are you up to driving yourself?"

"Hopefully by tomorrow. I get kind of dizzy at times, probably because of the fever, and my head is all stuffed up, but I'm taking Advil and drinking lots of water, so fingers crossed I'll feel better soon."

"Okay, but I'm coming over later to check on you."

"No, please…I look awful," I replied, reaching for more tissues.

"I'll take my chances," he stated firmly. "No arguments."

I sighed deeply. I really didn't have the energy to get into one of our spats and it warmed my heart to know that he cared enough about me to risk catching whatever I had. "All right," I agreed weakly. "Bring a gallon of chicken soup, please."

He chuckled. "You're on."

It took me another twenty minutes to get up enough strength to pad to the kitchen to feed the cats. Racked first with chills and then sweating profusely, I had little appetite, but decided I needed to eat something. The only thing that sounded good was a cookie, so I ate two and drank another bottle of water before collapsing into bed again.

I fell sound asleep only to be awakened hours later by the sound of rain pounding against the window. I squinted at the clock. Wow. Almost three. I'd slept half the day away. I rolled over and watched the rivulets of water trail down the pane in a kind of hypnotic trance. It was a perfect day to stay home in bed. I closed my eyes again but when I tried to go back to sleep, all I could think about was Ada Potts weeping, wringing her hands and pacing the floor, waiting for Duane to contact her. What if my suspicions about Nelson Trotter were correct and Duane was in serious trouble? Could I live with myself knowing I was at least partially responsible for him making the boneheaded decision to follow up on my suspicions by himself? My mouth went dry picturing Ada as a grieving widow and the mournful faces of those four little kids who might have to grow up without a father.

My grandmother had another wise saying: "*Never make a life-changing decision in a high emotional state.*" I knew her statement had merit, but my heart refused to listen. So, operating on pure emotion, I threw off the covers, slid out of bed and yanked on the blue jeans that I'd carelessly thrown over the arm of the chair the night before. I dug out a heavy, dark gray sweatshirt and then pulled on thick socks and hiking boots. As I picked up the Jeep keys and my coat, I should have additionally taken heed that it is also not a smart idea to make major decisions when one is delirious with fever. "Certifiable," I muttered to myself hoarsely. Yes, I was definitely certifiable, I decided, bouncing along the muddy, rutted surface of Lost Canyon Road, keenly aware that I had no business even being out of bed, let alone heading out on this questionable mission. At least it had stopped raining and patches of powder-blue sky appeared between the swift-moving cloud cover, which indicated at least a slight break in the series of storms headed our way.

A sudden pang of *déjà vu* invaded my body. Wasn't it just a few months ago that the unexpected consequences of what turned out to be a spine-chilling assignment in southern Arizona had ended up thrusting both Tally and me into a life-threatening situation? Thinking back on all the gruesome details now, we were both lucky to be alive. So, why I was doing this to myself again?

The answer was simple. In order to salve my guilty conscience, in order to have any peace of mind, at the very least I had to find out if Duane had actually gone to the Double G in the first place. If he was smart about it, which was debatable for him, he would not present himself at the Trotters' front door; he would approach the property from the Buckskin Trail entrance. If he had, his patrol vehicle would most likely be parked somewhere nearby. Was he on a stakeout? Was that the reason he hadn't called? Perhaps the void of cell service in that area? I liked that scenario.

I pulled to the side of the road and snatched my phone from the passenger seat. There was one way to find out if he'd been to the ranch house. Why not just call Wanda? But within seconds, disappointment filled me after waiting through five rings and Wanda's gruff voicemail greeting. No point in leaving her a message now. Instead, I tapped out Marshall's number. I wasn't expecting him to answer and he didn't, so I left him a detailed explanation about where I was headed, why and what I suspected was going on at the old mansion. Next, I called Tally's number and when he didn't pick up either, I left him a message as well before resuming my drive.

I didn't really think any further ahead than that as I zoomed past Youth Oasis, noting that the short reprieve of blue sky had already been erased as more storm clouds moved in again. It took another fifteen minutes of splashing along the puddle-littered, dirt road until I rounded a sharp turn and the entry gate came into view. I could just barely make out the gabled roof of the Gold Queen mansion above the treetops but then I got one of those stinging gut jolts. Hovering over the old house hung one of the oddest cloud formations I'd ever seen. My jaw dropped as I stared at a surreal scene that looked like it had been computer-generated—ominous, eerie, almost like a prophecy of doom.

Mesmerized, I gawked at the globular pattern of gray pouch-like protrusions clinging to the bottom of a giant thundercloud like pendulous toasted marshmallows. I'd only seen this rare cloud shape one other time in my life back in Pennsylvania and if my memory served me correctly they were called mammatus clouds. I thought I remembered reading that they were composed of mostly ice crystals and were usually a harbinger for advancing severe weather. Great. Just what I needed.

I cruised past the rear entrance to the Double G, searching the brush for any glimpse of Duane's vehicle on either side of the road for the next two miles. Nothing. Straight ahead, I caught sight of the entrance to the neighboring ranch. I hit the brakes. It seemed illogical that Duane would park this far away and walk. Assailed by doubt, I sat gripped by indecision. So, maybe I was wrong. What if he hadn't come here after all? Then where was he? I checked my phone, thinking I'd try Wanda again, but the NO SERVICE message on my screen nixed that idea. The realization that I was out of phone contact bothered me and I should have listened to my intuition urging me to get the hell out of there, but of course I didn't. Call it my sixth sense, a premonition, reporter's instinct, whatever; the insistent drumbeat of urgency roiling inside me was overwhelming.

I executed a sharp U-turn and drove back towards the Double G. About a hundred yards from the gate, I veered off the road into a grove of mesquite trees where I hoped the Jeep would blend into the landscape. Drenched in a cold sweat, I sat for a moment trying to clear the cobwebs from my head. What now? I needed to formulate some sort of plan. Come on! Think! I blew my nose again, swallowed two more Advil and chewed on a protein bar, hoping to amp up my flagging determination.

Assuming that Duane had come here and his vehicle was nowhere to be seen meant only one thing to me. He must have driven onto the Double G property. What other explanation could there be? If Duane had taken my advice and somehow secured a search warrant, he certainly could have done that. So, what should I do?

Considering the fact that I felt like death warmed-over, it took colossal willpower to summon enough energy to begin my search while the analytical part of my brain cautioned me that I was in no shape to be roaming around the desert hunting for him.

I forced myself to concentrate, making sure I had plenty of tissues, another protein bar and my cell phone.

I secreted the tiny LED flashlight in my bra and, just as a precaution, I shoved my handy-dandy knife into the side of my boot and slipped my handgun into my zippered coat pocket. I tried to hydrate myself as best as I could by drinking another bottle of water before sliding outside into the icy wind. I never in a million years thought I would long for those sizzling, furnace-like days of summer, but I sure did as I zipped my jacket chin-high. Then I stealthily made my way towards the gate—fully expecting it to be locked—and mentally prepared myself to climb through the barbed-wire fence. Much to my surprise, I discovered the gate unlatched and standing open a few inches with the heavy chain dangling towards the ground. What was this?

On full alert, I swung around in a circle, checking in every direction. With my pulse thudding in my throat, I slipped through the gate and closed it behind me. Walking as quietly as I could manage, I kept close to the bushes along the side of the road, looking behind me every few minutes, until I came to the impressive grove of trees I'd seen from the hilltop behind the mansion. Under ordinary circumstances, I would have taken the time to savor and photograph the natural beauty of the secluded pond hidden below the leafy overhang, but I only had time for a cursory glance as I moved ahead and the Gold Queen mansion materialized in front of me.

I could not have ordered up a spookier setting than the sight of the pointed gables silhouetted against the leaden sky. My growing apprehension intensified with the addition of the keening wind rattling the leaves of the cottonwood trees. My footsteps slowed. What on earth was I doing coming out here alone? I could only chalk it up to the fact that I wasn't thinking straight. I hesitated, carefully searching the area before stepping into the clearing. There didn't appear to be any signs of life, so I promised myself that I would take a quick look around and if I didn't find anything to indicate that Duane had been here, I was gone, pronto.

My search of the mansion's perimeter netted me nothing. Might as well face it. I was wrong. Duane had not taken my challenge after all and for that I felt a small measure of relief. But then, I thought, with a resurgence of angst, where was he? I retraced my steps towards the driveway. Thunder rumbled overhead and a few big drops smacked the top of my head. I looked skyward at the churning clouds, thinking that I needed to break this bad habit of getting myself caught in thunderstorms.

When the toe of my boot hit the edge of a deep tire track, I stumbled and when I regained my balance, I stared down at the cluster of depressions crisscrossing the clearing. It was only then that something penetrated my tired brain. There were an awful lot of them. I walked around the area slowly, studying the clear tread indentations that would most likely not have been as visible on a dry surface. There looked to be three different sets of tracks, which told me that the vehicles must have been here within the last twenty-four hours since the rain started. I knelt down and traced my fingers along the uneven grooves. There were two distinct sets of tire patterns, and a third that appeared to have a slightly narrower tread. Most likely one set of treads belonged to Nelson Trotter's pickup, but what about the other one? Could it belong to Duane's patrol vehicle? Judging by the sheer number and depth of the larger tire tracks leading from the road, it appeared that at least one of the vehicles had been back and forth several times.

I rose and noticed that one set curved towards the southeast side of the mansion. I shoved my cold hands into my coat pockets, followed them around the corner and looked up at the shuttered windows on the second floor. Even on this cold, windy afternoon I could clearly hear the continuous hum of the air conditioners. How strange was that?

I turned in the direction of the path I'd used to climb the hill behind the house and paused. Something seemed different. Ahead of me, parked at the edge of the thick foliage, stood a brown horse trailer. I searched my memory but could not remember seeing it there on my first visit. Interesting. The fresh tracks led right to it.

My heart began to beat a little faster as I approached the trailer and walked around it, finally stopping at the rear door. I peered through the slats. Empty. Seemed innocuous enough but…why park it here when the barn was near the ranch house two miles away? I looked around it searching for some answers to my questions when I noticed something curious. To me, it seemed as if the fountain grass leading towards the direction of the pond appeared to be slightly crushed down on either side, as if a vehicle had recently driven over it. If the horse trailer hadn't been parked in this particular spot, I would have never noticed this aberration from the clearing, which meant that was most likely the intent.

I closed my eyes momentarily, knowing what I needed to do. With trepidation, I steeled myself and high-stepped along the path of mashed, wet grass that led me into a dark tunnel of tamarisk and cottonwood trees. When I finally emerged into the shadowy light, the hair on the nape of my neck literally stood on end when a muted flash of lightning illuminated something big almost submerged in the murky water. "Oh no!" I gasped, tears filling my eyes. I flinched sideways at the ear-splitting crack of thunder that followed and, within seconds, another bolt of greenish lightning confirmed my worst fears. The familiar gold-and-maroon emblem of the Yavapai County Sheriff's Office clearly identified the vehicle tipped on its side as Duane's patrol SUV.

CHAPTER 24

For I don't know how long, all I could do was stare in abject horror. My heart drumming painfully in my throat, I rushed to the water's edge, but then stopped and stripped off my coat, socks and boots and rolled up my jeans before splashing into the cold pond. Totally fixated on my goal, I barely noticed the water temperature. "Dear God, please make him be alive!" My feet sank in the mud and the water was up to my thighs by the time I grasped the door handle. Rigid with fear, my breath ragged, I tried to prepare myself for the worst—the sickening vision of Duane's lifeless body.

Gingerly, I peered through the half-open driver's side window. Aided by multiple lightning flashes I saw no one inside and exhaled a slow, shuddery breath. While immensely relieved that he hadn't drowned, alarm gripped me as the next thought reared its ugly head. Where was he? I scanned the pond, but saw nothing floating on the surface and no signs of life except a few cows staring back at me from the opposite bank. Whoever had driven his vehicle here had executed a piss-poor attempt to hide it. Was there any doubt now that Duane had lost his confrontation with Nelson Trotter? Plagued by intense guilt, I had to consider the unthinkable likelihood that Trotter may have killed him or, at best, he might still be alive and was being held prisoner inside the old mansion along with Holly, Lindsay and possibly other victims.

On shore once again, I tapped out a series of photos and then used my coat to dry my feet. I slipped on my socks and boots, but my sopping, wet jeans clung to my legs like cold snakeskin as I collapsed onto the ground. Overcome with emotion, I just sat there and wept. I wondered if it was possible to feel any worse physically and emotionally. This whole fiasco was my fault. If I had kept my big mouth shut and not baited Duane, he would have never felt compelled to prove that he could master the situation single-handedly.

Too late to un-ring that bell. I needed to get my shit together. I brushed the tears from my cheeks with the sleeve of my coat, dug out tissues and blew my nose, thinking that I had what I'd come for—proof that Duane had been here. No way could this wait until Marshall showed up later tonight. It was time to seek help from somebody somewhere right now. Would the Prescott Police or a sheriff from a neighboring county respond to my call? Had Ada called the Department of Public Safety?

I checked the time. It was closing in on five o'clock, but seemed later than that because of the charcoal clouds and overhang of trees. I rose unsteadily and started for the embankment, but froze when I heard the familiar clatter of a diesel engine on the road. Seized by sudden panic, I crouched behind a bush and glanced up in time to see the familiar Last Roundup white pickup and trailer speed by. There was just enough daylight for me to make out the square-jawed silhouette of Nelson Trotter behind the wheel. Cognizant of the fact that the ex-con had most likely done something unthinkable to Duane, my inner voice screamed loudly for me to run. It would be downright perilous if he caught me trespassing on the ranch again, and this time with no phone reception to save me.

Cautiously, I pushed myself upward and with a final backward glimpse at the dark outline of Duane's capsized SUV in the pond, crept towards the road, but once again the heartbreaking vision of Ada and her children invaded my consciousness, turning my feet to lead. Nelson Trotter was not only a revolting pervert—he was a murderer.

Fueled by blinding rage, I abandoned my escape plans and retraced my steps to the horse trailer. When I looked towards the old mansion, I was shocked to see that the double gates on the chain-link fence stood wide open and the truck and trailer were backed up to the door. What the hell was going on? Not at the best angle to observe, I craned my neck and watched Nelson Trotter shoving something into the trailer. I got the impression that whatever it was must be heavy by the way he appeared to be straining and pushing with his shoulder. My heart rate spiked at the thought of what he might be stuffing inside.

He finally completed his task and disappeared inside the house. Within seconds, he rushed out carrying two plastic bags, which he also threw into the back of the trailer. He slammed the doors shut before hurrying inside again. He reappeared several more times, carelessly hurling boxes into the bed of the pickup. Then, he trotted to the cab, vaulted inside and turned in the direction of the bone yard. He sure appeared to be in a hurry. He'd left the gates open and I had not noticed him lock the door, which signaled his intention to return. I looked towards the road. Did I have enough time to get out of here before then?

Perhaps because my fever-numbed brain was working in slow motion, it took me another couple of seconds to grasp what I'd just witnessed. Was he in the process of destroying evidence? He must know that his lame attempt to conceal whatever he'd done to Duane would soon be discovered. And if my crazy theory was true, did that also mean that he would be moving his other victims somewhere else before additional law enforcement descended on the ranch? "Son-of-a-bitch!" By the time Marshall got here there might be zero evidence left to support my allegations? I'd look like an idiot. But, how would Trotter arrange to get rid of Duane's vehicle by tomorrow? Or, would he play dumb and say that Duane must have run off the road in the storm? By that time he could have disposed of the body and there would be no telltale tire tracks. My thoughts hopscotched around as I stood there trying to decide what to do. Was I really in any condition to make important decisions on anything?

My choice was made for me when a deafening crack of thunder split the heavens open and a barrage of rain came down hard and fast. A powerful blast of wind almost knocked me off my feet and hailstones the size of golf balls pelted me. I raised my hands to protect my face and thought I would pass out at the sight of a black, circular cloud descending towards the house. Good God! Was that a tornado?

Self-preservation kicked in, so I chose the only shelter available and launched myself inside the horse trailer. The top protected me from the majority of the downpour, but unfortunately, it had open side slats, so I was still bombarded by stray hailstones pinging and hammering against the metal trailer. Facedown in a pile of dried horse manure, my arms covering my head, all I could do was lie there and pray while the shrieking wind violently rocked the trailer like an out-of-control carnival ride. It seemed to rage on forever while I struggled to keep panic at bay. I flinched at the cacophony of booms, crashes, thumps and finally the sound of breaking glass. I had just decided that I was probably a goner when the volley of hail abruptly ceased. The rain diminished to a drizzle, the wind calmed and then complete silence ensued. Ever so slowly I pushed to my knees. Still giddy with shock, I edged a look outside towards the house, half- expecting it to be in ruins. It appeared to be intact except for a section of overhang above the front porch that had collapsed where the supports had broken.

There was debris everywhere. The whirlwind had scattered the piles of lumber like matchsticks, buckets of paint and other building supplies lay strewn about and I was astounded to see that the twister or microburst had picked up a ladder and hurled it partway through one of the ground-floor windows. That explained the horrendous crash I'd heard. There were also several downed trees; mounds of roof shingles, torn branches and leaves littered the flooded clearing along with mangled sections of the chain-link fence.

Thanking my lucky stars that I was still alive, I slid to the ground, thinking I'd best get out of there because I had no idea if or when Nelson Trotter might return. Moving as fast as my rubbery legs would carry me, I headed for the driveway only to pause and listen intently. Was that the wind or was I hearing the sound of a car approaching from the direction of Buckskin Trail? It wasn't the wind. Paralyzed by indecision, I just stood there as the engine noise grew louder and louder. I finally willed myself into action. My pulse pumping madly, I hightailed it back to the horse trailer, ducked behind it and peeked around just in time to see a silver SUV cruise past, splashing through deep puddles and weaving around the rubble.

Uh-oh. Walking in plain sight along the driveway was now out of the question so my original path towards the pond now seemed like the best and safest route out of here. I took off and got about twenty or thirty feet into the trees and paused. *A silver SUV!* I had to know who was driving it. I swiveled around, ignoring the little voice whispering frantically in my ear, "*Don't do this!*"

In the fast-fading light, I crept towards the front of the trailer for a better view and jerked to a halt. Nelson Trotter had returned. He and another man, whose back was to me, stood close together and appeared to be engaged in deep conversation. I could hear their muffled voices and fervently wished I could make out all of what they were saying, but I could only pick up bits and pieces like, "…vital for the success of…" and "…don't have much time…" then, "get him back here…" before they disappeared inside the house. Bring back whom? Duane? Did they have him restrained at another location? But if so, why bring him to the Gold Queen where it appeared they were in the process of clearing out the old house?

Moments later each returned with additional boxes,

which were loaded into the trailer and truck bed. After several more trips, they vanished inside again and, within seconds, a porch light flashed on and then a dim glow appeared in one of the upstairs curtained windows. Their surreptitious actions confirmed my suspicion that they were busy removing incriminating evidence. Infused with anxious frustration that I had no way to report my suspicions to anyone, all I could do was stand there helplessly as they appeared again and hurriedly heaved more items into their vehicles. Nelson Trotter then saluted his cohort and jumped in his truck, shouting, "Meet you back here in an hour!" then took off again while the second man turned to lock the front door. It wasn't until that moment, with his features faintly lit beneath the porch light, that the realization of who I was looking at finally sunk in. Dumbfounded, I stared at the familiar face of Dr. Raju Mallick.

CHAPTER 25

Still trying to wrap my head around what I'd just witnessed, I shrank back behind the trailer as Dr. Mallick's SUV rumbled past. My mind pivoted back to earlier in the week when I'd seen him talking to Nelson Trotter at the gate near Youth Oasis. And last night after the open house while sitting in my Jeep, I wondered, could it have been the taillights of the doctor's vehicle that I'd seen speeding towards the Double G? I ran a hand over my clammy forehead. This was insane! None of it made any sense. What could his possible connection be with Nelson Trotter? Was the doctor part of the human-smuggling conspiracy? If he was, did it mean he had been the second man at the Family Dollar store the night Holly vanished? His vehicle matched Aleta Gomez's description.

In the sudden silence, I turned back towards the pale glow in the upper window of the old house and wondered if it was possible that they were just removing construction materials from the interior. But if so, why now and why the rush? More importantly, however, was finding out what had happened to Duane Potts. While I was only guessing about his whereabouts, it was possible that he was being confined inside at this very moment. The logical thing to do would be to wait for Marshall to get a search warrant and then accompany him here tomorrow during the daylight hours. But, did I have time to wait? When the two men returned in an hour would they be transferring the women and possibly Duane to another location? I could not allow that to happen. Glancing at the lighted window again, I knew what I had to do and there wasn't much time. I needed to get inside before they returned. Fortunately, Mother Nature had recently provided the means to do just that.

The thickening dusk made it almost impossible for me to safely navigate the now treacherous space between my present location and the house, so I dug out my miniature LED flashlight and picked my way around the minefield of debris, sloshing through water and mud. It wasn't lost on me that all the tire tracks were now history.

When I arrived at the window where the ladder protruded, I paused and listened, hearing nothing but the constant drone of the A/C units. Feeling the cool air wafting from the interior of the house, I wondered again why Nelson Trotter needed to keep the place so cold. I took a firm hold of the ladder and tugged with every ounce of energy I could muster. After several agonizing tries, I was finally able to drag it out onto the ground.

Panting like a dog on a hot summer day, I fought off another dizzy spell and then searched around until I found a small piece of lumber, which I used to clear away the remaining shards of glass jutting from the frame. I stuck my head in the opening and trained my flashlight beam around what appeared to be the living room. Faded Persian rugs covered the hardwood floors; photos and paintings adorned the walls and it looked downright ghostly with the furniture draped in sheets. Because my nose was so stuffed up, it took a few seconds for me to become aware of the sickly sweet odor. I inhaled several times thinking that it smelled like flowers or perfume combined with an underlying foul odor, as if something was rotting. Had an animal somehow gotten in the house and died? Or perhaps a skunk was trapped under the house. One thing was certain: I did not smell fresh paint. I started to climb in the window, but then hesitated. Did I really want to do this? Entering a deserted old house alone felt like something a bunch of stupid teenagers would do in a low-budget horror film.

To be honest, if the fierce desire to find Duane and also prove my theory about Holly had not been so strong, I don't think I would have continued, but Duane's life could be at stake so there was no time to be faint of heart.

I checked the time. Forty-five minutes before they returned. Just to be safe, I'd give myself thirty minutes tops. There should not be any danger with both men now gone, right? I would simply make a sweep of the house and if I found nothing suspicious I'd be on my way. With a stern lecture to myself to not overthink the situation, I eased inside before I could talk myself out of it.

The irony of the moment was not lost on me. My longing to see the interior of the magnificent old mansion had been granted in the most peculiar fashion. The moment I stepped into the room, a wordless knowing settled over me likc a warm veil. Someone or something was here. Call it second sight, whatever, but deep inside I sensed a distinct presence in the house. I remained motionless, my breathing shallow, waiting, but only silence met my ears. Was I feeling the forlorn spirit of Glendine Higgins trapped within these ancient walls, or was it something more sinister? Had she arrived at my side to issue a warning or to welcome me?

"Is anyone here?" I called in a tense whisper. Apprehensive, I stood, listening. Dead silence. I took a quick look around and then moved to the next room. "Duane, are you in here?" Still hearing nothing, I shined the light around a small dining area and then entered a large kitchen. First, I checked out the wooden door to my left. The black knob appeared to be tarnished and dated, but the padlock looked new and shiny. Of course, I wondered why the door was locked, but with such limited time, I needed to continue. A quick peek into the cupboards yielded the usual dishes, cups and glassware. Drawers contained flatware and cooking utensils. The refrigerator held only a few cans of soda and a six-pack of beer. Otherwise, there were no signs the kitchen was in use. There went my theory. People have to eat, so if Nelson Trotter was holding these women hostage, how was he feeding them? Severe doubt gnawed at me, and when I'd finished my examination of the ground floor I knew three things for sure. There was nothing to suggest anyone was living in the house. I saw no evidence that any recent painting had been done or any other renovations. And unlike Nelson Trotter's warning that it was "too dangerous" to enter the house, everything looked perfectly safe to me. So why all the construction materials piled up outside, and where had the boxes and plastic bags come from that the two men had hauled out of here? It made me feel queasy knowing that

Dr. Mallick had some involvement in whatever shenanigans Nelson Trotter was up to.

I arrived at the foot of the steep staircase and shined my light up into the shadowy abyss. Tally was right. It looked spookier than hell. I had to give myself a mental ass-kicking. "Get a grip and get this over with." I'd climbed only a few steps when I succumbed to a horrific coughing fit that left me wheezing and weak-kneed. The excuse that I was just too sick to continue gave me a perfect out, but the urge to satisfy my unquenchable curiosity propelled me upwards. With each step I took the air temperature grew noticeably colder and the overpowering combination of flowers or heavy perfume and something else had my stomach clenching. What could have caused such a foul smell and why was the house so friggin' cold?

When I reached the landing, I veered off to my left, exploring several bedrooms and a dated bathroom featuring a pedestal sink with old, rusted fixtures and a chipped claw foot tub. Nothing of interest here. In the deep hush engulfing the old mansion, I moved along the hallway in the opposite direction, but stopped in my tracks. At the far end of a long corridor a dim ribbon of light shown beneath a door, capturing my attention.

I blew out a shaky breath and, with my pulse rushing madly, I tiptoed to the door and extinguished my flashlight. I bent down and felt icy air flowing along the floor. How totally weird. I leaned my ear against the door but heard only a humming sound. I listened for a couple of minutes and then, not knowing what to expect, I wrapped my hand around the crystal knob. The hinges creaked and squealed as I pushed the heavy wooden door open and peeked inside.

As my startled gaze roamed around the cavernous, ornately furnished room, I gasped in surprise. This room was different from all the others. Besides being as icy as a meat locker, it looked downright palatial, fit for a queen. Beneath rose-colored overhead lights and bathed in the golden glow of countless candles stood a massive, canopied bed draped with sheer saffron-colored curtains that wafted gently in the breeze from the window air conditioners. Every piece of furniture held vases stuffed with fresh roses. *And they were all pink.* Nelson Trotter's flower-filled truck the day I'd seen him at the old church entered my mind. So, this had been his final destination. Even though the scent of the blooms was overpowering, there was no escaping the other smell—a putrid odor so strong I had to pinch my nostrils to keep from gagging.

My mouth went dry as chalk when I spotted the dark outline of a human form lying on the bed behind the gently billowing curtains. At first my mind rejected what my eyes were seeing. Who would be sleeping in this frigid room? "Hello?" I called tentatively. No answer. "Duane?" No answer. "Holly?" No answer. No movement.

I had to dig deep to summon the nerve to approach the bed and part the curtains. Shock nearly choked me as I stared down at what looked to be a sleeping woman dressed in a long, sequin-covered gold gown. She lay still as a stone and did not appear to be breathing. A thin, gauzy material covered her face. Creepy-crawlies erupted all over my body. Who the hell…? She looked like a mannequin, or an Egyptian princess or…maybe the Gold Queen?

On the far side of the bed stood the oddest-looking apparatus I'd ever seen. It appeared to be about the size of a refrigerator except it had colored lines and numbers blinking on a monitoring device. It also had numerous dials, pulsing lights and an array of tubes sticking out of the sides. It looked like a piece of futuristic equipment that might be found in the laboratory of a crazed scientist.

My confused thoughts tumbled over one another. The bizarre scene was so removed from what I had expected to find, I just stood there transfixed; I was so numb with shock that I simply could not conjure up a rational explanation. And then it dawned on me. I must have stumbled upon one of Dr. Mallick's research experiments. But, what kind of a procedure could this be? Was he experimenting with cadavers before moving on to clinical trials in humans?

It was difficult to make out many details in the low light, so I snapped on my flashlight again. It was then I realized there was a needle inserted in the woman's left hand. She was receiving an IV drip. Perplexed, I followed the line upward to a metal bar with hooks attached to the wall where several fluid-filled bags hung. On closer inspection it looked like she had some sort of electrode attached to her right hand and the wires led to the weird-looking machine.

I shook my head in confusion and swung the light over to the nightstand. It was crowded with assorted bottles and vials. I moved the beam across the labels, not recognizing the names of any of the ingredients until I noticed a small, familiar vial. PHENOXYETHANOL. Wasn't this the same substance used primarily as a preservative in cosmetics? My mind whirled in circles as chills chased up and down my spine. I glanced back at the woman in the bed. What kind of wild research was going on here? From what I could deduce, it appeared that Dr. Mallick was administering

Phenoxyethanol in combination with other drugs. But, to what end? Preserve the tissue of this deceased woman? For what purpose?

I geared myself up for what I had to do next. I reached out and touched her arm. For sure, this was a real person. The skin felt pliable and soft. I wondered how long the woman had been dead. To satisfy my own curiosity, I placed my thumb on her wrist to check for a pulse. There was none.

I lifted up one of her fingers and it moved easily, showing no sign of rigor mortis. I couldn't help but notice the enormous diamond on her ring finger and thought that for a dead person she looked pretty damn good even though the wrinkles and age spots on her hand and forearm suggested she was not a young woman. So, who was she? I shined the beam towards her cloth-covered face, which was framed by long, dark hair. Trying not to freak out, I reached out and lifted the wet material. What I saw was so repellant, I didn't know whether to throw up or faint. My legs turned spongy, my stomach heaved and it was all I could do to stifle a scream of sheer terror. A network of intravenous drip lines and electrodes was attached to her cheeks, neck and forehead. Except for the rows of stitches along her jaw and hairline, her mask-like features appeared smooth, pale and kind of waxy looking. But…the most disturbing fact of all was that the young face did not match the aging body. "Oh no." I breathed. Either this was her doppelganger or I was staring into the clear, glassy eyes of Holly Mason.

CHAPTER 26

Macabre. Insane. Revolting. It took every ounce of courage I possessed to calm my stampeding heart and not bolt from the room. I stared in horrified disbelief at the lifeless, sunken features. What kind of monsters was I dealing with here? My thoughts scattered. I didn't know what to surmise from this ghastly display. It was unfathomable that Holly Mason had been murdered so Dr. Mallick could perform some sort of bizarre experiment by attaching her face to someone else's body. The idea seemed preposterous and yet…

I was shaking so hard, I thought my knees would buckle. I really needed to sit down. Weak and burning up with fever, I reached for the bedpost and put my head down until the nausea and dizziness passed. I wished I were more clear-headed because I was unable to fathom what exactly was happening in this room. One thing was certain. My theory about Holly Mason being kidnapped for the purpose of human trafficking was dead wrong. Instead she'd fallen prey to whatever horrific experiment Dr. Mallick was conducting here. A fearful urgency compelled me to get out of this chamber of horrors before he and Nelson Trotter returned, but the thought of hiking back to the Jeep was as daunting as climbing Mount Everest.

I checked the time. Holy crap! I'd been here forty minutes. I started for the door, but then my reporter's instincts told me to slow down. It was vital that I record this evidence before it was moved or destroyed. I had no doubt that they intended to remove the corpse and dispose of all evidence before Marshall could swoop in with a search warrant.

I whipped out my cell phone and began taking photos until another violent coughing spell interrupted me. Wheezing and choking, I finally caught my breath and was in the process of wiping my watery eyes and blowing my nose when I heard the floor creak behind me. Heart catapulting to my throat, I spun around and gasped. Was I hallucinating or was that Dr. Asher Craig standing in the open doorway? I blinked hard, but the apparition stayed put. "Dr. Craig?" I asked hoarsely. "What…what are you doing here?"

"I should ask you the same question," he fired back, his handsome features crinkling in an expression of bemused censure, his eyes coolly calculating. "You don't sound well, Miss O'Dell, and you don't take advice, do you?"

"What do you mean?"

"You should have followed my orders and stayed home." He advanced towards me. "Although now that I know more about your…obstinate personality, I guess I shouldn't be surprised to find you snooping around here."

He was the last person in the galaxy I expected to see. Thunderstruck, all I could do was stare at him as he strode to my side wearing a self-congratulatory smile.

"Ah…I see you're taking pictures of her." He sighed deeply and cast an affectionate glance at the woman. "How do you like her gown? I picked it out myself. She looks radiant, don't you think?"

Blindsided by his question, I just stood there speechless, unable to comprehend his words. He sounded so sincere; his demeanor seemed so pleasant that I thought he was joking until he repeated, "Well, what do you think? Does she look magnificent or what? Very lifelike, wouldn't you say?"

Icy tendrils of fear raced down my spine when it became apparent that he was not kidding. What was wrong with him? Even though I'd only met him a few times, I considered myself a pretty good judge of character. My impression had been that he was the epitome of an intelligent, educated, compassionate and refined individual. He had exhibited nothing that would have led me to believe that he was alarmingly unhinged. I finally found my voice and pointed a shaky finger towards the bed. "Are you talking about this…grotesque…creature?"

His smile dissolved and, eyes blazing with rage, he gripped my arm. Shoving his face close to mine, he said through gritted teeth, "Don't ever speak that way about her again, do you understand me? I will not tolerate you speaking ill of my wife."

Mounting fear exploded into full-blown panic. "Your…wife?" I stammered, breathlessly.

"You heard me," he answered, a gleam of pride lighting his eyes. "She is my pride and joy. Behold," he commanded, dragging me back towards the bed. "Thanks to my unparalleled surgical skills, she has been transformed into the most beautiful woman on this earth. And now," he went on, gesturing towards the odd, pulsing mechanism, "by harnessing Dr. Mallick's expertise and applying his forward-thinking vision, I believe that miracles are possible. In time, we will bring my sweet love back into this dimension."

A million goose bumps stung the back of my neck and my insides shrank into a cold ball. This man was psychotic. Did he actually believe they were going to bring this decomposing corpse back to life? Acutely aware that I was in grave danger, I tried to jerk my arm away, but he viciously twisted my wrist and yanked the phone from my hand. Even as muddle-headed as I was, in a nanosecond it flashed through my mind that in each case, the missing women's cell phones had vanished, making it impossible to track their location. Unwilling to become another victim, I decided I wasn't going down without a fight. With no thought of consequences, I lowered my head and propelled myself upwards, hitting him hard under the chin. Yelping with pain, he stumbled backwards and the phone clattered to the floor. I scooped it up and sprinted towards the door only to run headlong into Nelson Trotter. Sheer terror sizzled through me when he gripped my shoulders firmly and pushed me back to face him. "Well, lookee who we got here!" he taunted with a demonic grin. "I knew you were gonna be trouble."

"Let go of me, you freaking lunatic!" I shouted, fighting to squirm from his grasp without success.

With a harsh laugh, he pulled me close to his muscular body. "You're a real spitfire," he hissed in my ear. "I like that."

His words chilled my blood, imagining what horrific

torment awaited me. I screamed for help and managed to almost break away, but, laughing like a maniac, he pulled me back and pinned my arms to my side just as Dr. Mallick appeared in the open doorway. He stared at me goggle-eyed. "What…is going on here?"

"We have an unwelcome visitor that we must deal with," Dr. Craig answered coldly, rubbing his chin. With a death grip on my phone, I frantically pressed for 911, but he yanked it from my hand again. Crap! Bad move. I should have left it locked.

"I can't have you interfering in my work." He addressed Dr. Mallick tersely, pointing across the room at the monitoring device. "Make sure she didn't tamper with anything," before turning back to Nelson. "What's the boyfriend's name again?"

"Bradley Talverson, big shot cowboy over at the Starfire Ranch. Everybody calls him Tally."

A wily expression stealing over his features, he crooned, "He'll be getting a text from you now, Miss O'Dell." He scrolled through my contact list and started typing. "Too bad you've been called out of town on an important new assignment and won't be back for several days. How does that sound?"

He had no way of knowing that Tally was probably on his way to my place right now. Struggling harder to free myself, I shouted, "He won't buy it. He's smarter than any of you nutjobs."

The deadly gleam entering his eyes made me wither. "We'll see about that." He nodded curtly at Nelson. "Proceed with the plan. You know the drill."

"Hang on…there's no placc to lock her—"

"It doesn't matter," he snapped. "Stick with the plan. She can't get out."

"Wanda's right," Nelson yelled in my ear. "Our whole lives, all we do is take orders from your high and mighty ass and you never do any of the dirty work."

Coldly, Dr. Craig responded, "Shut up. Unless the two of you want to go back to jail, you'll do as you're told." He speared Nelson with a contemptuous glare. "Stop complaining. I pay you well and don't tell me you don't enjoy the perks of our special endeavor."

A defeated sigh. "You're the boss."

Nelson tightened his grip on me. Would they be openly discussing my fate if there were even a glimmer of hope that I would escape whatever mayhem they had in store for me? I renewed my struggle against Nelson, thinking wildly that if I could somehow get my right hand free, I could reach the firearm in my jacket. But just how did I intend to take down three men at once? Odds of escaping from this living nightmare seemed slim to none, but I had to try. I bit down on Nelson's fingers as hard as I could and hung on while he howled like an animal. Amid a barrage of expletives, he roared, "Meddling bitch!" before he punched me in the jaw and slammed my head against the wall. Stars exploded in my head and black shadows swirled before my eyes. Seconds before I lost consciousness, I heard Dr. Craig's terse command, "You insufferable moron! Don't injure her face! Glenny may need it soon."

CHAPTER 27

Half-awake. Asleep. Haunted by disturbing nightmares. I struggled to wake, but it felt like my eyelids were glued shut. I surrendered again to blessed sleep. I don't know how much time passed until I finally opened my eyes. What was that wavering light in my bedroom? Groggy and weak, I pushed myself to a sitting position, confused. Nothing looked familiar. Was I still dreaming? Slowly, very slowly, it began to pierce my foggy brain that I was not at home. Ropes of fear tightened around my heart as my gaze traveled around the shadowy room. Flickering candles tucked back in three arched alcoves explained the erratic light. Besides the candles, two dim wrought-iron fixtures mounted high against roughly-textured rock walls provided barely enough illumination for me to see my immediate surroundings. What was this place? It looked positively medieval, like some sort of ancient dungeon.

I tossed aside the blankets, swung my legs over the side of a small cot and sat there staring at the uneven stones on the floor until the surge of dizziness passed. Still feeling weak and sick, I wondered how long I'd been sleeping? I looked around the unfamiliar room again. With no outside light source, there was no way to know if it was day or night.

For some reason, the first thing that jumped to mind was the padlocked door I'd seen in the kitchen of the Gold Queen mansion. So...this must be the basement. Even with my stuffy nose, I could smell the musty odor of age and feel the chill, damp air, which confirmed my suspicions. Thoughts of the first missing girl, Krystal Lampton, popped into my mind. Was this where she'd been held hostage for two weeks before she had eventually escaped and jumped from a second-floor window? How had she avoided being caught by Nelson Trotter? Thinking about him triggered my memory. Everything came rushing back—the horrifying discovery of the candlelit room with the decaying corpse, my violent encounter with him and Dr. Craig. That was bad enough, but then I was struck by the profound realization that I still had no clear-cut understanding of what was actually taking place in that room.

My eyes now accustomed to the faint light, I focused on a small table nearby. Was I seeing correctly? I counted four bottles of water, a bowl of fruit and a box of cookies. Really? How generous of them to take such good care of me. Inexplicably, the story of Hansel and Gretel being fattened-up by the evil witch crept into my mind. So, they were planning to keep me alive...at least for a little while. My head throbbed painfully when I attempted to get up. I reached back and gingerly touched the tender goose egg on my scalp. Damn! Was that the reason I felt so woozy, or had Dr. Craig given me some kind of drug to keep me quiet?

"What have you done to yourself this time, O'Dell?" I moaned, burying my face in my hands while I struggled to organize my thoughts. If I only had my notes with me, it would make it so much easier to... *Wait!* Wait just a flippin' minute! It seemed like a giant leap of logic, but could it be possible that the elegantly-dressed corpse was the year-old, preserved body of Glendine Higgins? And... she had once been Dr. Craig's wife? When? Why did no one in town know about this? Why hadn't Clara or Wanda mentioned it? Why would a person of his stature marry a bitter, old recluse with a disfigured face? And why had he talked about her as if she were still alive? I stared blankly for a few seconds as pieces of the frightening puzzle began to fall into place. Was I way out in left field or was it conceivable that Dr. Craig was the mastermind behind the disappearance and murders of Krystal, Holly Mason and Lindsay Cole for the express purpose of...what? Using their faces as a substitute for Glendine's damaged features? But, for what reason? It seemed impossible, but it was the only plausible conclusion I could reach. And did he seriously think that Dr. Mallick was going to bring her lifeless corpse back to life where she would enjoy her new and improved face? What kind of a sick, psychotic mind would dream up a scenario that preposterous?

Dr. Craig's seemingly innocuous remark about the supple texture of my skin suddenly took on a new and monstrous meaning. If I coupled that fact with his expression of tender malice when he'd demanded that Nelson Trotter not injure my face, it made my gut contract in pure horror. What was it Dr. Craig had said just before I had lost consciousness? *"Glenny may need it soon."* The answer came to me in a flash. Was there any doubt that he intended to keep me captive until he needed my face for his sinister experiment on the cadaver? So, that answered the question of what happened to the three missing women. The scream of horror rose in my throat, but I clapped a hand over my mouth and willed myself to calm down. Breathe. Relax. Breathe. I reminded myself that panic was the natural enemy of rational thinking and would not solve my dilemma.

One thing I knew with fierce certainty. I had failed spectacularly. Somehow I needed to find a way out of this place before Nelson Trotter returned. I shuddered with revulsion at the thought of being alone with him. Remembering the taste of his blood in my mouth when I'd locked my teeth on his hand had me swallowing back waves of nausea. And that spawned the thought of how I'd gotten here. With a jerk of alarm, I wondered what he might have done to me while I was unconscious. Frantically, I patted down my clothing. The realization that I was still fully dressed and nothing appeared to be disturbed left me giddy with relief. But then, my spirits wilted. Son-of-a-bitch! My jacket was missing. I checked underneath the blankets and all around the cot. Nothing. With my weapon gone I had nothing with which to protect myself from the loathsome predator. Hastily, I checked my bra and, with sigh of triumph, pulled the tiny LED flashlight out. Next, I checked my boot. My knife was still secreted there. Not much of a defensive weapon, but better than nothing.

Spurred to action, I rose and drank a full bottle of water. Far from hungry, I forced myself to eat a banana and a handful of cookies, which gave me a little boost of energy. Okay. Time to figure a way out.

Aiming the bluish beam around, I made my way through the arched doorway and almost immediately spotted the stone steps. I shined the light up expecting to see a door, but instead saw only the blank wall. What? Steps to nowhere? But, when I moved the beam higher, it revealed a trapdoor in the ceiling. My breath deserted me when a pervasive sensation of dark foreboding paralyzed me. I wasn't in the basement of the Gold Queen. Had I gotten what I wished for? The clear recollection of Nelson Trotter strong-arming the door upwards before descending into the crypt beneath the old church streaked through my mind.

I climbed the eight steps to the top and pushed upwards with all my might even though I already knew it was a futile gesture. Nevertheless, I shoved and strained until I could no longer hold my arms above my head. Afraid of bringing on another coughing fit, I decided it was better to conserve what little energy I had left. Breathing erratically, I leaned my forehead against the wall, fully accepting the indisputable fact that my situation was worse than first imagined. I was in big trouble and I had no one to blame but myself. Once again, I'd waltzed right into a horrific predicament with my eyes wide open. When would I ever learn? Loving thoughts of Tally, family, friends, and my cats waiting for my return, paraded through my mind, piercing my heart with searing anguish. Odds were good that I would never see any of them again. Tears scalded my eyes and a sob rose in my throat. Fervently, I prayed to God for help as the irony of the situation occurred to me. Once again, I was in the perfect place to pray. And I did. Hard.

I have no explanation for the sudden sense of warm peace that enveloped me. Perhaps it was my subconscious mind, perhaps something else, but I felt it was telling me not to give in to the icy panic filling my chest or I would have no chance of survival. Somehow I needed to gather my wits and clear the cobwebs from my brain so I could think straight.

Desperately, I turned and pointed the light in the opposite direction and stiffened with surprise. Shrouded in deep shadows stood two rows of wood and stone coffins raised above the floor on short concrete pedestals. The casket-filled room matched the description Clara had recounted to me. There was no denying that I was trapped in the crypt beneath Our Lady of the Desert. That ominous revelation spawned another. Had she and Thena toured this windowless tomb in total darkness? Doubtful. I ran the flashlight beam up and down the wall until I found what I was looking for set back in a corner behind the railing. I reached out and flipped the light switch. Four naked bulbs bathed the space in pale light.

Morbid fascination led me down the stairs to walk among the final resting places of the departed souls. Focusing the flashlight beam, I walked along the row, noting the names and dates on the caskets: Glen Marlow Higgins, Anna Marie Kerrigan Higgins, Gary Morris Higgins, Gwyn Anna Higgins Trotter and several other names I did not recognize. But when I came across the plaque on the ornately patterned concrete vault of Father Robert Alton Kerrigan, I stopped in my tracks. The sobering phrase Clara had recited to me now held significantly more meaning. "***We were what you are; and what we are, you will be.***" While I knew the statement was true, I had no desire to join them in this silent, lonesome burial chamber.

At the far end of the row, I came across a tiny coffin resting on a shelf. I leaned in to read the inscription and my throat closed with emotion. ***Grace Irene Foley, Never Forgotten, Forever Missed.*** The dates showing her death at three months established that she was Glendine's deceased infant daughter. How tragic. Clara's description of this place was right on-target. It definitely was like visiting a dark, dirty and forgotten underground cemetery.

I remembered Glendine's final wish that she be cremated, so I trailed the light over urns of various sizes and shapes tucked into arched alcoves until I came to a beautiful, cream-colored vase adorned with flowers and angels. It looked fairly new and sat next to a plain wooden box with no identifying name. The dedication on the ceramic urn read: ***In loving memory of Glendine Marie Higgins—may she find peace in death that was denied in life.*** I wondered if the simple box adjacent to her urn held the ashes of the young priest for whom she'd mourned her entire sad life. The fact that the two containers sat alone and close together in the little domed nook seemed to confirm Glendine's final wish that she spend eternity with her first and only love. I hoped that was the case, but if my suspicions were correct, her earthly ashes did not reside there. That thought reminded me of Holly's deteriorating face sewn onto the older woman's corpse. A tremor of horror raced through me. That would be my fate if I didn't get my ass in gear. Now.

I shook off the aura of melancholy that hung over me and began to search in earnest. The area was larger than I had imagined. Along one wall, I spotted what looked like a damaged, but elaborately carved, confessional crammed between two concrete pillars. On either side of it were two doors, one solid, and one with a small, barred window. My hopes leaped. Did one of them provide a way out? I approached the first door and pulled on the handle until it creaked open. I shined the light inside, sweeping it over piles of broken pews, wooden crosses, boxes of Christmas and Easter decorations and other discarded items. In a nanosecond, I realized all the contents of the room were connected by spiderwebs the size of hammocks. A sudden movement in some of the silky grids nearby sent me leaping backwards. I shoved the door shut. Forget that! After a quick glance inside the confessional, which was also laced with webs, I quickly abandoned the idea of opening the second door. Even though the logical part of my mind cautioned me that, right now, spiders were the least of my problems, the illogical part argued there could be nothing worse than being trapped down here *and* having spiders crawling all over me. Best leave them in their secluded habitat.

Compelling myself not to give in to the dark despair that threatened to consume me, I continued exploring. At the furthest corner of the crypt, I reached a stone altar. The narrow beam revealed rows of half-burned candles, spent matchsticks and scraps of paper with faded prayers written on them. When I moved the beam higher, my pulse began to throb with excitement. Mounted against the wall was the flowing-robed figure of a woman, and above it a gilded plaque read: ***Genesis 45:7 God sent me before you to preserve for you a remnant in the earth, and to keep you alive by a great deliverance.*** "A great deliverance," I murmured in awe. So, this was the statue of St. Barbara that Clara had mentioned. Only because of her call did I understand the hidden significance of this Bible verse.

In one hand she held a silver chalice while proffering a golden cross in the other. I moved the light over her, viewing the statue from several different angles. Bravo to the sculptor, whoever he or she had been. Somehow, the artist had managed to create the impression that St. Barbara's compassionate blue eyes followed me no matter which direction I turned. Racking my brain, I tried to recall everything else Clara had told me. What was it she had said? St. Barbara was the patron saint of those at risk of sudden or violent death. Well, that certainly applied to me. But there was something else. Something else important. I closed my eyes and plumbed the depths of my memory trying to recall the contents of the conversation. Why, oh why, hadn't I paid more attention? Come on! Come on! What was it? Think! I don't know how long I stood there until the answer finally slammed into my brain. "Holy cow." If Clara's information was correct, St. Barbara held the key to my escape. Standing on tiptoe, I reached up and touched the gold cross. Hadn't Clara said that rotating it would reveal the entrance to the secret passageway that priests used to avoid being scalped by marauding Indian tribes?

But, what was the combination? One turn to the left and three to the right? Two to the right and three to the left? Or neither? I reached out and tried to rotate the cross. It didn't budge. If the story was true, the mechanism probably had not been utilized for a hundred years. I yanked harder to no avail and then stopped to rest for a few minutes before twisting again with renewed persistence. Employing every ounce of strength I could summon, I used both hands and practically hung my entire weight on it until I suddenly felt it move. Filled with elation, I murmured, "All right!" The cross now turned freely so all I had to do was remember the combination. I tried several different sequences of turns but nothing happened. I turned it again and again with no results. Finally, overwhelmed with teeth-gritting frustration, I collapsed on the floor, positive that I was doomed. Striving to calm my frenzied thoughts, I rested my forehead on my knees. Acutely aware of my dilemma, it was next to impossible to suppress my growing panic. Relax, I urged myself. Relax and open your mind.

There was no way to tell the passage of time, so I just sat there like a lump, sniffling softly before finally rising to my feet. "Help me out here, would you?" I pleaded, staring into St. Barbara's kindly eyes. "I need a miracle." I closed my eyes, and placed my hand on the cross. I allowed my mind to go blank and suddenly Clara's instructions echoed in my ears. *"Three full turns to the right and two to the left."*

With bated breath, I tilted the cross in the upright position and began the series of turns. My heart was locked in my throat with the last rotation to the left. If I had not been listening carefully, I would never have heard the faint click of a latch release. Was this for real? Hastily, I pointed the flashlight beam towards the rear of the altar and sucked in a startled breath. A dark crack approximately three feet high was visible in the rough, stone wall. Hardly daring to believe my good fortune, I flicked a glance back at St. Barbara and whispered, "Thank you."

Waves of gratitude and relief washed over me as I hurried to the spot and fell to my knees. Wow. What were the odds of being among the handful people of on earth possessing the knowledge to activate this ancient mechanical marvel? It had to be a gazillion-to-one. Hats off to whoever had designed this ingenious escape route. Eagerly, I pushed the small door open a few inches, then recoiled with surprise when a rush of warm, humid air hit me in the face.

The odd sensation triggered the memory of a recent sightseeing trip I'd taken with my family to southern Arizona. While there, we had visited Kartchner Caverns State Park near Benson. Not only had we toured one of the most magnificent caves I'd ever seen, but I had also wished I'd been around to report on the story behind its unexpected discovery. The fact that the two young cave explorers, fearing vandals would destroy the rare, pristine, "living" cave, had managed to keep its location a secret for fourteen years was in itself downright astounding.

With a sense of euphoria mixed with trepidation, I opened the door further and aimed my flashlight ahead into the black void. Not crazy about dark, enclosed spaces, I swallowed hard, struggling to dismiss my claustrophobic panic. I closed my eyes and drew in several calming breaths. Come on. You can do this. You *have* to do this. But doubt assailed me. Once I shut the door behind me was there any way to open it again? Would this passageway lead me to safety or would I wander about in dark, subterranean corridors until I starved to death?

Hesitating, I looked behind me at the outlines of the silent coffins. What choice did I have? Gruesome, certain death awaited me if I stayed. It was now or never. I moved the door a few more inches until the opening was wide enough to slip through. My hand shook as I moved the light in a wide circle. From Clara's description, I had been expecting some sort of man-made tunnel, but the notion that this might be an undiscovered cave was more credible when I caught sight of multi-colored stalactites drooping from the craggy ceiling. I blinked in amazement. Fascinating. And then something occurred to me as I stared down at my trusty little flashlight. Just how big was this cavern? From what little I knew, some caves could extend for miles consisting of multiple passages, irregular rooms, cramped holes, dead-end tunnels and sometimes underground streams or lakes. Because the air smelled fresh and it was damp and significantly warmer than the crypt, it seemed to confirm that this might very well be a "wet, still forming" cave like Kartchner Caverns, and most likely there was a second entrance somewhere. That fact would correspond with the legendary escape route for the endangered priests. But, how in the world did they know how to find their way around with no light? How was I going to find the exit and how long would it take? All questions I was about to find the answers to.

My mouth dry as sand, I dropped to all fours and began to crawl inside. Then I stopped myself. Wait. Be smart here. I backed out of the opening and made my way to the candlelit room where I'd started. I tugged the sheet from the cot, and then using my knife, I slit it in half and laid it on the floor. Next, I set the three remaining water bottles on it and added the fruit and cookies. Then I rolled them all into a snug pouch and tied it around my waist before wrapping one of the blankets around my shoulders for warmth. Better. Wiser. Now I was ready to roll.

My eyes now accustomed to the dim light, I marched purposefully back towards the door before I could change my mind. I had just passed by the second wooden door I had opted not to explore earlier when I thought I heard a scratching sound. My steps froze. I swung around and listened closely. I waited. Nothing. Weird. Had I imagined it?

But no sooner had I turned and headed towards the altar than I heard it again. *Thump. Scratch. Scratch.* I pivoted back and about jumped out of my skin when I noticed a slight movement beneath the door. My pulse shot through the roof. What was that, a rat or some other small animal? Whatever it was appeared to be trying to dig its way out from underneath the door. I couldn't clearly make out what it was, so I cautiously stepped closer and trained the flashlight directly on it. Spellbound, I stared in disbelief at human fingers clawing at the dirt floor.

CHAPTER 28

It took me several seconds to process and react to what I was seeing. *There was a person behind that door.* "Hello?" I called out guardedly.

The fingers vanished and there was no further sound. With stealth, I approached the door and pulled on the antique brass handle. It wouldn't budge, so I yanked harder. No movement. On closer inspection, I noticed the sturdy dead bolt lock. Unbidden, the memory of Nelson Trotter entering the crypt flashed through my mind. So, I'd been right all along. This hideous place is where he imprisoned all of his victims. Except I was the only one who actually knew what a ghastly destiny awaited. And, I had a pretty good idea who was behind this door. If I was right, she'd been locked in this hellhole for three weeks.

I knocked lightly. "Is your name Lindsay Cole?"

Following a long silence, a shadowed face appeared at the barred window. "Who are you?" demanded a female voice ringing with suspicion. "Are you working with that…

that sadistic…piece of shit?"

"No way. I'm in the same fix you are." I moved closer to the door, shining the beam upwards so I could see her features more clearly though the narrow slats without blinding her while allowing her to see me as well. "My name is Kendall O'Dell. I'm an investigative reporter."

Lank hair hung around her pretty face, which was much thinner than in the photo of her I'd recently seen. She squinted back at me skeptically. "Why should I believe you?"

"Good question. How about this? I spoke on the phone with your stepmother, Patty. She told me you hitched a ride from a truck stop and went missing."

Her sunken, fear-glazed eyes grew wide. "You're for real!" She burst into tears, quavering, "I've been praying so hard that someone would come for me! Where am I? How long have I been here? Why am I here?"

In just a few sentences I filled her in on the location and date, then gave her Nelson Trotter's name, but decided not to divulge the real reason she was being held captive. Why terrify her further?

She extended both hands through the bars, weeping hysterically. "Help me! You gotta get me out of here before he comes back! Please!" Her frantic shouts escalated to the point that it was freaking me out. I reached out and wrapped my right hand around one of hers.

"Lindsay! Calm down." I commanded harshly, waiting until her shrieks diminished to whimpers. "Listen to me! This door has a dead bolt lock on it and I don't have the key. But, I'm going to try to get out of here and go for help."

Still sobbing piteously, she begged, "No! Please! Don't leave me alone with him." She clung to my hand like it was a life raft. "You gotta take me with you."

Blistering anger flared up, almost choking me. It didn't take much imagination to figure out what that pervert was doing to her. I wanted to say something to lift her spirits, but for her safety and mine, I dared not tell her about the secret passageway. The less she knew the better. If Nelson Trotter learned of my escape route there would be no hope for either of us. My heart aching with compassion, I answered mournfully, "I'm sorry. I can't do that."

She jerked her hand away and began pounding on the door. "Help me get out of here! Please! Help me!"

Steeling myself, I shouted, "Lindsay! Do you have food and water?"

I had to repeat my question several times before she regained control. "Yeah," she finally responded, sniffling. "He brings me food and candles and stuff. That psycho even brings me flowers. Can you believe that? The asshole brings me friggin' flowers!" Her caustic laughter, edging on hysteria, echoed around the crypt.

Fearing she was close to losing it again, I called out, "I have to go now." I couldn't tell her that I had no way of knowing if I'd ever actually make it out or ever return to rescue her.

"Wait!" She extended a hand towards me again. "You promise you'll come back for me?" she implored beseechingly.

I squeezed her fingers and forced a positive note, pledging: "I promise." Weighed down by the awesome and unexpected responsibility of saving this poor girl, I prayed I'd be able to keep my promise. My mind zipped back to the sickening memory of Holly Mason's deteriorating facial skin and I suspected Dr. Craig would need a fresh face soon to fulfill his ghastly obsession to beautify Glendine's moldering corpse. And that brought to mind more questions without answers. What on earth was really going on in that room? Why did I get the impression that he was actually in love with a dead woman?

A sudden *clank* and scraping sound banished all thought. "Oh my God!" Lindsay gasped. "It's him!" I thought my heart was going to stop. No sooner had the words left her mouth than the trapdoor at the other end of the crypt swung upward and daylight poured in the opening. For a split second, I thought about running towards the blessed sunlight, running towards freedom, but just as quickly realized I was no match for Nelson Trotter.

Lindsay was still clenching my hand in a painful grip, so I jerked my hand free, murmuring fiercely, "I'll be back. Don't say anything." With the sting of excruciating fear and guilt, I left her there sobbing. I sprinted past the altar and without thinking about the consequences for another second I ducked through the opening, turned, closed the secret door with a definitive thud and switched off my light. Barely breathing, my pulse pounding furiously, I leaned my ear against it expecting to hear Lindsay's screams and him pounding against the other side of the little door, but I heard no other sounds.

Waiting there in pitch-black darkness, it seemed to take forever for my thundering heartbeat to subside. I don't know how much time passed while I crouched in abject fear of eventual discovery before I finally felt it was safe to move. My emotions a jumbled mess, I couldn't stop imagining what would have happened if he had discovered the underground passageway and me. Perhaps the legend of St. Barbara was true after all.

Gathering my fractured wits, I turned my flashlight back on, which now seemed unbearably bright in the total-blackness. I shaded my eyes and then shined the beam around the small doorframe, wondering if the clever architect had hidden a mechanism on this side. I trailed my fingers along the wall around the frame, but found nothing. And what if I had? There was no way I could return to the crypt now.

Acutely aware of the intense, impenetrable silence, the gravity of my situation sank in. The stark reality descended upon me like a thick, dark cloud that left my heart punctured with profound sadness. No second-guessing my decision now. I was on my own and flying blind. Literally. It would have been easy to succumb to the incessant dread clawing at me, but I urged myself to get a grip and get going.

At least I could stand upright in the small anteroom. Turning in a slow circle, I swept the light around, marveling at the surprising shapes and colors of the stalactites and stalagmites that surrounded me. But then I spotted something I could not identify in a far corner beneath a rocky overhang. What was that? I crept into the nook and stared in bemusement at the sight of what looked like mounds of old blankets. I knelt down and felt the material. Yep, wool blankets. Nearby sat a cluster of candles along with several wooden boxes. Curious, I opened one of them and stared in amazement at an assortment of dark stones and pieces of metal. I opened a second box filled with tiny pieces of wood and was reminded of my brother Patrick's Boy Scout Handbook describing how to start a fire with flints. This stuff had to be ancient and no doubt strategically placed here. I could imagine the fleeing clergy being in the same dilemma I was, except I had the twenty-first-century advantage of having an LED flashlight in my possession. But there was no way of knowing how long the battery would last. Six hours? Eight? Maybe ten hours max? What would I do then?

My hopes climbed when I opened a burlap sack containing more modern fire- starting paraphernalia—a box of matches like the ones my grandmother had in her kitchen. I looked over at the pile of blankets, wondering if this is where the priests had slept or…perhaps I had stumbled upon Glendine and Father Dominic's secluded lovers' hideaway. Thinking I'd probably never know the answer, I pulled out a limp, damp match and scraped it against the striker on the box. Nothing. I scraped a second one and still nothing. I tried countless more with no results. Useless.

With a sigh of frustration, I stood up and shined the light around to see if there was anything else I could use. Only then did I notice the letters carved on the far wall. I moved closer and aimed my flashlight at the words etched into the rock. ***John 12:36-37 Believe in the light while you have the light...***

Heeding the directive, I took two of the flint stones from the wooden box and slid them into the right back pocket of my jeans. But when I tried to shove four of the slender candles into the left pocket I felt something. Puzzled, I dug out a wad of papers. For a time, I stared blankly before realizing what they were—the tickets to the pancake breakfast. Tears blurred my eyes. Most likely it was an event I'd never attend. I dipped my head in sorrowful recrimination. If only I had not agreed to pursue this assignment, if only I had stayed in bed and not tried to find Duane. If only… *No!* No! I must not surrender to negative thoughts. I had two lives to save now.

Heightened determination galvanized me into action. Protectively clenching my flashlight, I turned and forged ahead, only to stop in my tracks. There were three entrances to the cave. How did the priests know which passageway to take? Two welcomed me with wide arched openings while the one to the far right looked dark, narrow and frightening. Mired in indecision, I stood there wondering what to do and then it struck me. What if the first two Bible quotes were meant to be clues, like a treasure map? Perhaps I'd best pay attention to the signs laid out before me. So far, St. Barbara had delivered me from violence and now I'd been advised to take heed of the gift of light, so logically, there must be another message around here someplace to guide me in the right direction.

I located it fairly quickly and could not help but admire the ingenuity of whoever had devised this clever system of subtle instructions. Carved on a smooth mound of rock were the words: ***Exodus: 15:6 Your right hand O LORD is majestic in power, your right hand O LORD shatters the enemy."***

"Exodus," I whispered, "Of course." Holding onto the belief that deliverance was at hand, I stooped low and entered the uninviting, dark cavity. After traveling what I calculated to be only a few hundred feet, and bumping my head untold times against the rough rock ceiling, I lost all sense of time and direction. In the absolute blackness, I couldn't tell up from down or right from left. The only sound was my tortured breathing and uneven footsteps. Feeling dizzy and disoriented, I sipped my precious water sparingly and then continued creeping along trying not to trip and fall until, much to my dismay, the passageway began to narrow. Oh, this was not good. On hands and knees, I crawled awkwardly through a constricted, zigzagging passageway that seemed to go on forever. Panting with exertion, I had to pause numerous times to rest. Oh no. Was I imagining it, or was my flashlight dimming? Fighting off tears of anxiety, I finally had to stop.

I rolled onto my back, switched off the flashlight, and clutching it against my chest, I stared into oppressive blackness so complete that I got a sober lesson in what it must feel like to be blind. Once again, I raged against my self-imposed predicament and thought about the reason I was in this terrible fix. Dr. Asher Craig. Just who was this psychotic mystery man? And what hold did he have over the Trotter twins? Remembering Nelson's spiteful assertion that he and Wanda had taken orders from him all their lives left me confused and baffled. I tried to recall everyone Tally and Clara had mentioned and could only come up with one possible answer. Could it be that Dr. Craig was actually the young cowboy that Glendine had supposedly been with the night her abusive boyfriend had mutilated her face? Who else could it be? Too tired to think anymore, I slid into a deep sleep.

When I opened my eyes after an unknown amount of time, it took me a while to first, realize that I was awake, because I could see nothing, and then to remember where I was. The complete blackness felt suffocating and it was a struggle to keep from hyperventilating. Would I ever get out of here? For some time, the acute sense of dread consumed me, holding me immobile, terrified to the point of numbness. But, I couldn't lie there forever. I moved my arm slightly and the feel of the hard flashlight against the palm of my hand gave me a faint hope. I snapped it on and shielded my eyes until they adjusted to the glare before pushing myself to a semi-sitting position in the cramped space. I needed to stay focused on my goal—freedom, Tally, all of my loved ones and my dear, sweet cats. What did the wooden plaque over Tally's desk say? **COURAGE IS BEING SCARED TO DEATH BUT SADDLING UP ANYWAY.**

With a groan of resolve, I resumed crawling along the ever-narrowing tunnel holding the flashlight in my teeth. My sore hands, rubbed raw on the sharp stones, stung like crazy, my bruised knees ached and my neck and back throbbed with pain. I wondered how much longer I could continue. Had I been in this subterranean corridor for hours or days? Feeling incredibly lost, I felt as if I were on an alien planet with no cell phone, no clock, no sunlight and no hope of returning to the sweet land above. But no sooner had that thought crossed my mind than the tunnel's circumference suddenly began to expand. Within a few yards, I was able to walk stooped over and then finally stand upright again. My sense of relief was profound, but short-lived. When I trained the light ahead at a tall, blank wall, my resolve deserted me. "It can't be." But, my eyes had not deceived me. I had reached a dead end.

CHAPTER 29

Excruciating desolation invaded every cell in my body. All I could do was stand there and stare in abject horror. How could I have made such a fatal blunder? How could I have so badly misinterpreted the biblical message literally carved in stone? Surely, the placement of the clues had been designed to guide the priests and others in harm's way to safety. My usual boldness and rational thought slowly seeped from my soul leaving me a quaking mass of pathetic cowardice. I sobbed bitterly. Never had I felt so helpless, so hopeless and so miserable. And I'd done it all to myself. "Had to get that adrenaline rush, didn't you?" I blubbered aloud. "You stupid, stupid idiot!" I wept until I couldn't weep anymore.

It was only when I stopped sniveling in self-pity that I was able to think rationally again. Wait. None of this was coincidental. Maybe I wasn't wrong. There had to be a way out of here. With supreme effort, I pulled myself together and began to search all the rocks nearby, but found no message.

Keep looking! But, after scouring every rock several times front and back, my courage began to wane again. I forced myself to stop and stand still. Okay. Think. Worst-case scenario, I could always retrace my winding route back to the room with the secret door. And then what?

Weak and spent, I sat down on one of the boulders and swept the light around the cave room, reminding myself again that if I was going to survive I must not give up. I must look for another sign. So far, there had been three, so why not a fourth? If I was interpreting the last quotation correctly, I was in the right place.

Concentrating solely on that thought, I got up and began to explore the area around me, looking behind every piece of cave art and every rock formation. I could not measure the passage of time, but my apprehension increased as the flashlight grew progressively dimmer. My hopes dashed, I had just about given up, when I shined the beam around a giant, bronze-colored column in one corner of the room. When I saw the words carved on the wall behind it I nearly shouted with joy. ***Psalm 119:105 Thy word is a lamp unto my feet, and a light unto my path.***

Expectantly, I moved the light downward and drew in a sharp breath at the sight of more candles and fire-making paraphernalia situated close to a dark, irregular-shaped depression in the ground. If I hadn't been in such a perilous situation, I would have been captivated by the astounding historical significance of what I had so far encountered. No time for that now.

I could only guess that the subtle suggestions within the quotations were calculated so that anyone familiar with the Bible would grasp the significance. Whoever designed this maze didn't want it to be obvious or the enemy would figure it out as well.

It wasn't easy squeezing through the small gap between piles of sharp rocks and the fragile column, but when I did, I aimed the light down directly into the crevice. I couldn't really see much, but my morale escalated when I felt the movement of air on my face. I glanced back at the candles, positive that they wouldn't be in this strategic location by accident. I had to be on the right track.

What choice did I have but to descend into this intimidating crater? Hesitation paralyzed me for long seconds, but I came back to the belief that others before me had embarked on this perilous journey. I hadn't seen any skeletal remains along the way, so why not assume they had been successful, right?

I picked up a stone, dropped it in the hole and heard an immediate thump. Okay. Not a far distance. I sat down and dangled my legs in the opening, gathering up my courage again. I could tell that in order to fit through the small gap, I would need to remove the stash of supplies from around my waist, which I did. I swallowed hard and looked down again. If I thought about it too long, I'd suffer a major claustrophobic episode, which might trigger one of my now rare asthma attacks. My heart was knocking so hard against my rib cage I could barely breathe as it was. "Just do it," I said aloud, gripping the flashlight in my teeth.

I said a fervent prayer and eased myself downward, dragging my makeshift bag behind me. I was only in the narrow tube of rock for a few seconds before I slid out and my feet hit sandy earth. Wow. Okay. So far so good. I tied the blanket around my waist once more and directed the light all around, stunned at the size of this new cave room. The array of rock formations was breathtaking and the ceiling was so high the beam of light didn't reach it. If I hadn't been in such a pickle, I would have been awestruck to be in the bowels of what I suspected was an unexplored cavern—most likely the same one the young explorers Wanda had chased away were searching for.

I wandered around aimlessly for a time, searching nearby rocks for another message until I stepped in something soft and gooey. I looked down, surprised to see mud. I moved the beam outward and beyond. Water. And a lot of it. "Holy cow," I murmured. Either I'd have to climb around this vast underground lake or wade through it. I picked up a stone and threw it, startled at how loud the plopping noise sounded in the dead silence. I tossed another pebble, but could not gauge how deep it was. No way did I have the stamina to swim.

The sight of all that water triggered my thirst, so I retreated to a drier area and allowed myself to drink the second half of one of the bottles. I didn't have much left, although the cave water was probably safe to drink with nothing around to contaminate it. My nerves were so jangled and frayed, my stomach in such an uproar, I had to force myself to eat the apple and two cookies before I wrapped up the remainder of my meager reserves in the blanket. Feeling only slightly rejuvenated, I moved the flashlight from side to side trying to figure out which direction I should go. I couldn't afford to meander aimlessly, because the beam was growing more and more faint. It was a monumental effort keeping panic at bay and I pleaded aloud, "Come on. Please show me another sign."

As time dragged on, I roamed around searching rocks further from the sinkhole for another clue, but found nothing. I felt like screaming from the combination of mounting fear and frustration, which would solve nothing. Inhaling as deeply as my tight chest would allow, I swung the light around again, halting in wondrous amazement when a radiant reflection caught my eye. I looked closer and my mouth fell open. "'And a light unto my path,'" I whispered, following the beam upward, illuminating what looked like a river of gleaming, white flowstone. What an idiot I was. The message had been right in front of me all along.

There was no way to scale the smooth, slick waterfall of wet rocks, so, my faith renewed, I began the arduous task of scaling the adjacent neighboring boulders. Up I went. Higher and higher. In my puny condition with the flashlight's battery life failing, the climb grew increasingly treacherous. At one point, I caught my toe in a crevice, lurched forward, and slammed my forehead into a jagged rock. Lightning bolts sizzled behind my eyes. Crying out with pain, I instinctively grabbed hold of the ledge and hung on until the dizziness passed. Shit! I'd nearly dropped the flashlight. Good God in heaven, when would this nightmare end?

Proceeding with extreme caution, it seemed that I had to pause every few feet. My ragged breathing finally brought on another coughing spell that forced me to stop until it passed. It seemed like I'd been climbing forever when I finally reached a semi-level area where I collapsed in a heap. Burning up with fever and overcome with intense fatigue, my hands shook as I gulped down more precious water. The only positive aspect of being so sick was that I wasn't my usual famished self.

Painfully aware that the battery wasn't going to last much longer, I pulled the flints and candles from my pocket and stared at them forlornly. How was I going to do this? In my entire life, I'd never done anything remotely like trying to start a fire from nothing. And even if I could muster up enough energy to create a spark, it wouldn't last long enough to light a candlewick. I needed something that would ignite easily. Wait! What about the cookie box? Hurriedly, I unwrapped the blanket and dumped the remaining cookies onto it. I tore the box into small pieces, but quickly realized it was unlikely that I could get enough of a spark to light cardboard. Maybe the blanket would ignite faster or… "The tickets!" I gasped. Never dreaming that I would need them for kindling, I dug the folded pieces of paper from my back pocket. This might actually work.

I shredded the tickets into tiny bits, scooped them into a pile, placed the candles nearby and began scraping the flint stones together. At that point it would have been so easy to give up and just lie down and wait for death, but even though I was exhausted beyond measure, I forced myself to keep rubbing the stones together, keeping Tally's face, serious brown eyes and signature crooked grin at the forefront of my mind.

Calling upon my last vestiges of willpower, I repeated over and over my grandmother's pronouncements that, far and away, I was most stubborn person she'd ever known. And lastly, I kept imagining Ginger's voice urging in my ear, "Come on, darlin' yank on them big gal britches and git 'er done!" My arms and hands ached so severely, I had just about admitted defeat when the tiny pile of papers suddenly burst into flames. Hardly daring to believe my eyes, I lit two of the candles and turned off my flashlight to preserve whatever juice was left.

My will to live rebounded, burning brighter than the comforting flames dispelling the blackness around me. "Hallelujah!" I crowed, immediately beginning a search of the area. It didn't take me long to find what I was looking for. Etched on a nearby rock, I read the words: **James 1:17** ***Every good and perfect gift is from above…***

"'Gift from above,'" I mouthed, filled with puzzlement until I noticed the huge mound of tiny, black pellets nearby. I knelt down and when it finally dawned on me what it was, grateful tears clouded my vision. Bat guano. I stood and held the two candles up as high as I could. Instead of feeling any fear, I doubted anyone else on earth could have been more overjoyed to spot the enormous colony of bats hanging from the cave ceiling. Staring in awe, my pulse pounding with anticipation, I whispered, "Hello, boys and girls. Show me how you got in here."

I searched my memory, trying to remember what little I knew about the furry, winged mammals. They hunted and consumed large quantities of insects by night and slept during the day. So, that meant it was still daylight, but I had no idea what time it was or how long I'd have to wait for feeding to begin. I think I'd read that in cold regions, they hibernate for winter, but did that apply to Arizona? Were they hibernating now or just sleeping? Only time would tell and I didn't have much of that left. Once all the candles burned out and my flashlight died, I'd be trapped in the dark with no hope of freedom. Somehow, I had to get back to my loved ones, my job and my life—and I had to stop Nelson Trotter and Dr. Craig or Dr. Mallick from murdering Lindsay

Cole. For Ada's sake, I must find out what happened to Duane and put an end to this insidious madness.

Still feeling rotten, the desire to sleep overwhelming, I fought the urge to lie down. I dared not close my eyes and allow the flames to burn out. But, I had to wait and see if the bats made a move. I passed the time reminiscing about my childhood, my family, my decision to move from Philadelphia to Arizona, my first meeting with Tally, Ginger, Tugg and all the gang at the newspaper. My heart contracted into a tiny, cold fist as I imagined each of them going on with his or her life without me. Grief threatened to consume me again, but then I heard it, the sound I'd been waiting for—the flutter of wings.

Inhaling an expectant breath, I set the candles down and picked up the flashlight. The beam was noticeably dimmer, but when I shined it upwards, there was just enough light to see the bat colony disconnecting from their roost and flying in one direction. I trained the light on them and the general area where they disappeared, probably twenty feet above me. Instinct told me this was it. No time to lose. I had to follow them right now. I needed my hands free to scale the rocks, so candles were out. I could only hope the flashlight would last long enough for me to find the opening. But then I had another thought. What if I couldn't fit through it?

Faith. Keep the faith, I urged myself. I lit the remaining candles, set them on the ground and, along with the dim beam, it cast enough light to chart a course upward. Clamping the flashlight between my teeth for what I hoped was the last time, spurred on by hope, fear and faith, I put hand over hand and bounded up the rocks like a mountain goat, all the while listening to the constant whir of bat wings now directly overhead. It was the most beautiful sound I'd ever heard.

Suddenly, fresh, cold air hit my face. I pulled the flashlight from my teeth and let out a whoop of exultation when the moon and stars burst into view. The bats were flying right along beside me now and I could feel the wind from their wings as I squeezed through an opening not much bigger than a basketball.

Laughing and crying at the same time, I crawled onto the ledge and watched my liberators vanish into the night sky. My breathing labored and shaking all over, I couldn't believe I was free. But, I wasn't safe yet. With effort, I corralled my wits and looked out in all directions, trying to figure out where I was. The position of the moon told me I was facing east and the terrific view of the valley below confirmed I was on a hilltop somewhere.

The battery in my trusty flashlight finally died, so with no firm plan in mind, and only the moonlight to guide me, I began to clamber downward in the bracing night air. Overflowing with happiness, gratitude, and tingling all over with jubilation, apparently I was moving way too fast and lost my footing. I scrabbled for a handhold on a bush, rock, anything as I tumbled and slid downhill. Frantically, I grabbed for another rock, missed, and then felt myself disconnecting from the ground and sailing through the air. Seconds later, I shrieked with astonishment when I plunged into a pool of hot water. In that instant, I knew exactly where I was.

CHAPTER 30

Nobody could believe it. Seconds after I posted the story it went viral, lighting up social media with all of the grisly details I'd been able to cobble together. The initial account of Dr. Craig and Dr. Mallick's grotesque experiment shocked everyone and devastated Lucinda, her family and Ronda. The equally grossed-out citizens of Castle Valley found themselves the focal point of yet another sensational, worldwide front-page headline. I wondered if the locals were developing a complex considering how many of these bizarre stories I'd unearthed in just the past year. I had no doubt that someone was already planning a movie version for this latest one. A horror movie.

Not surprisingly, the X-ray taken during my visit to Dr. Garcia the following day revealed that I was suffering from bacterial pneumonia. He prescribed antibiotics, a cough suppressant, fluids, and complete bed rest. I protested, but when he threatened to hospitalize me, I reluctantly agreed. Much to my relief, he also removed the remaining stitches from my chin.

I dozed on and off the first day, vaguely remembering Ginger fussing over me, bringing me soup, water, medications and caring for the cats who seemed perfectly content to stay in bed with me most of the time. I spoke briefly to Tally. He expressed profound relief that I'd escaped this latest caper alive, but I could tell by his reserved tone that he was not happy with me. Fearing I was still contagious, I discouraged him from coming over right away. I worried about Ginger too, but she waved away my concerns with a compassionate smile. "Don't be silly, darlin'! I ain't been sick with so much as a sniffle for ten years so I'll take my chances. Keep yer butt in that bed and git better." Her selfless generosity brought a lump to my throat and again I thanked God that I had a friend like her.

Sometime during the evening I awakened in a feverish sweat, startled to see Tally slouching in the doorway, arms crossed and staring at me. With only the night-light on I couldn't see him clearly but felt sure his eyes reflected a look of troubled censure. Before I could say anything, he turned and left the room. Feeling immediately deflated, I could only imagine what he must be thinking. "*What the hell is wrong with her? How does she keep getting into these awful situations? Is she ever going to settle down? Doesn't she care about how her actions affect me? Do I really want to marry this impetuous woman?*" Hot tears scalded my eyes and I sobbed quietly for a while until I began to stubbornly defend myself.

What happened wasn't my fault. Well…yes it was. But hadn't I taken every precaution? Apparently not, even though I'd let him and Marshall know exactly where I was going and went prepared with my flashlight, knife and a weapon. Okay, maybe the decision to crawl out of a sick bed and drive off into a massive storm to find Duane wasn't very smart. But, was I really thinking clearly? And in a million years, who could have ever guessed what was going on inside that old house? Granted, I should have never gone in, but at the time I strongly believed Duane was being held there against his will along with the missing girls I suspected were victims of human trafficking. I couldn't have been more wrong on both counts. And now, even though I had vowed to exercise caution after my last crazy assignment, I had still managed to almost get myself killed just to snag that all-important scoop, just as my dad had warned. Feeling more miserable than ever, I finally fell back to sleep and when I woke up late the next morning, the house and my heart still felt empty.

Later on after Ginger had arrived with breakfast, I sent Tally a text acknowledging that I'd made a big mistake. SO SORRY! CAN WE TALK SOON? By noon, he had still not responded, so I tortured myself the remainder of the day thinking I couldn't blame him for changing his mind. Had he run out of patience with my reckless behavior and decided to call off the wedding? I moped all afternoon, mentally thrashing myself for such utter selfishness and stupidity.

He finally messaged me that evening. STILL TIED UP WITH BUYERS. LET'S TALK WHEN U FEEL BETTER. CLOSE CALL. TOO CLOSE. LUV U. Typical of him, his message was short, sour and sweet. I felt like I'd been spanked and kissed at the same time.

I could only stand to stay in bed for three days, and after that I kept on top of things from home until I regained enough strength to return to the office. After risking life and limb to secure what turned out to be one of the most terrifying, baffling and complex stories I'd ever covered, I wasn't about to miss out on the new details coming to light daily.

Thinking back, what had seemed like a year in captivity was, in reality, less than twenty-four hours. Numb with shock, I'd crawled out of my impromptu mineral bath Monday night, miraculously uninjured except for scrapes, bruises and every single fingernail broken. Keenly aware that the distinctive cone-shaped mountains were less than half a mile from Our Lady of the Desert, I'd hurried towards the main road as fast as I could manage, aided solely by moonlight. Wheezing from exertion and trembling from the chill of cold, wet clothing plastered against my skin, I nervously kept an eye out for Nelson Trotter, who was most likely trying to hunt me down. Fortunately, I stumbled upon the campsite of two young men who turned out to be the cavers Wanda had ordered off the property earlier that week. After expressing alarm at my disheveled appearance, they listened to my terse explanation and agreed to take me home.

During the drive, I borrowed a cell phone, called Marshall, and after my brief description of events, he barked, "Damn it, Kendall! Can't you stay out of trouble for two seconds?" He then brought me up to speed on his activities. Based on my phone message, Ada's frantic inquiries about Duane and Tally's urgent call minutes after he'd received the bogus text from Dr. Craig, Marshall had awakened Judge Collins shortly after midnight and obtained a search warrant. He deputized Tally and several other members of the Search and Rescue team, and then descended upon the mansion in time to find Nelson Trotter and Dr. Mallick in the process of destroying and disposing of evidence. The two were detained and questioned. To save his own hide, Nelson Trotter denied knowing anything about Duane or me and quickly pointed an accusing finger at Dr. Mallick, who claimed he'd been hired only to assist Dr. Craig at Youth Oasis and work on his ground-breaking invention, nothing else. It was then they heard a single gunshot from within the mansion.

When Marshall and several of his team entered the upstairs bedroom they found Dr. Craig dead from a self-inflicted gunshot wound to the head and lying next to a woman's moldering corpse. They'd all been confounded and sickened by the discovery of Holly Mason's decomposing face. "I've come across some weird things since I took this job," Marshall admitted grimly, "but never anything like this."

"What about Duane?" I interjected tensely.

"No sign of him yet. Found his SUV in the pond. Divers didn't find anything."

I told him about the wolf I'd seen gnawing on what I believed to be a human bone and urged him to explore the bone yard ASAP where I suspected Nelson Trotter had dumped Duane's body. Then I asked if he knew about Lindsay Cole. He did not so I told him where to find her and they did. He also found my missing coat and cell phone stuffed in a drawer in Glendine's bedroom, signaling there had not been time to dispose of them before the authorities had arrived. But then Marshall solemnly conveyed the most disconcerting news of all. From what they could piece together, it appeared that when Dr. Craig realized law enforcement was on the scene, he had used my .38 to kill himself. Marshall promised that as soon as the investigation was concluded my weapon would be returned to me.

On the fourth day of my convalescence, Marshall brought my coat along with my cell phone, car keys, a casserole from his wife, and something else I had completely forgotten about. Following my directions, Tally and Ronda had taken my Jeep and located hers still secreted beneath the cluster of trees near the old mansion. Afterwards they met up at my house. While Tally and Ginger were out of the room Ronda quietly apologized for asking me to get involved in the search for Holly. I waved away her concerns, saying it was part of the job, and then presented her with the snippet of hair from Dolly's tail. Until that moment, I had never seen Ronda express much emotion. Her eyes brimming with tears, she thanked me and quickly left. It was nice to know that beneath her detached exterior beat a tender heart.

After she and Tally left, I fell into a blissful sleep only to be awakened when Lucinda showed up bearing containers of homemade soup, biscuits and cookies that she and her Aunt Polly had prepared for me. I thanked her, we talked briefly about the tragic loss of her sister and then she apologized for involving me in what turned out to be such a precarious situation. In a show of emotion much like Ronda she squeezed my hand and left with her eyes brimming with tears. Even though I'd come close to losing my life, I did not regret for a second cracking the convoluted case. No more beautiful young women would be killed and mutilated to satisfy Dr. Craig's sick obsession. I also realized that from that day forward, my relationship with Lucinda would be different. And that would be a good thing.

Shortly after she left, my parents called for the third time. After assuring them once again that I was in good hands, I'd barely hung up when Clara phoned to check on my welfare. It appeared that in a small community, an episode of this magnitude had an emotional effect on everyone. She was blown away when I told her the story of my captivity with Lindsay in the crypt, and I expressed my unending thanks to her for giving me St. Barbara's secret instructions to activate the hidden door. When I told her about the biblical clues in the cave that led to my escape, she exclaimed, "The Lord must have been with you, child! I can't wait to tell Jane. She will be over the moon." In a tremulous voice, she added, "Now I have something to tell you."

Good to her word, Clara Whitlow had spent hours leafing through her old yearbooks and finally discovered a photo of the blonde boy in the picture she had shown me that day at the library. My suspicion that the unidentified man in the photo with his arm draped possessively around Glendine was the abusive boyfriend proved to be correct. His name was Dillon Ashercroft. But the subsequent bombshell sent a seismic shock reverberating through me, the entire community and beyond. It answered the burning question that had been bothering me from the second that Dr. Craig had walked into Glendine's freezing bedroom. It put to rest the rumor that the lonesome, twenty-eight-year-old woman had been caught in bed with one of the ranch hands that fateful night. In fact, her young lover was actually Dillon Ashercroft's seventeen-year-old son, Craig—the man we knew as Dr. Asher Craig.

Admissions by Wanda and Nelson confirmed the rumor that Dillon had flown into a drunken rage, and, after soundly thrashing his son he'd thrown him out the door and turned his wrath on Glendine. Wanda stated that she'd never been able to forget Glendine's screams of pain and terror.

When Dillon emerged sometime later, splattered with blood, he threatened to kill the Trotter siblings if they ever ratted him out. In the meantime, Craig had gone to the kitchen, seized a knife and returned to the living room where he stabbed his father in the back. As he fell to the floor shouting obscenities, the Trotter siblings joined in, beating him with a poker and brass lamp while Craig continuing stabbing until Dillon stopped breathing. Clara's unexpected revelation shocked the hell out of me and spawned a fierce desire to continue digging until I got answers to the questions still haunting me.

The following Monday afternoon as the staff gathered in my office for our weekly meeting, it seemed as if the clusters of purple-and-yellow wildflowers outside my window had sprung up overnight. By that point in time, we knew who all the players were. We knew what happened and where it happened, but details on the how and why and exactly when were still trickling in as the investigation continued. Additional information from the Trotter siblings filled in more of the blanks, but, as in all cases where the culprit took themselves out, a host of secrets went with them and we were left to speculate. The more I learned, the more fascinating it was to realize that even now, forty years later, the long arm of the so-called Higgins family curse was still reaching out to ensnare innocent people, causing untold collateral damage.

Blunting the outcome of the grotesque events was one piece of phenomenally good news. Marshall and the search party did find Duane in the bone yard lying under the hind end of a dead horse. He'd been shot several times, but amazingly, was still alive. The doctors believed that the horse's weight helped compress the wounds and kept him warm. Thankfully, he was expected to make a full recovery. When Ada phoned to thank me profusely for saving Duane's life, the euphoria I felt lessened the heavy weight of guilt. She seemed understandably confused when I told her that she, in a roundabout way, had actually saved *my* life. She gasped with amazement when I explained what happened and how I had used the pancake breakfast tickets to start the fire that paved the way for my escape with the bats. Her voice thick with emotion, she praised God for both miracles. I agreed wholeheartedly.

After hearing that news, Jim had deadpanned, "So, you're saying Duane was saved by a horse's ass?"

"I…guess you could say that," I replied, waiting for the good-natured laughter to die down before continuing. "The sad irony is by exposing the truth, I ended up spoiling Thena's big plans and I'm worried that she's planning to withdraw her support." I didn't say it out loud, but even though she'd sent me flowers with a note telling me how distraught she was that I'd almost been killed carrying out her wishes, I felt I had lost the opportunity to smooth things over between us.

"I wouldn't be so sure of that," Tugg corrected me with an encouraging smile. "Thena's a pretty resilient lady and always seems to land on her feet. In fact, she told me while you were home recovering that she's already been in contact with a couple of well-respected cosmetic surgeons interested in keeping Youth Oasis up and running. And she's ninety percent sure Wanda is going to sell her the church and the surrounding property."

My spirits picked up even more when Tugg excitedly

waved the sheaf of papers I'd handed him hours earlier. "You may have unintentionally saved the day. There's enough material here to keep this series running for a month. Judging by the explosion of online subscriptions, there are a lot of people out there hanging on every juicy detail."

Jim jubilantly tacked on, "He's right! The number of hits and chatter on our social media pages is epic. I say keep the momentum going for two months."

"Right on!" Walter crowed, giving me an approving grin. "Maybe I see a book in your future?"

The barrage of praise heartened me, but then Tugg intoned seriously, "I do have one problem with this gawd awful story."

"What's that?"

"It's so damned complicated I'm having a devil of a time trying to follow all the twists and turns. I hope our readers can."

I shot him a wry smile. "I know. It's been a real headache trying to unravel this convoluted mess. I actually had to make a flow chart so I could try and understand each person's warped motivation and distorted thinking."

Tugg's old chair let out a ragged squeak as he leaned back and folded his hands behind his head. "Enlighten us."

I shuffled through my notes. "Okay, you already know the catalyst in this story. Glendine Higgins suffered her share of tragedy at the hands of other people, but she also made some really bad decisions. Her careless actions four decades ago set the stage, but her death last year really put this horror show in motion."

"I can simplify this for our readers," Jim offered airily, stretching imaginary letters in front of him. "Local psychopath murders women to steal their faces."

"Nice try," I answered dryly, "but I'm afraid it's far more multi-layered. It wasn't just any face; it had to be a beautiful face. This story contains every basic human emotion you can conjure up—love, hate, greed, jealousy, revenge and combinations of them all." I hesitated a few seconds before adding, "In the oddest sort of way this is a love story."

"A love story?" Walter burst out, incredulous. "We're talking about one depraved dude here masquerading as this…supposedly benevolent doctor." He made a face like he'd been sucking on a lemon. "I mean, who does something like that?"

"Asher Craig was definitely a master of camouflage," I concurred softly, glancing down at the page again. "Talented, a highly-regarded surgeon by day, besotted lover and deranged scientist by night."

Tugg remarked sarcastically, "Ya think? The guy belonged in a straight jacket. So, what was with all the flowers anyway? And why was the woman dressed like she was going to the prom?"

"We can only guess, but it appears that Glendine was his first love, a forbidden love, and he spent his entire life punishing himself for what happened to her. When he couldn't fulfill her pleas to make her beautiful in life, he attempted to do it after her death. He turned her room into a shrine, filling it up with flowers and candles and dressing her like a queen. He doused the sheets and her corpse with lavender oil to help diminish the smell of rotting flesh." I flipped the page and continued. "The medical examiner told me he'd even inserted glass eyes." I looked up at their attentive faces. "Are you ready for this? According to Wanda, he bought a diamond ring for her and performed his own marriage ceremony…post death."

Following a few seconds of stunned silence, Jim quipped, "Are you shittin' me?" He leaned forward, his impish blue eyes sparkling with mischief and whispered in a confidential tone. "Ya think the dude was banging her corpse?"

"Could be," Walter chimed in, laughing uproariously, "but no one's alive to tell!" The two men exchanged a fist bump while I swapped a look of speculative disbelief with Tugg.

"Geezuus!" he groaned, covering his ears. "I don't want to hear this stuff!"

"Yeah, but I'll bet our readers do!" Walter announced excitedly. "That fact alone will burn up the Internet!"

He was probably right. As long as it wasn't happening to them, people were endlessly fascinated by lurid stories like this one. As if I were addressing two ornery kids, I admonished them lightly. "So, do you guys want to hear the rest of this story or not?"

"Oh, puleeeez!" Jim begged, still sniggering, "I can't get enough."

I rolled my eyes and resumed. "Okay. I just hung up talking to Marshall a few minutes ago. They found human remains in the bone yard while they were searching for Duane and suspect they belong to Krystal Lampton, the girl that disappeared before she could testify against Nelson Trotter. They're waiting to receive clothing and hair samples from her foster mother to determine if there's a DNA match."

Tugg cut in thoughtfully, "Okay, now it makes sense. The Trotters closed off the back entrance because they couldn't take a chance on one of the other ranchers, or anybody else for that matter, finding her body."

"Not exactly, but I'll get to that in a minute. The gate was locked because they didn't want anyone snooping around the old mansion."

"Like you," Tugg said, flicking me an incisive grin.

"Yeah. Like me. Anyway, within minutes of Glendine's death, Dr. Mallick's mad experiment to bring her back to life began. Dr. Craig ordered Nelson to block the windows and install all those air-conditioning units to keep the room as cold as possible."

"Cold storage, like the morgue," Jim remarked matter-of-factly, wrinkling his nose in distaste.

"That was part of it. With his efforts bankrolled by Dr. Craig, Dr. Mallick began administering his own special formula designed to work in conjunction with that weird Frankenstein-looking contraption she was hooked up to. Dr. Craig was apparently desperate enough to believe that Dr. Mallick's trailblazing procedure could regenerate new cells by applying electrical impulses to constantly stimulate her brain and organs. Transfusing his special concoction of chemicals would theoretically help preserve her blood and keep the skin soft and hydrated."

Everyone stared at me speechlessly for long seconds until Walter exclaimed, "Who in his or her right mind would ever fall for such a truckload of bullshit?"

Grimacing agreement, I suggested, "Someone with a dangerous obsession. Dr. Craig's lifelong fixation with Glendine is the main reason he opened Youth Oasis in the first place. He maintained his home in Aguila so he could continue to secretly visit her over the years and arranged for several innovative surgeries in hopes of restoring her lost beauty. The clinic's close proximity to the mansion not only allowed Dr. Mallick to cover for him when he wasn't there, it made it convenient for him to monitor the flow of fluids, similar to the procedure used to embalm cadavers that are donated to medical schools for anatomy class. But he pushed it to a whole new level. The closest term I could find to describe that process is called anatomical wetting."

"That sounds obscene," Tugg muttered under his breath. "So doesn't that make Dr. Mallick an accessory to murder?"

"Not really," I answered, watching his eyes widen with surprise. "It was Dr. Craig's diabolical plan to begin the face transplants using unsuspecting donors. Dr. Mallick was told the cadavers were obtained from one of those body donation companies."

"Huh?" Jim grunted doubtfully. "So, we're supposed to believe that he knew nothing about Dr. Craig's scheme to have Nelson grab those girls?"

I grimaced. "So far, there's no proof to the contrary."

"Dead men tell no tales," Walter murmured thoughtfully, adding, "So…who actually killed those poor girls?"

"Dr. Craig," I replied quietly. "He used the same drugs on them that he used to sedate his patients, only he administered an overdose and then…well, you know."

"Good God in heaven," Tugg exclaimed, his mouth puckered in horror. "The psychological gymnastics people go through in order to justify the most heinous actions never ceases to amaze me."

I nodded agreement thinking how close I'd come to

being one of Dr. Craig's unwilling donors. "Wanda has a theory about that. Supposedly, Dr. Craig's mother fattened her bank account by cheating on his father while he was on the road. Even though he and Dillon didn't get along, he developed a deep-seated hatred for his mother. In his mind, the types of women who hung around truck stops soliciting for sex or drugs were simply whores like her and therefore expendable. Once Krystal's face began to decompose, Nelson Trotter was sent to find another beautiful face. Unfortunately, it was Holly Mason's."

"I get it," Walter intoned, somberly. "Trotter picked the girls up, imprisoned them at the old church and afterwards the bodies were dumped in the bone yard."

"Only Krystal's. When Wanda's son, Grayson, got too sick to work, Dr. Craig came up with the idea of having Nelson take over his duties for The Last Roundup. It would have been the perfect cover if he had transported her body to the county landfill and disposed of it along with his load of dead horses like he was supposed to, but because he's such a lazy SOB, it was faster to discard Krystal's body closer to home in the bone yard and keep the landfill fee for himself. Apparently when Dr. Craig found out, he went ballistic."

"So, where's Holly's body?" Jim inquired.

"Nelson isn't talking, but crews from the Sheriff's Office are searching the county landfill as we speak. And from the bone yard, they've recovered numerous plastic garbage bags filled with medical waste along with clothing and other evidence pertaining to Holly's murder and that of Krystal Lampton."

"There's something I still don't understand," Walter asked with a perturbed frown. "I don't get the weird connection between the Trotters and Dr. Craig."

"I was just getting to that." I flipped back several pages and filled them in on all the details surrounding the night of Glendine's attack. "The four of them made a solemn pact to never divulge what really happened. Craig Ashercroft fled to California and with Glendine's financial help began a new life. But it was also the beginning of a lifetime of recriminations, resentment, guilt and self-loathing."

Walter whistled softly. "So, they were all blackmailing each other."

"Correct. Each feared the other would divulge the truth and each used that leverage to get what they wanted from the other. When the Trotters both landed in legal trouble Dr. Craig was forced to bail them out and pony up for the high-priced attorney. In return, they were obligated to do his bidding, like caring for Glendine twenty-four-seven and then he forced them to participate in his insane scheme to resurrect her." I checked my notes again, adding, "FYI, Wanda was released yesterday for lack of evidence. Nelson's not so lucky. He's in deep guano with a host of charges against him and this time there's nobody to come to his rescue by hiring an expensive lawyer. Lindsay Cole's testimony alone will probably put him away for a lifetime."

Looking thoughtful, Tugg mused, "What about the three of them murdering Dillon Ashercroft? There's no statute of limitations in Arizona that I know of."

"That's true, but keep in mind they were all juveniles at the time and Wanda is claiming it was self-defense. Marshall told me she's actually relieved to be free of the guilt that has haunted her all these years and is prepared to face whatever the consequences might be. And that brings me to the second reason they couldn't have people trespassing around the Gold Queen mansion."

Everyone stared at me expectantly for a few seconds before Jim's eyes lit up. "Holeeeee guacamole! Don't tell me they hid the boyfriend's body there?"

I nodded. "In the padlocked basement. That's the reason Glendine chose to live there isolated from public view. She made sure no one ever discovered their secret and lived out the remainder of her life two floors above Dillon's decomposed corpse."

CHAPTER 31

Nothing quite matches the beauty and solitude of the Arizona desert. Riding Starlight Sky for the first time since my harrowing ordeal, I lifted my face skyward, treasuring the glorious sensation of being alive to enjoy the feel of warm sunlight and the gentle breeze caressing my cheeks. I rejoiced at the wide arc of sapphire sky festooned with cottony, white clouds and the dazzling display of spring wildflowers blanketing the rocky hillsides. Ever since my confinement in the dark crypt and claustrophobic cave passages, I appreciated everything I saw, touched, smelled and tasted. All of it nourished my battered soul, reminding me of those I loved and how precious life was.

Promising myself I would never, ever take anything for granted again, I glanced up at Sidewinder Hill, thrilled to see how much progress had been made on our house in just two weeks. During that time, I'd had very little downtime while I continued to recuperate from pneumonia, gathered more disturbing information on Dr. Craig's nefarious activities, and finally had a heart-to-heart talk with Tally.

As expected, he was both highly agitated and distressed by my impulsive actions, but probably no more than I was. After reaffirming our enduring love for each other we reached an undeniable truth. Neither of us was going to change. However, the gnawing fear that he might cancel our wedding plans was unfounded. He did have one solemn request, however: would I please consider giving up these types of heart-stopping assignments once we started our family? Still shaken to the core from my latest scrape with death, I promised him I definitely would. But until that time came, I planned to continue my career and vowed that I would try my level best to stay out of trouble. And I meant it.

As I angled Starlight Sky up the knoll towards our new house, radiant happiness flowed through me. Tally would be waiting there. The plan was to evaluate progress on the house and, afterwards, I hoped the romantic picnic dinner I'd prepared would help smooth over his ruffled feelings. Listening to the steady *clip-clop* of Starlight Sky's hooves on the sandy trail, my thoughts gradually returned to recent events.

Armed with the new information I'd gotten from Wanda and Marshall, the answers to several of my most vexing questions had come to light. Others most likely would remain a mystery forever.

One thing had bugged me from day one. Why had the new pastor of the church vacated the property so suddenly after only one year? The answer: Dr. Craig and Nelson could not risk another girl escaping from the Gold Queen mansion as Krystal Lampton had done. They needed a more secure place nearby. The crypt fit the bill perfectly, but even with a generous cash offer, Pastor Gates refused to sell. He was persuaded, however, after Nelson began terrorizing his wife and kids. First, by releasing countless venomous spiders into their house and when that didn't work, setting fire to it. Step two of their plan was fabricating Glendine's dying wish that her heirs acquire Our Lady of the Desert so that she could be interred forever with her first love, Father Dominic. Next, Nelson posted NO TRESPASSING signs and then positioned building materials around both the church and the Gold Queen mansion in an effort to keep people away from a supposed construction zone.

It was no surprise to learn that Krystal Lampton's personal items received from her foster mother confirmed a positive DNA match. Crews were still combing through the landfill, but hopes of finding Holly's remains were fading. It was also discovered that the light-colored SUV Dr. Mallick had been driving was registered to Dr. Craig. Marshall had floated several theories, one being that it was Dr. Craig who met Nelson at the Family Dollar store that night to pass judgment on whether Holly's face passed his beauty test. But since there was no video and Aleta's poor eyesight made her a questionable witness, his premise would remain pure speculation unless Nelson Trotter eventually divulged the truth. I thought Ginger's observation summed it up best. "Lord a mercy! Ain't it disappointin' when folks live down to your lowest expectations."

One positive outcome of the horrendous events was mending fences with Thena. We'd finally had a frank discussion where she admitted that she was still reeling from the aftershocks of the appalling revelations. I apologized to her for unintentionally ruining her plans, but she dismissed my concerns. I was elated to hear that Wanda had finally agreed to sell her the church and surrounding property. She excitedly informed me that she was also working on a plan with the State of Arizona to preserve the extraordinary cave and develop it as a tourist attraction, in much the same manner as Kartchner Caverns. Our Lady of the Desert would become the welcome center. The conversation ended on a happy note when she congratulated me on breaking the story and assured me that funding would continue, especially after the recent spike in online and print subscription, plus increased ad revenue.

I had put off until yesterday my visit to see Duane. Ada had called to tell me that he had come home and wanted to thank me in person for my "courageous" efforts to save his life. He seemed genuinely glad to see me and we talked briefly about his violent confrontation with Nelson and his subsequent night in the bone yard pinned beneath the dead horse. When I got up to leave, he held out his arms and asked if he could give me a "thank you" hug. Knowing a leopard never changes its spots, I did so reluctantly. It was an awkward embrace and I thought he'd never let go. I was hoping against hope that his motivation was sincere, but when he finally relinquished his hold, he managed to make sure his hand lingered on my breast as I pulled away. Yep. That was Duane. Smarmy as ever. He was going to be okay.

On my way out, with all four of her children gathered around, Ada pressed a small gift box into my hands. I tried to object, but she forcefully insisted. At home later I opened the box to find a beautiful ceramic angel along with her note that read: *Dearest Kendall, My children and I are eternally grateful to you for putting yourself in harm's way to save my husband and my family. Please accept this small token of our affection. I don't believe in coincidences. I believe the hand of God guided you.* ***Ezekiel 1:24 I also heard the sound of their wings like the sound of abundant waters as they went…*** Deeply touched, I reread the proverb several times. Everyone had remarked how resilient I was, how I'd bounced back following my traumatic ordeal, but the last words in her letter slammed into me, releasing pent-up emotions I'd kept under wraps all these weeks. I broke down and bawled like a baby, bemoaning the fact that I could not seem to stop myself from landing in trouble when my goal was always to do the right thing and maybe secure a great story. Would I ever learn? Always intuitive, my cats stared at me with wide, startled eyes and finally pressed themselves against me in an apparent attempt to comfort me. When I finally regained control of myself, I was emotionally and mentally drained, but felt much better. I soothed my furry companions and assured them everything was okay. I don't know why, but suddenly another of my grandmother's wise sayings came to mind. *"All's well that ends well."* And in this case, at least for Duane and me, she would have been right.

Starlight Sky's sudden whinny brought me back to reality just as we reached the top of Sidewinder Hill where I spotted Tally's pickup and attached horse trailer that we would use to transport Starlight Sky back to the stables. The sight of his tall, lean frame outlined in the doorway of the unfinished house filled my heart with fierce joy. "Hey, there, cowboy!" I called out, waving. Starlight Sky nickered her own greeting as he strode towards us.

"Did you work up an appetite during your ride?" he inquired, treating me to his disarming grin while holding the reins as I dismounted. "I sure did!" I replied, unhooking the saddlebag, announcing happily, "I'm having a splendid time gaining back that five pounds I lost. I've got plenty to eat and a nice bottle of wine."

"Sounds good to me," he answered lightly. Whistling a little tune, he removed Starlight Sky's bridle and saddle, slipped on her halter and tied her to the back end of the trailer where she could graze. Then, hand in hand, we toured the house. It still seemed a little unreal to me that I would soon be living in such a spacious place. We chatted about some of the upgrades we still wanted—quartz countertops, additional window coverings and top-of-the-line kitchen appliances—before I spread a blanket on the concrete slab and we sat down to enjoy our picnic. Long shadows stretched across the desert floor by the time we finished and walked outside to stand near the edge of the cliff overlooking the wide valley below. We had stuck to neutral topics during the meal, both of us skirting around the touchy subject I felt certain was uppermost on our minds.

We fell into a companionable silence until I couldn't restrain myself, finally blurting out, "Tally, are we going to be okay?"

He turned to me with a look of calm speculation. "I guess that's up to you."

"What do you mean?"

He blew out a heartfelt sigh. "I'm not sure that I'm going to be able to provide you with enough stimulation to keep you happy."

I leveled him a coy look. "You stimulate me plenty, cowboy."

A tight-lipped smile. "You know what I mean.

We've had this discussion before. Being a rancher's wife isn't going to give you that adrenaline boost you crave and I'm not crazy about how you go about getting it."

"It's not like I plan—"

He put up a hand to interrupt me. "I know you don't, but it's not like there isn't pattern here." He reached out and took my hands in his own calloused ones. "Listen, I think you are the most beautiful and determined woman I've ever met. You're definitely a handful, but…" he paused, apparently searching for words and then concluded with, "You're damn good at what you do and I'm not going to be the one to stop you. I admire the hell out of your persistence, your spunk, your passionate sense of right and wrong, all of it, but, if you don't mind," he murmured, pulling me into his arms, "I'd like to keep you around for a while, okay?"

The compassionate light in his eyes ignited a warm glow inside me. "I like that plan," I replied softly. "I love you, Tally. More than you'll ever know. Thank you for putting up with me." My heart bursting with emotion, I pressed my lips against his. When we finally drew apart, he held me at arm's length, locking his serious gaze on me.

"Tell me something. Does m'lady still want that turret added to the house?"

"What are you talking about?"

"You know, the turret you requested a few weeks ago."

Was that a glint of humor sparkling behind his eyes? I stared at him blankly until I remembered the flippant remark I'd made the morning he didn't show up to meet with our architect. With a self-conscious laugh, I admitted, "No. That was just me being my usual bratty self."

He feigned disappointment. "That's too bad. I was

thinking it would make an interesting place to spend our wedding night."

"You are a very naughty boy."

"Speaking of the wedding," he said, gently brushing wisps of hair away from my eyes, "have you picked out a location yet?"

"I can't decide. I'd like to have your input first." I listed the names of all the resorts Ginger had tentatively lined up, even floating her idea of getting married at one of the National Parks.

He gave me a noncommittal shrug. "Whatever you pick is fine with me."

"Well, you're no help," I teased, turning my attention westward towards the jagged purple mountains where Mother Nature was busily painting a breathtaking sunset. Awestruck by the spectacular beauty of the crimson sun sinking into a bed of butterscotch-and-ultra-violet-tinged clouds, it was then the answer came to me. Why hadn't I thought of this before? Why not be bold and do something different? Why not create a memorable event that reflected the true western lifestyle Tally and I loved so much? Barely able to contain my excitement, I turned back to him. "Who needs a National Park when we have this?" I announced, sweeping my hand across the blazing horizon.

He frowned. "Not sure I'm following you."

"I can't think of a more perfect place to get married than here at the Starfire."

"You mean right here where we're standing?"

"Yes. And on horseback."

His eyebrows shot up. "On horseback? Are you sure this is what you want?"

"Positive. And as Ginger would say, 'Y'all might as well get hitched up right.'"

Shaking his head as if he couldn't believe his ears, he tipped his hat up, wrapped his arms around me once more and as his lips lightly grazed mine, he whispered, "If that's what m'lady wants, that's what m'lady gets."

Sylvia Nobel bases all of her Kendall O'Dell mystery novels on stories plucked from newspapers, Internet or even first-hand information and then weaves the stories into her fictional novels, applying her unique spin on each suspenseful tale.

As much as she loves the craft of writing, she equally loves the thrill of getting out into the Arizona countryside to carefully research each exciting story.
FYI - The fictional town of Castle Valley is based on Wickenberg, AZ.

For Benevolent Evil, Sylvia traveled
to the Hualapai mountains in
Northwestern Arizona to explore the
old Gold King mansion.

Gold King Mansio
Photo: Mohave Museum of History and Arts
The Gold King Mansion was built early in 1929 by the Gold King Corporation.
corporation used this ornate structure to entertain wealthy investors and to house
mine foreman. The nearby Gold King Mine produced gold, silver, copper, and lead,
production never reached the level the miners had hoped for. The stock market cras
October 1929 brought an end to the mine and to the short-lived mansion.
The mansion's roof and walls are made of poured concrete, a construction techniq
rarely found in northwest Arizona mining camps. The structure was built in two stage
the western rooms were built first, and the eastern rooms were added later. The his
depicts the structure's early configuration.

C.H.COOK
MEMORIAL
FIRST
PRESBYTERIAN
CHURCH

Sylvia researches the historic C.H. Cook Memorial Church in Sacaton, Arizona.

Sylvia checks out the bone yard located on the Bumblebee Ranch near Bumblebee, Arizona.

Ranch manager Kelly Powell gives her some of the history of this unforgettable spot.

Sylvia traveled to the tiny community of Aguila, Arizona for additional research for Benevolent Evil.

FAMILY DOLLAR
COYOTE FLATS
CAFÉ
BAR
CAFÉ

UNITED STATES POST OFFICE

Sylvia Nobel currently resides in Phoenix, Arizona with her husband and five cats. She is a member of Mystery Writers of America and producer of the feature film, *Deadly Sanctuary*.